⚜HIGHLA

For generations, the Glen of Many Legends has been beset by strife and bloodshed as three Highland clans claim ownership to the land. The warrior chieftains are powerful, noble, and refuse to relinquish their birthright. But three cunning, beautiful lasses are about to band together to bring order and goodwill to their beloved homeland. Yet when the campaign moves from the battlefield to the bedchamber neither laird nor lass will be able to resist the passions unleashed...

⚜   ⚜   ⚜

PRAISE FOR
SUE-ELLEN WELFONDER

"Few writers can bring history to life like Sue-Ellen Welfonder! For anyone who loves historical fiction, the books in the Highland Warrior trilogy are a true treasure."
—**Heather Graham**, *New York Times*
bestselling author

"With each book Welfonder reinforces her well-deserved reputation as one of the finest writers of Scot romances."
—*RT Book Reviews*

...AND HER NOVELS

SINS OF A HIGHLAND DEVIL

"4½ stars! Top Pick! The first installment in Welfonder's Highland Warriors trilogy continues a long tradition of well-written, highly emotional romances. This marvelous novel is rich in love and legend, populated by characters steeped in honor, to make for a sensual and emotional read."
—*RT Book Reviews*

"Sue-Ellen Welfonder has truly brought legends and love to life...I cannot wait for the next two."
—**FreshFiction.com**

"A richly enjoyable story. Welfonder is a master storyteller."
—**ARomanceReview.com**

"One of the finest books I've read in a long time. The characters are so rich and vibrant, and Sue-Ellen Welfonder writes the most realistic descriptions of Highland battles. I was transported to the Glen and could almost smell the forest and the peat fires in the castles...I'm looking forward to the next story in the series!"
—**OnceUponaRomance.net**

A HIGHLANDER'S TEMPTATION

"Sue-Ellen Welfonder has written a wonderful historical romance that will make readers feel as if they have gone back to the past."
—*Midwest Book Reviews*

"[Welfonder] continues to weave magical tales of redemption, love, and loyalty in glorious, perilous mid-fourteenth-century Scotland."

—*Booklist*

"4 Stars! A fascinating, intriguing story that will definitely stand the test of time."

—*RT Book Reviews*

SEDUCING A SCOTTISH BRIDE

"4½ Stars! Welfonder sweeps readers into a tale brimming with witty banter between a feisty heroine and a stalwart hero....The added paranormal elements and sensuality turn this into an intriguing page-turner that fans of Scottish romance will adore."

—*RT Book Reviews*

"A great paranormal historical romance....Fans will read this in one delightful sitting so set aside the time."

—*Midwest Book Review*

BRIDE FOR A KNIGHT

"[Welfonder] skillfully draws you into a suspenseful mystery with wonderful atmosphere."

—*RT Book Reviews*

"Once again, Welfonder's careful scholarship and attention to detail vividly re-create the lusty, brawling days of medieval Scotland with larger-than-life chivalrous heroes and dainty but spirited maidens."

—*Booklist*

KNIGHT IN MY BED

"Exciting, action-packed ... a strong tale that thoroughly entertains."
—*Midwest Book Review*

DEVIL IN A KILT

"A lovely gem of a book. Wonderful characters and a true sense of place make this a keeper."
—**Patricia Potter, author of *The Heart Queen***

BOOKS BY SUE-ELLEN WELFONDER

Devil in a Kilt
Knight in My Bed
Bride of the Beast
Master of the Highlands
Wedding for a Knight
Only for a Knight
Until the Knight Comes
Bride for a Knight
Seducing a Scottish Bride
A Highlander's Temptation
Sins of a Highland Devil
Temptation of a Highland Scoundrel

TEMPTATION OF A HIGHLAND SCOUNDREL

SUE-ELLEN WELFONDER

FOREVER

NEW YORK   BOSTON

This book is a work of fiction. Names, characters, places, and incidents are the product of the author's imagination or are used fictitiously. Any resemblance to actual events, locales, or persons, living or dead, is coincidental.

Copyright © 2011 by Sue-Ellen Welfonder
All rights reserved. Except as permitted under the U.S. Copyright Act of 1976, no part of this publication may be reproduced, distributed, or transmitted in any form or by any means, or stored in a database or retrieval system, without the prior written permission of the publisher.

Book design by TexTech, Inc.

Forever
Hachette Book Group
237 Park Avenue
New York, NY 10017
www.HachetteBookGroup.com

Forever is an imprint of Grand Central Publishing. The Forever name and logo is a trademark of Hachette Book Group, Inc.

The publisher is not responsible for websites (or their content) that are not owned by the publisher.

Printed in the United States of America

First Printing: August 2011

10 9 8 7 6 5 4 3 2 1

With love and so many fond memories to Gerlinde Huber, dear and loyal friend of a lifetime, best-ever travel companion, pillar of strength through my worst days, and, so often, the first to share my smiles in the good times.

If I could, I'd turn back the clock to our Munich years, so full of joy and laughter. Kino nights and dinner at "our" Greek restaurant, browsing the Viktualienmarkt, drinking hot mulled wine on snowy nights at the Christkindlmarkt, girlfriend getaways to London, Dublin, Athens, Brussels, Vienna, and so many more shared destinations.

Always, you were there. And I know you always will be, wherever the road yet takes us. I love you dearly and am blessed to call you friend.

Acknowledgments

As with all my books, *Temptation of a Highland Scoundrel* was inspired by my lifelong love affair with Scotland, land of my dreams and home of my ancestors. My office might be an ocean's width from the mist-clad hills and windswept glens I love so dearly, but Highland magic is ever-present in the hearts of Diaspora Scots and when I write, time and distance blurs and I am there again, in the magnificent Scottish land- and seascapes I visit as often as I can and that become the settings of my stories.

For my Highland Warriors trilogy, I chose a place of exceptional grandeur, an area that's wonderfully remote even today. The Glen of Many Legends exists only in my imagination, but its inspiration was a rugged swath of the Western Highlands known in Gaelic as Garbh-chriochan, the Rough Bounds. Rich in legend and lore, this region is also blessed with a darkly romantic past.

Kendrew and his Mackintoshes relish that past and

they live by the old ways, proud of their ancestral ties to the pagan north. Of all the Glen of Many Legends, it is Kendrew's home that makes my heart beat fastest. Nought is a wild, edge-of-the-world kind of place. Defined by soaring peaks, filled with dark, blowing mist and masses of tumbled stone, Nought isn't for the faint of heart, but rather a land that should only be trod by those who savor cold air, strong winds, and a bracing dose of adventure. Like me, Isobel Cameron is drawn to such places. And although danger abounds at Nought, she uses her wits and her wiles to convince Kendrew that she is the heroine he needs, the only lady worthy of being mistress to a place of such savage splendor.

For the curious, inspiration for Nought's dreagan stones came from Scotland's Neolithic chambered cairns, in particular the Grey Cairns of Camster and other such prehistoric sites in Caithness. I doubt dreagans sleep in these impressive monuments, but walking there on a chill, misty day does make the notion seem possible.

If you can't decide, come bide a wee at Kendrew's fireside and listen to the tales of his seannachies. By night's end, when the wind dies and the peat embers turn cold, you might just believe....

Innumerable thanks to two women I owe so much: Roberta Brown, my agent and dearest friend. She's my champion in all weathers. And Karen Kosztolnyik, for her editing brilliance and her much-appreciated sensitivity. She deserves a castle made of gleaming amber. Karen and Roberta have my eternal gratitude. I couldn't do this without them.

Much love and thanks to my very handsome

husband, Manfred, who shields me from all ills. Valiant as a medieval warrior, he's my real-life hero. And my little dog, Em, for his snuggles, tail wags, and sloppy wet kisses. The world's oceans couldn't hold my love for him.

TEMPTATION OF A
HIGHLAND SCOUNDREL

The Legacy of the Dreagan Stones

❖

Many tales are told of a wild and untamed vale deep in the heart of the Scottish Highlands. Protected by high, rocky crags, blessed with rolling heather moors, and kissed by soft mist and the silver sheen of the sea, this fair place is known as the Glen of Many Legends. The name is well earned because the glen is steeped in myth and lore.

Since days beyond counting, the glen has been prized as a place that stirs the spirit and wakens a sense of wonder in all who tread this sylvan landscape. Three clans—MacDonalds, Camerons, and Mackintoshes—call the glen home. These clans feuded in the past but now share the vale grudgingly, biding the strictures of a recent truce.

Each clan believes that its corner of the glen is the finest.

Clan Mackintosh boasts that their holding is more.

They speak true. Their rugged, upland territory is home to the dreagan stones.

Strange outcroppings that litter the rough ground beneath Castle Nought, the forbidding Mackintosh stronghold that rises almost seamlessly from the bleak, rockbound cliffs that edge the glen's northernmost boundary.

No one knows the true origins of the dreagan stones.

Those of a fearful nature would rather not know.

Clan Mackintosh, ever proud of its fierceness, accepts several possibilities....

As odd things do happen on Mackintosh land, especially on nights of dark, impenetrable mist, it is generally believed that the unusual rock formations are sleeping dreagans—dreagans turned to stone, but able to come to life and wreak terror if they wish to do so.

Others claim the stones aren't just frozen dreagans, but also ancient warriors who were once the dreagans' masters. These were fearless men who protected the glen in a time when the world was young, but who were betrayed when one in their number was turned by greed, thereby inviting annihilation by evil powers stronger than any mortal men.

Some tales are even more chilling.

Graybeards who have lived long enough to be wise in such matters insist that the red-eyed glance of a stony-scaled dreagan marks a soul for death.

The dreagan stones are also known to scream. The sound is more like a roar, and on black, moonless nights, these chilling cries have been known to strike terror in the hearts of bold and courageous men. On such nights in this cold, inhospitable corner of the glen, even something as innocuous as a curl of mist holds menace.

Kendrew Mackintosh, clan chief, is proud of this legacy.

Dreagans do lie beneath the dreagan rocks.

At least, clan legend claims it is so.

Those tales say that one blast of a dreagan's fiery breath could melt Kendrew's formidable war ax in his hand. Or that a single swipe from the creature's stony, razor-sharp claws could cut down a score of mailed warriors. Kendrew's loudest, most fierce battle cry would be like the chirp of a sparrow next to the hill-shaking roar of a dreagan.

Now some whisper the beasts are stirring.

These tale spinners suspect the dreagans resent the fragile peace that has descended on the glen. Clan Mackintosh, after all, has always been a warring tribe. Mercy and quiet living runs against their heated nature and unquenchable thirst for battle and bloodletting.

If suchlike is true, Kendrew would welcome the dreagans' unrest.

He's already noticed something afoot.

Whatever the cause, the nightly rattle of shifting stones makes his pulse quicken. And the eerie growls heard on the wind call to his wild nature. He, too, is restless. Like the dreagans, he'd rather stir trouble than pace his keep like a caged beast.

A man was born to fight, not lie idle.

He needn't worry, because tragedy is about to strike, giving him ample cause to swing Blood Drinker, his huge war ax. Only along with sword-wielding foemen and stony-backed, fire-breathing dreagans, he'll be fighting a greater challenge than he would've believed.

His opponent is a woman.

And their battle begins in the shadow of the dreagan stones.

Chapter One

❦

CASTLE HAVEN

THE GLEN OF MANY LEGENDS

MIDSUMMER EVE 1397

*D*o *you believe Kendrew Mackintosh dances naked on
the dreagan stones?"*

Lady Isobel Cameron glanced across the well-appointed
bedchamber at her good-sister and, much as she tried,
couldn't keep the excitement from her voice. Her heart
knocked wildly at her daring. Especially when Lady
Catriona's reaction was to sit up straighter in her massive,
four-postered bed. She also pinned Isobel with a look that
held more than a hint of disapproval. Worse, there was a
flicker of sympathy in the depths of her dark blue eyes.

Isobel lifted her chin, pretending not to see.

Pity was the last thing she wanted.

Her heart was set on the Mackintosh chieftain and had
been for some while—as Catriona well knew.

It'd been her plan, and not Isobel's, that the two of them
and Kendrew's sister, Lady Marjory, should each seduce

and wed a man from one of the other glen clans. Only so could true peace be held.

Or so they'd agreed the previous autumn, in the bloody aftermath of the trial by combat. A battle to the death, ordered by the king to decide which of the three clans should be granted overlordship. When the fighting ended, the three warrior chieftains were still on their feet, their weapons held fast in their hands.

In his well-meant benevolence, King Robert III declared a truce.

He'd presented each chieftain with a charter for land the clans already saw as their own. And he'd left them with a not-too-subtle warning that any further unrest would result in severest punishment.

Banishment to a distant Hebridean isle was just one threat that—still—hung over the heads of every man, woman, and child of the glen.

No living soul in the Glen of Many Legends would risk such a fate.

Yet the men of the clans were quickly angered, their tempers easily roused.

Keeping peace fell to the women.

Catriona was now wed to Isobel's brother, James, clan chief of the Camerons.

It seemed a blessed union.

Isobel was meant to be the next bride.

And on the day the three women made their pact, she'd chosen Kendrew. What she hadn't done was tell her friends how much she secretly desired him. His wildness excited her, his adherence to ancient Norse ways calling to her own Viking blood—a legacy she was proud of and that her own clan largely ignored, much to her sorrow.

Only Isobel's heart quickened at the thought of distant northern lands full of cold wind, ice, and endless winters. She alone held a soft spot for the fearless, seafaring people who, legend claimed, gave one of their most beautiful young noblewomen as a bride to a distant Cameron chieftain. A war prize and peace offering, she'd forever sealed the clan's irrevocable bond with the pagan north.

Isobel felt drawn to that legacy.

So Kendrew, who often wore a bearskin thrown over his broad shoulders and favored a Viking war ax over a sword, fascinated her.

He flaunted his Nordic ancestry.

Isobel admired him.

Unfortunately, the attraction wasn't mutual.

Isobel brushed at her sleeve, willing her annoyance to fade. Unfortunately, she failed. Her wilder side, the part of her no one suspected existed, swirled and raged inside her, demanding attention.

"Kendrew Mackintosh is a howling madman." Catriona found her tongue at last, her tone proving she knew the source of Isobel's agitation.

Isobel flicked at her other sleeve, too irritated to care.

"It is summer solstice." She went ahead and spoke her mind, images of Kendrew's big, powerfully muscled body kissed by the glow of bonfires making her breath catch and her skin tingle. "The Mackintoshes celebrate Midsummer in the old way." She glanced at the room's tall window arches, her pulse quickening at the polished gleam of the twilight sky. "On such a night, I can't help but wonder if he really does leap naked onto the cairns."

"He is surely bold enough." Catriona smoothed the

bed covers, resting her hands atop her slightly swollen belly. "Everyone knows he's wholly untamed."

Isobel could've added more. She did imagine him standing proud in the heart of his rock-hewn land, cold mist blowing around him, the gold of his Thor's hammer and arm rings glinting brightly.

"He did fight ferociously at the trial by combat." She bit back how much his bravery impressed her. "The earth shook when he stamped the haft of his war ax on the ground after the battle."

"He is fearless, true enough." Catriona shivered when a chill wind swept the room, stirring the floor rushes. "Word is he can trace his line back to the Berserkers, Odin's bloodthirsty, half-mythic bodyguards.

"So-o-o..." She laced her fingers. "He could well be doing anything this night, including leaping naked onto his dreagan stones."

Isobel agreed.

But unlike her friend, she didn't find the notion disturbing.

The brisk air filling the chamber brought traces of damp earth and pine, just a hint of distant woodsmoke. Soon the first stars would start to glimmer. Beyond the thick pine forest that separated their lands, Mackintosh bonfires would crackle and blaze.

Those who prayed to Odin would gather. Men would touch hammer amulets and drink from mead horns. Blood would heat, passions rising as the revelry commenced...

Isobel's heart pounded.

"I wouldn't mind seeing Kendrew on those stones." She glanced again at the windows, the night's magic calling to her, making her restless.

"The sight would ruin you for life." Catriona sounded sure.

Isobel lifted her chin. "I think I'd be rather intrigued."

"Humph." Catriona leaned forward a little. "You'd feel otherwise if one of his dreagans took a bite out of you."

"Pah." Isobel dismissed the possibility. "They only live in legend."

"I've heard tales." Catriona persisted.

"Then you'd know they're said to fire-blast, not bite." Isobel regarded her levelly. "You just don't like Kendrew."

"That's true." Catriona held her gaze.

Isobel struggled against the urge to squirm, wishing her friend didn't have such a direct stare. "I've wondered"—she took a deep breath, then rushed on—"if the blue marks he carves on his chest and arms really are to celebrate each enemy he kills in battle or—"

"They are." Catriona tightened her lips. "I'm sure he also does it to look terrifying."

Isobel ignored her friend's comment. "Do you think he has the marks anywhere else?"

Catriona shuddered. "I'm sure I don't want to know."

"I do." Isobel did want to know, badly.

She was also sure the admission had turned her cheeks scarlet. She could feel the heat blooming there, branding her shameless. High-born, gently raised females weren't supposed to ponder the lure of bare-bottomed men. They especially weren't wise to crave the attention of a man as wild as Kendrew Mackintosh. And they should never imagine him whirling about naked in an ancient, pagan ritual that most decent folk had abandoned years ago.

Such thoughts were wicked.

But they filled her with prickling excitement.

And once the images had taken root, she couldn't banish them.

Nor did she want to.

The Mackintosh chieftain was a great giant of a man, burly, loud, and rough around the edges. An unapologetic scoundrel, he towered over most men and clearly enjoyed that dominance. Heavy, burnished copper hair swung about his shoulders, and when he flashed his fast, crooked smile, it was said that no female could resist his rascally charm.

He defied every danger and laughed in the face of death. He lived by his own rules. His strange blue kill marks made him look like a fearsome Norse god. And his prowess in bed was said to be even greater than his formidable skill on the field of battle.

Well-lusted, he was rumored to be insatiable.

Isobel shivered, delicately.

She could so easily see him sweeping her into his arms and whisking her up the turret stairs, ravishment and more on his mind. No man had ever even kissed her. She knew with a desiring woman's instinct that Kendrew's kisses would be hot, furious, and deliciously savage.

It was a notion that made her entire body flush.

She just hoped Catriona would credit the warmth from the bedchamber's crackling log fire as the reason for her heightened color.

The earlier breath of cold had fled, the wind moving on to rustle through the pines.

It was again stifling in the room.

By all reckoning, Catriona's travails weren't expected until the passing of another six full moons. A winter birthing seemed probable, possibly at Yule. Yet some of the older castle women predicted she'd need longer. A few argued less. Either way, no one was taking any chances.

Catriona carried the clan heir. And there wasn't a soul at Castle Haven not concerned with her comfort. A few, including her besotted husband, seemed worried that she'd freeze. Every few hours, or so it seemed, a kitchen lad came to toss a new fat log on the bedchamber's hooded fireplace. Torches blazed in every wall sconce, and a score of fine wax candles graced the room's two small tables, each dancing flame adding to the stuffiness.

There was even a small brazier placed near the bed, its coals glowing softly as pungent, herb-scented smoke rose to haze the air. Eye-burning, overheated air that Catriona seemed weary of breathing, for instead of quipping that Isobel shouldn't concern herself with Kendrew's arm-and-chest markings, she tossed back the coverlets and slid down from her bed. She crossed the room to the far windows where she breathed deep of the cool, evening air.

Isobel gave her a moment, then hitched her skirts and joined her. "They say Kendrew leaps onto Slag's Mound wearing only his Thor's hammer." She'd meant to say something else entirely, but she couldn't get Kendrew from her mind. Speaking quickly, the words left her in a rush. "Slag was the worst of all dreagans, the most dangerous.

"I've heard he could kill ten men with a single swipe of his long, stony-scaled tail." The thought made Isobel's nerves flutter. "Slag's cairn is where the Mackintoshes celebrate their Midsummer Eve revels. Storytellers say that if Slag wished, even now he could send scalding, sulfuric breath right up through the cracks between the stones, blasting anyone who'd dare come near his cairn. Kendrew watches over the festivities from atop those stones. He—"

"He is that crazed, I know." Catriona braced her hands on the broad window ledge and turned her face to the freshening wind. "Be warned"—she shot a narrow-eyed glance at Isobel—"if you knew how I've felt these past months, you wouldn't be thinking of men."

"Kendrew isn't just any man." Isobel stepped closer to the window, half certain she could feel the power of the fierce Mackintosh chieftain even here, coming to her on the night wind, beckoning.

To her, he was everywhere.

And ever since she and her two friends had carefully woven their plans, there wasn't a corner of the Glen of Many Legends where she could escape his image. No place where she wouldn't dream of his heated gaze devouring her, or how she'd love feeling his hands glide along her body. Or where she wouldn't yearn for the hot, turbulent desire that she was sure would sweep her if, just once, he'd seize her and crush her to him, kissing her hungrily.

This was a night for kissing.

Ignoring Catriona and her somewhat soured expression, Isobel straightened her shoulders, determining to keep her gaze on the well-loved landscape before her.

Although already evening, the sky shone with pearly luminescence, and the cool, pine-scented air felt rich with custom, legend, and magic. The hills rising beyond Castle Haven's walls shimmered in the strange, soft light. And— if she looked closely, opening her heart—she could almost see water nymphs bathing in the tumbling cascades spilling down the sides of the highest peaks.

Birdsong filtered through the trees, sweet and musical,

almost as if the tiny woodland creatures joined with the night's wonder to tempt her away, out into the enchantment of Midsummer Eve.

The world gleamed, expectant and waiting.

Isobel's pulse raced.

Then she made the error of glancing at her friend.

Catriona was watching her as if she could peer into her soul and see the urgency beating there, making her burn to unleash her desires.

"I wish you'd chosen someone else." Catriona's voice held a note that could've been regret or reproach. Turning back to the window, she fixed her gaze on a single star that sparkled like a jewel in the silvery sky. "When the three of us"—she meant herself, Isobel, and Kendrew's sister, Marjory—"agreed to each wed a man from a feuding clan, the idea was to keep peace in the glen through our unions.

"That will only happen if such marriages take place." She shifted her glance to where a second star was just winking to life. "Kendrew isn't a man to wed. Everyone knows it. He's in love with his war ax and—"

"It's only been a few months since our pact—"

"Nae, it's been over half a year." Catriona touched a hand to Isobel's arm. "Kendrew hasn't even spoken to you in all that time. The one visit he made us was brief and he didn't spare you a glance. He keeps himself locked away behind Castle Nought's walls where he surely spends his days sharpening weapons and making pagan sacrifices to Thor. James has invited him here, often enough.

"It would be a small thing to accept my husband's goodwill. Yet"—Catriona paused to take a breath—"he chooses to shun us all. Some even say he's planting poison-tipped stakes in the ground around his stronghold. He's been heard to say he wants to deter visitors from breaking his peace."

Isobel frowned. "He wouldn't do that."

"Pah!" Catriona clearly believed he would. "He'd challenge the Devil and all his ring-tailed minions if it amused him to do so."

"He has Berserker blood." Isobel secretly thrilled to his wildness.

"All the more reason you should consider someone else." Catriona clutched Isobel's hands, squeezing tight. "We've grown close since I married your brother and came here. You've become the sister I never had, and"— she released Isobel and stepped back—"I couldn't bear to see you unhappy. Kendrew will only hurt you."

"Nae..." Isobel refused the possibility.

She did shiver. The sensation that he was near her, all around her, strengthened. She touched the charmed amber necklace at her throat, wondering if Catriona's gift, or the magic of summer solstice, was the reason she felt so powerfully drawn to him this night.

"Kendrew would never cause me pain." She stood straighter, flicked her braid over her shoulder. "He doesn't frighten me and never will. Even Marjory has told us how fiercely he honors women and—"

"He'll be *honoring* plenty this night." Catriona returned to her bed, lowering herself carefully onto its edge. "Or what do you think Mackintoshes do at their dreagan stones on Midsummer Eve?

"They'll be doing more than dancing in a circle and leaping over bonfires." Catriona clasped her hands over her belly. "Be glad you aren't there."

Isobel wished she was.

"Do not think to sneak there tonight." Catriona's glance was sharp.

Isobel crimsoned. "I wouldn't dare."

"Nae?" Catriona lifted a red-gold brow.

Again, Isobel felt like squirming. But she forced herself to stand still. She also held Catriona's deep, all-seeing gaze. "I know better than to traipse off into the night, alone and unescorted."

"Indeed?" Catriona's brow arched a fraction higher.

"So I said." Isobel didn't turn a hair.

"Then you are less like me than I'd believed." Her friend's expression softened, the glimmer of pity returning to her lovely blue eyes. "With half the castle abed with a bellyache from bad herring and the rest down in the hall, deep in their cups because tonight is Midsummer, I would've thought you'd be tempted to slip away.

"I've done the like more than once, as well you know." Catriona's tone was quiet, reminiscent. "Back in the days before I was a settled, married woman. Now"—she splayed her fingers across the swell of her abdomen—"I do see things a bit differently."

"You're seeing them wrong." Isobel should've known Catriona would guess the thoughts flitting about in her mind this night. "I'm not going anywhere."

She hadn't actually planned to until Catriona's words made the idea seem possible.

Now . . .

She bit her lip, half afraid Catriona would tell James, causing him to rush out after her, if she dared to sneak out on her own.

But she so wanted to.

She turned back to the window, the night's sweetness beckoning. Midsummer magic steeped the air, the beauty of the luminous twilight combining with her desire to see Kendrew on the stones until her pulse raced as never before. Longing swelled in her chest, hot and insistent, tugging on long-buried needs deep inside her.

Across the room, Catriona sighed. "You truly do have your heart set on Mackintosh, don't you?"

"I…" Isobel took a long breath, knowing there was no point in denial. "Any other man pales beside him." She left the window and started pacing before the fire, a strange sense of triumph beating through her now that she'd spoken openly. "If I see him at his boldest tonight, perhaps I can learn how to attract his attention."

Catriona snorted. "You have breasts and a comely face. Catching his eye is the least of your worries. The problem is that"—she pulled a small pillow onto her lap, her brow creasing again—"a fast tumble in the heather is all you can expect from him."

Isobel didn't want to believe it. "You won James's heart—"

"James is not Kendrew Mackintosh." Catriona dismissed her objection, the words dimming the warm glow of hope that had begun to thrum in Isobel's breast. "I can see no good coming from you sneaking off to Castle Nought tonight. That corner of the glen is also fraught with other dangers. It's an unholy place, filled with weird mist and darkness. Bare rock and naked, jagged cliffs make it cold and forbidding. Mackintosh territory is nothing like Castle Haven and the wooded hills and waterfalls surrounding us here.

"Nought is a terrifying, unwelcoming place." Catriona

drew the little pillow closer against her middle. "They say the wind there carries ancient echoes of dreagan roars. I do believe that is true."

"I'm not afraid." To her amazement, Isobel wasn't.

Catriona frowned. "If something happens to you and James discovers I kept silent about you slipping away, he'll never forgive me."

"I never told you I'm going." Isobel brushed at her skirts, offering her friend the only defense she could against James's possible wrath. "Indeed, when I leave you, I'll be heading to my own bedchamber."

She didn't say that she'd simply meant to retrieve her cloak.

The crease in Catriona's brow deepened. But she held her peace, settling back against the bed cushions.

She did send a pointed glance at the small oaken table set before one of the room's colorful wall tapestries. The table was right next to the door.

"You know"—she looked back to Isobel, her blue gaze piercing—"that my condition keeps me from wearing my lady's dirk." She flicked another quick glance at the table where her jewel-hilted dagger glittered in the light of a wall sconce. "Everyone knows sharp objects might cause harm to a wee babe in the womb."

Isobel nodded, understanding her friend's unspoken message.

"Thank you." Isobel touched her amber necklace again, almost overcome by the rush of hope, giddiness, and excitement mounting inside her.

Then, before she lost her nerve, she cast another look at the shimmering sky beyond the window arches, and hurried from the bedchamber.

She snatched Catriona's dagger on her way out the door.

She doubted she'd need it.

But she didn't want her friend to worry. Unlike her, Catriona saw danger in Nought's mysteries, the dark and rock-bound landscape.

Isobel saw adventure.

And—she hoped—the love of a lifetime.

About the same time, but in the dread place of rock and shadow that Isobel and her friend had just been discussing, Kendrew Mackintosh stood in the middle of Castle Nought's cavernous great hall and stared at his sister, Marjory. Fondly known as Lady Norn for her striking Nordic beauty and Valkyrie-ish temperament, she lifted her chin, meeting his gaze with her wintriest smile. She also had the cheek to think that planting herself in front of the door would keep him from leaving the hall.

"You'll no' be stopping me from enjoying the night's revels." Kendrew folded his arms, incredulous as ever at her flashing-eyed boldness.

Then he grinned, unable to help himself.

"By Thor," he boomed, "you should have been born a man. If you wielded a sword as sharp as your blazing eyes, no enemy would be safe."

Marjory set her hands on her hips, her chilly mien not warming a whit. "You'll be spared my wrath as soon as you read James Cameron's missive." Sending a pointed glance at the parchment scroll resting atop a nearby long table, she began tapping her foot. "It's no great task. Break the seal and give him the courtesy of—"

"Odin's balls, I will!" Kendrew glared at her, his grin

faded. "Breaking thon seal and reading his foolery will only sour my mood. I already ken what he's after. This new letter will hold the same twaddle as his previous ones, and I'm having none of it."

"He only wants a few stones for the memorial cairn." Marjory bent another icy look right back at him. The little brown and white dog sitting beside her skirts eyed him with equal animosity.

Marjory glanced at her pet, and then back at Kendrew as if the teeny beast's opinion supported hers. "Send James the rocks and"—she curved her lips in an annoyingly superior smile—"he'll leave you be."

"Aye, he will." Kendrew swelled his chest. "But no' because I do his bidding, I say you."

Jaw set, he shot a glance at the hall's high, narrow-slit windows, his irritation increasing to see that the twilight was already sliding into night. The sky still shone with the fine luminosity of highest summer, but the hour was advancing.

The celebrations at the dreagan stones would be well underway.

"You did agree to send stones." Marjory proved she could be the most vexatious female he knew. "I heard you when we were at Castle Haven to discuss the cairn just a few months past. Everyone heard you."

Kendrew cut the air with a hand, ignoring her argument.

"I'd rather send Blood Drinker arcing into James Cameron's skull." He grinned again, liking the notion.

Blood Drinker, his beloved, well-used, and storied war ax, hadn't quenched his thirst of late. Giving his finely tooled blade a nice long drink of Cameron blood would do the weapon good.

"The bastard is a bane." He relished the shock on his

sister's face. "He'll no' be getting a single Nought stone for his cairn. Every rock here, even the smallest pebble, belongs where it is.

"Cuiridh mi clach 'ad charn." Kendrew waited for her reaction. "Have you forgotten that those words mean so much more than 'I will place a stone on your cairn?' Has it slipped your mind"—he stepped closer, frowning down at her—"that the old wisdom has little to do with carrying a rock to a man's final resting place and everything to do with vowing never to forget that man?"

When she flushed, Kendrew pounced. "Every stone on our land, be it on a cairn or in the bottom of a burn, recalls a long-past clansman. I'll no' disgrace their memories by seeing even a grain of Nought sand added to a memorial that glorifies our enemies."

Satisfied that Marjory couldn't argue, Kendrew folded his arms.

She recovered swiftly. "Word is Alasdair MacDonald sent enough stones to build a small house." Straightening to her full height, she tossed back her bright, sun-gold hair and raised her chin, defiant. "He—"

Kendrew snorted. "MacDonald is a worse snake than Cameron. With his sister now married to James, the bastard had no choice but to send Blackshore rocks. I do have a choice and Cameron knows what it is."

"He can't. You're ignoring his requests."

"That's my answer."

"The memorial cairn is to mark the battle site," Marjory persisted. Her dog stood, a cagey look entering his eyes as he started toward Kendrew. A wee creature she'd illogically named Hercules, the dog was clearly bent on performing a favorite irritating trick.

"Call him off, Norn." Kendrew glared at the dog, his manly dignity keeping him from leaping out of Hercules's leg-lifting range.

"Hercules, come here." Marjory used her sweetest tone.

The dog bared his teeth and growled at Kendrew, but then trotted dutifully back to Marjory, where he once again took his place beside her.

"He's annoyed by your grumblings." Marjory excused her pet. "And I'm disappointed by your stubbornness." She took a breath, all cold, northern ice again. Kendrew could almost feel the chill winds swirling around him. "You're deliberately undermining the peace in this glen. You know there's to be a friendship ceremony at Castle Haven in two months. If you refuse to send stones, the cairn can't be completed."

"Could be I'm for forgetting that slaughter ever happened." Kendrew grabbed his bearskin off the bench where he'd thrown it earlier and swirled it around his shoulders. "If I think about it, I just want to be there again." He strode right up to his sister, towering over her. "Only then I'd finish the fight, leaving no' a miserable Cameron or MacDonald on the bloody field."

"The king ordered peace." Marjory didn't back down.

Hercules growled again.

"Robert Stewart has his royal will." Kendrew stepped around them both and threw open the hall door. "And I"—he glanced over his shoulder at her—"am off to Slag's Mound to enjoy what peace is left to me.

"A pity you'll no' be coming along." At the moment, he was secretly relieved.

In such a mood, she'd ruin the festivities.

"Hercules was ailing this morn." She bent and scooped the wee dog into her arms, coddling him. "I'll not be leaving him alone tonight."

"As you wish." Kendrew shrugged, certain Hercules looked triumphant.

He knew a trickster when he saw one.

He was a master scoundrel himself, after all.

Glad of it—and proud, truth be told—he pulled the hall door shut behind him and stepped out into the glistening, silver-shot night.

Marjory needn't know he had other reasons for being so thrawn about the stones.

His stubbornness was Cameron's own fault.

The last time he'd visited Castle Haven, he'd told James of seeing several armed strangers. Thick-bearded men in helms and mail, they'd lurked about on a ledge overlooking the waterfall behind the Cameron stronghold.

James claimed his lookouts would've spotted any trespassers. He did send men to the falls. No strangers were found. James's tone upon reporting his guards' findings implied that Kendrew had mistaken water spray for the glint of mailed coats.

Kendrew said no more.

But he hadn't forgotten the slight.

Pushing his foe from his mind, he stepped deeper onto the broad landing.

Splendor greeted him, making his heart thud fast in his chest. Castle Nought's thick, impregnable walls rose seamlessly from the cliffs at the northernmost end of the Glen of Many Legends. And here, in the stone-cut arch of the lofty gatehouse, the whole sweep of his territory could be admired. But he knew that many short-sighted fools didn't appreciate the windy, steep-sided vista of rock and mist stretching beneath him. Those misguided souls thought of his home as a dark and benighted place, full of cold and menace.

Kendrew knew better.

True men thrived in such wildness.

Soft living created weak men. Those who cowered in gentler climes weren't worthy of their bollocks.

Knowing he was worthy of his and more, Kendrew reached for the heavy gold Thor's hammer at his throat and kissed the well-loved amulet.

The gods did well settling him and those who'd gone before him as the guardians of this rugged, mist-drenched corner of the Highlands. Tonight he and his people—and a few lusty, well-made lasses drawn to the raucousness from the surrounding hills and moors—would honor those gods, thanking them for their bounty.

Already, the bonfires were lit in celebration, flames leaping high against the sides of the high peaks hemming Nought land. The fires threw a pulsing, golden cast across the windswept ridges and the narrow, rock-filled vale, the contrast with the glistening silver of the night sky almost too beautiful to behold.

But Kendrew did, fierce pride coursing in his veins.

He loved Nought.

And he waited all year for Midsummer Eve.

It was a night of magic.

A time when—he was sure—even the dreagans sleeping beneath their stony cairns stirred and yearned for the days of yore.

Kendrew understood such longing.

And when he let his gaze sweep the great mounds of

jumbled rocks so many glen folk still feared, he knew he'd sooner take his last breath than call any other place home. He closed his eyes and breathed deep, reveling in the heady smell of cold air and damp stone, the tantalizing trace of roasting meat and woodsmoke drifting on the wind.

Joy filled him.

It was time to forget any fools who didn't appreciate Nought and let his own passions run free. Eager to be on his way, he bounded down the bluff's narrow stone steps and made straight for the jumbled outcroppings dotting his land, the heart of the dreagan stones.

This Midsummer Eve would be like no other.

He felt it in his bones.

Chapter Two

✦

Isobel's daring held until the Rodan Stone loomed before her.

She stared at the monolith, its sudden appearance through the mist both startling and unsettlingly ominous. She hadn't faltered once since leaving Cameron territory, and although she'd imagined eyes watching her once or twice, the feeling had been fleeting. If anyone had seen her slip away, she'd surely have been followed. But she'd only heard the rustle of her own passage as she'd hurried through the thick pine forest she knew so well.

Now...

The succor of Haven's woodsy-scented pines, rich, damp earth, and clean, cold-rushing streams lay far behind her. And Kendrew's Nought was living up to its fierce reputation as a grim place choked by rock and battered by wind. Little more than a few tussocks of stunted heather and ghostly looking birches grew here.

Worst of all...

She'd almost swear the Rodan Stone was glaring at her.

Set deep into the wild sweep of rock, scrub, and jagged peaks that defined Mackintosh country, the monolith seemed to warn that the fates weren't kind to those who dared trespass beyond this point. The brooding heart of this bleak, mist-shrouded corner of the glen stood near. And anyone venturing onward should take heed.

Isobel did pause. But she refused to let the hoary monument sway her.

Even so, her insides went a little cold as she eyed the stone.

Tall, eerily manlike, and more than a little menacing, the standing stone would've speared heavenward if it didn't lean at an odd angle. But the towering stone did tilt forward, giving credence to the tales that the monolith was actually a once-living man who'd been flash-frozen in the act of fleeing from the dreagans.

Rodan, the storytellers called that man. They claimed he'd been a long-ago Mackintosh warrior. He was one of the clan's revered dreagan masters, until the hungry beasts rebelled at the instigation of his greatest rival, another master of dreagans, who went by the name of Daire. That clan traitor—supposedly turned by greed—is said to have used darkest magic to spell the dreagans into attacking Rodan when he revealed that Daire was lightening Nought's impressive stores of silver and gold, and even lining his purse with the sale of Mackintosh cattle and grain.

Daire's nefarious deeds were paid in his blood.

Rodan was a clan hero.

And his stone had become a place of reverence for all Mackintoshes.

It also served as a boundary marker for dreagan stone territory, or so Isobel had always heard.

Just now, she was more concerned with what she felt. In keeping with the legends of Nought, thick mist rolled across the broken ground and the cold air held more than the sharp brittleness of a chill night. Something stirred in the swirling mist.

This time, she was certain.

She felt someone—*something*—staring at her as surely as the morrow.

And whatever it was, it was angry.

"Rodan..." Isobel whispered the stone's name, hoping to placate the long-dead dreagan master if it was his ill will prickling her nape.

She looked about, studying the lichen-grown boulders and sheer cliffs. Mist wraiths slid past granite outcrops and through the scattered birches of a nearby wood. It was easy to imagine a tall, dark shape hovering there, frowning at her from the shelter of the trees.

Little fantasy was needed to see a thick-bearded spearman, his mail coat shining through the whirling mist—until the mist shifted, revealing the *warrior* had only been the silver-gleaming trunk of a birch. His shield, moments before blazing brighter than the sun, proved nothing more than the silvery flash of a rushing stream.

Isobel shivered, all the same.

She knew from her family history that ghosts existed.

Clan Cameron had their own Scandia, once known as the Doom of the Camerons, until they'd learned the truth of her tragic demise. A gray lady, Scandia most often appeared when tragedy struck the family, but she wasn't the cause of those disasters, as the clan had always believed. She only sought to warn the clan of impending danger.

And perhaps—or so Isobel personally believed—Scandia simply wished to enjoy the ambiance of Castle Haven and the good cheer of men and women she'd once walked among and still viewed as her own.

Someone's mortal passing didn't mean the snuffing out of his soul.

Isobel was certain of that.

So she couldn't ignore the possibility that Rodan lurked near his stone and might see her, a Cameron woman, as a threat to his people.

"Rodan..." She stood straighter, speaking louder this time. "I know you're a clan hero." She touched her amber necklace, taking strength in the gemstones' smooth coolness. "I honor your bravery and—"

A whoosh of icy wind whipped past her, tearing at her cloak and then circling the stone before speeding off into the deeper shadows.

"Ack!" She brushed at her cloak and patted her hair, annoyed that the wind had loosened her braids. She'd taken care to twine blue silk ribbons through the strands and now one of the ribbons was coming undone.

"I mean no harm." She lifted her chin, hoping her voice sounded more firm than it did to her.

She also curled her fingers around her ambers, waiting for the enchanted stones to spring to life, lending their protection as she'd been told to expect of them. Catriona had sworn the ambers quivered and heated whenever a threat loomed near.

The necklace was still.

Forcing herself to be brave, she went to the Rodan

Stone and flattened her hand against the monolith's icy, age-pitted surface. "I've made a pact, see you? An oath sworn on sacred white heather and with two friends to ensure this glen is never sundered again.

"I haven't had much luck upholding my part of our plan." She chose her words carefully, keeping her hand pressed to the stone so the gods who ruled Midsummer Eve would hear her. "I'm hoping this night's magic will aid me. I mean no harm. I only want to see Kendrew." It wasn't the whole truth—she wanted his kisses, perhaps even more.

But she felt rather silly speaking to a stone.

"Once I see him, I'll leave." She hoped he'd see her and demand that she stay.

She'd accoutered herself to tempt him.

She wasn't here as an enemy.

And if legends were true and the storied stone—or Rodan himself—was guarding the entry to the dreagan stones, she wished the monolith and its spirit would note how carefully she'd readied herself to come here. She'd brushed her hair so many strokes that the long raven tresses gleamed like blue-black satin. And she'd not just bathed, albeit quickly, but had smoothed her body with rich, scented oils. She'd chosen a low-cut gown of sheerest silk, its deep sapphire color dark enough for modesty, though the soft fall of its clinging folds left little to the imagination.

She meant to leave her cloak at the edge of the dreagan stones.

Then...

She shivered and closed her eyes, refusing the notion that some fierce power here might prevent her from continuing to the heart of Nought territory. She could hear the revelry. Joyous shouts and laughter filled the air, raucous singing, and the roar of bonfires. Pipes screamed and drums rolled, the familiar music blending with the more primordial beat of what could only be scores of spear ends knocking on the stony ground.

She took a deep breath, her own wildness awakening, roused by desires older than time.

The chill wind blasted her again, its urgency making her heart beat fast in her chest. She could almost feel a rush of emotion beneath the freezing gusts, a powerful force seeking to prove its fury.

She gripped the stone harder, the wind nearly knocking her off her feet.

"See here..." She delved deep inside her, summoning strength.

She'd come so far. And she wasn't leaving just because Rodan and his stone apparently disliked her.

She meant to be triumphant.

But the cold wind mocked her, howling so that its scream blotted the din from the revels. For a moment, she imagined she again caught a movement in the birch wood, this time nearer to the edge of the trees. As before, it was the fleeting image of a tall, dark shape—the figure of a man—and with a furious glint in his eyes.

They were eyes as hard as stone.

And like the figure itself, they vanished when she blinked.

Still...

She could feel the specter's annoyance. Displeasure that thickened the air, souring the night's magic.

"You must see that my purposes are good." She slid a

hand down the side of the leaning stone, patting its solidness in reassurance. "I am intrigued by your clan leader. I know he is a bold and fearless chief, a fine man. And I want to win his heart."

At once, the air shifted around the stone, lightening. The icy wind careened away, sweeping up and over the crowding peaks, vanishing into the night. All sense of heavy anger lifted, disappearing as if it'd never been.

Whatever had tried to block her path was gone.

Or—her pulse quickened—had given approval for her to journey on.

And so she did, hitching her skirts and hurrying toward the distant red glow of the bonfires—the everstranger piles of tumbled rock known to be the final resting places of sleeping dreagans.

She spotted Kendrew at once.

Naked indeed, he stood atop the largest stone cairn. Mist and smoke from the bonfires blew around him, shielding parts of him from view as if the gods of such revels envied his splendor. He'd braced one hand against his hip and held his long-bearded ax in the other. It was a powerfully masculine pose and one that made Isobel's breath catch.

He truly was magnificent.

He breathed hard, his broad, well-muscled chest rising and falling as if he'd just finished the leaping, whirling dance she must've missed. The same wind that cloaked him in smoke and mist tossed his mane of rich auburn hair. And the blaze of the fires made his skin gleam like burnished bronze. His golden Thor's hammer glinted at his throat and the blue kill-marks adorning his powerful arms and his chest seemed almost alive, each jagged slash challenging anyone to doubt his fierceness.

Isobel's heart thundered.

A blush swept up her neck, staining her cheeks. Gloriously warlike, he looked ready to stand at Thor's side, fighting with the irascible Viking god at Ragnarok, the great battle at the end of the world that every Norseman knew would someday bring the Doom of the Gods. Kendrew's arms would be thick with gold rings of valor, his face fierce as he fought with all the Berserker rage of his race. The image came to her clearly, everything feminine in her responding to him and the heritage she prized so dearly.

Could she ever desire any other man after seeing him here tonight?

Sure she couldn't, she stayed in shadow, content for the moment to simply watch him.

As she did, the mist and smoke shifted, letting her glimpse a wicked scar that slashed down his abdomen. The scar was a remnant of the trial by combat, a cut he'd suffered at the hands of Alasdair MacDonald near the battle's end. She winced to think how close Kendrew had come to losing a part of him that all men prized so highly.

Women, too, she knew.

Caught in that age-old attraction, she wasn't surprised to feel ripples of appreciation begin to spill through her. Delicious currents of shivery female need spooling low in her belly as blood rushed in her ears. Her pulse grew so loud that she could hardly hear the thunder of the Mackintosh warriors' spear ends beating against stone.

Even the scream of the pipes seemed to fade, everything around her whirling away, including the cries of the many half-naked couples writhing in carnal ecstasy on the ground. Isobel's flush deepened, her awareness of the frolicking pairs adding to her inner heat and discomfiture. The open lovemaking both embarrassed and aroused her. But she kept her gaze on her heart's desire, her senses igniting until nothing else existed except Kendrew, so proud and magnificent, as he looked around, surveying the celebrations.

He hadn't yet seen her.

And when one of the women mating beneath the dreagan cairn nearest to Isobel tipped back her head and released a throaty cry of bliss, Isobel almost turned and hastened back the way she'd come.

She might want Kendrew.

But she wanted him for her husband.

She gulped as her gaze flicked over the scene of pagan debauchery. She wasn't sure he'd even glance at her with so many unclothed, willing women flitting about the great mounds of stones. Firelight gilded them, displaying their charms to advantage as they roamed about, seeking to entice new partners for vigorous tumbles in the heather.

The women were notably alluring. Females of skill and experience who'd come in from distant hills and moorlands to indulge in a good night's trade at the Mackintoshes' Midsummer revels.

It was a fest known for such delights.

Vibrant, beautiful, and lusty, they were joy women who made Isobel feel like a dim gray shadow. Her midnight tresses suddenly struck her as uninspired against so many flame-haired females, their unbound hair shining brighter than the bonfires. And although the other women were voluptuous, she doubted a single one came up to her chin. Their smaller stature made her feel clumsy and over-large. Kendrew would be a fool to waste such an enchanted night on her. Yet she'd come here with such hope.

Isobel frowned, not sure what she could do if he didn't notice her.

And if he did, would he find her lacking?

She was a virgin.

She didn't even know how to kiss.

"Kendrew!" A big, burly man tossed Kendrew a spear, laughing when he caught it midair and quickly took up the rhythmic stone-pounding, beating the spear end on top of Slag's Mound.

Kendrew grinned. He gripped the spear with enthusiasm, the merriment in his eyes setting off a flurry within her. Her doubts fled, replaced by something wondrous. A sensation that made her feel soft and warm inside, thrilling in a different way from the tummy flutters caused by catching a glimpse at his nakedness.

His smile showed her his soul.

And her heart split wide at the intimacy.

She understood the longing to uphold and honor the old Viking ways. The same Nordic blood flowed in her veins and, more than anyone she knew save Kendrew, she felt deeply bound to her heritage.

Sharing that bond with Kendrew was her dream.

A goal that meant as much to her as sealing glen peace with their union.

Their appreciation of northern ways would enrich their lives. She could feel their connection, even here in the shadows at the edge of the dreagan stones. The feeling was so strong that she wanted to hurry past the other cairns and scramble up onto Slag's Mound, capturing his attention. Once she did, she'd make him see how perfect they were for each other. But she remained where she stood, simply enjoying how his exuberance thrummed the air.

His passion beat around her, as much a part of the night as the stones and mist, the luminous silver sky. Surely twice the size of most men, he looked even larger up on the cairn. But it was his grin that made her path irrevocable, ruining her for all others.

She could love him so easily. Doing so would be as natural as breathing.

So she placed a hand on her heart and took a few steps toward the center of the dreagan vale and the high, stone-built mound.

"Odin!" Kendrew threw back his head then and roared the Norse god's name. "We honor you with our revels!" He raised the spear high, shaking it at the heavens. "Bless us this night and throughout the coming year!"

"Odin, Odin!" Everywhere, Mackintosh warriors took up the cry.

The pounding of spears on stone rang in the cold night air, the sound deafening, primordial.

Isobel felt the festival's magic building, the intensity of ancient, long-simmering powers. She watched Kendrew, every part of her tingling, fired with excitement.

The blowing mist and smoke swirled so thick now that she could hardly see more than his outline, big, powerful, and edged dark against the lighter gray of the haze. He kept the spear above his head as he shouted Odin's praise, his passion making blood scream in Isobel's ears. Her pulse roared, matching the beat of the spears, the flexing of Kendrew's arm as he thrust the spear heavenward.

She bit her lip, her world spinning until nothing existed except the two of them and the night's magic.

She knew she was breaking every rule she was supposed to live by.

She didn't care.

It'd been reckless to come here.

His nearness caused wild sensations to whirl inside her. Darts of pleasure danced between her legs, awakening her as a woman. The delicious tingles chased her modesty, urging her to be bold.

"Oh, dear..." She took a few backward steps, withdrawing into the deeper gloom, away from the entwined couples rolling on the grass nearby.

Sheltered by a cairn's shadow, she lifted her hands to her cloak pin, undoing the clasp.

I can do this... She kept the vow silent, willing courage to pour through her as she removed her mantle. It was her best, deep sapphire of lightest wool and lined with silk of the same dazzling color. She folded the cloak with care, setting it on a large stone.

Straightening, she smoothed the fine blue silk of her gown. She ran her hands down over her hips and then adjusted the perilously low cut of the garment's bodice. Wind helped her temptation plan, cooperatively molding the gown's fluid folds to her curves.

She might as well be naked.

How startling that the notion excited rather than embarrassed her.

No man had ever gazed upon her unclothed skin.

Yet...

Heart racing, she put back her shoulders and moved deeper into the narrow vale, heading straight for Slag's

Mound. If she meant to catch Kendrew's eye, she'd need to be quick. Three barely clad women were already gathered beneath the cairn, vying for his attention. He paid them no heed, still shouting Odin's praise and thumping the long spear's end against the cairn stones. Growing bolder, one of the women lifted her breasts, calling his name.

"O-o-oh, Kendrew," the woman trilled, "these be sweeter than anything in Valhalla."

Isobel felt a stab of resentment. She could never be so brazen, so direct. She preferred winning her man with a bit more finesse. Even so, she inhaled sharply, annoyance tightening her chest.

Bent on seduction, the other woman plucked on her bodice's already-loosened laces. With the ease of much practice, she pulled open her gown, revealing her eye-popping bosom in all its ripe glory.

"Oh, dear." Isobel stepped faster, scarcely aware of the wind that had just torn the last ribbon from her hair. Her braids unraveled and her hip-length tresses spilled over her shoulders and down her back, swinging free as she hurried toward the man she wasn't of a mind to share with anyone.

She knew they were a perfect match.

Soon—she hoped—he'd believe the same.

Even so, she felt a flutter of nerves as she nipped around the mound of stones, hot on the trail of the three skirling, hip-swaying women. Slag's Mound was immense, the largest of the dreagan cairns. Its great height cast a wedge of purple-black gloom so dense that Kendrew might not even see her if she jumped about waving her arms. Her rivals apparently felt the same, sashaying out of the murk even as Isobel stepped deeper into the cairn's shadow.

Frowning, she hitched her skirts and hurried on, only to hear a sudden skitter of stone and feel a whoosh of air as Kendrew jumped down from the cairn, landing right in front of her.

"Sweet, bonnie lass." He looked at her, his eyes alight with a bold recklessness that made her pulse leap. He didn't show a hint of recognition.

In the gloom of Slag's Mound, he didn't know her.

Isobel crushed a twinge of disappointment. She hadn't wanted him to recognize her. Not at first, anyway. Her plan was to captivate and then win his heart before her name could sour him.

Still . . .

She'd helped tend his wounds after the trial by combat. It rankled to think he'd forgotten her. Or else the cairn's shadow and the whirling mist hid her face better than she would have thought.

She also didn't know where to look.

The mist and smoke cloaked him well, yet standing so close to her, his nakedness was startling. She could feel his masculinity wrapping round her, dark, intimate, and almost predatory. His scent, so virile and male, made her senses reel. Delicious tingles stirred low in her belly, warming and exciting her.

As if he knew, his smile turned wicked. "Are you one of Odin's handmaidens, come down from Valhalla to tempt me?" His tone was teasing, the words bold. "If so I am yours."

"I—" Isobel blinked, nerves stealing her tongue.

He grinned, stepping closer. "Say you are mine."

She nodded, stunned by her daring.

Looking pleased, he tossed aside the long spear and

snatched a discarded plaid off a clump of heather. He slung the plaid across his shoulder, as if he knew the proud sweep of its folds would only enhance his power-fully muscled chest. His eyes glinted in the smoky air, his gaze raking her from the tumbled disorder of her hair to where she still held the hem of her gown hitched above her knees.

"You take my breath." His voice was low and deep, full of appreciation. "I knew this would be a Midsummer Eve like no other."

Isobel stood frozen. She knew hot color blazed on her cheeks, but hoped the shadows were deep enough so he wouldn't notice.

She couldn't speak.

Every witty and seductive quip she'd tried to memo-rize on the trek here vanished as if her mind were filled with bog cotton.

"Where have you been all the e'en?" His gaze was on her face now, his eyes dark with passion. She could feel his nearness, burning her like a physical touch. A smile lifted the corner of his mouth, deepening into a grin that made her heart flip. "If you're no' from Valhalla, are you one o' the lasses up from Rannoch Moor?"

Isobel knew he meant the light-skirts known to flock to Nought's Midsummer ribaldries.

It was whispered he journeyed often to Rannoch Moor.

Isobel's entire body flushed at the thought. By the way the joy women cooed and preened, she was sure Kendrew was a welcome visitor to their beds. Everyone knew they were accomplished sirens, able to deplete a man with a flick of their knowledgeable fingers, a single sultry glance. Her-self…She still couldn't get her tongue to work properly.

Worse, her heart seemed to have leaped to her throat, lodging there so that even breathing proved difficult.

"I didnae see you earlier." His voice deepened, the rich timbre rumbling though her, melting her. "For sure, I would've noticed."

"I..." She touched her ambers, taking comfort in the stones' cool stillness. Catriona's enchanted necklace didn't see him as a threat.

Their approval gave her courage. "I came late. It took a while for me to get here."

That was true.

She just didn't say where she'd started her journey.

To her surprise he frowned, his gaze flicking to the jagged cliffs soaring above the cookfires where whole oxen were roasting on spits. "You'll no' have trekked through the glen on your own?"

"I know the glen well." Isobel couldn't keep the pride from her voice.

Kendrew's face remained somber. "It is a fair place. But not without dangers." Once more, his gaze went beyond the cookfires. "Peril is known to follow lasses as beautiful as you, especially on nights when spirits are high and the mead flows so freely."

"I wanted to see you." The truth slipped past Isobel's lips.

"So you did, aye?" He stepped closer, so near she could feel the heat pouring off the hard muscles of his big body. "And now I see you. Your creamy breasts tempting me"—he let his gaze dip there, then lower—"and the curve of your hips.

"I would see more of you." He touched her cheek, his arm brushing lightly against the side of her breast.

His caress sent streams of pleasure through her. The graze of his arm against her breast made the silk of her gown pull across her nipples, the friction almost unbearable. Her body warmed, her skin tingling as her senses came alive with awareness.

"Will you be on the stones again?" It was all she could think to say.

He shook his head, his eyes locked on hers. "I think not."

Isobel bit her lip. It was clear that he also didn't recall her voice.

He did want her. Desire rolled off him, thick and potent. Even the air between them sizzled. There was no doubt that she intrigued him. More than that, he was hungry for her. She could see that in his eyes. She thrilled to the knowledge, eager to feel his arms slide around her.

Isobel swallowed, wondering how long she could keep his attention before he remembered her. If they moved away from the cairn's shadow, he surely would. She couldn't let that happen yet. She also didn't brush back her hair, allowing the wind-whipped strands to shield her face. She detested deceit, but she had to get close to Kendrew.

He repeatedly refused her brother's invitations to Castle Haven.

This was her only chance.

Every moment that stretched between the battle and now flashed across her mind. Loyalties and honor weighed down on her even as hope beat wildly in her breast.

She couldn't fail.

She'd entered into a sworn pact, even kissed the sacred bloom of white heather, vowing to seal glen peace by wedding an enemy chieftain. She'd chosen Kendrew. Her heart had swiftly agreed, knowing no other man would please her more. If she could tempt him now, making him want her so fiercely her name wouldn't matter...

Her palms went damp at her daring.

He held her gaze. "I've no need to return to the stones. The gods have blessed me well this night." The look in his eyes made her feel desired. "In truth, they've ne'er been so good to me."

A twinge of guilt stabbed her.

Not that she was actually tricking him. The temptation of Kendrew Mackintosh was good and necessary. It was something he'd thank her for later. After she'd had a chance to entice and bewitch him, winning his heart before he thought to guess her clan allegiance.

She just wished he'd grab her and kiss her, quickly before she lost her nerve.

Instead, he did what she'd most dreaded.

He asked her name.

And as he did, a small party of mailed, thick-bearded men looked on from the shelter of a thrusting outcrop beyond the cookfires. Armed with swords, shields, and spears, they ignored the tantalizing smell of roasting meat that kept drifting past on the wind. Their noses twitched with the scent of something much more tempting.

"She's the Cameron's sister." One of the spearmen, a tall brute with shaggy black hair and a broken nose, pointed his spear in Isobel's direction. "She—"

"I told you her name back at the Rodan Stone when the bitch looked right at you." Ralla the Victorious, so named because he'd never lost a fight, used his own spear to knock down the other man's weapon. "She is a maid of rank and riches. And"—he flashed another look at her—"we'll no' be touching her this night."

Tor, the black-haired man with the crooked nose, bent to snatch up his fallen spear. "Thon amber necklace she wears is worth more than the coin-hoard promised us for this night's work."

A third man spat on the ground. "I'd like to see her brother's face if we sent him those ambers wrapped around her severed neck."

"And what would happen then?" Ralla couldn't believe his men's stupidity.

The ground-spitter swelled his chest. "James Cameron would see that for all his arrogance, he's powerless. He'd recognize that there are others whose strength is greater. Others like us and—"

"Aye, so he would." Ralla nodded, feigning agreement.

Grinning, the ground-spitter whipped out his sword, testing its edge on his thumb. "I've ne'er used this on a woman. The thought makes me—"

"It shows what a fool you are." Ralla gripped the man's wrist, twisting his arm until the blade clattered onto the rocks. "If anyone takes their pleasure with the Cameron she-witch, it'll be me.

"This night"—he slammed the end of his spear into the ground—"we retreat. The bitch's presence changes our plans. The Mackintoshes are the fiercest fighters in the glen. Their chief isn't as mead-taken as we'd hoped to find him, but we could still wipe them out if we wished. A bloodbath with the Cameron's sister caught in the middle..."

He let the words trail off, waiting until his men lowered their spears.

"Such folly would only unite the three clans." Ralla looked round, pleased to see understanding finally sink into his men's thick skulls. "We're hamstrung until we've broken the Mackintoshes' fighting power. Once we have, we'll crush the Camerons and MacDonalds like snails beneath our heels. That's when we'll feast on their oxen and take our ease with their women."

His men greeted the words with varying degrees of enthusiasm.

"I be hungry for both now." A burly man whose arms were well ringed with gold plucked a dirk from beneath his belt and used the tip to pick at his fingernails. "I wouldn't mind feasting on—"

"You'll taste my fist and more if you make trouble." Ralla stepped toward the other man, not surprised when his bravura faded.

Ralla hadn't earned his by-name for naught.

"The Mackintosh saw you a while ago." The other man waved his dirk in Kendrew's direction, the challenge proving he had more bollocks than Ralla believed. "He took a hard look at us, he did."

"The bastard was blinking ash from his eyes, no more." Ralla refused to admit that Kendrew might've seen him. Such a slip would be a first in his long and illustrious career of villainies.

"Say you." The dirk-wielder thrust his knife back beneath his belt, dusted his hands.

"I do." Ralla yanked his spear from the peaty ground. "Now we're gone from here. We'll wash the glen with Berserker blood on another day, I promise you."

Turning, he walked away, taking a narrow goat path that wound along the deepest defiles of Nought's formidable peaks. He went swiftly and with sure, long strides, knowing his men would follow.

Ban, the dirk-wielder, caught up with him first. "I know how to handle uppity females. I'd have the Cameron bitch after you're done with her."

"And so you shall," Ralla agreed. "But not before the others."

No man would want her once she'd been at Ban's mercy.

Ralla treated his men equally, showing no favoritism. Only so could he expect men to carry spears for him. He was a fair and generous leader. When the time came, they'd all enjoy Isobel of Haven.

Then they'd send her to hell.

Chapter Three

⚜

She'd already lost his attention.

Isobel watched Kendrew's brows draw together as he glanced past her to where the largest cookfire blazed near the rocks at the base of Nought's highest peaks. Well-burning torches circled the fire pit, lending to the festive air, and a whole ox roasted in the fire's leaping flames. The wind was just turning, treating them to the tantalizing aroma of perfectly done meat. Yet Kendrew frowned as if eyeing a cauldron of warty toads seasoned with newt fingers.

His gaze flickered over the soaring cliffs, red-gold in the firelight. He took a step forward as he stared, his fists clenching at his sides. But then his face cleared and he turned back to her.

"Your name, sweet." His smile flashed as he came closer. Holding her gaze, he touched her face again, this time gliding his knuckles along her cheek and then down her neck. "I'd know what a lass as fair as you is called."

"I am Isobel." Her voice was strong. In this, a point of honor, she couldn't lie. Though she wished he hadn't prodded her. "Isobel of—"

"Of the Ambers," he decided, fingering her necklace, clearly thinking she was a joy woman from Rannoch Moor. "'Tis a fitting name."

He released the gemstones and gave her another of his crooked smiles. "Though I vow you are worth a thousand such baubles."

Isobel's heart pounded. "The necklace was a gift."

"No doubt." His gaze dropped to her bosom, lingering there before returning to her face. "And I would reward you with a much greater treasure. Some say"—he leaned in, lowering his voice—"that all the world's gold lies buried beneath the dreagan stones."

Isobel lifted her chin. "I do not want your wealth."

She didn't.

She wanted him.

So she looked into his eyes, directly. "Riches have little meaning to me."

"Then you are a maid like no other." His smile deepened. "Now I know the gods have looked after me this e'en."

"Perhaps they desired us to meet?" Isobel couldn't believe her boldness.

"The gods are aye wise." Kendrew's voice was rough, his eyes dark with hunger. "They ken what's good for a man."

"Aye, they do." She took a breath, struggling not to sweep her hands against her skirts, dashing the dampness from her palms.

She couldn't lose courage now.

Not when desire crackled in the air between them, filling her with hot, shivery anticipation. Blood racing, she glanced about, the tremulous sensation increasing when she saw they were alone.

All around them, the spear-thumping continued, the sound oddly muted as if the stone-knocking belonged to another place and time. The scream of pipes, drum beats, and raucous laughter came loudest from near the cook-fires where carousers were gathering to dance.

Yet here, beneath Slag's Mound...

Isobel glanced at Kendrew, and then back at the empty landscape. She saw only broken rock, heather, and bracken. The dark peaks that pressed so close, guarding the tight stony vale. The land's fierceness quickened her blood. She almost felt light-headed.

Nothing but shadow and mist surrounded them. The drifting smoke, so redolent of roasting meat and laced with just a trace of sweet, heady mead. All else was still, the world holding its breath.

The isolation was thrilling.

She should be alarmed, her maidenly sensibilities on high alert, urging her to run. Instead, she ached to touch Kendrew's muscled chest and arms, tracing her fingers along his blue kill-marks and then gliding her hands lower, learning his mysteries as he kissed her deeply.

"Perhaps the gods make mistakes." It was a feeble attempt to regain her ladylike dignity.

She failed miserably.

"Norse gods?" Kendrew laughed and shook his head. "They make mischief. And they make merry." His lips curved in a slow, dangerous smile. "Erring isn't in their nature. They see and know all. It's no good thing to ignore their wisdom." He stepped closer, his body almost touching hers. "We daren't offend them."

Isobel met his gaze, aware of the implication behind his words.

He wanted her.

And he meant for them to enjoy the same wild and uninhibited carnality going on throughout the narrow vale, beyond the wall of mist and the shielding bulk of Slag's Mound where couples whirled and danced around the bonfires. And then—she knew—they fell in a tangle of arms and legs onto the cold, stony ground, mating furiously.

That was what he wished to do with her.

He could mean nothing else.

"Oh, dear." Isobel's nerves surfaced, unwelcome and annoying, but there all the same.

He gripped her chin then, his gaze piercing. "You tempt me greatly, Isobel of the Ambers. I'd have you here and now, before Odin and in the shadow of Slag's Mound."

He slid his thumb back and forth over her lower lip, softly. The caress sent shocking waves of pleasure spilling through her, hot and sweet. He arched a brow, clearly waiting for her consent. For all his roguishness, no one denied how much he respected women. He'd go no further unless she indicated that she wanted more.

And she did.

Guilt lanced her. Gently bred women weren't supposed to feel lust. But she'd felt such a strong physical attraction to him since the trial by combat. Even more powerfully, his boldness drew her. His Norse blood proved irresistible. They shared so much.

He was a man like no other.

And the look on his face as he touched her lip so gently was making her burst with longing.

Isobel shivered, knowing she was lost. "Yes..."

She let her voice trail off, not quite brave enough to put such wanton desires into plain words. He surely knew what she meant.

Proving it, he grinned. "Then come here." He pulled her close, so near that she was crushed to his hard-muscled body. Sweeping a hand down her back, he splayed his fingers over the curve of her bottom, drawing her against him. She felt his arousal now, his hardness pressing sensitive places, stirring need within her. "Let me kiss you."

"Then do." Her voice was stronger this time, his touch melting her. He traced her jaw with his thumb and her skin warmed there, tiny shivers slipping down her neck and lower. She gazed up at him, her breath catching at the fierce desire in his eyes.

"Och, I will kiss you and more. This is a night to amuse the gods, and ourselves." The red glow from the bonfires glinted in his rich auburn hair and made the heavy gold of the Thor's hammer at his neck gleam brightly. He'd never looked more wild, or so appealing.

"I want you, lass." He stroked her cheek. "Ne'er you worry."

"I'm not worried." She wasn't.

She was excited. The sensations she felt gathering inside her, heady and delicious.

He looked down at her, his broad shoulders blocking out the high peaks behind him, narrowing the world to just the two of them. "That's good, because we're about to set fire to the heavens."

Isobel blinked.

Kendrew grinned, the laughter lines at the corners of his blue eyes deepening. "We'll light a blaze to warm the mead halls of Valhalla."

Isobel's heart flipped. "Valhalla, yes..."

Then, somehow, she found herself backed against the high, stone-built cairn, his hands braced on either side of her head as his mouth descended, slanting roughly over hers. His kiss was hot, deep, and bruising. Her entire body caught flame and she twined her arms around his shoulders, thrusting her fingers into his hair. She needed and wanted him so much. Her heart beat faster, blood thrumming in her veins as she parted her lips, letting his tongue plunge deep to tangle with hers in a kiss more heated than her dreams.

Somewhere near—or distant, it was hard to tell—a great rumbling of stone shook the earth, the low, thundery sound echoing along the stark and jagged cliffs hemming the rock-strewn vale.

"Dear saints!" Isobel froze, her eyes flying wide.

Tremors rippled through the ground and even the polished silver sky seemed to quiver. Around them, the swirling smoke and mist eddied, caught in an unseen wind as the stone-thunder slowly faded.

Kendrew broke the kiss, sweeping her up in his arms and turning away from the cairn. "See there"—he looked down at her, his smile flashing—"the dreagans are taken with you, Isobel of the Ambers. That was their roar just now, praising your beauty."

Isobel smiled. "I thought they didn't exist?"

"Who is to say?" He shrugged away a more direct answer. "Though"—he bent to kiss her brow—"I'll no' have you frightened. More like, thon rumble was a bit o' rock rolling down the brae."

"I'd say a landslide." Isobel glanced at the cliffs, so dark and brooding.

"Aye," Kendrew agreed, then fell silent as he followed her gaze. Another frown touched his brow, but briefly, disappearing almost faster than she'd noticed. "Falling rock is no' uncommon here."

Isobel shivered. The air was cold and damp now, and...

Somehow her bodice laces had come undone. Her gown gaped wide, open to her waist. Night wind kissed her skin, raising chill bumps. Kendrew was pulling her sleeves down from her shoulders and freeing her arms, releasing them from her gown's constraints. His plaid was still in place, the red-based tartan bright against the whirling mist. The contrast made her feel even more vulnerable.

"Oh..." She forgot all about rock-thunder.

"Odin, but you're lovely." Appreciation shone in Kendrew's eyes, his gaze devouring her. "Let me look at you, see the bounty the gods have sent me."

"You are looking." Isobel could feel her face coloring.

"So I am." He didn't deny it.

He did snatch up what looked like a black-furred blanket and tossed it over his arm, the dark pelt cooled by the night's chill.

Isobel knew why he'd grabbed the fur and the knowledge slammed through her. Anticipation made her heart pound. Her emotions unraveled, whirling until nothing mattered except his strong arms holding her and the way he kept lowering his head to kiss her hair. He rubbed his face against the side of her neck, breathing deep as if he were scenting her, perhaps savoring her taste.

Her skin prickled at the scintillating thought. Stunning expectation beat through her, shivery warmth that lit across her nerves and caused a languorous, weighty sensation deep inside her.

She almost forgot to breathe.

He smoothed back her hair, leaning down to nip at the soft hollow beneath her ear. Slow, tight heat wound through the lowest part of her belly, making her tremble. She caught her lip, certain she'd never felt anything quite so wondrous, so tantalizing.

He grinned. "I could eat you whole, be warned. I'd start at the top of your head and make my way down to your sweet, wee toes, tasting every place in between. The gods know I'm tempted." He slung the fur over his arm and started down the side of the cairn, his strides sure as he crossed the stony ground.

Isobel darted a look at the blanket. Wicked images of them naked and entwined on the dark-glistening fur flashed across her mind.

Surprisingly, she didn't feel a shiver of shame.

She did have to tamp down her doubts. A well-lusted man, Kendrew's blood likely heated for any comely female. Attracting him hadn't been hard. Pleasing him once he started kissing her again, when he'd no doubt pull her tight against the hard, masculine length of his body, and if—she darted another look at the fur—they were to lie down together, pressed skin to naked skin...

That was a different matter.

She didn't want to disappoint him.

"My bearskin," he spoke then, catching her glance at the

pelt. "No maid has ever lain upon its fur." His gaze raked
her breasts, his expression so heated she would've sworn
liquid flames were bathing her. "Not till you, this night.

"You make me burn for you." He stopped before a
patch of heather, sheltered by the cairn. His eyes darkened as he looked at her. Then he tossed the bearskin onto
the ground and lowered his head to kiss her, still holding
her clutched tight in his arms.

This kiss was just as roughly demanding as before, hot,
hungry, and crushing. Full of tongue and breath, it was also
shockingly intimate because he swept a hand across her
breasts, rubbing and squeezing, as he plundered her mouth.
He took her nipples between his thumb and fingers, rolling
and pulling the tightened peaks. She arched in his arms as
sensation raced through her, the pleasure almost too intense.

"That's my lass . . ." He was palming her now, his big,
calloused hand so sweet against her skin. He kept kissing
her, his heady male scent flooding her senses, making her
dizzy. His tongue was masterful, sliding and dancing with
hers, coaxing her to respond.

And she did. She even rocked her hips, giving herself
up to the ancient, time-honored needs welling inside her.
Womanly cravings that urged her on to the heated, carnal
bliss she knew only he could give her. Powerful yearnings that felt so natural, that all her inhibitions spun away,
leaving only raw, aching desire.

He set her on her feet and pushed the hair back from
her shoulders. "Sweet lass, what have you done to me?"
Pulling her close, he kissed her face and her throat. Then
he swept lower, dragging bold, urgent kisses across the
top swells of her breasts, grazing her nipples with his
teeth. "You turn my head as no other."

"I am glad." She plunged her fingers into his hair, holding him against her breasts, melting when he swirled his tongue across her nipples.

Somewhere stones rumbled again, but the sound was more distant this time, muffled by the thickening mist rolling down from the higher mountains.

Still...

Isobel shivered, a flicker of ill ease slipping down her spine.

Kendrew didn't seem to notice.

Instead, he dropped to his knees on the bearskin and pulled her into his arms, lowering her back against the pelt. Heavy mist drifted between them and Slag's Mound. Almost impenetrable, the fog hovered, blotting the cairn and the other strange outcroppings from view.

Now was Isobel's chance.

She reached for him. "Please." She spoke boldly, hoping he'd be fast and eager so he wouldn't notice her purity before it was too late.

"Och, I'll please you, Isobel-lass." He lifted her hand to his mouth and kissed her palm, nibbling the flesh beneath her thumb. Then he laced her fingers with his and raised her arm above her head, looking down at her in a way that set her blood to racing.

"My only wish is to pleasure you." He leaned over her, his eyes dark as he slid his free hand down her side and lower, gripping the hem of her gown and pulling it upward, baring her legs.

"This night and"—his hand slipped between her thighs, cupping her neediest place, squeezing—"mayhap a few more nights if you'll stay."

Isobel stiffened, his words reminding her that he still

believed she was a light-skirt from Rannoch Moor. But he was moving his fingers over her most intimate place. And the thrilling tingles rushing over her chased the worries from her mind. His touch seared her, giving her breathless, almost dizzying pleasure.

"O-o-oh…" She turned her head, closing her eyes. She reveled in the tantalizing magic of his hand lighting across the very top of her thighs, then stroking and teasing her secret places. Each questing touch proved wickedly exciting. It was exquisite bliss, and she wanted to drown in the wonder of every new sensation.

Nothing had prepared her for such headiness.

Feeling almost intoxicated, she started rocking her hips again. And she made no protest when he lifted her knees and urged them open. His caresses turned hotter, more deliberate, as he explored her intimately. Tingling heat curled low in her belly, a startling tension that quickened her breath. She felt exhilarated, aware of something urgent and desperately necessary that hovered just beyond her reach. And whatever it was, she wanted it.

"Kendrew…" She breathed his name, stunned that this between them was so much greater than she'd expected at Castle Haven, in Catriona's bedchamber.

This was…

Magic.

Tempestuous passion beyond her wildest imaginings, and so right that she knew their connection swept past their carnal attraction and straight into the deepest corners of their hearts. She felt that, knew it by the glowing happiness spreading through her, warming her soul.

The shocking pleasure between her thighs turned into an exquisite, aching hunger as his fingers drifted over her. He looked deep into her eyes as he touched her, and the dark passion smoldering in his gaze intensified the intimacy.

She arched her back, pressing against his hand. Her entire body felt hot, heavy with yearning. "Dear sweet saints—"

"No' yet, precious." His voice was low and deep, roughened by lust. "We've the whole night before us."

Isobel's heart skittered. Again, she felt a flutter of nerves.

She wanted so much more than this one night.

But she'd think of that later, when the moment came to tell him her clan name. Just now she was lost in sensual awakening, tumbling deep into a sweet, mind-numbing abyss. Then he circled his thumb over a spot that gave her such prickling, concentrated pleasure she'd swear the stars fell from the sky to glitter around them.

"Sweet lass…" He nipped her ear, and then claimed her lips in a deep, open-mouthed kiss. His tongue tangled with hers, desire mounting.

"I could kiss you all the night through." He stretched out beside her now, rolling on top of her, stroking the insides of her thighs until she let her knees fall even wider apart, welcoming him.

Anticipation rippled through her, taking her breath when his manhood nudged her where his fingers had teased her only moments before. Hot, granite-hard, and as silky-smooth as her gown, that part of him slid back and forth against her, the intimacy scalding.

"Isobel of the Ambers, you are beautiful." He pulled her skirts higher, bunching her gown about her hips, freeing her of that last shred of modesty.

She didn't care, glorying in the heat of his big, strong

body looming over her. She even reveled in the rush of cold air on her naked, most private places. And how he deepened their kiss, letting his tongue slip slowly in and out of her parted lips, the sinuous gliding a preparation for what was about to come.

She was ready.

This wasn't a sacrifice, but something she wanted desperately.

Then he was reaching down between them, positioning his length to claim her at last.

"Kendrew..." She didn't care if he heard the yearning in her voice. She did slide her arms around his shoulders, gripping tight, urging him on.

Her heart was splitting.

Then he entered her and that part of her split, too. Fiery, stinging heat stabbed into her vitals, her innermost place clamping tight, protesting the intrusion. He froze above her, his head thrown back, and his neck and shoulder muscles straining. A terrible, snarl-like growl rumbled low in his chest, escaping through his clenched teeth as his manhood jerked against her softness. Molten warmth touched her, damping her thighs.

His seed?

Surely so, but he didn't move. He just drew a quick breath as if in agony. Isobel knew he was partly inside her. The burning pain was too great otherwise. It hurled sharp waves across her most tender places, squeezing her chest, stealing her breath.

"Don't stop." She curled her hand around his neck, pulling his mouth back down to her, kissing him deeply. She put all her passion in the kiss, hoping to distract him from her annoying tightness.

The pureness she knew would turn him from her.

"It's been a while, see you..." She twirled her tongue around his, holding the back of his head, not letting him pull away.

She tried to sound worldly. She even nipped his lower lip, hoping to seem seductive, knowledgeable in the ways of men and pleasuring them.

"Then you're no' ready." He broke her kiss, lifting up on his arms to look at her. "And I—no woman has e'er driven me to spill so..." He didn't finish.

He was frowning.

"I thought..." His face was fierce, confused, and disappointed.

"There's nothing wrong," Isobel lied, not daring to tell him she was a maid.

"Humph." He didn't look convinced. Far from it, he pushed up on his knees, reaching for her raised skirts, surely meaning to pull down the gown, covering her.

Before he could, his eyes rounded and he leaped to his feet, staring down at her as if she'd grown horns and a long, forked tail.

"Sakes!" He jammed his hands on his hips, suspicion all over him. "You weren't 'not ready,' you were a virgin! And a lady, I'll vow." He sounded livid, his eyes blazing. "Why else wear such a dagger on your thigh?"

"Dagger?" Isobel blinked. She'd forgotten Catriona's bejeweled lady's dirk, strapped near the top of her right leg. And, she realized, hidden by her bunched skirts until this moment.

"It's for defense." She spoke true. "No lady would traipse through the glen without—"

"So it's true." The horror on Kendrew's face alerted her to her mistake.

Isobel sat up, horror washing through her, too. "Times have been fraught here of late." She tried to deflect his attention from her gaffe. "There were broken men about mere months ago, making trouble after the trial by combat. Even in Rannoch Moor, one hears—"

"You are no Rannoch wench." He threw his plaid back over his shoulder, brushing angrily at the folds. "Thon women have no need to protect themselves from brigands. They greet every man gladly. Nor"—he was scowling now—"would they possess such a dagger as yours.

"Such a woman might earn an amber necklace, aye. A pretty bauble for a night well spent." His voice was cold, the words harsh. "She wouldn't own a gem-crusted lady's dirk. A dagger of such worth could buy her a fine house in Glasgow, servants to attend her. She'd turn her treasure into good, hard coin. Only a true gentle-born female would carry such a blade strapped to her thigh."

The look he gave her was like a fist to the heart. "Or will you be denying it?"

Isobel scrambled to her feet, shoving her arms into her sleeves. "The dagger is not mine."

"I dinnae believe you." Kendrew folded his arms, a different man than moments ago. His face grew as hard as the dreagan stones, his eyes as dark as the mist. "I also doubt your name is Isobel."

"It is." Her heart was sinking, the night's cold suddenly icy, the bright silver sky now gray and dismal. "The dagger belongs to my good-sister, Catriona. She didn't think I should make the journey here without—"

"Great Odin's balls!" Kendrew's brows shot upward.

"You're Isobel Cameron!" He reeled back as if someone twice his size had punched him. All color drained from his face, his expression setting off a flurry of panic inside her. "You're Cameron's sister. How could I not have recognized you?"

He shook his head, disbelief rolling off him. "And now I've sullied you. A great regret."

"No." Isobel started forward, reaching for him. "You've done nothing I didn't desire." Her voice cracked, shameful heat stinging her eyes. "I wanted to see you tonight so I slipped away—"

"You didn't come here to be ravished." He slammed the ball of his palm against his forehead, pacing back and forth in front of her. "Never in my life have I lain with a virgin, a daughter of good house. I've prided myself on my restraint, challenged other men, even banishing a few from my guard when they caused the fall of an innocent. Now..."

"Nothing has happened." Isobel knew that wasn't true.

The world was ending.

Pain lanced her chest, making it so hard to breathe. His rejection stunned her, plunging her into darkness. She felt chilled, hollow inside. She should have been more patient, waited until he finally heeded her brother's invitations, came to Haven.

Now...

She swallowed, wishing the burning in her eyes wasn't making it so difficult to see. "Nothing terrible happened," she said again, trying to banish the awful look from his face. "You didn't—"

"I touched you." He whirled to face her. "That's enough. I stole your most prized possession. I—" He broke off, looking ready to murder.

"You didn't hurt me." Isobel went to him, touching his arm. "Please, it is Midsummer Eve. I am fine and no harm was done. Can we not just—"

"I don't pillage virgins." He jerked away from her, stepping back as if she'd scalded him. "Nor do I touch ladies of any sort. Not even the ones who'd willingly share their charms. I thought you were one of the Rannoch women. And if this hadn't been Midsummer Eve, if I hadn't been so muddle-headed from the revels, I'd have seen right away that you're no common light-skirt.

"I would've sent you home to Castle Haven faster than you can blink. And"—he crossed back over to her, towering above her—"that's what I'll be doing now. You'll be on your way as soon as I gather a few stout men to escort you. I'd take you myself, but that's no longer wise."

"You're making a grave error." Isobel lifted her chin, getting angry now.

"My mistake was jumping down off Slag's Mound." He glared at her. "Be sure I'll ne'er do anything so fool-hardy again. For certain I'll no' commit such nonsense with James Cameron's sister."

"I am Isobel." She held his gaze, knew her eyes were blazing. "Simply Isobel."

"You are—" He snapped his mouth shut, his brows lowering in a ferocious scowl.

"I am a woman who admired you." Isobel kept her back straight. "I have done so a while. And this night I also desired you, greatly." She flipped her hair over her shoulder, striving for dignity. "I see no shame in what happened between us."

"You speak plain." The coldness of his tone squeezed her like a vise.

"I always do." She lifted her brows infinitesimally. "Someday you might realize that such a quality is worth even more than a woman's breasts, the over-ripe charms of a female who 'greets all men gladly.'"

She lifted her chin and tugged on her sleeves, adjusting them. Then, because the devil was riding her, she gave him a small, chilly smile.

He looked at her, his mouth set in a hard, tight line. "Dinnae think to try such foolery again, Lady Isobel. I'll no' be responsible for my actions if you do."

Isobel hardly heard him.

His words didn't matter. It was his expression that made her heart lurch. The bitterness in his tone that let her know how much he regretted what had happened.

Quite possibly he detested her.

She was now more than halfway in love with him.

And she'd ruined everything. Her only option was to get away from him, leaving his sight and land with as much pride and grace as she could muster. And that wouldn't be easy with her eyes so bright and her chin threatening to quiver, her bodice laces still loose and her hair tumbling to her hips in wild disorder.

She looked a fright and felt worse.

But she was also a Cameron.

A daughter of the Glen of Many Legends, and she did have steel in her blood. She possessed the strength of generations and an iron, unbending will. And even if she bled rivers inside, she'd be damned if anyone would know she'd been so terribly wounded.

So she took a deep breath and shook out her skirts, preparing for a grand exit. "There were three Rannoch Moor lovelies looking for you earlier." She used her coolest, most ladylike tone. "If you hurry, you might catch them before another of your men takes the opportunity. I do believe"—she glanced round, then pointed to the bonfires—"they went that way."

Not surprisingly, he looked to where she gestured.

Isobel took advantage, hitching her skirts and marching away through the mist and rock whence she'd come. She didn't hurry and she kept her back straight, her head high, as she made her way over the broken ground. She could feel Kendrew's furious stare boring into her. But she didn't glance back, not giving him the satisfaction.

They'd meet again, she knew.

And the next time she'd wield a more powerful weapon than lust. She knew him better now. And she suspected that the one thing he most wanted was the very thing he professed to avoid: a lady.

She was that, as well he knew.

He already desired her.

Sooner or later, he'd accept what they'd both learned this night, however ghastly the encounter ended. They were perfect for each other. And their passion, now unleashed, would drive them back together.

It was only a matter of time.

Chapter Four

❖

Above the thick silence of Castle Haven, Isobel heard the thudding of her heart as loudly as if she stood again in the midst of Midsummer Eve revels, the primordial knocking of Mackintosh spears on rock still ringing in her ears. The sound followed her through the glen, as did the agitated rush of her blood. The latter increased when she'd gained enough distance from Nought territory to quicken her pace without denting her pride.

The last thing she'd wanted was for Kendrew to see how deeply his rejection stung her.

A lady kept her dignity always.

Straight-backed, calm, and ever in control was her credo.

But here, in the confines of her bedchamber and in one of the smallest, most still hours of the night, there was no one to see her. And so her emotions were in turmoil. Her heart refused to quiet. The rapid pounding would soon bruise her ribs, she was sure.

And that would happen with good reason.

Kendrew had made her a woman.

They'd crossed a line. And no matter what happened now, her life was forever changed.

Shivering in the chill air—she stood naked before her wash basin and pitcher—she reached for the cloth she'd been using to bathe herself. Even in the dim light of a single night candle, she could see that her body was now clean. But the linen bore stains. Like a man's battle wounds, the blood smears stared up at her, demanding redress.

Reminding her with a rush of emotion that she had no choice but to pursue her goal of making Kendrew want her with the same fierce yearning she felt for him. Futile as her hopes now appeared, she couldn't cast them aside with a quick flick of her wrist.

She suspected he would think less of her if she did.

Kendrew wasn't a man to appreciate weakness.

Only strength would impress him.

A thrill raced through Isobel at the thought of how much he'd impressed her.

She could still feel how her skin warmed beneath his hands. Echoes lingered of the delicious tingles brought on by his touch. Recalling his deep, oh-so-rousing kisses set her heart aflutter. She wanted him to pull her against him again, cupping her face and slanting his mouth over hers, ravishing her. Truth be told, she'd always want him, because any way she turned it, the answer remained the same.

The evening's tumult beneath the dreagan stones had been so much more than intimate embraces and desperate, scintillating kisses.

Their desire stretched beyond pure need and fest-night

carnality. Something reckless and elemental had sprung to life in her when she'd seen him cloaked in smoke and mist high atop Slag's Mound. With his war ax glinting and a long spear clutched in his hand, he'd looked able to conquer any foe. He was a man who'd never be bested, a warrior as implacable as the rock of his land. When he'd leaped down in front of her, the world had fallen away beneath them. It'd been a moment like nothing else in her life.

When he'd claimed her, sealing their bond with one look from his blazing blue eyes, the night's magic was theirs. His bold gaze had branded her heart, body, and soul.

As she'd known would happen.

She'd just believed he'd be equally affected by her.

Now she knew better.

And even the solace of her much-loved bedchamber couldn't ease the pang of acknowledging that truth. Usually, her room's lightness swiftly chased her cares. She loved the chamber's loftiness, set as it was near the top of the tower. And with its bright white-painted walls, tall, arched windows, and colorful silk hangings, the room was one of the finest at Castle Haven. A fire always burned in the grate, though the peats were presently little more than softly glowing embers. The earthy-rich scent of peat blended well with the strewing herbs of the floor rushes, lending a warm, cozy air.

If her brother's dog, Hector, visited the chamber—he was sadly absent now—the old dog's company made her quarters all the more welcoming.

This night, for the first time she could recall, her bedchamber felt cold and empty.

Her pristine bed, as yet untouched, seemed to chastise her for her foolishness.

Yet she'd started the night with such hope.

It still beat inside her.

Her skin prickled with annoyance. Disappointment lanced her, taunting and painful as the room's chill swept her. Gooseflesh rose on her arms, reminding her she was still unclothed.

Trying to ignore the sting of defeat, she grabbed a length of drying linen and began scrubbing her body, dashing away the remaining droplets of water. Her brow creased when she looked down and her gaze lit on the tiny mark on the left side of her lower belly. Angled between her navel and her inky-black female curls, the dark brown mark was a beauty spot. Or so she liked to tell herself.

It was shaped like Thor's hammer.

And ever since she'd first noticed the mark, she'd felt its purpose was to remind her to always follow her heart, staying true to the Nordic heritage many in her family would prefer to forget.

Isobel remembered gladly.

And the hammer mark was one reason she'd believed her attraction to Kendrew would blossom into the grand and passionate love she'd been so sure they'd find together. She trusted her instinct as surely as she put faith in Catriona's enchanted ambers.

But the necklace didn't warn against broken hearts.

And Kendrew hadn't even glimpsed her Thor's hammer beauty mark.

She doubted he'd have cared.

She'd have to make him.

There could be no doubt he desired her. Now she'd

have to prove she offered more than a sensual challenge. That she was strong, bold, and capable of great daring. A woman worthy of walking at a warrior's side, her head high and pride in her heart.

She was that woman.

The problem was that having failed at the revels she didn't know where to go from here. They'd forged a history and it wasn't just deeply intimate, but awkward. A debacle filled with searing passion, harsh words, and charged with unpleasantness. Yet now more than ever, she knew they belonged together.

Their brief moments of bliss had been wilder, more exhilarating than her most brazen, uninhibited imaginings about him.

She even admired his refusal to soil a lady.

Much as that particular trait thwarted her plans.

Wishing he weren't quite so noble, she tossed aside the drying cloth and pulled a fresh chemise over her head. Who would've thought desire and yearning could sweep her to such heights and then send her plummeting into a dark, painful abyss all in one night? She'd hoped a touch of Midsummer Eve magic would've worked in her favor, aiding her plan of temptation and helping her to seize the love and happiness she'd waited for so long.

Now...

She smoothed her chemise into place and moved to the window arch, wishing she could begin her adventure again, but knowing that, even if such a wonder were possible, she wouldn't change anything she'd done.

If need be, she'd admit to Catriona and Marjory that they were right to warn her away from Kendrew. That she wasn't likely to fulfill their sworn pact. Her choice weakened their vow to secure glen peace. All that she knew in her heart, and the truth weighed on her.

But she refused to feel shame.

Instead she embraced each memory she and Kendrew had made this night. They'd caught fire, intimacy coming swift, shocking, and wondrous. Even now, need burned inside her. Images of his smile, him reaching for her, flashed across her mind, heating her blood.

She could feel his embrace, their desire flaming.

His big, strong hands gliding over her, gripping her waist, then splaying his fingers across her hips, pulling her roughly against him...

"Dear, sweet mercy." She bit back a sigh, took a deep, steadying breath. Starlight shone through the window, glossing her bedchamber's lime-washed walls. Chill air poured inside, lifting tapestry edges and scenting the room with pine. She longed for the mouthwatering aroma of roasting meat and the tang of cold, damp stone. The rush of Kendrew tightening his arms around her.

She could almost taste his kisses.

Restless, she stepped deeper into the window alcove, her heart tripping as she placed her hands on the ledge. The night remained magical, the whole of the glen washed in silver and blue. Wind whistled through the pines, the familiar sound soothing her. The pleasant scent of damp, pungent earth teased her senses. And the heavens still shone like mother-of-pearl, the low clouds gleaming as if lit from within. A soft red haze glimmered in the distance where Kendrew and his warriors were likely still knocking their spears on stone.

She refused to think what else they might be doing.

She did lean out the window, welcoming the cold

night air on her skin. Chill wind raced around the curved tower, rippling her hair and reminding anyone awake at this unholy hour that even at high summer, the long cold nights of autumn would soon be upon them.

Shivering, she rubbed her arms. Autumn was when she'd vowed she and Kendrew would wed. After tonight, she doubted he'd even speak to her again.

She'd made a muddle of her dreams.

Worse, she'd endangered a vital oath, damaging a link that would've been solid if she'd chosen a man less obstinate and wild than Kendrew.

The men, women, and children of her clan might not know of the pact with her friends. But their ability to sleep at ease depended on the plan's success. Centuries of unrest proved the fragility of truces. One false word or narrow-eyed look could throw fat onto the feud-fire. Old grievances would flame anew, possibly unquenchable. Her bond with an enemy husband should've strengthened glen peace.

She couldn't fail.

But before she could decide her next move, something stirred in the trees beneath her window. A large dark shape similar to the hazy form she'd glimpsed near the Rodan Stone on the boundaries of Nought land.

"Dear saints…" She gripped the stone ledge of the window.

Her breath snagged and the fine hairs on her nape lifted. The figure—whatever it was—drifted from tree to tree, little more than a deeper blur against the shifting mist. Yet real enough to chill her insides and send a flurry of shivers rippling down her spine.

But when she blinked, the shadow was gone.

Someone *was* in the room with her.

She straightened, her senses alert. The rustle of movement was unmistakable, as was the sound of the door scraping across the floor rushes, then the soft stirrings of a woman's skirts.

Isobel released the breath she'd been holding. Relief swept her. No dark shadow-form had slipped from the pinewood and crept up the stairs to her bedchamber. A waft of gillyflower perfume revealed her visitor's benevolence.

"Catriona." Isobel swung about to face her friend. "You startled me." Her nerves were jumping. "It's late. I didn't think—"

"Did you see him?" Catriona closed the door behind her, her eyes glinting in the room's dimness. "Was he on the dreagan stones? Naked?"

"He was." Isobel could see him still. And she was surely flushing crimson. So she turned her coolest gaze upon Catriona and hoped she wouldn't notice her discomfiture. "You should be abed at this hour."

"Pah! You should've been more careful." Catriona thrust her rushlight into an iron ring on the wall by the door and came into the room. "I told you no good would come of such folly. You were seen."

"Not by James?" Isobel washed hot and cold, alarm gripping her.

"Be glad it wasn't him." Catriona placed her hands on her hips. In her soft-falling night robes, the swell at her middle was more than apparent. The look she bent on Isobel was full of reproach. "One of the kitchen laddies and several guardsmen saw you flitting through the trees. There was quite a stir in the hall."

Isobel's stomach gave a lurch. "When did they see me? Just now, coming back?"

"Nae, when you left." Catriona went to Isobel's undisturbed bed and settled herself onto the edge of the high mattress. "I've been watching for you the night through. I can't say if anyone else saw you return. Everyone should be sleeping. James certainly is, or I wouldn't have been able to come here to warn you."

"Is he angry?" Isobel knew he'd be furious.

"When he first heard, I feared for you." Catriona was blunt. "If he'd guessed where you'd gone or"—she leaned forward—"why you went there…" She didn't finish and there wasn't any need.

Everyone knew James's opinion of the Mackintoshes.

He especially disliked Kendrew.

Scoundrel was the kindest name he ever called him. Most were so vile that heat crawled up the back of Isobel's neck just recalling them.

Catriona's opinion wasn't any higher. "James spoke of the Nought revels at supper, saying that such debauchery is a blight on our glen."

"Oh, dear…" Isobel risked a look at the little oaken table so close to where she stood, hoping her friend's observant eye wouldn't light on the stained wash linen. To her mind, the cloth screamed for attention, lying so near to the night candle as it did.

Worse, the candle glow fell across the bloodied cloth. One could almost believe it did so with diabolical purpose, hoping to damn her.

Debauchery.

The word made her throat go dry. She'd found the revels exhilarating. The pagan excitement hadn't repelled her, but fired her blood. Even the dreagan vale—thought of as bleak and terrible by so many—had quickened her pulse. Never had she felt more alive, so filled with passion. With the exception of how things ended, what happened between her and Kendrew had been wondrous.

She regretted nothing.

But Catriona was watching her, her gaze sharp.

Isobel tried not to squirm. She did feel her chest tightening. Her friend's perusal made it difficult to breathe.

And she was sure the wash linen was coming to life, winking at her and blazing red, bright as a brand.

"No one followed me." She forced herself not to edge in front of the table. "Surely if James was riled, he would've sent men after me. More like, he would've gone himself, leading the search."

"To be sure, he would've done..." Catriona glanced at the long-dead fire, the peat ashes still glowing faintly. "If he'd thought it was you."

Isobel blinked. "But you said—"

"The gods of Midsummer were with you." Catriona turned back to her. "Those who saw you reported that you vanished before their eyes. They believed you were Scandia. Her ghost does resemble you."

That was true.

And Catriona spoke with authority for she was one of the few souls at Castle Haven who'd actually seen the famed Clan Cameron haint. The first time or two, she'd also believed she'd seen Isobel. She'd confirmed their like appearance. Once believed to herald doom, Isobel's long-dead ancestress was now known to be benevolent.

But Scandia hadn't been seen in months. Not since the days of the trial by combat. She was thought to be at peace now, roaming the glen no more.

"There was a mist gathering when I left." Isobel pushed

her hair behind her shoulder, striving to look calm, untroubled. "It was thickest along the edge of the pines, swirling and gray. If someone saw me enter the wood, it could have looked as if I'd disappeared. Did James"—she had to ask—"believe I was Scandia?"

"He did." Catriona regarded her levelly. "After I told him I'd seen the ghost, too."

Isobel felt a stab of guilt. "You lied for me?"

Catriona nodded. "Only this once, be warned. I did so because we swore on a sprig of white heather to each wed a man of a feuding clan. For the weal of all, as it were." Her eyes narrowed, her tone turning steely. "I wed your brother, becoming a Cameron. You chose Mackintosh and I felt honor bound to support you. But I'll not tell James another falsehood. If he presses me, I'll speak true."

"You are too good to me." Isobel meant it. "I won't put you in such a position again."

"You're giving up on Mackintosh?" Catriona's face brightened.

Isobel felt her own brow furrow. "I am not."

She turned again to the window, careful to keep her back straight. Better to gaze out at the heavy mists of the small hours than watch her answer cause her friend's face to cloud over. Even the eerie shadow-form she'd seen earlier would be preferable.

Behind her, she heard Catriona sigh.

Below her window, the night mist swirled and eddied. Cold wind still whistled around the tower. Low, fast clouds sped across the dark green tops of the pines and somewhere a burn cut through the deeper heather. Isobel could hear the rush of water in the stillness. But no strange shadows drifted from tree to tree.

There *was* a dark giant shape.

Not at all wispy, it looked big, bold, and menacing.

Isobel inhaled sharply, chills racing over her.

She caught a flashing glint of gold. Then—her eyes rounded—an equally bright sheen of silver.

She knew who was down there.

And there he was...

Kendrew striding purposely out of the mist, the golden Thor's hammer at his throat shining like a beacon. He'd come dressed for war. Gold rings banded his powerful arms and his huge Norse war ax was strapped across his back, the weapon's arced blade gleaming.

Isobel gulped.

He strode forward, making straight for the base of the tower as if he had every right to be there. When he stopped, directly under her window, he looked up at her, surely aware that she'd seen him.

And she had.

She also saw that he carried her discarded—nae, her *forgotten*—cloak over one arm. His proud face was set in hard, fierce lines.

Isobel could feel the blood draining from hers.

She froze, staring down at him.

Anyone who happened to glance out a window, or a guardsman who might yet be patrolling the battlements, would see him. Just as they'd recognize that he held her fine, blue woolen cloak. A gift last Yule from James and Catriona. And a treasure she'd meant to sneak back and retrieve when everyone was at the morning meal.

As if he guessed her mortification, Kendrew thrust his arm in the air and waved the mantle like a poled banner on the battlefield.

Isobel gripped the edge of the window, her heart in her throat.

She was surely going to die.

Any moment the floor would tilt and then split wide, plunging her into hell.

Instead, she heard a soft stirring behind her. "You'd best tell me what happened." Catriona's voice was no longer reproachful.

It was steeped in sympathy.

And Isobel had a good idea why.

"Don't pity me." She whipped around, not about to budge from the window. If she blocked the entry to the embrasure, Catriona wouldn't be able to get close enough to see Kendrew waving her cloak in the air.

"You know that I must." Catriona's gaze was on the bloodstained wash linen. "How can I not feel for you? Thon cloth gives me reason aplenty."

Isobel lifted her chin. "I am not sorry."

"I'd hoped there might be another cause for such bleeding." Catriona's gaze was meaningful. "Perhaps"— her voice turned hopeful—"a female matter?"

"It was a female matter." Isobel was amazed she could hear her voice above the roar of her pulse in her ears. "But it was not the womanly reason you mean. I think you know what happened."

Catriona did.

Isobel saw it all over her face.

"James mustn't know." Isobel thought she caught the crunching of footsteps on gravel from beneath her window. Her knees began trembling when the sound came again, proving she wasn't mistaken.

Kendrew was surely parading back and forth before the tower, hoping to cause a confrontation.

Her cloak would be streaming in the wind behind him, drawing eyes.

Moisture began to bead Isobel's brow.

Any moment a horn would blare, calling men to arms.

"You cannot tell James." Isobel was getting frantic. "Not ever—promise me."

"Isobel..." Catriona started to reach for her and then let her hand drop. "He would demand the bastard marry you. That's what you've wanted all along. Or"—she tilted her head, frowning—"did Kendrew hurt you? If he did, if he forced himself on you, then—"

"He did no such thing." Isobel could feel the blood burning her cheeks. "What happened just did. I'll not have him made to wed me because of it. An offer must come from him. And only because he—"

"Because he loves you." Catriona managed to put a world of impossibility into the four words.

Isobel ignored her own doubt. "That is my hope, aye."

Catriona arched an eyebrow, not needing words.

"He desires me greatly." Isobel's defense sounded weak even to her. A man as well-lusted as Kendrew likely ate a different woman for breakfast each morning. "I only need to think what to do next and—"

A loud *scrunch* on gravel, followed by skitter of pebbles, came from outside.

Catriona narrowed her eyes and glanced around, blessedly at the closed bedroom door. "Did you hear something?"

"Nae." Isobel's heart stuttered, her pulse beating wildly at her throat. It was all she could do not to spin around and yank the window shutters into place.

She did step forward and take Catriona's arm, guiding her across the room. "Come," she said, pure nerves giving her a burst of strength, "and I'll tell you what happened." Catriona would give her no peace otherwise. "But only if you sit on my bed. You do look a bit pale and tired."

She'd never looked more beautiful.

Catriona's skin glowed and her flame-bright hair shone like garnets. Breeding became her. Unfortunately, she remained just as headstrong as ever. If another noise floated up to the window, Catriona would be at the ledge, leaning out, in a heartbeat.

Isobel couldn't allow that to happen.

So she settled Catriona on the edge of her bed, plumped a few pillows around her, and took a good deep breath. Then she told her friend everything, leaving out nothing. She even spoke of her jealousy of the light-skirts from Rannoch Moor, how Kendrew's touch and his kisses had left her aching for more. Most damning of all, she revealed that just when the sweetest bliss began to claim her, he'd shoved her from him, rejecting her.

When she finished, Catriona was frowning.

"Mercy, Isobel. It is worse than I thought." Her opinion wasn't reassuring.

"I'll think of something." Isobel hovered, not about to let her push to her feet and wander anywhere near the room's three window embrasures.

Kendrew would be visible from any one of them.

Damn the man!

She needed to go down and speak to him.

Catriona was tapping her chin, her expression thoughtful. "Perhaps there is hope for the howling madman after all. He did act the gallant, all things considered. Who would've thought he'd abandon his pleasure?"

Isobel blushed. Her friend's words brought a rush of vivid images racing across her mind. The hot smolder in Kendrew's eyes as he'd reached for her, pulling her against him, kissing her so deeply.

Then...

She swallowed. "It is said he holds women in high esteem. Ladies, that is."

"It's also said that he has Berserker blood running in his veins."

"So?"

"Such men have a streak of untamed wildness in them. As Odin's own bodyguard, Berserkers were fearless fighters. Once the battle lust was on them, nothing could hold them back from an affray."

Isobel flicked at her sleeve. "We saw how ferociously Kendrew fought last autumn. No one who witnessed the trial by combat would doubt his prowess on the field."

"Indeed." Catriona slipped down from the bed, smoothed her night-robe. The flickering light from the night candle illuminated her face, showing how her blue eyes sparked with purpose. "Some might say that you have stirred his blood lust, pushing him beyond restraint. I'm thinking he'll not be able to resist the challenge."

"He already did." Isobel couldn't forget the horror on his face as he'd leaped away from her.

"You shocked him." Catriona drew her night-robe more securely about her shoulders. "Once he's recovered, he'll come looking for you.

"You've become the battle." She moved to the door, set her hand on the latch. "But unlike his usual opponents, your weapons aren't swords, spears, and axes. You must fight him with a woman's cunning and wit, using your charms and his need for you to best advantage."

Isobel bit her lip, watching as her friend cracked the door and peered out into the dimness of the landing. Apparently satisfied, Catriona lifted her hand-torch from its ring on the wall and opened the door wider, stepping over the threshold into the shadows beyond.

"Only so will you succeed." She looked back at Isobel, eyeing her critically. "You must want him badly enough to fight him."

"I do." It was the truth.

"I wish you didn't. But you do, so I'll just warn you to be careful." Catriona held her gaze for a long moment and then closed the door.

Isobel stood beside the bed, listening to her friend's footsteps fade as she made her way down the corridor. She also heard the renewed *crunch* of a much bolder, heavier tread rising up from beneath her tower window, the sound sluicing her with agitation.

She must be careful, Catriona had warned.

Too bad that just now, with Kendrew marching about beneath her bedchamber, his mere presence threatening to make everything even worse than it already was, she really did want to challenge him.

In truth, she must.

So she crossed the room and pressed her ear to the door, waiting until the sounds of Catriona's retreat stilled and she heard nothing but silence. Then she dressed as swiftly as she could and slipped from her room, hurrying down the winding tower stairs much more quickly than she had climbed them only a short while ago.

With luck, she'd reach Kendrew before anyone spotted him.

And then...

She didn't stop long enough to consider what she intended to do beyond snatching her mantle and sending him on his way.

She did know she wouldn't shy from using any and all weapons at her disposal. He'd given her no choice by coming here, disrupting her night peace and causing a commotion that could start a clan war. If she greeted him like a fury, it was his own fault and no one else's.

The battle between them already raged.

And she was ready to fight.

Chapter Five

❦

"You are a scoundrel!"

Lady Isobel marched out of the narrowly arched postern gate and came forward at speed, waving a hand at the rich blue cloak snapping in the wind above Kendrew's head. Somehow she managed to look like a queen, all elegance and grace, despite her long strides and the hot color staining her face. Barely restrained fury sparked in her great dark eyes and—Kendrew could hardly bear it—her silky, blue-black hair spilled free, swinging about her hips.

Her beauty took his breath, her spirit and vibrancy touching him much too deeply.

He could so easily succumb to her.

Cast aside the niggling doubt that warred with his more honorable reason for coming here.

Instead he ignored the heat racing through his veins, damned her ability to rile him, and wondered if any female had ever stirred such hunger in him.

She was a vixen through and through.

And he was...

He didn't want to know. It suited him better to just watch her storm toward him, starlight shining on her long, unbound hair. Her anger only brought out the worst in him, warning that he'd find himself in serious trouble if he allowed her closer than an arm's length.

Already, he couldn't tear his gaze from her.

So he braced himself, aware that he was much too smitten. His wits addled because she was so annoyingly delectable. His good sense scattered by the all-too-fresh memory of the feel, scent, and taste of her.

"A scoundrel, do you hear?" She reached him then, the flush on her cheeks almost heating the air. "Many say worse, calling you a howling madman. Now I see they weren't erring."

"Aye, they weren't." Kendrew fought the upward tilt at the left corner of his mouth. It was all he could do not to grin outright.

He was proud of the names folk called him.

And fury became Isobel.

Fetching color lit her lovely face and her eyes blazed with so much challenge he truly was hard pressed to keep his lips from twitching.

The shawl she'd flung about her shoulders—apparently in haste—wasn't knotted and fell loosely, displaying her magnificent bosom in a way that wasn't good for a man. The lush swells of smooth, creamy skin proved more than enough provocation to squelch his smile.

His loins tightened painfully, making it all the easier to glare at her.

She returned the displeasure, her tempting lips setting

in a firm, angry line. "My cloak, if you please." She extended her arm, her hand palm up. "I'll have it now and spare you brandishing it like a trophy pennant."

"Ah, but it is a prize, eh?" Kendrew lowered his arm but didn't relinquish the fine blue mantle.

Instead, he swept her a bow. " 'Tis glad I am to see you again, too, Lady Isobel. I feared I might be tromping to and fro out here till the morrow."

"You fear nothing, I'm sure." She snatched the cloak as he straightened, shaking it before she folded it over one arm.

"Or"—she lifted her chin, her tone icy—"can it be my brother scares you? Is fear of James why you came here wearing a war ax?"

"I rarely go anywhere without Blood Drinker." Kendrew glanced past her to the tower, eyeing the stout walls up and down. "His blade is sharp and e'er thirsty. If your brother or any of your kinsmen wish to come out and challenge me, you'll see how much I fear them. Blood Drinker willnae leave you in doubt."

The high flush on her cheeks deepened. "You should not have come here. It was foolish."

"And you, lady, are a female who drives men to fool deeds." Kendrew clenched his hands to fists at his sides, fighting the urge to grab her to him and kiss her. "I'm thinking you do it gladly."

Her chin came up again. "I didn't ask you to return my cloak. Truth is"—she turned and sailed off toward the mist curling along the edge of the wood, leaving him no choice but to follow her—"I can't imagine how you knew it was mine. There were other ladies at your revels."

"Not the sort who'd possess anything so fine."

Kendrew stepped around into her path, preventing her from pressing deeper into the pines.

The wood surrounding Castle Haven was thick and vast, the tops of the great Caledonian pines keeping out even the silvery sheen of the Midsummer night sky. The trees' massive girths offered numberless hiding places, absolute privacy. The last thing he needed was to be alone with her in a dark, secluded place. The way just looking at her made the ground seem to tilt beneath his feet warned him how dangerous that would be. He was a scoundrel, after all. And his restraint was swiftly unraveling. His blood was hot, his temper primed. Her swaying hips, the clean, spring violet scent wafting around her, and the shining skein of her unbound hair were all conspiring to bring out the beast in him.

She was torturing him.

And the pain was worse than any hooded executioner could inflict on a man.

"I was going to return for the mantle in the morning." She was folding it into a lump, the movements making her breasts bounce. "There was no need—"

"There was every need." The words came harsher than he would've preferred.

"Oh?" She settled the *lump* against her hip. "You are not my keeper."

"To be sure, I am not." Kendrew dragged a hand through his hair, torn between the desire to strangle her or kiss her. He did glance at the nearby shadows, the high ramparts of her brother's castle, half-certain that bastard's henchmen would be spying on them.

"After what happened"—he refused to put such a disaster into words—"I did feel a need to follow you here. No lady should traipse through the night alone." His words put a defiant spark in her eyes. "Or can it be that you weren't unescorted after all?"

There. He'd broached the possibility that gnawed so unpleasantly inside him.

"I don't understand." She looked about her, taking in the dark outline of the tower against the silver-washed hills, then the silent, night-glistening trees looming behind them. "I am not afraid of the night or this glen. I told you I came on my own."

"So you said, aye." Everything in Kendrew's gut rebelled against pressing her. The puzzled look on her face didn't support his suspicions. And—damn her—her nipples were chill-hardened, the thrusting peaks dangerously apparent. Yet he needed the truth. "Could it be your brother sent men to escort you? That they trailed behind you, watching over you without your knowledge?"

He didn't say he suspected James of trying to bait and trap him, that he wouldn't put it past the rival chieftain to have used Isobel as a lure.

He could've ordered his men to wait for him to fall for her charms and then rush from hiding to thrust a spear into his back. Such a scene would've given the Camerons good reason to start a ruckus at the revels, a time when Kendrew's own warriors would be ale-taken and vulnerable, not at their fighting best.

He'd been sure he'd seen mailed spearmen on the far side of the vale, lurking behind an outcrop.

Through the smoke and mist, he'd thought they were Camerons.

If they'd been there at all, for he'd blinked and they were gone.

Uncertainty didn't sit well with him.

So he'd come here—for that among other reasons!

Now...

The innocent outrage on Isobel's face made him feel like an arse.

"Are you calling me a liar?" She glared at him and he had to tamp down his own ire.

"I speak plain, my lady. You could have come escorted." He didn't care that he towered over her, his face set in his most fearsome scowl.

"I didn't." Undaunted, she met his gaze, her eyes unblinking.

"Then I am gladdened you returned here safely." He wanted to kiss her, savagely.

"You said you'd send guardsmen to escort me." She tossed back her hair, causing it to ripple like ebony silk about her shoulders, the ripe curve of her hips. "Why did you come yourself?"

He'd told her once.

He wasn't going to do so again.

He did glance up at the clouds and mist, the few stars glimmering high above. There wasn't a place on her body he trusted himself to rest his gaze just now. "My men were enjoying themselves." That was true. "I didn't want to call them away from their pleasures."

"I understand." She gave him the smallest smile, almost regal. She didn't seem to realize that the laces of her bodice were coming undone, revealing such a wealth of smooth, creamy-white skin.

There was also a shadowy hint of nipple, so tempting in its tight, puckered state that raw, burning lust shot straight to his groin. Need raced through him like sheeting fire, out of control.

He ground his teeth, trying not to notice.

"I truly do." Her tone was as queenly as her smile.

"Do what?" He didn't follow her, his mind distracted by the pounding at his loins. The nipple he could see most clearly, just inside her loosened bodice.

She would be the end of him, he knew.

He'd sooner face a score of wild-eyed, ax-swinging Berserkers. Opponents he could face on equal ground. And then cut to ribbons one by one, feeding his blood lust and battle frenzy, taking his mind off her dark, oh-so-wickedly luscious nipples.

"Why..." There was something suspiciously soft yet warlike in her tone. "That I understand you had your own pleasure to attend, away from your men and their ribaldry." She flicked a glance at the stretch of gravel and stone beneath the tower. Silvery light from the Midsummer sky spooled across the ground there, so that the little forecourt seemed to gleam almost accusingly.

Kendrew knew what was coming.

Guilt stabbed him.

The beauty before him tilted her head, her elegant brows winging upward. "What could be a greater thrill than risking my good name by acting the madman beneath my window?"

"Thon was no act." Kendrew scowled at her, seeing no need to tell her he'd hoped her brother would appear. He might not have whipped out Blood Drinker, having no mind to unduly frighten her. But breaking a few choice Cameron bones would've done him good.

James deserved no better.

But the bastard's sister was looking at him in a way that made the satisfying and respectable pastime of bone breaking seem shameful.

Her disapproval reminded him anew why he wanted nothing to do with ladies.

Stepping back—he needed distance from her—he hooked his hands in his sword belt and cleared his throat, loud and manfully.

"It was your good name I was thinking of when I returned your cloak, Lady Isobel." That was true enough, among his other reasons.

"Indeed?" She lifted a brow.

"Someone would've found it, see you?" He glanced at the silken blue *lump* tucked beneath her elbow. Even scrunched into a bundle, the mantle's richness caught the eye. "There's not a soul at Nought who wouldn't know such a fine raiment ne'er hailed from Rannoch Moor.

"Tongues would've wagged." He spoke bluntly, knowing she couldn't deny the truth. "Now no one will have cause to be long-nosed. You have your mantle returned and—"

"We can just forget what happened?" Her eyes flashed dark fire at him. "Go on as if nothing—"

"So would be best, aye." Kendrew felt the heat of her anger clear to his toes.

For a moment, he thought she was going to strike him. But she only went rigid, her back straightening as she took a long, deep breath.

"Tell me"—her gaze locked with his—"that you are not so cold."

"I am." He didn't hesitate. "I am that and more, my lady. Ne'er you forget it."

"I doubt I could." She put back her shoulders, taking a breath.

Before she could argue further, he turned and strode

into the mist. He went swiftly and silently, using his skill at moving unseen through shadows to ensure that she wouldn't be able to follow.

He suspected she had the courage to do so. He just hoped she wouldn't.

What he wanted was for her to despise him.

Only then would she be safe.

Isobel stood as calmly as she could, her gaze on the shifting mist where Kendrew had been a moment before. For such a big, broad-shouldered, and—it must be said—swaggering brute of a man, he'd disappeared into the shadows with astounding swiftness. And he'd done so with such ease and so noiselessly that she almost wondered if he possessed the Berserkers' ability to change shape, slipping through the night as wisps of thin, dark mist, undetected as they passed right beneath their enemies' noses.

It wouldn't surprise her. To her mind, he could do anything.

Just now, he'd infuriated her.

So she kept her chin raised and her face set in her most controlled, unaffected mien. She didn't trust him not to whip around and bellow another insult at her. If he did, she intended to be prepared.

Cold indifference would slice him deeper than swoons or tears.

She couldn't abide simpering females and thought even less of those who started weeping at the drop of a pin. So her only recourse was to stand proud until she was sure he was well and truly gone. Then she'd lift her skirts and stride coolly back to the tower.

What she'd do then...

She hoped that after a few hours' sleep, she'd be able to decide her next move.

It was just a shame that her blue silk cloak now held his scent. Each breath brought him back to her, flooding her senses with shockingly vivid images. She was reminded of the hot glide of his hands on her naked flesh, his tongue tangling so provocatively with her own, until each scandalous memory spread ribbons of tingly heat low in her belly.

She should no longer desire him.

Guilt wound within her. He was her family's most dreaded foe. This night he'd proved he was worthy of the worst slurs hurled after him.

But when he smiled, his teeth flashing white in his roguish face...

"Damn him." Isobel felt the air around her hum with her annoyance.

Who would've thought need and matters of the heart could be such a plague? A misery that clawed at tender places and made her head ache. Even the cool night air seemed unbearably hot. The back of her neck throbbed, the skin heating as if set afire.

It was all most terrible.

And yet...

Even when his face had hardened so fiercely and he'd called her a liar, she'd still found him the most shamelessly appealing man she'd ever seen.

Isobel resisted the urge to scowl.

Instead she took a deep breath and let it out slowly. She remained still, listening. Her ears caught no sound except wind soughing through the pines, the soft tumbling of a nearby burn, and from farther away, on the other side of Castle Haven, the muffled roar of the falls that spilled down a gorge in one of the higher peaks. Not even the cracking of a twig broke the night quiet.

She was alone.

And now that she was, she wanted nothing more than to return to her bed, pull the covers over her head, and sleep long and dreamlessly.

So determined, she started forward, certain that no day in her life had ever been, at turns, so wildly perfect and perfectly horrid.

"Now you see your folly." Kendrew's deep voice came from behind her. He gripped her elbow, preventing escape. "The danger you ignore."

"Gah!" Isobel jumped.

"How easily I surprised you." He tightened his fingers on her arm. "Did you ne'er hear that the men of Nought are aye one with the shadows? Such talk is true." His tone held pride, his arrogance palpable. "I could have you over my shoulder and gone from here by now if I'd wished."

"So you are the threat?" She deliberately mistook his meaning.

"There are others with night-walking skills." He was close, his breath warming her nape, tickling strands of her hair. "But no one does it better than me."

"I see." She turned to face him as slowly as she could, dignity demanding she not spin about. She ignored the leaping of her pulse, the fast, uneven beating of her heart. She hadn't heard a twig snap. He couldn't be standing right in front of her.

But he was.

And although she wouldn't have believed it possible,

he looked angrier than he had earlier. His brows were down-drawn and a muscle twitched in his jaw. In truth, he appeared almost murderous.

Isobel kept her gaze on his face, trying not to blink. "Should I fear you or those other night-walkers?"

"Any man would be a threat to you, running about as you are." Eyes narrowing, he flicked a glance over her. "Are you no' aware that your gown is undone? That a man"—his gaze lingered on her breasts—"loses his wits when faced with such temptation?"

"Is that why you came back?" She glanced down. Her bodice had come open, the laces loose and allowing the edges of her gown to gape wide. The white rounds of her breasts were plainly visible, her nipples wholly uncovered. Worse, her nipples were drawn tight and straining against the cold night air, almost as if they sought attention.

"No' to ogle you, my lady." He gave her a smile that was anything but warm. "You needed to see how easily you could be taken."

"No one has ever bothered me until you." Isobel yanked her bodice together and started fastening the laces. Unfortunately, Kendrew's steady perusal unnerved her so greatly that her fingers shook and she couldn't tie the ribbons properly.

She did manage to make two knots.

Her breasts pressed against the taut ribbons, the knots cutting into soft flesh. And—she wanted to sink into the ground—her nipples thrust even more now, pointing straight at Kendrew.

She risked a glance at his face and wasn't surprised to see his expression had darkened, his gaze still locked onto her breasts' straining peaks.

"Now see what you have done." His voice was deep, roughened with desire.

Isobel swallowed, recognizing the tone from the revels. His eyes smoldered, his jaw hard set as he drew a dirk from beneath his belt. Then, without taking his gaze off her bosom, he sliced the knotted ribbons.

"There." He shoved the dagger back into its sheath and stepped away from her. "You'll have to hold the gown together until you get back to the tower and reach your quarters. If you dinnae..."

He let the words trail away, not needing to finish.

His meaning burned the air between them. The way his eyes gleamed in the dimness told her everything. It was a look that made her heart beat faster and everything female in her prickle with excitement.

And he knew it.

"You'd best cover yourself." He sounded pained. "You've two good hands, by Thor. Put them o'er your breasts. Now."

Isobel did. She splayed one hand over her breasts and used the other to clutch the edges of her bodice. But as soon as she touched her fingers to the welling curves, his scowl deepened. Wheeling about, he turned his back to her. Then he ran a hand through his hair and tipped back his head, glaring up at the heavens.

"Begone, Lady Isobel." He flung out an arm, pointing in the direction of Castle Haven. "This moment, lest I—"

"Do what?" Isobel couldn't believe her daring as she stepped around him. Ignoring his outthrust arm, she eyed him up and down. "Shall you turn into the Berserker everyone says you are?"

"Have a care, lass." He shook his head, slowly. "You dinnae want to provoke me."

She did.

She'd gone too far to retreat. He'd accused her of speaking falsely. She needed to show him that he was a liar, denying their attraction. Challenging him was all that remained to do. This was war and her weapons were...

"Provoke you?" She stepped closer, her pulse quickening as his heady male scent swirled around her. Virile, earthy, and just a bit dangerous, the hints of clean, cold air, wood smoke, and man thrilled her. She hoped that her scent, essence of spring violets, would prove as irresistible to him. Her unbound hair and state of dishevelment should also work in her favor, fuddling his wits.

He'd already implied the possibility.

"Perhaps..." She tilted her head, taking advantage. "I would enjoy seeing you go Viking. Or"—she let her gaze flick over him again—"are you not as wild as one hears?"

"You tread dangerously, lady." A muscle in his jaw jumped, proving it. "'Go Viking' is what Norse raiders did when they assaulted our coasts and isles, as well you know, I vow. A Berserker's rage was nothing of the kind."

He leaned toward her, his voice a growl. "Their fury was a terrible thing. As is mine, be warned."

"Oh, I am." Isobel resisted the urge to lift up on her toes and kiss him.

He was that close.

And his anger was building, his clenched hands white-knuckled now.

"You are"—he grabbed her shoulders and hauled her against him, his grip fierce—"the most infernal, pestiferous lady I have ever known!"

Isobel felt a surge of triumph, her entire body coming alive. Her heart hammered, beating crazily in her chest, victory so sweet.

"I would prefer lady of spirit." She circled her arms around his shoulders, hoping to prove her point. "You, too, should beware. Norse blood also runs in my veins. I am just as fearless as you."

"Foolish, more like." He seized her chin and slanted his mouth over hers in a hard, furious kiss. Hot, crushing, and taking the breath from her, it was a kiss full of anger and thrumming, unchained need. And so glorious that a floodtide of exhilaration swept her, especially when he plunged his tongue into her mouth, his taste and the intimacy making her cling to him, demanding more.

She kissed him back with fervor, twining her fingers in his hair and pressing into him. She wanted to drink him in, savor the essence of him, the feel of his large, powerfully muscled body melded to hers. Her heart almost stopped when he pulled her even closer, so fast against him that her feet left the ground.

"Kendrew..." She floated on a glittering cloud, dizzy. She nipped his lower lip, then curled her tongue around his, teasing, enjoying.

"Enough!" He tore his mouth from hers and stepped back, looking fierce. "Go now, you she-vixen. If you dinnae"— he shoved a hand through his hair, his chest heaving—"I swear I'll carry you to thon forecourt beneath your tower walls and finish what we started at the revels. And I'll have you again and again until I'm sated, no' caring who sees."

Isobel's ardor vanished. "You wouldn't dare."

His arched brow said he would. "Doubt me at your peril."

"I would be ruined." Isobel placed a hand to her breast, covering her gaping bodice. She didn't miss that, this time, he didn't lower his gaze.

"You should've thought of your good name before you went to Nought." He towered before her, big and menacing. "For sure, before you came out here, half undressed and with your hair spilling down everywhere."

He folded his arms, his black scowl daring her to deny it.

She couldn't.

That truth sent heat washing the length of her. Even the tops of her ears burned. Rarely had she been so mortified. And she had no one to blame but her own scandalous self.

It was a galling admission.

But it gave her the strength to stand tall.

"You are a bastard, Kendrew Mackintosh." She flipped her hair over one shoulder.

"Nae, I am not." His voice was tight. "But I am many other things, 'tis true."

Isobel's chin went up. "Then prove that you are a nightwalker and disappear again."

Not waiting, she turned and made straight for the tower's silver-washed forecourt and the postern gate just beyond. She went as proudly as she could, taking care to keep her head high and her back straight. Above all, she refused to glance over her shoulder.

Something told her that if she did, he'd make good his threat to ravish her beneath the castle walls, in view of all and sundry.

And if she didn't wish to see blood spill between him and her brother, she'd let him.

As things stood...

She simply stepped through the arched entry into the tower and ascended the winding stair to her bedchamber, not pausing until she had bolted the door behind her. Only then did she release the breath she'd been holding and face the worst truth of the night.

If she'd had the sliver of a chance to win Kendrew's heart, she'd ruined it now.

He not only rejected her for being a lady. He now despised her because she didn't behave like one.

It was the last turn of events she'd expected, a new and daunting obstacle that wasn't at all promising. But she'd think of a way to surmount it, just as she always did.

This time would be no different.

She'd make sure of it.

Deep in the pinewood Isobel had just left, a large, dark shape waited until she slipped inside Castle Haven and Kendrew's footfalls faded into the mist. The steps—not so noiseless to one such as him—wouldn't have stirred a mouse. Yet caution was never misplaced. Only when empty silence spread through the cold night air did the hazy form emerge from the trees to hover at the wood's edge.

Just as he'd done earlier on his beloved Nought land when the lovely, raven-haired Cameron woman stopped at the Rodan Stone.

She'd seen him then, looking his way and even speaking to him.

Something warmed inside him at the recollection. Something good, even though he knew he couldn't truly feel such a long-dormant sensation. In memory, he recalled the like very well. And he missed such things, he did.

Once, in distant days so long ago the first dew hadn't yet kissed the land, his living heart had aye been filled with honor, loyalty, dedication, and pride. Love, too, though not for a woman as is the wont of most red-blooded men. As a dreagan master, he'd had nary a moment for frivolous pursuit. His mortal life had been devoted to duty and the magnificent sweep of jagged cliffs, cold, deep mist, and jumbled boulders he was sworn to protect.

It was a responsibility he'd taken seriously.

And one he'd shouldered gladly.

A weight he bore even now, though only in spirit, as things were.

The figure frowned—if the filmy, wraithlike form he crafted with all his not-so-impressive strength could even be called a figure. The shape was the best he could manage, given his circumstances.

At least he could still think, and that was a blessing for which he was most grateful.

Even if his mind-wanderings often caused him pain.

He *was*.

And that was quite a wonder. The alternative, a dull, black, unthinking void, would be a greater tragedy. Keeping his dark thoughts in rein was definitely the lesser evil, compared to not existing at all.

Now someone else knew of him.

Although...

The fetching Cameron lass didn't quite have the right of it. Even so, her acknowledgment of him at the Rodan Stone was an event to savor. He just wished her encounter with his kinsman, Kendrew the Wild, as he liked to think of the lad, hadn't run so ill-fated.

Not that he'd watched, of course.

As a man of noble sensibilities, he'd discreetly with-
drawn as soon as he'd seen where the two were heading.
But one such as he picked up on nuances. Ghosts, insubstantial as they are, detect faint ripples in the atmosphere
unnoticed by those still weighted and burdened with mortal bodies. When things went bad between the young pair,
he'd felt the night air quiver in distress, then the deep,
rolling shockwaves of their angry emotions.

Their upset had buffeted him, making it difficult to keep
his wispy form from dispersing. This was always demoral-
izing, for he enjoyed drifting about in the same huge, powerfully built shape he'd once kept hard-muscled and so very
well trained. Then, as now, he'd appreciated having bright
mail glinting from his broad shoulders, and he'd taken pleasure in lining his arms with fine, gold rings. Such adornments were recognized as signs of a man's valor and prowess.
And that wee spot of vanity he'd granted himself, for he'd
earned his warrior's reputation. He'd had both his long sword
and his war ax hanging at his waist, and he wore them still.

Even if no one but he was aware.

A man's pride never left him, after all.

Nor his need for justice, though such were thoughts
best left for another day. At present, he was again concerned for the lovely young Cameron maid who—he was
sure—had hung her heart on his gruff and swaggering
kinsman. A lad who clearly needed some sense and chivalry knocked into his thick, too-stubborn skull.

To the lad's credit, he had followed the lass to her home.

Even if he'd largely done so because he wrongly suspected the cravens who'd hidden behind an outcrop at the
revels had been James Cameron's men.

He'd come here, and that counted much.

And as happened so often whenever something monumental seemed about to occur, Kendrew just had to arrive in the moment when Isobel appeared to have noticed *him* in the wood beneath her window.

The figure frowned again and then released a long sigh. For sure, he'd trailed the maid to be certain she reached her part of the glen safely. But he'd also hoped to delve deeper into her seeming ability to sense his presence, even see him. If she could see him, she might be capable of sensing others such as him.

And what a wonder that would be.

But before he could drift over to her tower's little forecourt, his hot-headed kinsman had burst onto the scene waving her cloak in the air as if he'd never learned the first shade of manners.

The figure shuddered, wishing not for the first time that he could resume physical form just long enough to share a bit of his hard-earned wisdom.

When the last earthly breath is drawn, one finally realizes that life itself was the prize. Each day should be enjoyed to the fullest, and all a man should care about leaving behind is the good of his name.

Kendrew—by the look of matters—needed to learn that truth.

And *he* had matters of his own to attend.

He couldn't lose heart. Nor could he allow distractions, for his personal reasons for walking—nae, drifting about the glen—meant a great deal to him and were of such import that he couldn't dally.

The dreagans were stirring.

He'd heard them this night—in his realm that was possible—praise all the gods.

He'd cross paths with Lady Isobel again soon, he was sure. Indeed, he'd make a point to do so. He could not let things stand as they were.

She'd erred greatly in calling him Rodan. And that mistake needed correcting.

His name was Daire.

And once, back before memory began, he'd been the greatest dreagan master of them all. In his heart, that hadn't changed. But now he was also something else. And it was a distinction that rode him hard and kept him from peace.

He was the only soul who knew the truth of the dreagan stones.

Chapter Six

❦

It was the chill wind blowing down off the cliffs that woke Kendrew hours later. Another factor was the horror of dreaming that a huge, mail-clad warrior with a hard, grim-set face was bending over him and glaring at him with fierce, piercing eyes. Most times, he'd welcome such a challenge. No man swung a blade with more gladness. Each new enemy killmark he carved into his arms or chest was a badge of honor. He cowered from no man. And he knew no fear.

But in his dream, he'd been unable to move.

The granite-faced warrior somehow pinned him in place with his stare, stealing his ability to fight and reducing him to nothing better than a bug caught in the web of a spider.

Worse, when he tried to glower back at the man, he found he could see right through him!

"Guidsakes." He rubbed his eyes, shuddering. And it was then that he realized the third reason he'd wakened in such a foul mood.

His bedchamber wasn't just cold as an ice-crusted burn in winter...

His bed was full of rocks.

"Bluidy hell!" He shot up from his bearskin, seeing his folly at once. He wasn't abed at all. He'd been so vexed with Isobel that—he now recalled, wincing—upon returning to his own territory, he'd snatched his fur cloak from where he'd left it and climbed Slag's Mound, choosing to sleep atop the great stony cairn.

Passing the night beneath the stars seemed preferable to returning to Castle Nought where he'd risk his men catching a look at his soured expression and subjecting him to endless ribbing.

Having his sister needle him was an even worse prospect.

He just hadn't counted on the night turning so cold.

He'd also overlooked how much he'd miss his own many-cushioned bed. The great four-poster that had belonged to his father, his grandfather before him, and many other Mackintosh lairds was massive and carved of rich, age-blackened oak. Finest linens made the bed sumptuous. Furred coverlets—furs much softer than his bearskin—ensured warmth, as did the bed's proud tartan curtaining.

A small, equally splendid table stood close by, always dressed with a fresh ewer of mead and a precious silver-and-jewel-rimmed drinking horn.

He felt a surge of pride, thinking about his room's luxurious trappings.

He might be a warrior like no other. But he did appreciate his comforts.

Just now, he jammed his hands on his hips and looked

round, not surprised to find himself alone. The whole of the dreagan vale stretched empty. Thick, gray mist hid the tops of the cliffs, while a smudge of light in the overcast sky proved the sun had risen. The chill wind that had disturbed him whistled eerily. Some good soul had doused the bonfires. And the air, already thick with the scent of damp earth and old stone, held traces of cold ash. Nowhere did he see a hulking, fierce-eyed assailant, seethrough or otherwise.

More's the pity, because if the man had been real, he would've relished a good fight.

Ever since he'd left Isobel, he'd been itching to break something. And the few hours of sleep he'd managed hadn't lessened the urge. If anything, he was more riled than before. His regrettable sleeping choice hadn't just given him a rip-roaring backache. He now faced the unpleasantness of entering his hall to even more questions than he would have done hours ago.

"Thor's thundery arse!" He glanced again at the cloud-darkened sky, the smudge of lighter gray he knew to be the sun. Its position showed that the morning was no more.

The day had crept well past noontide.

His hall would be abuzz.

But none of the louts who'd soon accost him would've seen Isobel's blue silken cloak. That problem, he'd dealt with soundly. Her good name would not be smirched. That was all he cared about. She'd also answered his other reason for tromping through the glen. He didn't trust her brother farther than an ax blade could fall. But he didn't doubt Isobel's word that no men had accompanied her.

Of course, believing her made the men he'd seen at the outcrop a mystery.

A damned unsettling one—unless his eyes were failing him.

Kendrew's mouth twisted. His head was beginning to pain him as much as his aching back.

Scowling, he snatched up his bearskin and slung it around his shoulders. Soon every stone in his beloved vale would sprout a clattering tongue and scold him for his lies. The truth was surely stamped on his throbbing forehead. Isobel Cameron intrigued him.

He wanted her badly.

He could still feel her warm and pliant in his arms. Her taste lingered on the back of his tongue. The image of her full, round breasts kept blazing across his mind's eye, tormenting him until such need gripped him that he could hardly breathe.

Yet he'd sooner cut off his best piece than go near her again.

A *lady* was the last female he wanted on Nought land or anywhere close to him. His sister was the sole exception. As a Mackintosh, she was born and bred in the shadow of the dreagan stones. Her flesh and blood were hewn of granite, her spirit weaned on cold wind and blowing mist. She thrived in darkest winter and was as strong-willed as a Norse frost giant. She also wielded her tongue as wickedly as Mackintosh men swung their war axes.

Marjory was, in a word, fearless.

Any other gently bred women...

Kendrew blotted Lady Isobel from his mind and leaped down from Slag's Mound. It was time to return to his hall. If anyone so much as looked cross-eyed at him, he'd soon regret his mistake.

He was in a vile temper.

And Blood-Drinker was thirsty.

Kendrew knew his arrival at the keep would be worse than expected as soon as he reached the steep stone steps to Castle Nought's lofty gatehouse. He could feel an ominous *humming* in the air even here, at the bottom of the cliff stair and well below the rock-girded stronghold. Bracing himself, he took the narrow steps two at a time, prepared for anything. His gut told him his sister waited in the shadows of the castle's arched entry. Or perhaps she hovered on the other side of the stout, iron-studded door, waiting to pounce when he stepped inside the hall.

Either way, she'd have words for him, he knew.

She always did.

And she didn't hesitate to share them.

His lips twitched as he imagined her ire. Her blue eyes would flash and she'd tap one foot, her color rising as she upbraided him. Every man in the hall would turn to watch, some amused, others embarrassed. And if the gods really meant ill with him, Marjory's wee pest of a dog, Hercules, would run circles around him, snapping at his ankles. It would be an unpleasant scene.

But her fuss would serve her naught.

He hadn't achieved his fierce reputation by allowing himself to be cowed by a woman.

Nor was he of a mood to be pestered.

But when he assumed an indifferent mien and stepped into the gatehouse, the two guards on duty only nodded from their posts. The men had been leaning against the

wall, no doubt recovering from the revels. They straightened now, their bloodshot eyes and the hint of stale ale
in the cold air proving he'd guessed rightly. Neither man
showed awareness of discord inside Nought's walls.

Kendrew knew hell awaited him.

The prickles at his nape told him so. He liked to think
such warnings had been passed down to him from his
Berserker forebears. Wherever such niggles came from,
he knew not to ignore them.

Turning, he swept a glance over the rocky expanse
stretching beneath him. But if any mailed spearmen
dared slink about his land, hiding behind outcrops or
cairns, there was no sight of them now.

Nothing stirred at Nought except cold, blowing mist.

Yet his neck niggles remained.

So he took a deep breath, flung open the door, and
entered his hall. "A good morrow to all," he boomed,
striding forward as if nothing was amiss.

And—he blinked—nothing was.

Return greetings sounded in the colorful, mead-reeking
hall. Men lined trestle tables, most of the warriors eating
bread and cheese. Some slumped forward, dosing with
their tousle-haired heads resting on folded arms. Several well-burning logs blazed in the huge, double-arched
hearth. Orange-red fire glow glinted off the round, brightly
painted shields and weaponry that decorated the hearth-
side wall, while torchlight flickered across the richly col-
ored tapestries and animal skins adorning the hall's other
three walls. As so often, cold gray mist slid past the high,
narrow slit windows.

It appeared a day like every other.

Even Gronk, his favorite castle dog, behaved as was

his wont at this quiet hour of the day. A great wolflike beast with a shaggy black coat and silver eyes, Gronk sprawled before the fire, gnawing a giant meat bone while Marjory's wee Hercules hopped around him like a flea, begging attention. As always, Gronk ignored the tiny dog. His only acknowledgment of Kendrew's arrival was a single, quick ear twitch.

Gronk's bone held priority.

Kendrew understood.

It was good to have a purpose.

His goal was to find out why the hall seemed such a haven of peace when the skin on the back of his neck still prickled so incessantly. He also needed to discover his sister's whereabouts. A glance around the cavernous, smoke-hazed room—and then another, just to be sure—revealed Lady Norn wasn't present.

That boded ill.

Her absence meant she was up to something.

But before he could lift a hand and rub his nape, deciding his next move, a cool, feminine voice spoke at his shoulder. "By all the heather, you must've enjoyed the revels greatly, returning only now."

Kendrew whipped around to face his sister. "I'd be enjoying myself still if you hadn't come creeping up on me out of nowhere."

Some of his men sniggered. A few shifted on the trestle benches or coughed. Grim, Kendrew's captain of the guard, was passing and cuffed him on the shoulder. A burly, tough-looking man, Grim was so named because his eyes were the same deep gray as the mist that so often cloaked Nought. Just now, he winked, not breaking stride as he made his way to a table against the far wall.

Kendrew itched to join him.

Grim was his most trusted friend. He was a man who, despite his name, was aye full of laughter and could lift any man's spirits with a wink and a smile. Kendrew could've done with a few of Grim's more colorful jests, anything to take his mind off a certain tall, well-made beauty with dark eyes and long, blue-black hair.

But he stayed where he was, his gaze fixed on his sister. "No good comes to maids who slink through the shadows."

He meant that, by God.

Marjory met his stare, cool as ever.

"I've been here all along." Her tone held just enough smugness to fire his temper. "You'd have seen me if you'd looked well. Or have you forgotten"—she tilted her fair head, watching him—"that you're not the only Mackintosh able to night-walk?"

"Humph." Kendrew clamped his jaw, unable to argue.

He did chide himself.

He had forgotten that Marjory, like all their blood, could slip about in the shadows, silent and unseen for as long as she desired to remain undetected. Some Mackintoshes, himself in particular, could even pass through a bustling bailey or thronged great hall without a soul taking note. Though, he wouldn't deny, it was a skill that required much concentration and practice. Night-walking was a gift laid in Nought cradles, a legacy from the clan's long and mysterious past.

Marjory also possessed the irritating power to make him feel like a wee lad again, a mischievous boy caught doing something he'd been warned to leave alone.

Truth was he'd done just that.

He'd touched the forbidden, even sullying a lady. It scarce mattered that she'd deliberately provoked him, tempting him beyond the limits of any man and not even backing down when he'd made her aware of the danger. All that counted were his actions.

He'd behaved like a beast.

Marjory was eyeing him sharply, as if she knew.

"I wasn't night-walking." He looked at her, unable to keep his brows from snapping together. "I was sleeping. Alone on top of Slag's Mound, if your long-nosed self wants to know."

"Indeed?" She turned all innocence.

Kendrew saw right through her. "So I said, aye."

"And have you nothing else to say?" She bent to scoop Hercules into her arms when the little dog bolted up to her. "Perhaps about James Cameron's request of stones for the memorial cairn?"

"Hah!" Kendrew snatched an ale cup from a passing kinsman and tossed down the frothy brew in one swift gulp. "So that's what you're about. Still harping on that string, eh?" He slapped the empty cup on a table, dragged his arm over his mouth. "I'll no' be changing my mind and all your needling won't make me."

Now more than ever, he wasn't setting foot on Cameron land again.

He did fold his arms, abandoning any attempt at maintaining an air of goodwill. "No' so much as a thimbleful of stone dust will be leaving Nought. I've told you why often enough. *Cuiridh mi clach 'ad charn.* 'I will carry a stone for you,' as the wise words go. We both know it means 'I willnae forget you.' Not a one of our forebears will be dishonored by seeing stones he trod or rocks from his cairn carried off to grace a memorial on enemy territory."

The pronouncement made, Kendrew fixed his sister with his most intimidating scowl, determined to glower her—and her infernal gnat of a dog—away from his sight and out of his hall. Leastways until he'd had time to slake his thirst and address his hunger.

His stomach was rumbling, and if he didn't soon eat, someone would suffer.

Marjory seemed bent on being that person.

"A pity you're so stubborn." She shook her head, feigning sympathy. "I vow King Robert will be most grieved when word reaches him that you refused to serve the glen's peace. He might even be so wrought that he'll renew his threat to banish us all, then—"

"There *is* peace in the glen." Kendrew glanced round the crowded hall, letting his stare challenge anyone to say otherwise. "Every day I refrain from taking my men hallooing through the heather, slashing swords and swinging axes, peace reins in these hills."

He suspected he'd soon be doing just that if strange men truly were prowling the glen.

But he wouldn't make a fool of himself by heading out with a war band until he was sure.

"I'm no' breaking any truce." The words were his only nod to Marjory's needling.

A few grunts and mumbles came from the hall's darker corners. The enthusiastic assent Kendrew hoped for—cheers and many elbows thumping the tabletops—didn't come. Not a single foot stomp. Nor the clatter of good Mackintosh steel rattling in scabbards.

Even Grim held his tongue. The big man lounged on

a trestle bench, his long legs stretched to the fire. He was calmly sipping ale and appeared to be studying the hearth flames. Gronk, the furry traitor, sat next to Grim, surely expecting a treat now that his meat bone was gnawed bare. Grim loved animals and always carried twists of dried meat to feed any dogs who begged a morsel. He slipped one to Gronk now, not taking his eyes off the hearth fire as he fed the dog from the leather pouch at his belt.

Other warriors were equally occupied, their attention elsewhere.

Kendrew frowned, his temper rising.

No one met his eye.

Hercules did, baring his little-dog teeth and snarling deep in his tiny chest.

Marjory shifted him in her arms, not turning a hair herself. "You say the present quiet is peace? The kind that will last once the horrors of the trial by combat fade? If you do, be warned. Everyone in this hall feels differently."

"Bah." Kendrew dusted his sleeve. "There isn't a man here who'd cross me."

Hercules growled again.

Lady Norn smiled, petting his head. "Your men know what's at stake."

"Stoking Cameron's pride, naught else." Kendrew jutted his chin, the prickles at his nape now replaced by a nice, angry flush. "I'll have no part of that. His head is already swelled enough to fill the glen."

Pleased by his wit, he threw another look over the smoky hall, hoping for his men's agreement.

Again, no one responded.

Grim was gone, no doubt heading for the kitchens, where a certain plump serving lass supplied him with the dried meat twists for dogs. The wench gave Grim other treats as well, everyone knew.

Gronk prowled past the tightly packed tables, head low and tail swishing as he sought another dog-loving treat-giver among Kendrew's warriors.

Kendrew might've been air.

For all intents and purposes, he was as insubstantial as the rings of smoke curling along the hall's heavy, age-blackened ceiling rafters. And this was one time he was not night-walking. A man should be noted when he stood in the middle of his own hall.

So he drew himself up to his full height and put back his shoulders. "I'll no' surrender to Cameron's whims." His voice rang, reaching every corner. "Not this day, nor on the morrow. All he'll get from me is my sword rammed down his throat. If"—he hooked his thumbs in his sword belt—"I don't first use my ax to lop off his head."

His boasts went ignored.

Beside him, Lady Norn folded her hands, standing so straight she might have swallowed a broom. "If you do, you may as well behead us all."

"Dinnae tempt me, Norn." Kendrew flushed hot and cold, his annoyance welling. "Men need a little bloodletting now and then. Aught else isn't natural."

Even those words failed to stir his men.

Kendrew glared at them, half wondering if he'd walked into the wrong hall.

Yet this was Nought.

The men were his own, even if most of them were applying themselves to their bread and cheese with gusto, pretending not to have heard him. Some scratched sudden itches or hid behind their ale cups. Silence came from those with their heads on the tables, though one or two suddenly emitted such loud, fluting snores that he was almost of a mind to jab them with the pointy end of his sword, just to prove they were awake.

And men called him a scoundrel.

He was to be pitied, he was.

That was the way of it.

"You speak of James Cameron's whims." Marjory lowered Hercules to the rush-strewn floor and straightened, smoothing her skirts. "Because of you, he's relinquishing his plan to erect a memorial cairn with—"

"Hah!" Kendrew slapped his thigh, his good humor restored. "Like as not, thon cross-grained seaweed-eater Alasdair MacDonald threatened to take back his Blackshore stones on hearing that I'd no' be sending any from Nought."

"He'd never do that." Marjory's tone was cool. Her cheekbones washed pink. "The MacDonald is a man of honor. He and Laird Cameron are agreed to—"

"*Agreed, are they?*" Kendrew's levity vanished. "How would you know what those two cravens are planning?"

Marjory's chin went up. "They aren't cravens. And there will be a memorial at Castle Haven. But now, because of your refusal to send stones, the cairn will be built of rock from Cameron and MacDonald land."

"By thunder!" Kendrew stared at her. "You opened Cameron's letter."

She didn't deny it.

Half disbelieving, Kendrew looked on as Marjory extracted the parchment from a silk purse hidden in the folds of her gown. She held out the scroll, showing that the seal was broken. A snarling dog could still be seen in the cracked red wax, his image stamped deep and true.

It was clearly Cameron's missive.

The beast was Skald, the ferocious dog that also graced the Cameron banner and had done so for centuries.

Kendrew frowned. His sister's defiance didn't surprise him at all.

"Here, it was meant for you." She wriggled the parchment at him, causing the broken seal to jangle on its dangling, red silk ribbon.

In the flickering torchlight, the scroll minded Kendrew of a writhing snake. But he took the epistle, annoyed that just touching something from Castle Haven made some deep, dark part of himself wonder if he was about to be struck down by a thunderbolt.

Marjory lifted a brow, giving him the horrible notion that she'd read his mind.

"She's a bold lassie, our Norn," a deep voice called from a nearby table, breaking the men's quiet.

The man sounded proud. As if the far-famed Lady Norn hadn't just snapped a seal, but faced down an army of helmed and jeering spearmen.

Several other warriors chuckled, but most held their tongues.

The silent men were wise, for they knew the peril of Kendrew's Berserker fury.

The others...

Kendrew tossed a scowl at the chucklers, quickly ending their mirth.

"So you did read the letter." He turned back to Marjory.

"Someone had to." She didn't blink. "Be glad I did. You'd have put us all at risk otherwise. You can't allow things to remain as they stand. It won't do for the other two glen clans to erect their own memorial."

"Why not?" Kendrew rather liked the idea.

He also took pleasure in irritating the buggers.

"Because"—Marjory paused as Gronk sidled up to them and dropped onto his haunches with a gusty, big-dog sigh, indicating he'd been unsuccessful in finding treat-givers—"King Robert is sure to hear that the memorial cairn is missing Nought stones. He'll know why and before we know it, we'll have his Lowlanders loose in the glen again. And this time they'll come to tame you."

Kendrew snorted, not about to answer such nonsense.

His sister took a breath. "Or worse, they'll come to haul us all to the Isle of Lewis, as they threatened last time if we didn't hold our peace."

"Pah! You go too far, Norn." Kendrew reached down to rub Gronk's ears. "King Robert is an intelligent man. He'll know my keeping away from Camerons and Mac-Donalds is more than honoring a truce." He straightened, folding his arms. "I dinnae need to send stones to Castle Haven to prove aught."

"You should send them because it's right."

"Keeping Blood Drinker sheathed is all the righting I'm willing to do." Kendrew spoke firm, his words final.

Cameron and MacDonald could build a bridge to the moon with stones from their own territories. As long as he wasn't troubled, it was no matter to him, save that he was glad to have done with such foolery. Perhaps now there'd be no more Castle Haven couriers darkening his door at all hours, bringing letters he had no intention of reading, then requiring sustenance before they took their leave.

No reason for him to see Lady Isobel Cameron.

He should be joyous.

Instead, his heart lurched. And his reaction unsettled

him so much that he stepped around his sister, marched across the hall, and threw the scroll into the hearth fire. Only when the edges had blackened and nothing but ash remained did he stride back to Marjory.

His step was light now, satisfaction coursing through his veins.

The odd sense of something amiss was gone.

"That was not wise." Marjory narrowed her eyes as he approached, showing her displeasure.

Kendrew flashed a smile, just to annoy her. "Wise men aren't known for enjoying life."

"And you are?"

"At the moment I am, aye." He rocked back on his heels, feeling himself again for the first time since he'd entered his hall.

"There are ways a man can take his pleasure without burning other men's words."

"Thon was what I think of James Cameron and his bellyaching for stones." Dusting his hands, he kept his smile in place. "I'll be posting an extra guard or two out by the Rodan Stone. Any Cameron courier who seeks to pester me with more such fool missives will be turned away before he can penetrate our territory."

He might also send Grim, trusting him and no one else to also watch for a certain raven-haired Cameron female.

She'd already proven she made her own rules.

So he'd have to show her that he was a master at breaking them.

But before he could head for the high table to relish the prospect, thunder sounded in the distance and rain began hissing against the ledges of the hall's narrow, high-set windows. The wind rose and several of the wall torches sputtered, spewing ash and smoke. Kendrew frowned, chills once again rippling along his spine. Beside him, Gronk leaped to his feet, his hackles also rising.

Kendrew eyed his dog, the beast's ill ease fueling his own.

"See?" Marjory cast a glance at him. "Even Thor is displeased by your stubbornness."

"He'll be more annoyed by women who dinnae ken when to hold their tongues." Kendrew was sure of that. He touched his hammer amulet all the same, certain as well that it wouldn't hurt to show reverence.

The odd sense of something being not quite right was back, the hall seeming a shade darker, and cold, almost as if a great shadow had swept inside, blotting the light and chasing all warmth.

Kendrew ran his thumb over the heavy gold of his Thor's hammer. If the gods in Norse Asgard were indeed wroth, it wouldn't be with him.

But as soon as he lowered his hand, the hall door flew open and several of his warriors burst in from the storm. Patrol guardsmen, they carried swords and spears. Their faces were as dark as the weather, their long hair and braided beards wild and wind-tangled.

Grim was with them, looking equally shaken.

And it was Grim who closed the door and hurried toward Kendrew as the other guardsmen sheathed their swords and propped their long spears in a corner.

"Odin's balls!" Kendrew sprinted forward, meeting his friend halfway. "What's happened?"

"One of the cairns was disturbed." Grim dashed rain-drops from his brow. "I was heading for the kitchens when the patrol guards pounded up the cliff stair. They were out by the farthest bounds of the dreagan stones when they heard a great rumbling and then the sound of falling rock." He glanced over his shoulder at the guardsmen, then back to Kendrew. "They said the ground shook and—"

"A dreagan cairn has been damaged?" Marjory joined them, all rapt attention.

Grim nodded. "So it would seem, my lady. The guards—"

"Thunder rumbles and stones are aye falling hereabouts." Kendrew's head was beginning to pound again. "The earth is also known to shake at times. Or"—he glanced at the guardsmen, still in the entry—"did the men see anyone around the dreagan cairn?"

"They saw no one." Grim glanced at the guards, who all shook their heads, confirming his statement. "The cairn was split in two, its stones fanning out to both sides, littering the ground all around. One or two of the men think only a dreagan breaking free could've caused such damage."

"Bah!" Kendrew made a dismissive gesture. "Dreagans haven't roamed since the world was young. More like some cravens broke open the cairn hoping to find the treasure buried beneath. Though"—he glanced round—"all here know that tale, too, isn't likely."

He set his hands on his hips to deter argument.

He knew the direction it would come from, too.

A crafty look had entered his sister's eyes the moment Grim mentioned the scattered stones. Marjory might be strong-willed and even fearless—as was every Mackintosh, after all—but she also had one glaring trait entirely her own.

She couldn't hide her thoughts.

"Come, I'd speak with the patrol guardsmen." Kendrew gripped Grim's arm, leading him toward the other men before Lady Norn could vex him any further this day. "We'll send men to search for trespassers and a second party to repair the dreagan cairn."

Men, no doubt mailed and carrying long spears, had destroyed the cairn.

And Kendrew would find the truth.

Failure to do so would mean he'd have no choice but to ride to Castle Haven and Blackshore to warn the other two chiefs that strangers were on the loose, wreaking havoc in the glen.

That was something he hoped to avoid.

He did not wish to see Lady Isobel again.

Yet he would if he couldn't solve the dreagan cairn mystery. The risk of Isobel falling prey to skulking marauders couldn't be allowed.

Even a *howling madman* had honor.

He just never would have believed that his would bring him to such a lamentable pass.

Damn the lass and the wretched hold she had on him.

He didn't want her.

And as a man of honor, it irked him beyond belief to know that wasn't true.

Chapter Seven

⚜

A sennight later, Daire drifted to and fro in front of the Rodan Stone, hoping he hadn't lost his touch as a grand dreagan master. It seemed a possibility, all things considered. Seven days now, he'd tried to track and find Borg, the young dreagan who'd crept from his nest when the marauders tore away the stones from his cairn, searching for treasure. A pity they hadn't seen him.

The sight might've chased the blackguards out of the glen.

But the once mighty dreagans roamed only in Daire's realm now.

And with his earthly life stolen from him before he'd been well trained, Borg was surely having trouble finding the way back to his damaged cairn. Daire could feel the beast's distress, his aimless wanderings. Yet, as with Daire's other attempts to use his long-dormant skills, he seemed doom to failure.

This was his fourth visit to the Rodan Stone.

He'd been that certain he'd find the errant dreagan here.

It was true that evil-doers returned to the scene of their villainy. And it was equally true that the wronged and dispirited were also drawn to the place that had brought them such grief.

Or so Daire believed.

He certainly spent too much time at the Rodan Stone.

Though his reasons were many and he hoped Rodan knew he came, treading the ground his old friend-turned-bitterest-enemy no longer dared.

It scarce mattered that he didn't exactly tread, his wispy feet no longer capable of the act.

He came and that was enough.

Just now he paused to fold his equally insubstantial arms, once so powerfully muscled. His face hardened as he watched mist curl past the tumbled rocks and heather that marked this supposedly sacred corner of the dreagan stones. Not that anything associated with his archrival, Rodan, could hold even a breath of holiness.

This was tainted ground.

The only reason the bastard's pillar leaned so shamefully was that the gods saw fit to prevent such a craven from standing upright.

Rodan was bent for eternity.

And that was meet justice for his perfidious nature.

Pleased by the crooked angle of Rodan's monolith, Daire straightened his own back and held himself as erect as one such as he could. On this, the seventh day of his search for Borg, he'd taken care to polish his mail, imagining the heavy steel links shone with the flashing brightness of the sun on the sea. He'd also donned his great plumed helm, ensuring that its steel caught the eye. The many gold rings on his arms gleamed and sparkled brilliantly. And his long sword and war ax should also attract Borg. They were weapons that any dreagan would know and honor.

Or so Daire hoped.

But the stillness around him was complete. He could've been in the grayest, most silent heart of Niflheim, the Norse abode of the dead. And although he was no longer a powerful leader of men, guarding Nought with his warrior's skill and prowess, his wits hadn't deserted him. His memory was long, stretching back to days when boulders were little more than tiny, wind-driven kernels of sand.

Now, hoping his great knowledge would serve him again, he pressed both hands to his heart and closed his eyes. Then he summoned his remembered images of the young dreagan he wished to lead back to safety.

It wasn't easy.

Other memories flooded his mind, wringing his soul and making his heart squeeze. But Borg needed him most now. So he willed away everything else and used the powers vested in his ghostly state to send a wordless command to the wandering dreagan.

"Come, lad." Daire spoke aloud this time. He lifted his once-strong voice, even though the words echoed through the glen as a cold, hollow wind, nothing like the call of a living, mortal man.

Mortal he wasn't.

But he did live, as did Borg, who wasn't very mortal either.

If the young, known-to-be-clumsy dreagan possessed a whit of sense, he'd heed the summons.

"Borg, my little friend"—Daire smiled, knowing the creature was ten times his size, if not larger—"I am waiting for you."

It was then that he heard a rustling in the heather. Angling his head, he caught a skittering of pebbles, then the unmistakable crunching of heavy, beclawed feet on stone. The earth shook and the air shivered, filling his realm with the well-loved, never-forgotten sounds that heralded a dreagan's approach.

Daire's heart brimmed with gladness.

Borg was shuffling toward him, already less than a dozen paces away.

"Borg, there's my good dreagan." Daire praised the beast, his voice low and soothing, full of love.

The dreagan's long tail began to swish, flattening heather and scattering stones.

"I am here, lad." Daire's chest was so tight he could hardly speak. "Soon you'll rest again, safe in your own good den."

Borg snorted, puffs of fire and smoke showing his trust.

He came forward slowly, the same shimmering mist that swirled around Daire also rippling along the dreagan's huge, lumbering body and trailing in his wake. His scales and the high, fan-shaped ridge on his back gleamed like quartz-shot granite. His lack of scars proved his youth. Borg's great head was close to the ground, his eyes full of doubt, as if he feared reproach. But his tail kept gliding from side to side, the sight making Daire's spirit soar.

Borg was glad to have been summoned.

He was happy to be found.

Reaching Daire at last, the dreagan leaned into him, snorting his relief. He nudged Daire's shoulder, seeking affection like a long-lost dog. Daire gave it lavishly, praising the dreagan and petting his massive side. Then Borg's whole body quivered as he began to rumble deep in his chest, his pleasure clear.

Daire swallowed hard, wishing…

He pushed the thought aside, feeling guilty because he was indeed very pleased to have this dreagan answer his call. He also had a duty to see Borg across the narrow vale to his ruined cairn.

"Your home is not looking so fine at the moment, my friend," he warned the dreagan, still stroking the gritty, rock-hard scales. "But I know a few words that will help you sleep well again despite the discomfort. And"— he hoped this would prove true—"Kendrew the Wild, himself, who lairds it in Nought these days, is out now, searching for the men who disturbed you. He's set others to repair your nest.

"Come now." He started forward, pleased when the dreagan obediently followed. Together they strode through the heather and rock, making for the far side of the vale. "Soon you will be home, once again sleeping beneath a fine blanket of stone."

Borg leaned into him again, blowing out a grateful breath.

"Aye, that you will, my wee one." Daire patted the dreagan's shoulder. "The good men of Nought have their hearts in the right place. Even if"—he started forward again, Borg with him—"they don't know you truly exist."

What they needed was to tell their chief to get his head out of his hindquarters.

But Daire kept that sentiment to himself.

He doubted Borg would appreciate such man-woman matters. And the truth was that Daire was certainly no expert in the like either. But he knew well when a man was making a fool of himself.

Ghost or no, he hadn't forgotten his talent for keeping order in the glen. Kendrew the Wild needed watching and guidance. A bit of fatherly direction, even if too many centuries to count stretched between them. Kendrew's late father rested peaceably, his spirit content and not deigning to roam Nought at all.

So the task fell to Daire.

And he already had a very good idea how he could set the stones rolling, as it were.

So he smiled as he and Borg continued across the heathery, rock-filled landscape. He even imagined the whirling mist glittered a bit in approval. And there was much to celebrate, after all. For the first time in so long, he'd once more proved himself successful as a dreagan master. Soon he would also help Kendrew the Wild and the lovely, raven-haired maid who ached for him.

Then, as all good things happened in threes, perhaps he'd triumph over his own great tragedy.

Glancing at Borg trudging along beside him gave him hope.

That alone was a wondrous feeling.

Very fine, indeed.

A fortnight later, in the great hall at Castle Haven, Isobel stopped prodding at the plump, green herring she couldn't bring herself to enjoy and turned to face her good-sister and dearest friend. Catriona had been eyeing her, one red-gold brow lifted suspiciously, ever since she'd taken her place next to Isobel at the high table.

Truth was Catriona had been watching her closely every day of the past two weeks. Just now she was doing it in a way that made Isobel want to squirm.

Instead, she frowned.

"What is it?" Isobel set down her eating knife. "Have I grown a wart on my nose?"

"You haven't touched your herring." Catriona took a demonstrative bite of her own. "They're quite good. Beathag seasons them much better than our cook at Blackshore." She dabbed her chin with a linen napkin. "Can it be that fish disagrees with you?"

"I'm not hungry." Isobel hoped she didn't sound peevish.

She did take a deep, long breath, ignoring the tantalizing food smells. She was grateful for the earthy sweet scent of peat wafting from the brazier set in a corner of the dais. Peat smoke always soothed her. She secretly believed a trace of it ran in every Highlander's veins.

Peat was one of their secret weapons. Like the scream of pipes, a breath of peat smoke made Highland hearts beat fast and true, turning them invincible.

Sadly, at the moment, even the magic of peat failed her.

The longing inside her was an ache, strong and insistent. Since Midsummer Eve, her heart's yearning had turned unbearable, sharp and cutting as the edge of a sword. And she knew only one way to assuage the need clawing at her.

Green herring, peat, and even well-meaning friends weren't enough.

She wanted Kendrew.

Yet the world conspired against her.

Leaning forward, she glanced down the long table to where her brothers James and Hugh, fondly accorded the honor of clan storyteller, discussed the memorial cairn with Alasdair MacDonald. Seeing them speak so energetically, agreed and content in their plans, made her want to clench her fists and pound on the table to stop their blether. More than that, she itched to let the steam rising inside her shoot straight out of her ears.

She had no desire to cry. Only women without a backbone resorted to tears.

But she was seething.

All around her the hall teemed as it did every noontide. Men warmed the trestle benches, eating and talking. Noise and clamor reigned, the mood boisterous and jovial. The hearth fire blazed and torches burned, hazing the air. Kitchen servants bustled everywhere, hefting platters of food and ale jugs. Dogs barked and scrounged, playing in the aisles between the crowded long tables.

No one guessed the turmoil inside her.

Determined to keep it that way, she sat up straighter and assumed her calmest mien. She even smiled at Beathag when the stout old woman sailed past the high table with a basket of fresh-baked bannocks. Smelling delicious, they might've tempted her any other time.

She almost called out for the cook to return so she could have one. A honey-smeared bannock would be easier to eat than herring. And Beathag did make the finest bannocks in all Scotland. Her skill was legend.

But at the other end of the table, James clapped Alasdair on the shoulder and rose from his laird's chair.

"Kinsmen, friends!" His deep voice rang out, commanding attention. "Blackshore"—he glanced at Alasdair—"and I have good tidings."

A hush fell over the long tables as Alasdair pushed to his feet as well. The same air of purpose and satisfaction surrounding James also lit the MacDonald chief's face. The two men, bitter foes only months before, stood together like brothers. Their alliance, born in blood and fury, had blossomed, their bond now carved in stone.

Isobel tried not to frown. Her breath did catch, her chest tightening.

"You mustn't be wroth." Catriona reached for her hand, trying to lace their fingers.

"I am well," Isobel fibbed, pulling away. She didn't want sympathy. She knew what was coming. And she'd meet it with a raised chin and all the poise of her station.

She was a lady, after all.

If Kendrew were here to remind her, she'd blister him with iciest grace, scalding him with frost. But he wasn't, so she kept her gaze fixed on her brother and Alasdair. They, too, deserved a bit of chilly disdain.

"We are to have a fine cairn." James's words made Isobel's heart lurch. "We'll have a base of MacDonald stones as Blackshore is the glen's southernmost holding. Haven stones will serve as the middle, representing this stronghold at the glen's heart. We'll mix our stones with Blackshore's to make the cairn's crown.

"I propose placing the memorial where King Robert's royal viewing loge stood. That spot"—he looked again to Alasdair, who nodded agreement—"has the best outlook over the battling ground."

"So be it." Alasdair lifted his ale cup, showing approval.

"If all men are in accord…" James paused, raising a hand as men cheered. As one, they thumped tables with their fists and stamped their feet on the rush-covered floor. Some rattled swords or beat dirk hilts on trestle benches, the noise making dogs bark. The uproar was deafening. Not a single protest was tendered.

Even Isobel's quiet-spoken brother Hugh, who preferred scribbling tales to swinging steel, was thwacking the table edge with the flat of his hand.

James and Alasdair grinned.

Their triumph made Isobel forget her wish to appear calm and ladylike. Narrowing her eyes, she shot daggers at her brother. She also aimed a peppered look at Alasdair, just for good measure.

They were in this together. Both men's behavior went beyond unjust.

A cairn without Mackintosh stones couldn't be declared a true memorial.

Kendrew and his Berserkers had also fought in the trial by combat. Mackintosh blood had flowed as freely as Cameron and MacDonald blood. Nought losses drenched the ground as red as the fallen of Haven and Blackshore. Everyone knew Kendrew was a proud and stubborn man. Work on the cairn should be delayed until he relented and sent stones.

Anything else was dishonorable.

And it was her brothers' and Alasdair's plans that ruined her appetite.

It had nothing to do with the irksome welling in her chest each time the sun dipped behind the hills, reminding her that another day had passed without her having an opportunity to see Kendrew.

She knew he desired her.

But she couldn't make him love her—and bring peace to their clans—if he kept himself from her.

Furious that he was doing just that, she stabbed a piece of herring and popped it into her mouth. The briny taste almost gagged her, but she forced herself to swallow. She usually loved herring, especially when it was so fresh. Now, nerves kept her stomach tied in knots.

She winced and reached for her wine cup, hoping to dash the taste.

"I couldn't bear food either, not at the beginning." Catriona leaned close, breaking into Isobel's misery. Her voice was low, commiserating. "Green herring was especially troublesome."

Isobel nearly choked on her watered wine. "I am not *troubled.*"

"No?"

"So I said." Isobel slapped down her cup, her face heating. "Dear saints, but you have notions."

"With reason, I believe." Catriona set a hand to her own thickening middle. "I am concerned."

"Shhh…" Isobel glanced down the table again, relieved to see that none of the men looked their way. "There's no need for worry. I told you—"

"You told me enough." Catriona folded her napkin and placed it carefully on the table. "Mackintosh is like a wild beast. Wholly uncontrollable. Such men need only glance at a woman and she'd—"

"Well, I didn't." Isobel's cheeks burned. She almost wished she had taken his seed. Then she would've had something of him. "He did not…I am not—" She didn't finish, afraid her voice would crack if she did.

"You are sure?" Catriona sounded doubtful. "I have heard that such men are more potent than most." She edged closer, whispering against Isobel's ear. "Some folk believe even the air around them will quicken a womb."

"Pah! I've never heard the like." Isobel pulled back, almost knocking over her wine cup, drawing eyes.

Turning aside, she feigned a cough to explain her clumsiness and the color she knew must be staining her cheeks.

Worse, Catriona's words brought a rush of scandalous images. Particularly vivid, the memory of her on her back with Kendrew's big, naked body over hers. She saw again his powerfully muscled shoulders and chest, the swirly blue marks he carved into his flesh. She still thrilled to recall them lying skin to skin, his heated gaze burning her.

Yet...

He'd desired, taken, and then rejected her.

Isobel touched a hand to her belly, her deepest places forever branded by the waves of pleasure that had spooled through her in those wondrous, bliss-drenched moments. The memory was enough to madden her.

Beside her, Catriona blanched. "Dear saints. You are—"

"I am not." Isobel pressed Catriona's foot beneath the table. "Hush, before someone hears you." Lowering her own voice, she spoke what she knew to be true. "There is nothing growing inside me except anger, if you'd hear the way of it. That's why I'm not eating. How can I when everything has turned so horribly wrong?"

"You could make it wonderfully right." Color began blooming on Catriona's face again. She looked so pleased that Isobel knew to dread her next words. "There are some fine, braw men at Blackshore," Catriona mused, tapping her chin. "I suspect Lady Norn will want Alasdair, but there are others. Worthy men, proud, honest, and not bad looking—"

"No." Isobel was firm.

"There are times we must choose between what we want and what is best." Catriona proved her own stubbornness. "Kendrew Mackintosh will only bring you sorrow. He already has, from what I'm seeing."

"You don't know him."

"And you do?"

"I believe so." Isobel flicked an oatcake crumb off the table. "He lives by the old ways. He does things with a flourish, scorns weakness, and honors his Norse ancestors. If he blusters, he—"

"He roars and bellows." Catriona helped herself to another oatcake, creating more crumbs. "Mackintosh is as wild and untamed as a rogue Highland bull. To be sure, he lives by the old ways. Pretending to be a Berserker makes it easy to ignore honor and duty."

"I doubt he pretends at anything." Isobel was sure he didn't.

He made no pretense when he'd spurned her.

"Come, he's not worth your tears." Catriona stood, drawing Isobel with her. "If you're not going to eat, let's leave the men to their ale and blether."

"I am not crying." Isobel blinked hard. If fury had caused her eyes to brighten—always a possibility—she didn't want anyone to mistake what they saw.

Cameron women didn't weep.

Few Highland women did, if their blood was true.

And like her sisters of the hills, she would sooner eat a bowlful of pebbles than shed a single tear.

"You look more distraught than I have ever seen you." Catriona wouldn't leave be.

"Livid is what I am." Isobel didn't deny it, certain her annoyance pulsed around her like a bright red cloud.

"Anger has its uses, I agree." Catriona took her arm. "Sadly, yours won't serve any purpose except to turn you into skin and bone if you keep refusing to eat your supper."

"I'm not refusing, just not hungry."

"So you said." Catriona led her away from high table and down the dais steps, into the crowded hall. With a surprisingly brisk step for an increasing woman, she maneuvered them around a knot of tussling dogs, past two tray-bearing kitchen wenches, and then toward the tower stair.

"Fresh air is good for the soul." Catriona flashed a glance at her. "A walk on the battlements will refresh us both. Cold as the day is, perhaps the wind will wipe a certain scoundrel from your mind."

"I have put him from my mind." Isobel had never told a greater lie. "I wouldn't have mentioned him at all if you hadn't asked what ails me."

"I had to ask." Catriona released Isobel's arm as they neared the arched entrance to the winding stair. "That's what friends do."

Her gaze flicked to the softly gleaming necklace at Isobel's throat. "I'll not see you hurt. If my ambers won't warn you of the peril that is Kendrew Mackintosh, then I shall. You are too fine a lady for his ilk."

Isobel coughed for real this time.

She also bit her lip, burning to blurt that her gentle birth was the problem.

Kendrew would've slaked their passions fully had she been common born.

He wanted a woman as bold, reckless, and uninhibited as he was. She'd seen such females at the dreagan stones, the evening of the revels. And while she might thrill to nights of cold, dark mist, her Viking blood quickening at the bite of sharp, winter wind, she wasn't at all like the light-skirts Kendrew favored.

Not by any measure.

"Don't look so glum." Catriona paused just inside the stair tower. "Your face will freeze and you'll go through life looking soured."

"Bah." Isobel smiled, unable to help herself. Then she laughed, the lightening of her spirit was so welcome. She gave Catriona a quick hug. "I'm ever so glad we're friends. Whatever would I do—"

A horn blast ripped through the hall, shrill and jarring.

Both women froze, shouts rising from outside the keep. Men leaped to their feet, grabbing their sword hilts. Isobel drew a swift breath as the alarm echoed from the rafters, hollow and chilling. Then the hall door swung open and a handful of guards rushed in, their faces grim.

"Mackintoshes!" The first sentry hurried forward, nearly tripping in his haste to reach James and Alasdair. "They're a small party, riding hard from the north and spurring down the slopes like they've got wasps stinging their backs. They'll be here anon. And"—he gained the dais, panting—"they're armed for war."

"Heathen bastards!" A huge-bearded MacDonald standing near the stair tower spat onto the rushes.

"The cloven-footed cliff-climbers cannae be trusted farther than a dirk's end," a Cameron agreed, his words starting a rumble of growls throughout the hall.

"I told you Mackintosh is a craven cur." Catriona gripped Isobel's arm. "He grabs that horrid ax of his as quickly as he pulls out his—"

"Catriona!" Isobel flushed, knowing fine what her friend meant to say. Words that burned deep inside her chest, hurting more than was good for her because she couldn't refute them. "He is not coming to swing his ax."

She ignored the rest of her friend's comment. It pained her to think of Kendrew's lusty reputation. How often he was known to visit Rannoch Moor.

She wanted him for her own.

"The Mackintoshes will mean no harm." She spoke with confidence, willing it so. "I am sure Kendrew is bringing stones."

He is also here because of me.

Isobel knew it. And the knowledge made her heart race, filling her with hope and joy. Soaring happiness so great it was all she could do not to dash from the hall and run outside to greet him.

"Stones don't require a battle-ready escort." Catriona didn't share her enthusiasm. "They're coming to stir trouble, you will see."

"Take your seats, all of you." James's voice reached them from the dais steps where he stood with the guards. "Nought men are aye armed. I vow they take their bluidy axes to bed with them." He paused as the snarls and grumbles in the hall turned to hoots and sniggers. "Whate'er they're about, they won't be coming here to fight. No' with just a few men against a stronghold manned with a stout garrison and plenty of MacDonald warriors as well. Mackintosh might be crazed, but he isn't a fool.

"More like"—James glanced at Alasdair—"he read my last letter and finally saw the folly of withholding Nought stones from the memorial."

"He'll have his own reasons and purpose." Alasdair folded his arms. "If he's bringing stones, it's because he sees profit in doing so."

"We'll accept them all the same." James was firm.

Alasdair didn't argue. But the tight set of his jaw showed that he preferred a Cameron-MacDonald cairn over a three-clan tribute.

"See?" Catriona's voice held pity again. "Even if Mackintosh wanted you, he'd always cause dissent in our clans. Alasdair is furious, though he won't say anything. I know that look on him."

Kendrew does want me. Isobel had to bite her tongue to keep from arguing.

She did see that Catriona's brother wasn't pleased. But Alasdair wasn't her concern. Her whole attention was on the big, fierce-eyed man just filling the open doorway to the hall. The sentries hadn't lied. Kendrew was dressed in all his battle glory. Mail shone from his broad chest and his silver-and-gold arm rings gleamed bright in the torchlight. His long sword hung at his side and he wore his Norse war ax strapped across his back.

His bearskin cloak made him appear twice as large as he already was. The Mackintosh warriors at his heels looked equally huge and fearsome.

As did the Cameron house guards, armored, stern-faced men who poured from the shadows to form a tight,

narrow line on either side of the newcomers, flanking
them as they entered the hall.

"Cameron—I salute you!" Kendrew made straight
for James, ignoring the sentries. "I come in peace." He
reached behind his shoulder, plucking his war ax from its
halter and offering it hilt first to James as a sign of truce.
"And I bring you stones and a warning."

"The stones, I accept." James nodded, ignoring the ax.
"Your warning is no' welcome. We have no need of your
counsel, or concern."

"My concern is no' for you." Kendrew flipped the huge
ax as if it weighed nothing and thrust it back into the halter at his shoulder. "There are others in your household I'd
no' see sundered or harmed."

James didn't blink. *"Others?"* He flashed a look at
Isobel. "Who at Castle Haven matters to you?"

Isobel's pulse beat wildly at her throat, every inch of
her skin heating. Any moment Kendrew would name her.

But he didn't, not even glancing her way.

Instead, his face hardened. "My caution is for those
most vulnerable: women, bairns, and old men. A dreagan cairn was damaged these past days. We searched for
whoe'er tore the stones apart, but found no one.

"Even so, you'd best tread with care." He fixed
James with a bold stare. "If you or any of your folk
are foolhardy enough to ignore my warning, I'll no' be
responsible."

"You and your like have caused havoc since before
time was." That was Alasdair, his voice cold. "Many ter-
rors we've suffered have come from Nought. Why, if brigands are on the prowl, a threat that would put my folk at
risk, would you come here to warn me?"

"I'm asking myself that, the now." Kendrew folded his arms, his scowl turning black as the ceiling rafters.

"Could be"—he looked round, frowning at any Cameron or MacDonald who dared meet his eye—"I wanted you to have your damty stones so you'd stop pestering me with unwelcome ghillies bringing letters every other e'en."

"My couriers were less than a score." James bridled.

Kendrew stared back at him. "And my honor obliges me to advise you to have a care with the stones. They hail from the damaged dreagan cairn. Could be the beast, Borg is his name, might be for wanting them returned. Could be he'll come here and—"

"Could be you're full o' Highland wind!" a deep voice boomed from near the hearth fire.

Hoots and guffaws circled the hall.

Kendrew looked pleased to have used legend to stir a commotion.

James reached down to pat the head of Hector, his ancient dog, when he tottered over to lean into him. "I'd sooner worry about my dog turning into a slavering beast than fear a dreagan."

"Think what you will." Kendrew shrugged, unfazed by the jeers and sniggers. He did glance at Hector, his gaze flickering over the dog's bony frame. "I told you once already that I saw spearmen up at the falls behind this keep. You"—he shrugged dismissively—"chose not to believe me.

"That is your folly, no' mine." He fixed James with a stare. "The stones will be here shortly. They're in a cart and once they're in your hands, I'm washing my own of you and your memorial."

In the shadows of the stair tower, Isobel dug her hands into the folds of her skirts, gripping tight lest her fingers tremble with ire. She also took care to keep her back straight and her face expressionless, should Kendrew turn his head and look her way. He knew she was here. Prickling awareness rippled between them, scorching the air even if he deigned to keep on ignoring her.

Annoyance flared in her, hot and swift. This was not how she'd wished their next meeting to be.

He'd even acknowledged Hector.

She'd seen his face soften when he'd glanced at the old dog. Yet he avoided looking at her as if doing so would turn him into a pillar of salt.

"Now you see him for the bastard he is." Catriona stepped closer, resting a hand on Isobel's shoulder. "He has forgotten you already."

"Nae, he just doesn't care." Isobel pinned him with an icy stare, willing his attention.

Kendrew continued arguing with James and Alasdair, just now refusing James's less-than-enthusiastic urging to return to Castle Haven for the memorial cairn's soon-to-be-held dedication ceremony.

Isobel might have been a dust mote.

A speck of lint on his sleeve or—her blood began to rush in her veins, her temper rising—a smear of mud on the sole of his shoe.

"Your cheeks are red and your eyes are catching flame." Catriona curled firm fingers around Isobel's arm, pulling her deeper into the shadows. "I do believe it's time for our walk on the battlements. Now, before he does look this way and sees you so upset."

"I'm fine." Icy cold claws squeezed Isobel's heart,

iron bands clamping round her chest, making it hard to breathe. "And I am not going up on the ramparts."

"You can't stay here in the gloom, staring at him." Catriona tugged on her arm.

"I won't be." Isobel broke free. "I'm away to my bedchamber."

Catriona's eyes widened. "The stair tower to your room is across the hall."

"I know." Isobel tossed back her hair, a little thrill at her daring already lifting her spirits.

"You'll have to pass Kendrew." Catriona's brow furrowed.

"So I will." Isobel shot another glance at the scoundrel. Then she took a deep breath. "He's about to see what it feels like to be air."

"Don't be foolish." Catriona snatched at her arm, but Isobel was faster, gliding purposefully out of the shadows and into the crowded hall.

Her bravura faded before she'd taken ten steps.

Kendrew's back was turned.

Worse, James, Alasdair, and Hugh crowded around him, leading him toward the dais, in the opposite direction from her path. Hector, the clan traitor, slinked along behind them, sniffing at Kendrew's heels.

Isobel's hands curled to fists, annoyance sweeping her like sheeting fire. But she kept her chin raised and didn't break stride, crossing the hall with as much dignity as she could summon. Without looking back, she entered the turnpike stair and climbed to the third landing. There, she paused beside an arrow slit so the cold night air could cool her face. Only when the heat began to ebb did she start down the long, dimly lit passage to her bedchamber.

Frustration accompanied her every step.

She should have provoked a meeting, challenging Kendrew to admit his intent, one way or the other. But doing so would've caused a clan fight in the hall. Blood would've spilled, she'd have been ruined, and—she couldn't ignore the possibility—men could've died.

Isobel frowned.

Despite everything, her heart still pounded just from having seen him. Her body responded, craving his arms around her. Need filled her, tingly awareness that flickered along her skin. Recalling his kisses melted her even now, when she was so angry she couldn't see straight.

She was also seeing things that couldn't be.

She stopped, staring as the wall ahead of her rippled and shimmied, rolling like waves on the sea. A huge tapestry hung there, its colorful width lifting in an impossible, unseen wind.

"Sweet holy heather." Her eyes rounding, she reached for her amber necklace, gliding her fingers across the polished gemstones.

The ambers were cool and still, withholding any hint of danger.

Sure the enchanted necklace erred, she started to back away. She knew of another, less direct route to her bedchamber. A secret passage through the thickness of the castle walls, its entrance...

"Agh!" She remembered now. The hidden passage opened here. And someone was inside, trying to force the damp, age-warped door behind the tapestry.

Isobel's blood ran cold. No one used the murky wall-tunnel.

Yet the scrape of wood on stone filled the quiet. As did

the rattle of the old door's rusted latch. Then the heavy woven cloth was flung aside and a big, dark shape pushed into the corridor.

It was Kendrew.

And although he didn't reach for his war ax, he did look angry enough to murder.

Chapter Eight

❦

"Felicitations, my lady." Kendrew bowed his head ever so slightly, his eyes glinting in the corridor's dimness. "We have business. Privy matters best aired here, away from the ears of your kin."

"Any matters between us ended when you returned my mantle." Isobel stared at him, her heart thundering.

"You know that isn't so." He flexed his shoulders, as if throwing off the closeness of the secret tunnel. Somewhere, he'd also cast away his bearskin, but he was still so huge and burly that he diminished everything else around them. He wrapped his hands around his sword belt as if he knew and was pleased to use his great height and width to crowd her.

"I know no such thing." Isobel wished he wasn't so large, so disturbingly virile.

"You are no' a good liar, Lady Isobel." He gave her a bold, provoking look that sent shivers rippling all through her. Chills that stirred wicked, tantalizing sensations she didn't want to acknowledge.

She shook her head, still stunned that he could be here, three floors above the great hall and having just burst out of a centuries-neglected hidden passage only Camerons knew existed.

"What are you doing here?" She struggled against the urge to draw back.

He arched a brow. "Did you no' hear me?"

"How can anyone not hear you?" Isobel let her gaze flick over him. She also held her ground, refusing to be intimidated. "More like, you're ignoring my question. You have no right to be here."

"I say I do." His tone implied he made his own rights. "And we will have words. I'll leave you after we've spoken. Till then..."

He stepped closer, towering over her. A rushlight gilded his rich copper hair and slanted across his mailed chest, casting him in a devilish red glow. The hellish sheen suited him, spilling over his big, hard-muscled shoulders and arms in a way that weakened her knees. Unfortunately, his fierce expression revealed that she probably didn't want to hear whatever he wished to say.

So she looked at him narrowly. "I think you'll leave me now."

"I think not." He didn't budge, blocking her escape.

"I have nothing to say to you." Isobel made to sweep past him.

"You will." He clamped strong fingers around her arm. "And you'll speak true. If you dinnae, I'll keep you here until you do."

"You wouldn't dare." Isobel knew he would.

He glanced up and down the passage, surely aware that it was a well-trodden corridor.

"Dinnae tempt me, lass." He gave her a look that sent alarm clear to her toes.

Isobel flipped back her hair. "I wouldn't dream of it," she lied.

"You'd best not." He tightened his grip on her wrist, a warning. "No good would come of it."

"That I know." She'd never spoken truer words. Already, her pulse leaped just from his grasp on her arm. Tingly heat sparked in her belly, spooling low by her thighs. Trying not to notice, she glared at him. "You are wild, heathen, and dangerous."

"So men say, aye." A thread of cold wind blew through an arrow slit, lifting his hair about his face. "Women…" He looked down at her, one corner of his mouth curving. "They say other things."

"I know what they say." Isobel's chin went up. She was not going to discuss his joy women. Just thinking of them twisted her insides and made her feel as if tiny daggers were stabbing her heart.

"You know prattle." His brief smile vanished, his blue eyes suddenly hard as winter ice. "I would know if I've a need to speak with your brother about something other than his memorial cairn?"

Isobel blinked, hoping she misunderstood. "I'm sure I don't know what you mean."

"I say you do." His gaze dipped to her belly. "Though I'm thinking all is well with you."

"To be sure, I am well." Isobel could hardly speak, rivers of heat washing through her. Only this heat wasn't the exciting kind. A terrible mix of frustration, embarrassment, and anger, it welled inside her, hot and damning. "There's no reason for you to offer me the courtesy of"—she forced herself to breathe—"saving my reputation."

"You are sure?" He didn't release her, his expression intense. "It's only been—"

"It's been long enough." She rushed the admission. "I know nothing happened. I am not..." She couldn't bring herself to finish.

Not that there was a need.

Kendrew's face cleared swiftly, showing he understood. "Odin be praised."

"Indeed." Isobel glared at him, his relief insulting her to the core.

Ire gave her the strength to pull free of his grasp. Stepping back, she dusted her sleeve demonstratively, hoping to show her disdain.

"Now that you've heard what you wished to know, you can tell me how you knew of the wall-tunnel." She held his gaze, sure that her eyes gleamed like an evil shrew's.

She didn't care.

He deserved to be set upon by a host of talon-fingered, grizzle-headed crones who'd cackle with glee as they hastened him to the coldest, blackest level of hell.

"Well?" She lifted her brows, waiting. "How do you know Haven's secrets? I'm sure you didn't ask James how to waylay me."

"I told James I didn't trust his stable lads with Mackintosh horses. He thinks I went to the bailey to care for the beasts myself."

"That isn't what I asked you."

"I told you once that Mackintoshes can night-walk." His mouth twitched, as if suppressing a smile. "How do you think I amused myself as a lad? Many were the days

I came here and crept about these walls, in high fettle because no' a one of you knew I was about.

"All castles have secret squints and wall passages." Now he did grin. "My cousins and I wagered who'd be the first to discover yours."

"And you won?" Isobel didn't doubt it.

"I did." He looked mightily proud. "The memory served me well this day."

Kendrew only wished his good sense had served him better, a regret that pained him even more when the high-spirited minx swished past him to flip back the tapestry, revealing the wall-tunnel's warped and wormwooded door. He didn't care a whit about the pitiful door or the dank, cobwebby passage beyond. But Isobel, with her glossy black hair spilling down over her shoulders and her face flushed, was a sight to behold. The hint of fresh, spring violets trailing in her wake was a torture no man should endure.

He frowned at her, annoyed that such a comely female could be so vexing.

She was worse than a pebble in his shoe.

Ignoring his scowl, she gestured at the tunnel door. "Your fine recall can guide you back down to the great hall, where your arrogant presence is surely missed."

Her dark eyes blazed at him, the agitated rise and fall of her breasts proving that she possessed more weapons than her raven tresses and delectable scent.

She did have a magnificent bosom.

And she had no idea how close he was to pulling her into his arms and tearing open the ties of her bodice, just so he could again gaze upon her luscious, dark-tinted nipples. Only this time he'd do more than look at them. He'd lick and nip them, grazing the hardened peaks with his teeth until she writhed against him. He wouldn't stop there, also devouring another wildly alluring part of her. The notion tightened his groin painfully.

And that unwelcome throbbing made it easier to keep glowering at her.

"The hall awaits you." She shook the wall hanging, sending up puffs of dust.

"We're no' done talking." He blinked against the dust cloud, willing his ache for her to subside. "You can let the tapestry fall, unless you wish your arm to cramp from holding it aloft."

"Oh!" The color in her cheeks deepened. But she released the wall hanging, the fury in her eyes spearing straight to his heart.

"That's better." He wrapped his hands around his sword belt again, needing a reminder that he was a warrior untamed, a *Berserker*. And that until she answered a certain other question, he couldn't trust her. He'd handle his desire for her later, with a good, bone-chilling dip in an icy lochan on the ride back to Nought.

As to why upsetting her pinched his heart, making him feel a worse scoundrel than the blackest rumors about him…

That was a matter he'd simply ignore.

For now, he looked down at Isobel, hoping his face was fierce enough to hide what she did to him. "Tell me true. Did you spell Borg's stones?"

She blinked. *"Borg's stones?"*

Kendrew nodded. "You were in the hall when I spoke of Borg. The damaged cairn is called after him, has been for centuries. Dinnae try to—"

"I'm not trying to do anything." Her eyes snapped, her outrage singeing him. "I'm surprised you knew I was there. You didn't so much as glance—"

"You should know why I didn't look at you."

She rushed on as if he hadn't spoken. "I know nothing of your dreagan legends, Borg, or his stones." She waved a hand in the air. "And I wouldn't know how to spell a dung beetle. If I had such talent, you'd be a croaking toad and I'd be safe in the peace of my bedchamber."

"Then I thank Thor you are no' so blessed." Kendrew wished she'd stop eyeing him through her thick, black lashes. Her apparent innocence annoyed him, making him feel like a great, bumbling ox.

Still...

He needed to probe further. "Someone cast dark magic over Borg's stones. The topmost rocks wouldn't stay in place when we rebuilt his cairn. They kept rolling to the ground, no matter how we set them. No' all the stones either, just enough to fill a cart."

He watched her carefully. "If no' you doing the spelling, it's well known that Gorm and Grizel, the Makers of Dreams, dwell in the high moors behind Castle Haven. They favor Camerons." He couldn't keep the suspicion from his voice. "Could be they were persuaded to work mischief to provoke us at Nought."

The words fell hard from his tongue.

Her light, clean scent kept wafting past his nose, reminding him of how her warm, smooth-skinned body had felt beneath him. All her lithe suppleness and the soft, plump weight of her full, round breasts in his hands. Then the wonder of those breasts pressed against his chest, her gasps of pleasure when...

He pushed the memories aside before the accompanying stirrings at his loins could worsen into something more formidable. Better to think of the fabled ancients said to spin all the world's dreams—who, most annoyingly, were sworn to watch over Isobel's clan.

Blessedly, he'd heard enough fireside tales of the two to envision them. And the image of a tiny, wizened crone and a small, long-bearded man with an elfin face and a whirr of iron-gray hair swiftly chased all misplaced twinges of lust, clearing his mind.

He took a deep breath, relieved. "I ken the pair are half-mythic and—"

"Gorm and Grizel are real." Isobel flicked a speck off her sleeve, her eyes gleaming with annoyance. "Their home, Tigh-na-Craig—*House on the Rock*—exists, as does Gorm's Cave with its Pool of Truth. All tales about them are true. But they are peace-loving souls. Neither of them would use their spelling skills to do harm." Looking up, she let her mouth curve into a challenging smile. "They wouldn't plague anyone undeserving, that is."

She eyed him boldly, implying that he deserved the full force of the fabled pair's witchery.

"You are a minx, Isobel Cameron." He stepped closer, bracing his hands on the wall either side of her, trapping her against the tapestry. "I warned you already that I'm no' a man for you to provoke."

"I didn't follow you up here." She puffed a strand of hair off her face, bristling.

"Would you rather I'd asked you in the hall if my seed quickened inside you?" He gripped her chin, forcing her to meet his gaze.

"You accuse me of bespelling stones belonging to a

dreagan cairn I never heard of." She ignored his question, returning his stare with the same fury that raged in him. "Then you dare to turn your suspicions on ancients you've never met and know nothing about."

Kendrew looked down at her, the throbbing at his loins returning with a vengeance. "If I *dared* what I'd like, sweet, it would no' be asking about stones that won't stay in place or two hoary souls who surely know their time is better spent keeping you out of mischief than plaguing me and the good folk at Nought."

"You've had what you wanted. You can return to the hall." She leaned against the wall, pressing her shoulders to the tapestry to put distance between them. Unfortunately, she only caused the silk of her bodice to stretch enticingly across her breasts. The gown wasn't as wickedly low-cut as others he'd seen her in, but...

Her infernal nipples were taut, twin peaks thrusting proudly, demanding attention.

"Damn you, Isobel." Kendrew couldn't breathe. His entire body tightened, a torrent of need rushing through him, making him crazy. "I have no' *'had what I want.'* I hunger with wanting and"—he reached to cup her breast, then jerked his hand away before he could touch her—"you ought to be glad I can restrain myself."

She had the cheek to smile. "I believe you are a master of restraint."

He stepped back, very close to losing control. "If you or your Makers of Dreams had naught to do with Borg's stones, then I'll leave you with one last warning."

"Indeed?" Her smile didn't falter.

It was cold enough to frost him.

Breezing past him, she paused beneath a rushlight. The

flickering glow limned her, doing wicked things to her silky blue-black hair and lush, oh-so-tantalizing curves. Kendrew suspected she stopped there deliberately, hoping to taunt and torment him.

And she did.

"See here, lass." He clenched his fists at his sides, knowing that if she so much as blinked wantonly, he'd be on her in a heartbeat. "Someone—*or something*—caused the stones to keep rolling off the cairn.

"Whoe'er spelled the stones could be dangerous." He didn't care if he frightened her. Fear would spur her to heed his words. "No one was at the cairn save me and a handful of my most trusted men. None of us touched the stones once they were set atop the cairn. Dark magic is about in the glen and you'd be wise to have a care."

He purposely avoided mention of the traces of a campfire he and his men had found, deep in a defile cut through Nought's most inaccessible peaks.

He'd handle that threat on his own, without frightening her.

He also held back that his sister believed the Norse gods in Asgard were responsible for the stones repeatedly falling off the cairn.

Marjory thought it was the work of prankster Loki.

A jest to irritate and—Marjory had been smug when she'd said this—to prod him into "doing the honorable thing" and seeing the stones delivered to James Cameron for his damty memorial.

There had been just enough stones to fill a cart.

No more, no less.

Kendrew's mood blackened. It galled to think the gods would side with Camerons.

"I'll keep your warning in mind." Isobel didn't look the least concerned. "Not that I intend to set foot in Nought territory ever again."

"Then we are done, my lady." Kendrew inclined his head, already reaching to fling back the tapestry and duck into the foul-smelling excuse of a tunnel Clan Cameron called a hidden passage. "I'll no' trouble you again. See that you do the same and—"

Thump. Thump. Thump.

Heavy footsteps and the deep voices of two men floated up the winding stair. Their clumping and low-spoken converse echoed through the passage, coming ever closer. Any moment they'd reach the landing...

"That's Hugh, my brother, and a cousin." Isobel clapped a hand to her breast, her gaze darting to the still-empty turret arch. "If they find us—"

"They won't." Kendrew lifted the tapestry and pushed open the door to the wall passage. "In with you and"— he put a hand on her back and urged her inside the dark space—"be still until they've passed."

"Oh!" She spluttered, flashing him an indignant glance over her shoulder.

"Hush." Kendrew nipped into the passage with her, closing the warp-wooded door behind them. Hugh Cameron and his cousin were already in the corridor, the noise of their approach unmistakable in the tunnel's darkness.

The blackness swirled around them, dank, thick, and filling with the scent of spring violets.

Kendrew's blood raced in response. "Odin's balls."

"You said we must be quiet." Isobel's voice came from much too close, her shoulder bumping his arm. The movement sent another waft of violet past his nose.

"It's your scent, damn you."

"My scent?"

"Aye." He glanced her way, catching the gleam of her eyes in the darkness. Praise the gods he couldn't see the rest of her.

He did stand still, trying not to breathe. But his lungs rebelled, mocking him as he inhaled deeply, drinking in her light, clean fragrance. His vitals stirred, urgent desire sweeping him.

Outside, in the corridor, Hugh and his cousin paused near the tunnel entrance. Their muffled voices filtered through the tapestry and the wooden door, revealing they were praising a lusty laundress named Maili who—according to the two men—enjoyed airing her skirts and was highly skilled at carnal pleasuring.

Kendrew frowned, trying to block his ears as well as not breathe.

Colorful tales of a maid's oral talents weren't what he needed to hear.

"Oh, dear..." Isobel sounded equally pained.

"Shhhh." Kendrew turned, placing a hand over her mouth.

It was a grave mistake.

Her soft, warm lips pressing into his palm was torture. The silken spill of her hair brushing across his wrist roused him beyond restraint. Cool and sleek, the satiny strands branded him as surely as if she'd set an iron to his flesh. He released her at once, lowering his hand with the lightning speed that had won him battles.

But it was too late, his best warring skills tromped.

The damage was done.

Furious, he clenched his jaw to trap the growl rising in

his throat. His wits must've abandoned him. He should've entered the secret wall-tunnel on his own, leaving Isobel in the corridor. Her brother and cousin would've passed by her without a word.

Now...

The fusty passage struck him as much tighter than before.

He knew it was darker.

Total, complete gloom that made it easy for certain images to whirl across his mind. Just as the closeness ripped away his restraint, letting desire surge so fiercely he feared he'd break Isobel if he did cast aside caution and pull her into his arms.

"I think they're leaving." She whispered the words, daring fate when her soft breath teased his neck.

Kendrew didn't move. A low *humph* was his only reply. Speech was no longer possible with the warm curve of her hip pressing against him, her damnable violet scent invading his senses.

But she was right.

The sound of retreating footsteps proved Hugh and her cousin were moving down the passage. Relieved, Kendrew reached to yank open the secret door just as Isobel sidled past him to do the same.

Only, in the tightness of the tunnel, she didn't *sidle* far.

"Oh, dear..." She froze, surely aware that she'd just rubbed the fullness of her breasts across his chest. "I'm sorry." Her voice sounded breathy, excited, and not at all remorseful. "I didn't mean to—"

"Lady Isobel, I say you did." Kendrew gripped her arm, pulling her back in front of him. "I doubt there is aught you do without deliberation."

She huffed, straining away from him. "You don't know me at all."

"I know you better than I wish." Kendrew held her by the waist, his fingers splayed across her hips. In the narrow tunnel, her back touched the wall, her breasts crushing against him. Her hair spilled everywhere, liquid silk, intimate and sinuous. And this time, he wasn't of a mood to ignore temptation.

"You are"—he lowered his head and nipped her earlobe, trailed kisses down her neck—"a born seductress." He kissed the curve of her cheek, then wished he hadn't, because her skin was so smooth and warm, enticing. "But I'm no' a man to hide in shadows.

"Suchlike runs against my nature." He straightened, setting firm hands on her shoulders, ignoring the sweet glide of her hair across his fingers. "Yet I dinnae think you'd wish me to kiss you out in the corridor, on the other side of thon door? Or down in the great hall with your brother and everyone else looking on?"

"No, that isn't what I wish." She took a deep breath and Kendrew sensed rather than saw her frown. "What I want—"

"I ken what you want." He gripped her chin, lifting her face to his even though she couldn't see him in the darkness. "Such passions are no' good for you. You're better off in your ladies' bower, stitching fancy borders on linens."

"Then step aside so I can go there." Her voice snapped with anger, just as Kendrew had hoped.

Releasing her, he edged past her, pulling open the tunnel door before he damned his chivalry and hitched up her skirts, taking her against the wall as his painfully tight body roared for him to do. She wouldn't fight him. Far from it, she'd welcome him, sliding her arms around his neck and kissing him deeply, urging him on.

He could quench his need for her so easily.

Leaving her now would damn him to sleepless nights, endless longing, and regret.

His honor—such as it was—won the battle.

"Wait till I'm down the stairs before you leave the tunnel, Lady Isobel." He did his worst, stepping out into the dimly lit corridor.

"What?" She burst from the secret passage, grabbing his arm. "You can't go down the stairs. Are you mad? Someone might see you."

"I'll say I lost my way returning from the stables." He shook off her grip and started along the corridor, making for the turnpike stair.

"Kendrew, please..." Isobel didn't come after him.

Kendrew kept on, not looking back.

"You are mad." She hissed the words, angry now.

Kendrew smiled, giving his steps a swagger. Anger was good. Thinking him crazed, even better. His smile widened when he reached the turret stair and stepped into its shadows.

He welcomed the gloom.

The dimness would hide him from view if Isobel dashed to the stair's entry and peered down to watch his descent. With luck, she wouldn't see him nip into the secret tunnel at the next landing.

It was best if she thought he'd boldly marched down the stair.

Mad as she believed him, uncaring if he caused her woe.

What a pity that he did care.

Worse than that, he didn't think he could stop.

*   *   *

Even as Kendrew made his way through Castle Haven's much-too-low, much-too-narrow secret wall passage, this time heading back down to the great hall, his long-passed but still lively ancestor, Daire, drifted to and fro in a quiet corner of the battlements. He'd always appreciated the contemplative benefits of pacing. And just now, he needed to decide if there was hope for Kendrew.

He believed so.

The notion put a smile on his once-proud face.

He hadn't been so sure the night he'd watched over Kendrew as he'd slept atop Slag's Mound. The lad's fury had thickened the air, even as he'd tossed and turned on the rocks, snoring worse than a dreagan.

Now...

Daire could scarce contain his excitement.

In life, he'd worked hard to forge peace between the glen clans. A keen judge of character, he'd secretly selected brides from both Clan Cameron and the Mac-Donalds for carefully chosen Mackintosh warriors, including the chief of his day. It'd been a grand undertaking and was almost ready for fruition when Rodan's treachery ruined everything.

All Daire's work had been for naught.

No marriages took place between the pairs he'd been so sure would wed well together.

And the enmity between the three glen clans only grew, worsening down the ages.

Now...

Kendrew and Isobel were better suited for each other than any of the pairs Daire had tried to match in his day.

So a strong sense of accomplishment welled inside

him. If such were possible, he was sure that his heart would beat faster, his pulse quickening. He did fancy that his ghostly mail gleamed with particular brightness, reflecting his satisfaction and delight.

It was just a shame that there was no one to share his high spirits.

Once, there would've been.

A true and loyal soul he'd loved more than his life.

We will never be parted. His own long-ago promise echoed in his mind as he paused by a merlon in the notched parapet wall. Lifting a mist-thin hand to his brow, he looked out across the wooded slopes of the hills, then to the high, heather-grown moorlands rolling beyond. Nothing stirred as far as his eye could see.

You can depend on me always. More of his words, slipping out from the deep, hidden place where he kept them, knowing well that dwelling on sorrow only deepened the pain.

But he had known glory for a time.

And he'd enjoyed the most pure and wondrous love.

That was long ago, sadly.

This day held one of the small triumphs that came his way now and then. So he allowed himself his pride. Even a bit of spectral daring, leaning out through a crenel opening to catch a better view of the great, roaring waterfalls that spilled down the hills behind Castle Haven.

The Cameron holding was a bonny place.

Perhaps not wild and rugged enough to attract anyone from Nought, but nothing was impossible.

He hadn't lived all these centuries without learning that truth.

So he braced a hand against the edge of the merlon and

kept watch as he always did, hoping he wasn't missing anything of import.

It was hard to think with so much clean, cold air blowing across the parapets. Like all Mackintoshes, he relished sharp weather. The keening wind was music to his ears, easily distracting.

And he really did need to keep his thoughts on Kendrew and the raven-haired lovely.

From what he'd seen, things weren't anywhere near settled between them. Admittedly, he'd left them to their privacy when they'd embraced in the tunnel.

He'd expected them to kiss, even hoped fervently.

They'd argued instead.

Tempers rose before Daire could flit more than a pace away. And then he'd been obliged to keep an eye on them. Having taken on their cause—life as an Otherworldly being did turn boring at times, necessitating such engagement—it was in his best interest to observe them.

Only so could he be of service.

He'd already performed a most astonishing feat, causing the top stones of young Borg's nest to keep rolling off the cairn until enough rock accumulated to make a cartload. That wonder filled him with pride. Sadly, it'd also cost him quite a bit of strength.

But he'd managed the journey here all the same.

His reward was great.

He now knew that Kendrew's heart was softening toward the fetching Cameron beauty who—beyond all doubt—was such a well-suited bride for him. There could be no other reason that he'd ignored her so fiercely upon his arrival in the Castle Haven hall. Nor could anything else have spurred him to once again suffer the tight confines of the secret passage, if not to protect Lady Isobel.

Kendrew did care for her.

If he didn't, he would've ravished her in the tunnel. Yet he'd resisted. He'd behaved nobly, even if he'd allowed Lady Isobel to believe otherwise.

Daire understood the lad's reasons.

So there was hope.

He just didn't know how to go about ensuring that the pair met again soon.

Kendrew had most adamantly declined the Cameron chief's invitation to participate in the upcoming dedication ceremony for the memorial cairn. His gallantry slipping, regretably, the lad had even thrown back his head and laughed, announcing his beard would grow past his ankles before he'd return to Castle Haven.

Then he'd left in a huff.

Daire had tried to stop him, to no avail.

His ghostly powers only went so far. And his remarkable bit of stone magic at Borg's lair truly had left him drained. So he hovered where he was, sheltered by the merlon and the wall of an empty guardhouse. He also sent a prayer to Asgard, asking the gods not to let the strong wind rushing across the parapets whisk him back to Nought.

He wasn't ready to return.

Castle Haven's battlements truly did offer a wealth of opportunity for scouring the landscape. Set as the stronghold was, in the heart of the Glen of Many Legends, the view of the surrounding woods and hills proved irresistible.

He didn't often get down this way.

And now that he was here, he needed to take advantage.

It would be a wonder, but there was a possibility that the thick pines around Castle Haven held more than mist, shadow, and the smell of resin.

If so...

Daire lifted a wispy hand and dashed his cheek. Hope was a beautiful thing.

He wasn't abandoning his.

Chapter Nine

❧

"W*here's Grim?"*

Kendrew glanced sharply at Talon, the warrior riding beside him. Rocky outcrops loomed before them, marking the edge of Cameron land and the beginning of the more rugged, far superior sweep of Nought territory. The small party of Mackintoshes rode hard, making good time since leaving Castle Haven. Until now, they'd also kept together. And Kendrew wasn't of a mind to halt. Not with his stronghold so near. His hearth fire beckoned, as did a warm meal and a cup—or several cups—of good thirst-quenching ale.

So he lifted his voice, pressing Talon when he didn't respond. "Grim." Kendrew's gaze flicked beyond the other man's shoulder, searching the high, steep cliffs and rocky ground. "Have you seen him?"

"Grim?" Talon blinked.

"He was just here." Kendrew's brows lowered as Talon reined closer.

"Aye, so he was..." Talon trailed off, frowning. A powerfully built man with a square, strong-featured face, he looked as puzzled as Kendrew. "I cannae say I saw him ride away."

"Then find him. He'll no' be far." Kendrew's jaw hardened as Talon nodded and then spurred off, disappearing into the mist at a fast canter.

Of all men to go missing, Grim was the most likely to vanish for reasons sure to foul Kendrew's mood.

The flat-footed craven thrived on vexing him.

Next to Lady Norn, that was. She lived to annoy and outwit him, plaguing him at every twist and turn, her iron will as unbreakable as Nought granite. There were times a body could fancy she'd been sired by the massive boulders that littered Nought ground and not their long-dead parents, gods rest their souls.

Kendrew eyed the nearest outcrop, the hoary stones cracked and pitted, seeming to glare at him accusingly. He didn't see any mailed and wild-eyed spearmen hiding there. But he could well believe his sister sprang from such origins. A nefarious changeling his parents had found red-faced and bawling in a bed of pebbles.

Their father had been too ugly to have spawned a maid of such fair beauty.

Norn's tongue was too sharp for her to have been born of their sainted mother's womb. Which meant Marjory was an interloper.

Whatever she was, Kendrew's blood quickened to be on Nought ground again. Breathing deep of the cold, stone-scented air, he felt his heart swell, pride surging as he rode past the first clusters of broken stone.

Thrusting boldly from the naked earth, the jumbled

rocks were just a hint of the wonders to come. Deeper into the wilds of his holding, Rodan's Stone would claim the eye, quickly followed by Drago's Lair, the cairn said to belong to a midsized, three-legged dreagan the talespinners loved to claim still roamed Nought.

Legend told that Drago walked to prove he could.

Drago was the beast seen most often at Nought. To be sure, those glimpsing him were storytellers, graybeards, and men deep in their cups. But all swore that when Drago walked, he went about proudly, bumbling through the heather, crunching over stones.

No one feared the storied beast.

Mackintoshes, at least, knew that the three-legged dreagan's prowling was a matter of dignity and not a search for his next meal.

Drago had no need to scavenge, after all. Grim supplied him with all manner of supper leavings from Nought's tables, regularly raiding the castle stores to fill whole creels with everything from barely gnawed meat ribs to entire sides of roasted oxen if the lout could steal one from the kitchen firespit without Cook catching him. Grim also nabbed barrels of herring and other pickled fish when he thought no one was looking.

No creature small or large went hungry at Nought.

Grim cared for them all.

It scarce mattered that deer or other woodland creatures, and not a dreagan, enjoyed Grim's offerings.

A romantic at heart, Grim appreciated the fancy of feeding a dreagan.

At the moment, neither Grim nor a needy beastie could be seen. Talon had also disappeared, the clatter of his horse's hooves faded. Nothing stirred on these outermost fringes of Nought except cold, blowing mist. Great, billowing curtains of damp grayness that—to Kendrew's delight—were always darker and denser than the mist found anywhere else in the Glen of Many Legends.

All was quiet.

And Talon was no man to tread gently. Unless he chose to night-walk, as all Mackintoshes were like to do when the need or desire rose.

Now...

Something was amiss.

Kendrew frowned, narrowing his eyes to better peer through the mist. The silence boded ill. The rocks, heather, and crags returned his stare uncompromisingly, the rough terrain showing its most sullen face.

Lifting a hand to his brow, he stared harder.

He was better at being sullen than any hoary, lichen-covered boulders.

His eyes were excellent.

In the distance, he could just make out Rodan's Stone, leaning precariously into the whirling gray. As usual, no one lurked there. For some reason, the air around the standing stone always held an unpleasant chill, leaving some to speculate that Rodan, the clan's greatest hero, was perturbed by the tilt of his monolith.

"Rodan must be about," a deep voice claimed from the tight column of riders behind Kendrew. "The cold's slicing my bones, it is."

Another man barked a laugh. "You're chilled because Kendrew made us leave Castle Haven before you could pull a certain flashing-eyed serving wench onto your knee."

"She was already there, you arse," the other man

snarled. "A bonnie piece she was, too. Plump and warm, all woman and wanting me."

More laughter rose from the men.

Kendrew refrained. They were almost level with Rodan's Stone and—his head began to throb—he'd swear the monolith leaned more than the last time he'd been here. Indeed, he was certain.

"I swear there's frost on my danglers," the first man complained again. "Rodan's sour at us. Ho, Kendrew." He raised his voice, calling from the end of the column. "Mayhap we should fix his—"

"Nae." Kendrew bit back a shudder.

It was superstition that kept the clan from righting the stone.

Twisting in his saddle, Kendrew looked down the line of riders to the man who'd spoken. "What gods willed, shouldn't be undone."

But—he decided as swiftly—if Grim were up to mischief, no such law would apply to him.

The oversized lout might be Kendrew's most trusted friend and captain of the guard, but he enjoyed thrusting his nose into places not good for him. And he did so much too often. Grim was a natural-born meddler who should've been a woman, with all his interfering ways.

A pesky feeling told Kendrew his friend was up to no good.

Talon would've returned with him by now if that weren't so.

Only a moment before, Grim had been riding at Kendrew's side. The three of them, Kendrew, Grim, and Talon, had led the column of men. They'd jested for the last mile or so, chuckling about the look on James Cameron's face as they'd taken their leave of Castle Haven. Grim, especially, had laughed at Kendrew's vow that his beard would grow past his ankles before he'd set foot there again.

Then, as they'd neared their own land and the mist thickened around them, the air turning brittle with cold, they'd all sighed in pleasure.

The only thing a Highlander loved as much as his own bit of home glen was returning there after he'd been away. Even after such a brief excursion outside Nought bounds, Grim had edged his steed closer to Kendrew's and reached over to thump him on the arm at their first sight of Nought's soaring cliffs filling the sky before them.

Now Grim was gone.

Unease curled around Kendrew's heart, gripping tight. For the most inexplicable reason, he was sure his friend's absence had to do with Isobel.

Even here, in the wilds of Nought's dreagan vale, her spring violet scent haunted him. He could still feel the sweet warmth of her curves pressing against him in the secret passage; her soft, tempting lips parting for his kiss, inviting him to ravish her; her heart beating so hard against his chest as he'd held her, her breasts...

He tightened his grip on the reins, fury boiling inside him.

He was a fool.

Maddened by her charms, the spirit and boldness he admired so much more than was wise, he'd let matters with her reach a dangerous point. It was a place he should never have gone. With her wiles and allure, she'd maneuvered him onto treacherous ground that would open up and swallow him whole if he wasn't careful.

The sad truth was he didn't want to be wary of her.

He simply wanted her.

"Damnation." He scowled into the mist, glaring at the gray swirls sliding so innocently down the high, rocky cliffs to roll across the ground.

A pity that since Midsummer Eve he was beginning to believe there was nothing at all innocent in his beloved Glen of Many Legends.

Isobel had spelled him.

And he hoped to the tops of Thor's thundery ears that she hadn't also worked her magic on Grim.

It would be like the bastard to conspire with her.

Grim was as susceptible to females as he was to needy animals.

He wouldn't grasp that Kendrew was so eager to put Isobel from his mind that his head would soon split. She filled his thoughts too greatly.

"Ho, Kendrew! Grim is well." Talon's strong voice rose behind him, the words echoing off the cliffs.

Kendrew reined in, whipping his horse around.

Talon was almost upon him, spurring across the stony ground, his plaid flying in the wind. All men eyed him as he neared, a broad smile twitching his lips.

Relief sluiced through Kendrew. Even though Talon grinning was anything but a pretty sight.

He pulled up swiftly, looking untroubled as he resumed his place beside Kendrew at the head of the line of riders. Looking pleased, he drew an arm across his brow, his eyes sparking with amusement.

"Took me a while to find the loon, it did." He tugged on his plaid, smoothing the folds.

"Where is he?" Kendrew didn't miss that Talon had returned alone.

"Och, he's back in the birchwood no' far from Rodan's Stone." Talon jerked his head in the direction from whence he'd come. "He's after a stray cattle beast wandering in the trees and wants to herd it back up into the grazing hills before the creature loses his way."

Kendrew frowned. "I didn't see any cattle when we rode past the birchwood."

Talon snorted. "Grim would find a beast in need if he were buried in a muck heap."

"Then we'll no' be waiting for him."

"I wouldn't."

Kendrew looked ahead of them, eyeing the cold, dark mist as the other men snickered. He couldn't blame them for their hoots and guffaws. Grim could take down a score of men in battle and not lose a wink of sleep. But if he found a dead newt, his heart broke.

Nor did Kendrew doubt Talon. A shrewd fighter and warrior of renown, Talon wasn't a man to spin tales. If he'd seen Grim fussing over a cattle beast, that would be what Grim was about and naught else.

Still...

The odd prickles at Kendrew's nape were back, his hackles rising as the little group nudged their horses and rode on through the rocky vale. And with each *crunch* of his steed's hooves on the cold, stony ground, he remained sharply aware of everything around them.

Something was afoot in the Glen of Many Legends.

It had nothing to do with Grim, Drago, or even Rodan and his tilting stone.

And even less with Lady Isobel.

His temples began to throb anew, images of her in the clutches of some faceless, unknown danger tightening his chest and making his blood boil. She wasn't the woman for him, but he did appreciate her. She was a lady apart, different from any female he'd ever known.

He'd become quite the fool.

But if any harm came to her, he'd find the perpetrators and make such foul work of them that only their dead eyes would remain to feed the ravens.

Unfortunately, his bravura was dashed like a dousing of cold water when the great, frowning fortress that was Castle Nought loomed into view. Veiled in mist, only a few of the stronghold's narrow windows showed flickers of light. But the gatehouse was ablaze. Scores of torches burned inside the entry arch and on the ramparts, the flames casting a garish, red-orange glow over the high walls and much of the rugged crag that formed Nought's stony base.

Hell couldn't look more terrifying.

But the vision at the top of the cliff stair did.

Kendrew's brows snapped together in a fierce scowl. "Odin's balls."

Beside him, Talon gave a short laugh. "Norn looks most pleased with herself, what?"

"Humph." Kendrew couldn't argue.

He did know a greater dread than if he were once again at the trial by combat, beating his sword against his shield and eagerly waiting to face the slashing bite of Cameron and MacDonald steel.

His sister didn't look pleased.

She beamed.

Her fair face and shining hair gave her the appearance of an angel. *A triumphant angel*. And even though he couldn't see her eyes at this distance, he could feel the victory in their sparkling blue depths.

There wasn't anything amiss in the Glen of Many Legends.

His unease came from Lady Norn.

And if he had any doubt, the little dog clutched in her arms proved him right. Hercules's canine grin was even more jubilant than Marjory's.

The wee beastie loved to needle him.

And just now Hercules looked more pleased than if he'd watered the inside of Kendrew's shoe.

Kendrew squared his shoulders, his pulse racing with annoyance. "Thon she-vixen can be damn glad she isn't a man." He could hardly speak for the growl rising in his throat. "If she were, I'd sever her head just to wipe the smugness off her face."

"I rather like her smile." Talon sounded smitten.

Kendrew shot an annoyed glance at him. "It's not her face you're staring at, you lecherous bugger."

"So it isn't." Talon had the nerve to agree.

Ignoring him, Kendrew kneed his horse and galloped straight for Nought's stables. He dismounted swiftly, tossing the reins to a startled stable lad and then running for the cliff stair, taking them two at a time until he reached the high gatehouse and his fair sister.

"What's the meaning of this, Norn?" He went toe to toe with her, fixing her with his fiercest glare.

"The meaning of what?" She smiled sweetly, stroking Hercules's tufted head.

"You waiting for me at the top of the cliff stair." Kendrew took a step closer, his hands fisting.

"I was taking the air." She tilted her chin, inhaling deeply to illustrate. "You know I love chill days full of cloud and mist."

"I know you—"

Hercules showed his teeth, snarling.

"Tell your pet squirrel to contain himself or I'll feed him to Gronk for supper." Kendrew scowled at the little dog.

"Gronk loves Hercules." Marjory's eyes twinkled when Kendrew's dog trotted over to them and dropped onto his traitorous haunches at Marjory's feet. Not even glancing at Kendrew, the big dog looked up at Hercules, his gaze full of adoration.

"See?" Marjory sounded most pleased. "Unlike you, your dog knows who is good to him."

"I ken fine what's good for me. And dinnae talk in riddles." Kendrew took her elbow and ushered her through the gatehouse and into the hall, his fearsome stare daring Hercules to bite him.

The dog didn't.

But Kendrew would've preferred the sting of Hercules's sharp little teeth to the air of satisfaction swirling around his sister.

"Now"—he steered her through the hall, marching her up the dais steps to the high table—"tell me why I've had prickles jabbing at my nape ever since riding onto Nought land? It's your doing, I'm sure."

"O-o-oh, to wield such power…" She placed Hercules on the floor at last and then made a great show of settling herself in her chair.

"You dinnae need such craft." Ignoring his own chair, Kendrew planted his hands on the table edge and leaned toward her. "Your usual scheming does well enough."

"It does, yes." She looked up at him, at last tossing down her gauntlet.

Kendrew straightened, folding his arms. "What have you done, Norn? Tell me true, for I'll no' be asking you a second time."

"You won't need to." She held his gaze, wholly undaunted. "I'm very pleased to tell you."

"Then do."

But instead of speaking, she peered about the torchlit hall, her lovely brow creasing in mock concern. "I do not see Grim." She returned her gaze to Kendrew, something in her tone making his innards quiver. "Did he not return with you?"

"Nae, he didnae." Kendrew's face grew hot, the back of his neck catching fire. "He's herding a stray cattle beast back to the grazing."

Marjory's golden brows winged upward. "Is that what he told you?"

"Nae. He disappeared like a wraith on our ride back here, there one moment and gone the next." Kendrew's head was going to explode. "He didn't tell me aught about spurring off to chase lost cattle. That's what he was doing when Talon went to look for him."

Marjory didn't turn a hair. "So Talon—"

"*Talon!*" Kendrew whipped around to face the crowded hall, his voice booming. A terrible suspicion was building in his chest. "Where are you, you conniving—"

"I am here." Talon stepped onto the dais, looking irritatingly innocent.

Kendrew glared at him. "Tell my sister how you found Grim herding a stray cattle beast in the birchwood. She seems surprised to hear—"

"I never said I saw him with the beastie." Talon's expression remained guiltless. "I told you what Grim told me, is what I did. He was alone, looking for the cattle beast. The poor creature slipped away from Grim just before I caught up with him."

"That's what he told you?" Kendrew could well imagine the scene.

Talon's nod proved him right. "So he said, aye."

"And you believed him?"

"Why shouldn't I?" Talon shrugged his big shoulders. "We all ken how he is with animals."

"Aye, we all ken how he is." Kendrew pulled a hand down over his chin, well aware that Grim's trickery had nothing to do with his love for four-legged creatures.

"You." Kendrew turned back to his sister, who was very carefully buttering a bannock. "I'll hear what's afoot now, before you do aught else."

Reaching across the table, he snatched the bannock and tossed it to Gronk. "Speak."

Marjory cleaned her fingers on a napkin. When she finished, she looked up, meeting his gaze. "Grim helped me deliver a letter to James Cameron. He wasn't chasing stray cattle. Indeed"—she took a breath—"there wasn't any such beast in the birchwood at all.

"Grim rode back to Castle Haven with my letter." She sounded so proud. "Except, of course, the missive is worded as if it comes from you."

"What?" Kendrew could hardly see for the tiny red dots blurring his vision.

When it cleared, Norn was buttering another bannock, a small smile playing across her lips.

"I do believe you heard me." She took a delicate bite of honey-smeared bannock. After swallowing, she dabbed her mouth with a linen napkin. "Grim kindly agreed to ride back to Castle Haven, bearing a letter I gave him before you left here to go there.

"As I am lady of the keep, he could hardly refuse." She spoke calmly.

Kendrew could hardly breathe. Any moment he was going to roar louder than a dreagan.

Throughout the hall, men stopped eating and drinking. All eyes and ears turned toward the high table. Heads swiveled, necks craning as everyone vied for a good view of the dais. As she did so often, Norn was steering the scene in her direction just as surely as the winter winds blew as they wished across northern lands.

It was beyond bearing.

"I will kill Grim." Somehow Kendrew managed to speak.

"You'll do no such thing." Marjory gave him a steady look. "Grim is your friend. What you'll do, and soon, is to thank us both for addressing matters you can no longer ignore and maintain this house's honor."

A muscle began twitching in Kendrew's jaw. "And what *matters* remain that you haven't already needled me about? I did just return from taking Nought stones to that fool Cameron for his bluidy memorial."

"We should have given Cameron a fine taste of Mackintosh swords, axes, and spears." Talon spoke Kendrew's mind. "He'll no' be changing even when the last sunrise blazes across this glen."

"So is the way of it." Kendrew swelled his chest, pleased to have an ally.

Growls of assent circled the hall, men's voices loud against Clan Mackintoshes' long-time enemies. Even Gronk, sprawled on the rushes at Marjory's feet, lifted his great head and snarled, low and deep.

"Cameron will aye be an ornery arse." Talon again took Kendrew's side. "Some men are too thrawn to e'er change."

"Indeed." Marjory pinned Talon with a frosty stare as he dropped down on a trestle bench and used a whetstone to sharpen his dirk blade. "A man too stubborn for his own good also harms his clan."

Talon's lips twitched, his gaze flashing to Kendrew.

Kendrew's brows lowered mightily. He refrained from commenting on his sister's latest jab at him. Ignoring her barbs was one of his most effective weapons against her pestiferous tongue.

Regrettably, she simply inhaled deeply, clearly preparing for another assault.

Kendrew braced himself, wondering not for the first time what he'd done to be plagued with such a vexatious, iron-willed sister.

"We agreed to peace in this glen." She looked straight at him, the coolness of her gaze making him want to tug on his plaid and shuffle his feet like a lad whose voice hadn't yet deepened. "The stones for the memorial were a start, yes. But they weren't enough. Your continued resistance to accepting harmonious, neighborly relations with—"

"You go too far, Norn." Kendrew cut her off before she could voice the words *'relations with Camerons.'* Had she done so, he would've flushed crimson, shaming himself before all and sundry.

Marjory wasn't finished. "I will go as far as needed to make you see reason. You are staining the good Mackintosh name. And"—she let her gaze flick over him, critically—"you are earning yourself the reputation of an ill-bred, unmannered lummox."

"What stood in your letter to Cameron?" Kendrew used his lowest, most dangerous tone.

It would serve Norn well if he frightened her.

Instead, her chin went up. "Why, your apology for behaving so abominably at Castle Haven, of course." She held his gaze, cool as rain. "The letter is worded to express regret that you didn't realize you'd been so rude until after you'd ridden away, hence Grim, acting as messenger, sent by you even as you hastened back here."

Kendrew started to speak, but didn't trust himself.

He did stare at her, well aware that his eyes were surely bulging and that the flush he'd hoped to avoid was sweeping his entire, outraged body. He could feel the heat welling inside him, racing across his skin. He'd surely turned bright red and he didn't care.

Any moment steam would shoot from his ears.

"Be gone from my sight, Norn." He didn't recognize his voice. "I'll no' have you before my face just now."

"It's your face I'm trying to save." She didn't even blink. "You must hear the rest."

"There's more?" Kendrew's brows shot upward.

"Oh, yes." Marjory lifted her wine cup to her lips and sipped delicately. "The letter ends with your sorrow that you so erroneously declined attending the memorial cairn's dedication ceremony. It continues with your promise to—"

"Dinnae tell me it says I'll attend?"

"It does."

Kendrew stared at her, speechless. Around him, the hall went dim, spinning away. His entire world blurred to a whirling blackness studded with flashing red dots that blazed so brightly they hurt his eyes.

When the hellish sight faded, Norn was smiling at

him. She sat poised as a princess at the high table, her hands folded serenely in her lap.

"You do agree that you must go?" Her tone didn't hold a whit of sympathy.

"Like hell I must." Kendrew put a hand on the table, needing its support.

The red-studded blackness might've gone, but the hall still seemed to spin around him.

"Give me one reason I should." He hoped to thunder she wouldn't mention Isobel.

"Why, your honor, of course." She hit him with her best weapon. "If you stay away now, having said in ink that you'll attend, your name will be forever sullied."

"I ne'er wrote any such missive." The argument was Kendrew's only defense.

"Everyone at Castle Haven believes you did." Marjory's smile didn't falter.

Kendrew was doomed.

Every word his sister spoke was true. And he did care about honor. More so the clan's good name than his own, but still... however he turned the wretched matter, there was only one outcome.

Marjory had once again tricked him.

He would attend the memorial cairn's dedication ceremony at Castle Nought. And when he did so, he'd act as if he participated of his own free will. Anything else would shed a dark light on his sister.

And that he couldn't allow.

It was just a shame he'd have to face Isobel again. In truth, the notion was terrifying. He knew already he wouldn't be able to resist her.

Worst of all, he didn't want to.

*   *   *

And even as Kendrew paced his hall, his face dark and his hands fisted, fury roiling inside him, another Nought soul faced his own battles. And like Kendrew, he knew the bitter taste of losing. Though many men would lift their brows in surprise to know that Slag, Clan Mackintoshes' most famed and feared dreagan, struggled against frustrations even the fiercest beast couldn't quell.

Nor could he pace about angrily, spewing smoke and fire, his much-dreaded roar echoing through the dreagan vale, making the rocky, broken ground and even the high, bare cliffs tremble beneath his wrath.

Such days were long gone.

Truth be told, they were so far in the distant past that he sometimes found it hard to recall just how ferocious he'd been. Or that one glance from his fiery red eyes had struck terror into the hearts of men.

Now, in the dark and dank confines of this dread cave where he was so regrettably trapped, all he could do was roll his great stony-scaled body hither and thither. At times, he took especial care to stretch his legs and wriggle his long, claw-tipped toes. Even if he wasn't going anywhere, it was beneath his dignity to suffer muscle cramps in limbs that once made the earth shake.

Such spasms also hurt.

So Slag did what he could to relieve them.

Once, long ago, he'd have been better able to cope with such agonies. Not that he'd been plagued by many weaknesses back in those carefree days he missed so much. If he was honest, and dreagans always were, he'd only been hampered by one truly shameful shortcoming.

Unfortunately, his worst failing had brought him to this pass.

The sad fate of being trapped by the cold, hard stone he loved so dearly—dreagans were hewn of stone, after all—but unable to roam the beloved, mist-hung vale that was carved so deeply in his heart.

Even stone hearts bled, as well he knew.

And second chances were the stuff of dreams: elusive, bittersweet, and definitely not within the reach of a dreagan, however big and mighty.

Here, where he was, he almost wished he'd been the smallest of his kind and not the largest.

His life, such as it was, would've been easier to endure.

But he was where he was and also as huge as he was.

And he had only himself to blame that he was here.

So he did what he always did—unable to do aught else—and pushed his feet against the rock-hard wall of his nest, giving his toes one last wriggle. Then he let his scaly eyelids drop, blotting the impenetrable blackness that pressed around him so cloyingly.

Sleep would soon come and spend him a few hours' numbness.

Hours that—to a dreagan—could last a hundred years or more.

Not that Slag minded, not now.

Oblivion erased cares, and the horror of being wedged into a tight, confining place he couldn't escape. And most blessed of all, when he slumbered, he couldn't scold himself for the embarrassing truth that had landed him here.

On the never-to-be-forgotten day when the traitor Rodan had brought evil to the vale of dreagans, his all-consuming greed driving him to unleash unspeakable terror on Nought as his unholy henchmen shouted dark curses and ripped open dreagan cairns in search of the treasure they'd hoped to find there...

Slag had run.

Instead of rearing up on his great hind legs and fire-blasting Rodan and his minions, Slag had clamped his tail between his legs and fled.

But it hadn't been Rodan and his hell-fiend friends who'd frightened him.

The day—Slag would never forget—had been cold and dark, the sky low and black with angry, boiling clouds. Wind tore through the vale, bending trees and flattening the heather. Rain spat and hissed, peppering the ground. And lightning split the heavens, thunder booming worse than any dreagan's roar.

It'd been too much for Slag.

And instead of rearing up and roaring, doing his part to quell Rodan's villainy, he'd run. He'd taken off as fast as his legs could carry him, seeking shelter not from Rodan and his perfidy, but from the one thing that terrified him more than all else.

Thunder and lightning.

Slag, once the mightiest dreagan of them all, had a humbling secret.

He was afraid of storms.

Chapter Ten

⚜

A sennight later, Isobel stood on the battlements of Castle Haven, her face tilted to catch the night wind. The air was clean, cold, and smelled of pine, the brisk freshness good for her soul. Stepping closer to the wall, she rested her hands on the ledge and looked out across land loved by Camerons for centuries. The reasons were manifold, going deeper than time could reach. The Glen of Many Legends was special, filled with magic and wonder. Silvery mist drifted across the hills and moorland, and stars glittered against a sky that shone like polished silk.

Surely there was no more stirring place.

Despite Kendrew's warning, nothing terrible had happened and no strangers had been seen prowling about. If anything, the glen was more lovely now than ever.

Pride flared in Isobel's breast, the nightscape invigorating her, making her pulse quicken.

She inhaled deeply, appreciative of the beauty around her. She also clutched a parchment scroll, pressing the letter close to her heart, just as she'd done every night for the last seven nights, ever since Kendrew's messenger, Grim, delivered such unexpected tidings.

A huge man, fierce looking, but with striking gray eyes the color of winter fog, he'd sworn that every word of the missive was true.

Kendrew would attend the memorial cairn's dedication and friendship ceremony.

Isobel wanted to believe.

Already, the cairn stood at the top of the trial by combat's battling ground, placed where King Robert and his sparkling entourage had watched the slaughter from their brightly painted, pennon-topped royal loge. The memorial was magnificent, each stone placed with love and pride. Clan MacDonald's Blackshore stones made the base. Cameron offerings provided the cairn's middle. And Kendrew's portion from Nought served as the top layer, though the crown held mixed stones from the lands of all three clans.

Tears, blood, and honor bound the stones, while devotion to the Glen of Many Legends gave the cairn depth and meaning that no Highlander could look upon without his eyes misting.

The cairn was a sight to behold.

Beautiful to the eye, poignant to the soul, and—Isobel so hoped—a reminder that the glen clans would thrive only if they banded together, united in their dedication to one another and the land so dear to them, fierce in their commitment to face all outside threats as one.

She, Catriona, and Marjory were the beginning. Their secret pact would blossom, sealing the glen's peace—and sanctity—for all generations to come after them. Children would be born of these unions, strong, proud sons and beautiful, high-spirited daughters of the glen, their legacy then passed on to their own descendants.

It was a good plan.

And to Isobel, so much more than a means to ensure that harmony reigned in the glen. The truth was she wanted Kendrew with a passion that threatened to consume her. She was falling in love with him.

Perhaps she already had?

Whatever her feelings, even if he remained obstinate and loving him would rip her world apart, she'd still follow him anywhere. She'd do so because their souls beat in tandem. Her feelings for him burned so hotly in her chest that only true love could flame so desperately, filling her so completely that she couldn't even breathe without his name whispering across her heart.

Closing her eyes, she imagined his powerful, rock-hard arms sliding around her, holding her tight. His intense blue gaze piercing her, his kiss...

"Oh, please..." She curled her hands on the cold stone of the ledge, her heart aching.

They were so perfect together.

She just needed to prove it to him.

And if his letter spoke true—she didn't need to reread the missive, each word echoed in her heart—then she'd soon have another chance to win his affection.

He already desired her. There could be no denying the attraction between them.

But she wanted his love.

Half afraid such a wish was beyond her reach, she leaned against parapet walling, her gaze lowering to the newly raised cairn.

No one stirred on the erstwhile fighting ground. The hour was late. And although the night sky still held the shimmering glow of summer, folk rose early at Castle Haven. Most of her kinsmen were abed, her family unaware that she held these nightly vigils—just herself, Kendrew's letter, and the burning hope that kept her going.

She needed these quiet moments.

They helped her trust in the parchment. And in the assurances of a burly, tough-looking warrior with kindly gray eyes who'd laughed when she'd suggested the letter must be a mistake.

He'd said he knew Kendrew better than most.

And that Kendrew had vowed on his life not to miss the ceremony.

But Catriona's borrowed amber necklace had quivered at Isobel's throat the first time she'd touched the parchment. The stones had warmed and hummed, giving off the warning she'd been told indicated danger.

Yet she'd felt in her heart that Grim was honest.

A good and well-meaning man, for all that his face could only be called rough-hewn and somewhat frightening. Or that he wore his thick dark hair wildly tangled, his visage made more fierce thanks to the half-score of tightly woven braids plaited into his great, black beard.

She did trust him.

Even so, something made the ambers quicken. And she doubted it'd been Kendrew.

He only posed a danger to her heart.

Could the enchanted gems be cautioning her that his presence at the cairn festivities would leave her emotions in a worse turmoil than she was already in?

Before she could decide, she heard the soft scrape of a shoe against the stone flagging of the parapet walk, then the gentle rustling of cloth, announcing that someone had joined her on the battlements.

A woman.

And if it was Catriona—out of her bed and braving the steep, winding stairs to the parapet, risking limb and the child she carried beneath her breast—Isobel would have sharp words for her friend.

But when she turned, rather than scold Catriona, she found her jaw slipping.

Beathag, the cook's wife, stood on the other side of the battlements. The stout woman's back was turned to Isobel and she appeared to be staring at the cataracts that splashed down a gorge in the hills not far from the castle's curtain wall. Beathag's dark cloak blew in the wind and the night's luminous silver cast turned her iron-gray hair the gleaming white of newly fallen snow.

A freshening drift of cinnamon wafted from her, carried on the wind.

Isobel sniffed, frowning.

Beathag usually boasted one of two scents: salt herring or a trace of fine, roasted meat. Sometimes she also carried a hint of wood smoke from the kitchen fires.

She never smelled of cinnamon, claiming the costly spice made her sneeze.

"Beathag..." Isobel started forward, and then froze when the woman turned. "Dear saints!" Isobel clapped her hands to her face, staring at the woman—*a crone*—who was definitely not Cook's wife.

"Beathag is sleeping peaceably in her bed." The woman smiled, her blue eyes twinkling in the starlight. "I needed a guise to make my way up here, see you?" She winked, looking pleased. "Some folk still be shuffling about down in the great hall. It wouldn't do if they saw me.

"A guise was needed, aye." The crone cackled.

"A guise?" Isobel's heart galloped.

Shrinking in size before her eyes, the woman wore her snowy white braids wound on either side of her head. Small black boots, impeccably clean, graced her feet, and her wrinkled cheeks held a touch of pink. A half-moon brooch of beaten silver gleamed above her heart. And it was upon seeing that shining crescent that Isobel's surprise became wonder, relief sweeping her.

"Grizel." Isobel quickly crossed the wall-walk to join the tiny woman, the female half of the mythic pair known as the Makers of Dreams. "I don't believe I've seen you since I was a child."

"So you remember, h'mmm?" Grizel preened, the rose in her cheeks deepening. "'Twas a fierce fever you had, it was. With your mother gone away, the saints rest her soul, who better than me to sit with you, eh? Could be I also murmured a few healing words o'er you."

She winked, her ancient eyes crinkling. "It did no harm, what?"

"No indeed." Isobel smiled. Images from those long-ago days flashed across her mind, vibrant, real, and becoming clearer the deeper Grizel peered into her eyes. "You sang to me and helped me sleep."

"Ones such as me aye help." Grizel's thin chest puffed a bit. "That's why I'm here. But you'll already be for knowing that, eh?"

"I know you wouldn't come without good reason." Isobel didn't want to say more.

Grizel and her partner, Gorm, were good souls. But sometimes they took spoken words too literally. A carelessly turned phrase could land one in a precarious situation if the well-meaning Makers of Dreams granted a wish uttered without consideration.

Grizel put her hands on her hips, the glint in her eye proving it. "You've grown into a wise lass, you have. Such prudence will serve you well."

Isobel did her best not to frown. Grizel's words weren't encouraging. Indeed, they made her belly knot and set her heart to thumping nervously.

"Will I have need of caution?" She broke another rule of dealing with the Makers of Dreams.

Questions were never asked directly.

Grizel and Gorm loved riddles.

"You are asking the wrong person, alas." Grizel's merry tone took the sting from her words.

"I see." Isobel didn't see at all.

"You shall, anon." Grizel sounded sure.

Isobel was anything but certain. But she knew not to try to rush the ancient for an explanation.

Whatever Grizel wished her to know, she'd reveal in her own way and time.

Unfortunately, instead of enlightening Isobel, she turned back to the parapet wall. Lifting her chin, Grizel once again seemed to be peering at the silvery waterfall plunging down the gorge.

Isobel stepped up to the wall beside her, waiting.

The smile tugging at the crone's lips showed that joining her at the wall was what she'd wanted Isobel to do. Pleasure almost rolled off her, the scent of cinnamon swirling around them.

"It be a fine night, h'mmm?" Grizel flashed a sidelong look at Isobel.

"Surely no more magical than at Tigh-na-Craig." Isobel tempted fate by mentioning the name of the Makers of Dreams' cottage. Hidden away where few men would dare wander, even if they could gain entry to the mysterious high moor where Grizel and Gorm lived, House on the Rock was a low, white-walled cottage nestled among a jumble of boulders at the base of a soaring cliff.

Isobel had never been there, but she knew powerful magic was said to permeate the cottage.

Even the peat smoke said to stain the walls and fill the cottage's interior purportedly held enough spelling to put a soul into a slumber that lasted centuries. If, of course, Grizel and Gorm wished to burden themselves with such a long-term visitor.

Just now, Grizel appeared entirely absorbed in the cataract splashing down the nearby hillside.

"Tigh-na-Craig's magic can be found everywhere." This time she didn't glance at Isobel as she spoke. "All the Highlands hold wonder. One needn't trek far away, high over inaccessible moorland, to discover enchantment. Ofttimes"—her voice took on a mischievous note—"the like is right beneath our noses. We just need to look."

Isobel's pulse leaped. "I'm always looking for magic."

She was.

Her fascination with Norse culture and legend was one reason she'd been so drawn to Kendrew. Like her, he appreciated the old ways. He believed in the spirits of rock and wind, the ageless wisdom in the glen's deep forests of pine, birch, and oak. The power of the tides was something he didn't doubt, nor the mystery to be found in high, boggy moorlands, or atop rocky crags veiled in mist. If he were here, he'd know where Grizel was leading her.

Isobel couldn't begin to guess.

Until she followed the crone's gaze and saw the magnificent white stag standing on a large boulder near the bottom of the waterfall.

"Laoigh Feigh Ban." Isobel gasped, using the Gaelic name for the magical beast. The immortal white stag, Rannoch, so named after the wild stretch of dark, impenetrable moor said to be his original home.

Now he was Grizel and Gorm's pet and helpmate.

Isobel touched a hand to her ambers as she stared at him, her heart thundering. "It is him, isn't it?"

"Rannoch?" Grizel's tone held affection. "Aye, that be him. He thought it might be doing you good to see him this night."

Isobel refrained from asking how Grizel knew the white stag's mind.

In truth, she wouldn't be surprised if he talked.

He did turn his proud head to stare at her, his ears twitching with curiosity. From high above, starlight fell across his pure white pelt, gilding him and letting him shine as if lit from within. His rich, liquid-brown eyes touched Isobel deeply, his steady gaze holding hers as if he could see to the roots of her soul.

"He's trying to tell you something, he is." Grizel put a hand on Isobel's arm, gripping tight. "Can you no' hear what he's saying?"

"Nae, I—" Isobel broke off, not wanting to admit that she heard only the whistle of the wind through the pines and the rushing water of the falls.

She did catch a faint whiff of Rannoch's musky, earthy scent, dark and primeval.

And...

"Oh, dear." Isobel's eyes widened, a thought popping into her mind. Her breath caught, snagging in her throat. "I do believe..."

Instead of finishing, she turned to Grizel, sure her cheeks were blazing. "He wouldn't be here because of his name, would he? Is that why he's staring at me like that?"

If so, the riddle would never be solved.

She wasn't about to tell Grizel why the word *Rannoch* made her blush.

"There be much afoot thereabouts." Grizel scratched her chin, clearly pretending to consider. "Down Rannoch Moor way, I mean."

Dear God, she knew.

Isobel whipped back around, facing the parapet wall again. "I'm sure I don't know what goes on in Rannoch." She did see that Rannoch the white stag no longer stood on a rock beside the waterfall.

He'd moved to the battling ground, very near to the new cairn.

And his gaze was now fixed on Grizel, as if willing her to join him.

"He'll be for home, it looks like." The Maker of Dreams stepped back from the walling, smoothing her cloak, the gesture sending up a hint of cinnamon. "His work is done here, after all."

She winked. "Don't be telling Gorm I told you Rannoch wished to mind you of his old home. Thon he-goat harps at me for days if I spoil a riddle."

"Then don't worry, please." Isobel reached to touch

Grizel's arm but somehow the old woman was already on the threshold of the door to the tower stair. "You haven't ruined the riddle. I can't imagine why Rannoch would wish me to think of that moor."

She really couldn't and didn't want to know.

But Grizel's eyes glinted in the shadows, her rosy-cheeked face full of mischief. "Ah, but you cannae know, *mo ghaoil*." She called Isobel "my dear." "Perhaps you'll need to ask someone who has the answer.

"Just dinnae fash yourself"—Grizel backed deeper into the gloom—"if what you hear is grim."

On the words, Grizel vanished, slipping away into the dimness of the stairwell. Though when Isobel hurried to the tower door arch, there was no echo of the old woman's descending footsteps.

She was simply gone.

Isobel leaned back against the cold stone of the wall and sighed. Frustration rose in her breast, maddening, and leaving her almost wishing the fabled crone and her enchanted stag hadn't paid her a visit.

They'd only confused her.

Their magic—for such an encounter could only be that—hadn't worked for her. She might be wildly excited to have seen the two at all. But she could live to be a hundred and wouldn't guess what they'd wanted her to know.

Until she drew her cloak tighter and stepped into the stair tower to make her way down the winding steps and back to her bedchamber.

The answer came when she reached the first landing and Grizel's parting words echoed in her mind: "...if what you hear is grim."

Grim.

Isobel stopped where she was, once again clutching Kendrew's letter to her breast. Her heart beat faster, certainty making her pulse race.

Grim, the big, tough-looking Mackintosh warrior, was the answer to Grizel's riddle. For whatever reason, Grizel and her pet stag wanted Isobel to speak with Kendrew's friend about Rannoch Moor.

And she would.

Hopefully on the morrow as the friendship and dedication ceremony would begin at first light. If Kendrew came as he'd promised in his letter, his captain of the guard would surely accompany him.

Isobel would corner the man.

Then, at last, the tides would turn in her favor. Grim knew something of great import that was crucial to her winning Kendrew's heart.

Her own heart welling with gratitude, she rushed back up the steps and dashed out onto the battlements, hurrying to the parapet wall.

But the fighting ground with its proud new cairn and even the hills and moors beyond loomed empty. The night-silvered landscape stretched still and silent around her. She couldn't call out a thank-you. Nor could she raise her hand to wave farewell.

Grizel and Rannoch were gone.

But they'd left their magic with her.

So she curled her fingers tighter around Kendrew's letter and took a deep breath of the cold night air, this time catching a trace of deer musk and cinnamon.

Then even that hint of her visitors faded.

It didn't matter.

Something told her they knew she'd solved their riddle.

She just hoped she'd also be able to appreciate whatever Grim would tell her.

She knew with a woman's instinct that everything depended on his words.

"You will behave nobly?"

"Humph." Kendrew stiffened on hearing his sister Marjory's admonition. Sitting straighter in his saddle, he squared his shoulders and clamped his jaw. He refused to cast a sidelong glance at the pestiferous she-vixen riding so regally beside him. His grunt had earned her wrath. He could tell even without looking.

"We're in Cameron territory now." She minded him of what he already knew. "The friendship and dedication ceremony is of great import to the weal of us all. You'll be expected to participate in the festivities. And"—she urged her garron closer—"you must do so gladly, without shaming us."

Kendrew forgot his vow not to glance her way and shot her a glare.

He wasn't about to answer her.

His fierce mien sufficed.

Some of the men riding behind them chuckled. One or two cursed the Camerons. Kendrew ignored them all, his attention on picking a way through the thick pines that clogged Haven land. The trees were a botheration, making the journey tedious. He much preferred the grand, rocky sweep of Nought with its soaring cliffs and brooding skies.

His land wasn't marred by damp, cloying woods that spoiled views.

Knowing Cameron land was so plaguey made his mouth twitch with satisfaction.

They deserved no better.

"It will do you no good to ignore me." Marjory spoke as if she didn't realize her continued needling put her in mortal danger. "You are only hurting yourself with your fool stubbornness."

Kendrew snorted. "Dinnae tell me what I'm doing."

He knew it fine himself.

He suffered enough just riding on Cameron ground. His head ached and pounded and had done for the last hour. Ever since he and their mounted party of soon-to-be memorial cairn celebrants had put their beloved Nought land behind them and entered Haven territory.

He didn't need Norn's pestering worsening his day.

It was already the most galling of his life.

A sudden skirling of pipes and a volley of shouts reached them from somewhere ahead, beyond the damty trees. The din grated on Kendrew's nerves. Such tumult meant the folly that was James Cameron's and Alasdair MacDonald's friendship and cairn dedication ceremony loomed before them, loud, raucous, and unavoidable.

Kendrew scowled, deliberately slowing his horse.

Marjory noticed.

"We are late." She took a breath that could only be called peeved. "They will have started at sunrise. It is now well past noontide."

"Is it now?" Kendrew glanced at her, feigning astonishment just to annoy her. "I did think we'd make better time. A pity if we've missed the ceremonies."

He hoped they had.

Doing so was the reason he'd pretended to have misplaced Blood Drinker earlier that morn. All knew he never set foot outside his stronghold's wall without the huge

Norse war ax. Making the household search for the weapon had taken up much of the morning. Only after several hours did he sneak back up to his bedchamber and retrieve his beloved Blood Drinker from beneath his bed's mattress.

It'd been a good trick.

Regrettably, it hadn't been good enough to last the whole day.

"Lady Isobel will need to bless Blood Drinker." Marjory cut into his thoughts, her voice smooth as silk.

Kendrew jerked, his chest tightening as if clamped round with a white-hot, iron vise. "She'll no' be laying a finger on Blood Drinker."

Nor would she be touching him, if he could help it.

"You needn't worry." His sister's pleasant tone said otherwise. "She won't have to touch the ax to bless him. She'll only sprinkle water along Blood Drinker's haft and blade."

Kendrew reined in sharply. "There'll be no water-sprinkling either."

"It's an important part of the ceremony." Marjory paused as another round of cheers rose from beyond the trees. "The blessing water is a blend of water taken from Clan MacDonald's Loch Moidart, the waterfall behind the Cameron's Castle Haven, and"—her smile sweetened—"from one of our own Nought burns, of course."

Kendrew stared at her. "And just where did Clan Cameron get Nought burn water?"

"Why, Grim delivered a flagon along with your letter." Marjory's smile didn't falter. "Did I forget to tell you? My apologies, if I did."

"You know you didn't tell me." Kendrew was going to

explode. "And"—he glowered at her—"because we're yet alone, amidst our own kin, I'll remind you that I did no' write that letter.

"I'll deal with the theft of our water when we return to Nought." He didn't trust himself to glance at Grim.

If he did, he might cut off the bastard's ears and make him eat them.

He did tighten his hands on the reins until his knuckles shone white. "Clan Cameron and the brine-drinkers some folk call MacDonalds can be glad we're here to stand at the edge of their fool ceremony.

"Odin can have my balls if I do more than that." Pleased by his wit, he grinned nastily.

"You'd be wise to lower your voice." The oh-so-terrible Lady Norn dropped her own to a whisper. "Or do you wish to shock Lady Isobel with your crudeness?"

Kendrew burned to shock the wench. Maybe then she'd leave him alone.

For the moment, he turned his wrath on his sister. "Thon raven-haired she-devil is—"

"She is just there, at the edge of the trees." Marjory lifted a hand, waving at someone behind Kendrew's shoulder. "I do believe she has the blessing water. She must be waiting for us to arrive."

Kendrew set his jaw, his entire body flashing hot, then cold.

He was not going to glance around.

He glanced at the wood's edge. His heart slammed against his ribs when he did.

Isobel stood there. And she looked more like a pagan sacrificial offering than the great gem-studded chalice she held in her hands.

Kendrew swallowed hard, his blood roaring in his ears. He stared through the trees at her, his traitorous knees nudging his horse forward, in her direction. She looked right at him, her breasts rising and falling with her breath. Her dark gaze moved over him, studying him from the top of his head to his toes, seeming to see right inside him. His loins clenched, pounding with a response that was more feral, more primal than a rutting stag.

She'd dressed to madden him, choosing a pure white gown overlaid with a shimmering tunic of sheerest silk, shot through with sparkling threads of silver and gold. A woven belt of the same colors dazzled low on her hips, drawing his eye to the one place he had no business looking because just the thought of her lush triangle of inky-black feminine curls would bring him to his knees.

Unfortunately, the wickedly designed gown offered no surcease if he looked above her waist either. So low-cut that the top rounds of her creamy bosom were displayed in all their glory, the gown's bodice had surely been designed by the devil's own seamstress.

He couldn't see her dusky nipples, praise all the gods in Asgard.

But he knew they were there.

And that was a fate almost worse than death. It was all he could do not to swing down from his saddle, storm over to her, and tear open the gown's silver-and-gold bodice laces, feasting hungrily on her breasts' sweet, tempting crests until he'd sated himself.

If ever that was possible.

He sorely doubted it.

And—Thor help him—he didn't know how he'd come to be off his horse and bending a leg to her.

But somehow he was doing just that.

"Laird Mackintosh, I greet you." She looked at him from beneath her sooty, black lashes, watching him bow as if such obeisance was her due. A corner of her mouth tilted ever so slightly as if she knew how sorely he desired her, how easily she scattered his wits.

Kendrew caught himself swiftly, straightening. "A pebble in my shoe, see?" He lifted his foot, shaking it vigorously. "Damty nuisance, the like, what?"

"A shoe pebble?" She raised an elegant black brow, her tiny smile fading.

"Nae, I meant—" Kendrew snapped his mouth shut, wishing women wouldn't twist words into their own irksome meaning. He started to say so, but Isobel's attention was already elsewhere.

"Lady Norn." She looked past him to his sister, smiling warmly now. "It is good of you to come."

Marjory rode closer, beaming. "You knew we would. Indeed"—she glanced at Kendrew, and then back to Isobel—"we're honored."

It was all Kendrew could do not to snort.

He did lower his foot to the ground, feeling suddenly foolish.

"Aye, we are that, Lady Isobel." Grim flourished her a grand bow. "Greatly honored," he added, sinking ever lower in Kendrew's esteem.

Grim was taking an especially high risk when he eyed Isobel appreciatively, his admiration putting a hint of rose on her cheeks.

Kendrew glared at him, but the lout pretended not to notice.

"A-hem." Kendrew hooked his thumbs in his sword

belt, swelling his chest a bit. "We're clearly too late to cause a bother," he announced, flashing an annoyed glance at his other men, who were also dismounting. "We'll be on their way then, leaving you be."

"Oh, we cannot do that." His sister slipped down from her saddle with a grace that made his blood boil. Gliding forward to stand beside Isobel, she turned an infuriatingly innocent smile on him. "Don't you see that Lady Isobel has the blessing chalice ready for you?"

I'll be blessed when I ride out o' here. Kendrew meant to snarl the words, but his tongue wouldn't oblige him.

He did manage to snap his brows together. "I see more than you know, Norn."

"Then you'll see how good it is we're here to honor the cairn." His sister proved how well she maneuvered him into corners.

"Are you no' done with the like?" It cost him all his strength to bend his gaze on Isobel. "The pipes are screaming and we heard cheers a while back. I dinnae care to make you repeat—"

"The younger lads have been holding wrestling competitions." Isobel turned a smile on him that sent another rush of heat pouring straight into his groin. "James and Alasdair are waiting for you at the cairn. Their swords haven't yet been blessed. No one wanted to proceed without you."

"My sword doesn't need blessing." The argument was his last defense. "I scarce use a brand."

She shifted the large blessing chalice against her hip. "James and Alasdair agreed that you could have me bless your war ax."

Kendrew looked at her, feeling the earth open beneath his feet. "They are generous."

They were bastards of the highest order.

"If you'll come with me now…" She glanced over her shoulder at the throng, a rowdy mix of plaid-draped, bearded Camerons and MacDonalds crowding around tables set with viands and ale.

Only the top of the memorial could be seen rising above the heads and shoulders of the celebrants. Three tartan banners covered the cairn's stones. Kendrew's face heated to see his own clan's colors. Grim had no doubt secreted a length of Mackintosh pride in the travel pouch he'd used to carry Nought water and a letter Kendrew hadn't written.

Unfortunately, before he could think of a worse punishment than forcing the lout to eat his own ears, a heady drift of clean, spring violet scent wafted past his nose, duly enchanting him.

His heart began thumping. "Blood Drinker doesn't take to…" His protest died when sunlight slanted through the pines, shining on Isobel's sleek raven hair.

He stared, unable to look away as the sun danced over the gleaming strands.

Unbound, glossy, and begging to be touched, Isobel's hair tumbled over her shoulders, spilling to the seductive curve of her hips.

For one crazy-mad moment, he envied the sunlight, touching her shining tresses so intimately. He knew how the silky skein felt in his hands and his fingers itched to once again enjoy the pleasure.

But he caught himself quickly, assuming his most hardened expression. "Blood Drinker doesn't take to waiting," he amended his cut-off sentence.

Earlier, he'd meant to say that his ax didn't like consorting with enemy swords—only breaking their inferior steel blades in two.

Now...

His only recourse was to put back his shoulders and stride purposefully over to his most hated foes and their fool pile of stanes.

He would not allow Isobel to escort him.

He'd rather cut off his own ears and eat them than endure the torment of walking closely beside her. The humiliation of having everyone present see the truth in his eyes: that he was so besotted with the wench that he could hardly breathe for wanting her.

So he started boldly forward, swaggering deliberately. He also let his chin jut at an arrogant angle. His sister, Grim, and the rest of their contingent could follow as they desired. Or remain in the wood, for all he cared.

Lady Isobel...

He knew without glancing at her that she kept pace with him. And that her head was lifted with the same degree of pride as he held his own.

She had more spirit than some men he knew.

And he was torn between the urge to turn and march away from her and the urge to pull her into his arms and kiss her roundly. But as he began leaning toward ravishing her, imagining her face if he were to grab her here, in front of her kin and friends, James and Alasdair turned his way, looking at him from where they stood before the cairn.

Both men held naked swords, clearly waiting for Isobel and the water blessing. They nodded in greeting, their welcome somewhat stilted. Until Alasdair's eyes widened, his smile turning into a grin as his gaze flew past Kendrew to light on someone behind him.

Alasdair's sword slipped from his fingers and he dropped it anew when he bent to snatch the blade off the ground. Suspicious, Kendrew turned to see who'd reduced the proud MacDonald chieftain to a bumbling oaf.

It was Norn.

Her own sparkling blue gaze so fixed on Alasdair that she didn't even see him glaring at her.

His dander roused, Kendrew noted that his sister appeared unaware of everything else around her. Her gaze was locked on Alasdair, as if she and her clan's mortal enemy existed in a world all their own.

Kendrew had never seen such a look on her.

He did whip back around before anyone saw him gawping. Now he knew why Norn had gone to such lengths to ensure they attended the ceremony.

It hadn't been about honor and the clan's good name.

She'd hoped to see Alasdair MacDonald.

And that meant only one thing.

He'd have to find a husband for her, and soon.

It was a task he'd set upon with relish. He'd do so as soon as he managed to rid his own mind of Isobel Cameron. And that was an undertaking he wasn't sure he could master, if the truth were known.

As if she knew, Isobel flashed a triumphant look at him and quickened her step, moving ahead of him so that he had no choice but to observe the enticing sway of her hips as they neared the cairn.

"Good men," she greeted her brother and the Mac-Donald, "see who has joined us at last…"

She turned, gesturing with her free hand. "The

Mackintosh of Nought, with his warriors. And"—she flashed a significant look in Alasdair's direction—"his sister, Lady Marjory."

It was then, seeing the look Isobel and Norn exchanged, that Kendrew knew which way the wind blew in this, his beloved Glen of Many Legends. When they both sent a similar look at Lady Catriona, sheltering from the wind in a nearby pavilion, he was sure.

The womenfolk were banding together, conspiring against him.

Not that it would do them any good.

He was on to them now, aware of their trickery.

And he had no intention of being led on a merry chase. He hunted and cornered his own prey, as Isobel would soon discover to her peril.

Her very great peril.

Chapter Eleven

❧

In the next glen, far from Kendrew and the three women conspiring against him, Ralla the Victorious held court in the great hall of Duncreag, Clan MacNab's proud stronghold. A massive, wind-lashed eyrie every bit as daunting as Nought, Duncreag sat so high on a sheer, rocky crag that clouds and mist often hid its walls from view. As at Nought, a steep and narrow path led to the well-guarded gatehouse, but unlike Kendrew's stone steps, where each tread cut into the cliff face, access to Duncreag was more like a goat track that wound its way up the bluff.

Visitors were few because Clan MacNab was aye at odds with its neighbors.

And any foe who dared to come unannounced would be met with a rain of fire arrows before he had climbed the first twist of the treacherous castle path.

Duncreag's impregnability suited Ralla well.

He didn't believe in making life easy for his enemies. Nor was he above having done with one of his own men if he suspected treachery. He wasn't going to leave this world by a knife between the ribs as he slept.

In truth, he rarely slumbered.

Sleeping wolves didn't catch much prey.

And Ralla was a hungry man.

This night he was also jovial. Proving it, he rapped his empty ale cup on the high table and leered at a young, bare-breasted slave girl plucking a harp in a shadowy corner of the dais. "You, Breena, fetch us more drink!

"I am thirsty, make haste!" Ralla laughed, banging his cup more vigorously when the slave tried to cover her breasts as she stood. A timid village girl taken during a raid in Ireland, she blushed red as her hair when she had to step out of the corner's sheltering murk.

"The fate spinners have been kind to us, lass." He grinned as if she appreciated his triumph. "I am told Mackintosh rode to Haven after all. And"—he looked round at his men—"he took his best warriors with him!"

The hall burst into peals of laughter, though some men snarled slurs and challenges.

Ralla beamed.

"We know what happens when a bear doesn't watch his den." He pinched Breena's hip as she darted past him toward the kitchens passage. "The men we sent back to Nought will ready a fine welcome for his return. Then"— he lifted his voice, looking round—"while he's spluttering and reeling, we sweep in for the kill."

"What of the other two clans?" Tor, a crooked-nosed brute of a man, spoke around a beef rib, the juices glistening in his beard. "I've my eye on Lady Isobel's amber necklace. After I've plowed her other delights!"

"She's mine, you arse." Ban, an equally huge man

whose thick arms were lined with gold rings, glowered at Tor. "I'll have her after Ralla, and if you think otherwise, I'll gut you faster than you can blink. You'll be raven fodder, good for no woman."

"You ask of the other glen curs?" Ralla snatched the ale jug from Breena when she returned and then tipped the ewer to his lips, drinking from the jug. "'Tis Cameron and MacDonald flesh that will soon be feeding carrion, that I say you. After their cairn ceremony, they'll be drunk on glory. Their high spirits will weaken them, dulling their wits. When they hear we've choked the Mackintoshes on their own blood, they'll be too stunned to react swiftly.

"By the time they do reach for their swords"—he slammed down the ale jug, grinning—"it'll be too late. We'll be all over them."

His men roared approval, sharing his mirth.

In the dais corner, Breena crept back into the shadows, trying to hide her nakedness behind her harp. Her efforts only drew Ralla's amusement.

"Dinnae cower so, lass." He leaned toward her, wagging his bushy brows. "When our work here is done and the Glen of Many Legends runs red with blood again, purged of its vaunted heroes, our lord will come to reward us. If you please him, he may take you with him to his own keep—a place much finer than this cold pile o' stanes!"

On his words, Breena slunk deeper into the murk.

And at the top of the high table, in a seat of honor, an old man with thinning hair and a straggly beard turned furious eyes on Ralla the Victorious. Leaning forward, he growled objection to the insult.

But Ralla only grinned, waving his ale cup in the old man's direction as if saluting him.

"Tor!" Ralla glanced at Tor. He sat nearest the gray-beard, Archie MacNab, the clan chief. "Give our friend more ale. He looks in need o' a drink."

"I'd rather use his bones to put a few new dents in my sword." But Tor stood, cracking his knuckles menacingly.

Then he went to the old man's chair and, a bit more roughly than was necessary, pulled a filthy cloth bind from the chief's mouth.

"Drink, you ancient bugger," he growled, pouring a cupful of ale down Archie MacNab's throat. "Celebrate, for we're growing bored with you. Soon we'll be sending you to join your sons in the corpse pit."

Still proud, all things considered, Archie spat the ale in Tor's face.

His daring earned him a hard cuff to the head.

And as he sagged in his high-backed laird's chair, Ralla laughed.

Across the heather miles, in the heart of the Glen of Many Legends, the air was filled with a very different kind of conviviality. The high point of the memorial cairn dedication was about to begin. And although most faces shone with pride and satisfaction, one most vital guest of honor—namely Kendrew Mackintosh—scowled fiercely enough to darken the lightness of the day.

Isobel tried not to notice.

She prayed he'd reconsider his stance, accepting the need for lasting peace.

The cold knot in her belly warned he'd remain stubborn.

But she could be just as unbending, so she took a deep

breath, readying herself for what could prove to be the most critical battle of her life.

It was a fight to win her heart's desire.

And to undo the ravages years of strife had brought to the glen.

All around her, people stirred, edging closer. Above them, high on the ramparts of Castle Haven, banners snapped in the wind. Dogs barked and circled, bounding forward with wagging tails as if they, too, were eager to hear the blessing she'd been honored to speak.

The moment was here.

Kendrew's frown deepened as if he knew.

Isobel took a breath, beginning...

"In honor of those who came before and for the weal of those yet to come, raise your swords." She lifted her voice, speaking clear and true. "And your war ax," she added, glancing at Kendrew. "Once the blades touch, we'll commence the glen water blessing."

She wasn't sure, but she'd almost believed Kendrew growled in his chest.

He did let his gaze slide over her, eyeing her as if they were alone and not surrounded by jostling men and women from all three clans. Screaming pipes, running children, and excited dogs. Everything disappeared except his big, strong body so improperly close to hers, and the boldness of his scrutiny. His gaze was also a hungry one, dark with appreciation, intimate and knowing.

He made her burn.

Heat swept her entire body, from the roots of her hair to the tips of her toes. She forced herself to hold his gaze. But it wasn't easy, feeling so vulnerable. The intensity of his perusal almost convinced her that he could see through the layers of white silk and gold-and-silver veiling she'd chosen to wear for the occasion.

She did keep her back straight, her shoulders proud. Her heart raced at the way he looked at her. His eyes smoldered, his mouth set in a hard, challenging line. She needed all her will not to blush. Hoping she wouldn't, she tightened her grip on the heavy chalice in her hands and tried to think only of the blessing she was about to perform.

She even imagined the still-covered stones of the new memorial cairn held a collective breath, waiting eagerly for the honor.

The afternoon wind quieted, dropping just enough for her to catch the low roar of the cataracts that spilled down a gorge on the other side of Castle Haven. She could easily believe that the glen water taken from the falls wished to lend a voice to the ceremony.

The notion was pleasing, and not at all impossible.

Magic did happen on such fine days.

Especially here, in the Glen of Many Legends, where wonders were never far.

So she held up the large silver chalice, pleased when the sun glinted off the colorful gemstones on the vessel's rim. Each jewel dazzled, offering a blessing to the power of the three waters.

"As water and earth unite, so will the joining of these three blades ensure peace, friendship, and a common purpose to all those here." She spoke the sacred words, lowering the chalice.

Her brother James and the MacDonald chieftain, Alasdair, dutifully extended their weapons. They stood side by side, swords in hand, the long blades shining in the afternoon light. An expectant hush fell over the assembled crowd, men and women edging closer, all eager to be a part of the long-awaited friendship and dedication ceremony. Cameron and MacDonald pipers strutted to and fro beneath Castle Haven's curtain walls, blowing gustily.

Kendrew didn't move.

Isobel risked a glance at him.

No longer looking at her, he'd fixed his gaze on the edge of the pines. It was the spot where the woodland path led back to his Nought lands. His fierce expression showed that he'd rather be there now.

He was also quite magnificent. Ire stood him well, the hard set of his jaw only enhancing his appeal.

His arm rings and fine mail coat shone brighter than the gemstones on the blessing chalice's rim. Wind caught his rich auburn hair, tossing the gilded strands about his broad, powerfully muscled shoulders. Equally distracting, the golden Thor's hammer at his throat gleamed with a brilliance to rival the sun, drawing eyes as if the amulet deliberately sought dominance.

And although Isobel knew he wasn't that much taller than her brother or Alasdair—both large, well-built men— he appeared to tower above them.

The slight thrust of his chin proved that he noticed her perusal.

Tamping down her irritation—he was known for causing havoc, after all—she turned to her brother and Alasdair. She nodded once, giving them the signal to bring their swords together.

Both men did, their blades meeting with a clear ring of steel.

Kendrew still stood as if carved of granite.

Murmurs of unease began circling through the crowd. Hector, James's dog, dropped onto his haunches and gave a weary, old-dog sigh. Hector's friend, Geordie, a likewise ancient beast who belonged to Alasdair, began to bark. Leaving Hector's side, Geordie took several stiff-legged paces toward the three men, his hackles rising as he fixed a suspicious, unblinking stare on Kendrew.

This time Kendrew did move. But only to toss a look at his friend Grim, who took two twists of dried beef from a pouch at his belt and then tossed the treats to the disgruntled dogs, quieting them both.

James and Alasdair frowned.

Apparently pleased to have annoyed them, Kendrew folded his arms, his face turning stony again.

"The ax, if you please." Isobel stepped more closely before him, some of the precious glen water sloshing over the chalice's rim because she'd moved too quickly in her irritation. From the corner of her eye, she saw Catriona toss back her hair, pinning a chilly stare on Kendrew.

Isobel inhaled sharply, fixing him with a look of her own. "Your ax," she said again. "We can't proceed until—"

"Thon ax is rusted in its straps." A MacDonald standing near the cairn spat on the ground. "Belike we'll no' be having any friendship with Mackintoshes, what? No' if their chief is too weak to heft his weapon."

"Too simple-minded," another MacDonald declared, looking round as if proud of his wit.

Several of his kinsmen chortled. One or two of them made similar quips.

The Mackintosh warriors put their hands to their sword hilts, their faces darkening.

Kendrew's lips twitched. Or so Isobel thought—the flash of amusement in his eyes was so fleeting that she couldn't be sure it'd been there at all.

He was enjoying himself.

No one else seemed to have noticed.

James's mien was solemn, his stance before the draped memorial cairn proud and respectful.

But a muscle jerked in Alasdair's jaw at the mention of Kendrew's Norse battle-ax. He narrowed his eyes, his displeasure at Kendrew's inclusion in the ceremony more than apparent.

Ignoring them both, Kendrew stretched his arms and noisily cracked his knuckles. Isobel shot him a warning look, but that only made him cock a bemused brow as he rolled his powerful shoulders, showing no hurry to reach for the ax strapped across his back.

Isobel straightened her own shoulders, keenly aware that all eyes were turned on her. "Your weapon, Laird Mackintosh," she spoke coolly, pretending not to see the challenge in his clear blue eyes.

He was deliberately provoking her.

"My ax is Blood Drinker." He still made no move to retrieve it. "He likes hearing his name."

Some of his warriors chuckled. Gathered near the viands table, they thumped one another's arms, amused by their leader's obstinate behavior.

"By whatever name, he will drink no more, blood or otherwise, if I slice his haft to bits with my sword." James scowled at Kendrew, his knuckles whitening as he gripped his brand tighter.

Beside him, Alasdair snarled low in his throat. "Unholy goat-men, cliff-climbers no' worthy of—"

"Blood Drinker, then." Isobel ignored their slurs, keeping her gaze on Kendrew as she did as he bade, naming his ax. "I cannot perform the water blessing if you do not offer me your weapon."

"That I have already done, my lady." Kendrew's words sent heat creeping up her neck, his meaning so obviously not the great bladed ax he wore. "By coming here this day," he added, mischief sparking in his eyes.

"Then please..." Isobel's pulse skittered wildly. His taunt recalled scintillating images, memories of them lying together, tightly entwined...

"That would no' be wise." A corner of his mouth tilted upward. "Me, pleasing you—"

"I'll have your gizzard for my dog's supper." James shot him a fierce glare, his earlier restraint gone.

Kendrew grinned, not taking his gaze off Isobel. "As you wish, though I'd prefer something much finer for my own feasting."

"Kendrew..." Marjory stepped beside Isobel, her eyes like sapphire ice. "You shame Nought and all we stand for." She spoke beneath her breath, her voice only loud enough to be heard by those standing close. "If you don't cease, I am no longer your sister."

"Dinnae tempt me, Norn." He still didn't look away from Isobel. "No' that I can think of anything else with Lady Isobel before me."

Isobel lifted her chin, sure her face was aflame. "These are the waters from our lands." She raised the blessing chalice, hoping to return the crowd's attention to the ceremony rather than the dangerous exchange between her and her clan's erstwhile greatest foe.

The man who, even now, took her breath away, firing

her blood and making her desire nothing more than to be held in his arms. Kissed long and deeply, his hands roving over her, sweeping down her back, and then clutching her hips, pulling her close...

She cleared her throat, feeling Kendrew's gaze like a flame on her skin. "The powers of the joined waters, their peace and protection, must flow over the blades of your united weapons."

"So be it." Looking away from her at last, Kendrew stepped back, his gaze snapping to the MacDonald man who'd jeered that his ax was "rusted in its straps." "Let no man say that Nought might won't stand to protect this glen." He reached over his shoulder, whipping out the great, long-handled war ax with lightning speed.

"I will cut down any fool"—he swung the ax around as if it weighed nothing, pointing the long-bearded ax head at the gawping MacDonald clansman—"who dares claim otherwise."

The man bristled, straightening his back. "I say what I will."

"No' if Blood Drinker takes your tongue before you can spew a word." Kendrew grinned when the sun glinted off his weapon's ax head.

The polished blade shone in challenge, gleaming bright as his mail.

"You see he is thirsty." Kendrew took a step toward the man, letting the edge of the ax blade nudge the man's wide leather belt.

"Threats are no' wished here, Mackintosh." James's warning went unheeded.

"A word o' caution, no' threat." Turning back to James and Alasdair, Kendrew swept his huge war ax in a circle, taking in the crowd. "From this day onward, Mackintosh strength guards all."

The vow made—Isobel noted that he spoke only of the glen, not the other two clans—he hauled back to swing Blood Drinker in a whistling arc, bringing the big blade down onto the joined blades of James's and Alasdair's swords with such speed that Isobel feared he'd knock the swords out of the other two men's hands.

But the ax head lit down as gently as a feather.

Kendrew grinned, his flourish drawing appreciative gasps from the celebrants.

Neither James nor Alasdair flinched, their iron-willed calm surely meant to show Kendrew that they were equally bold. Warrior chieftains just as worthy to wield power in the glen they all shared.

In seeming acknowledgment, Kendrew raised one hand, using the other to keep his ax blade atop James's and Alasdair's weapons. "Then have done with your ceremony." He spoke to Isobel, but his voice carried, deep and strong. "Blood Drinker wearies of consorting with mere swords."

Isobel bit back a smile. "Then he shall now be revived through the power of our glen water."

"Humph." Kendrew's brows lowered. "So he may, as long as his steel isn't pitted by the taint of Blackshore or Haven water."

"Kendrew!" Marjory glared at him, and then flashed apologetic looks at James and Alasdair. "He doesn't mean—"

"I do." Kendrew's tone was mutinous. "If I find a single speck of tarnish, there'll be a price to pay."

"As there will be if we must keep suffering your blether." Alasdair flicked his wrist in warning, causing his sword—a blade known as Mist-Chaser—to ring against Blood Drinker's long-bearded head.

"You'll be free o' me anon, brine-drinker." Kendrew twisted his own wrist, letting his war ax force Mist-Chaser down a few inches.

"No' soon enough." Alasdair jerked his arm, lifting his sword back into place.

Isobel glanced at Marjory, still standing so close beside her. Then she flashed a look at Catriona, who was now making her way through the throng, coming to join them before the memorial cairn.

Her friends' gazes were locked on the three chieftains.

This moment was one they'd worked hard to make possible. Though—Isobel was sure—James and Alasdair would erroneously believe that the idea for the cairn and the celebrations was their own.

The women of the glen knew better.

And they couldn't let their brothers ruin what they'd achieved. Their efforts and hearts' blood should spread gladness throughout the glen and prove long-lasting, leaving a legacy of peace for all time to come.

If this day's ceremony failed, their hopes would be dashed, slipping ever farther from their grasp.

And that was a tragedy Isobel couldn't allow.

So she kept her chin raised and smiled determinedly as Catriona finally reached her and Marjory's sides. She gave her two friends a tiny nod, knowing they'd understand her unspoken message.

Kendrew could balk all he wished.

He didn't stand a chance against the battle pitched before him.

He was outnumbered three to one.

Chapter Twelve

❧

Hoping the sacred number three would prove fortunate, especially for a trio of—she truly believed—such well-meaning and deserving women, Isobel again raised the blessing chalice, this time using both hands to hold the gleaming vessel high above her head.

She pretended not to see the hint of doubt in her friends' eyes.

Hoping to encourage them, she let her faith in their pact shine in her own eyes. The renewed stubbornness glinting in Kendrew's fierce-eyed stare gave her a most satisfactory boost. If he noticed her strength, that she'd thrown down a gauntlet and was battle-ready, the war was half won. He might not care for her methods, but he was sharp-minded enough to know when he'd met a greater opponent.

Praying it was really so, Isobel squared her shoulders and rushed on, calling out the age-old words she'd been practicing for days.

"Powers of water, strong and everlasting, bless these weapons and the men who yield them, keeping them true and ever faithful to the sacred glen whence you come."

Lowering the chalice, she dipped her fingers into the bowl, sprinkling water on the two sword blades and the head of Kendrew's long-bearded ax.

"As the Old Ones have willed and blessed our truce"—she took a breath—"so mote it be."

"So mote it be," James and Alasdair agreed in unison as they raised their swords to the heavens.

Kendrew humphed and shook the water droplets off Blood Drinker.

When he started to turn away, Isobel stepped in front of him, blocking his escape. "The three of you must take your banners off the cairn." She kept her voice low, hoping that none of the celebrants noticed he'd tried to stride away. "The blessing isn't yet complete."

"Plague take your ceremony." He shot an angry look at Alasdair, snorting as the other chief used Mist-Chaser to whip the MacDonald banner off the cairn, much to the delight of his clan's pipers, who were now blowing more gustily than ever. "I am done here."

"We are only beginning." Isobel slid a glance at Marjory, who nodded encouragement. "If you'll just remove the Mackintosh tartan—"

"'Tis myself I'll be removing. And"—he glared at his sister, his scowl blackening when he saw she'd stepped closer to Alasdair—"my fool sister who will no' be running after web-footed brine-drinkers."

"You are the one who is running." Isobel raised her chin, letting her eyes spark with challenge. "The great

Mackintosh Berserker, your arms and chest carved with pagan kill-marks, fears using his ax head to lift a piece of cloth from a pile of stones."

For a moment, his eyes narrowed, his mouth setting in a hard, tight line. But then he threw back his head and laughed, loud and boldly, drawing eyes. Men and women turned from watching James sweep the Cameron plaid from the cairn, looking on as Kendrew spun Blood Drinker in a fast and furious figure-eight motion. Then, with a grand flourish and at eye-blinking speed, he used the curved ax head to hook and whip the Nought banner off the stones.

"My banner, fair lady." He bowed low, extending the long-handled ax to her, offering the banner. "I give it to you, a token of my esteem and admiration."

Isobel set the blessing chalice on a plaid-draped table and accepted his banner, her heart thumping as she gathered the silken length over her arm.

She wanted to touch her fingers to Kendrew's face, tracing his lips and chasing the hard, cynical set of his mouth. Her heart, everything she was, ached to remind him of their kisses, the bliss they'd shared.

Happiness she knew could be theirs if only he wasn't so thrawn.

"So you can be a gallant, as well as stubborn." She held his banner close, the silk chilled from the wind. "Perhaps you will also—"

"I am no' a chivalrous man, Lady Isobel." He held her gaze, looking deep into her eyes. "I am only a man who knows what is best for you. Keep thon banner and each time you gaze upon it, remember no' to trespass on wild places where no maid as fair as you ought to tread."

"I am no longer a maid." Isobel refused retreat, the loud skirl of the pipes and the general din allowing her to speak freely.

"You remain a lady." Kendrew was firm, his tone final.

Looking past her, he inhaled sharply when his gaze lit on Marjory. "My sister shall stay a lady as well." He moved to step around her, clearly bent on separating Marjory from Alasdair. "I'll no' allow her to—"

"She is only giving him the ale offering." Isobel watched her friend hand a large earthen jug to the MacDonald chieftain. "The ceremony is threefold. Alasdair will now bless the cairn with ale, ensuring harmony and good cheer for the glen and our clans.

"Catriona, my good-sister, will present James with a bowl of freshest milk so he can honor the stones with the fruits and bounty of our glen and"—she felt her cheeks warming—"the future children of our land who, we all wish, shall live together in peace and prosperity for all the generations stretching before us."

"You said three blessings." Kendrew folded his arms. "I only heard two."

Isobel took a breath, her fingers clutching his banner for courage.

Kendrew cocked a brow, waiting. "Speak, lass, or I am gone from here in a blink."

"The third blessing is yours." She explained quickly, not giving herself a chance to falter. "You must pour the remaining glen water on the cairn." She glanced at the chalice, sure the gemstones around the rim shone brighter than before. "The combined powers of the three waters will seal the blessings and end the ceremony."

"I am to have that honor?" Kendrew's brow arched a fraction higher. His tone made it sound more like an annoyance than a privilege.

"It was hoped you'd accept." Isobel wasn't about to tell him she'd argued with her brother and Alasdair to secure such an honor.

Or that she'd outsmarted them by implying the last blessing would be of lesser significance.

She knew it was the most important.

Nothing else mattered—except that Kendrew complied.

And then—she fervently hoped—that he'd agree to stay for the celebratory feasting.

Unfortunately, the tense line of his jaw warned he was about to storm away. Or that steam would shoot from his ears any moment, ruining the glee of the celebrants, who were already circling the cairn in a joyous, foot-stamping dance, wild, carefree, and happy.

"Hail to the glen!" The revelers shouted the chant, holding hands as they rounded the memorial *deiseal*, moving in the direction of the sun. "Peace to our lands! By the gods' will, so mote it be!"

"So mote it be." James and Alasdair stood side by side before the cairn, the ale jug and bowl of milk, respectively, held high in their hands.

When they tipped the ale and the milk onto the stones, a great cheer rose from the circling dancers. The pipers went wild, strutting proud, their red cheeks puffing with all their lung power.

"It's time." Isobel's heart thundered. "Four little words, 'so mote it be,' and then..." She let her voice trail away, sharply aware that Kendrew's expression had turned fierce.

"Old women like your Grizel should chant such drivel." A muscle jerked beneath his eye.

As before, he didn't move.

But his gaze slid to the jewel-rimmed chalice, his hesitancy giving Isobel hope.

"Please." She touched his arm, pressing his rock-hard muscle. "If Midsummer Eve meant anything to you, anything at all, then do this for me."

He inhaled audibly, releasing the breath slowly. "You go too far, Lady Isobel."

"Would you care about a woman less bold?" She stepped closer, letting her breasts brush his mail-coated chest. "One too afraid and simpering to—"

"Damn you." He jerked back as if she'd scorched him, and then took three long strides to the viands table. Frowning blackly, he snatched up the blessing chalice and marched back to the cairn, where he tossed the vessel's contents onto the waiting stones.

"So mote it be." He made the words sound as if they'd choked him.

If anyone noticed, they gave no sign.

Everyone around the cairn cheered, the dancers whirling faster, faces shining in the excitement of the moment. Only two souls stood quiet, their countenances glowing with a wholly different kind of exhilaration. They were Marjory and Alasdair, standing at the edge of the crowd, looking at each other as if no one else existed.

When Alasdair lifted a hand to stroke Marjory's hair back from her face, Isobel knew trouble would erupt.

"Leave them be." Isobel grabbed Kendrew's arm when she saw he'd spotted them. "They are only talking."

"Say you." He pulled free, flashing another look at

the pair. "Talking they are now, aye. And a moment ago he was touching her hair. We both know what happens next." He took her chin, tilting her face to his. "Dinnae think to defend her. I'll no' have my sister tainted by a MacDonald.

"I'm fetching her from the bastard's clutches"—he released her—"and then I'm taking her home to Nought where she belongs."

Isobel's heart sank. "But the feasting—"

"Your carouse will go on without Mackintoshes." He started toward his sister, glancing back only once. "You should be glad to see the last of me."

"No, wait..." Isobel set his banner on an empty bench near the viands table and made to go after him, but a firm grip to her elbow stopped her.

"He'll no' be taking her anywhere, my lady," the deep voice behind her sounded amused.

Grim.

Isobel froze. Her gaze was still on Kendrew's broad, silver-glinting shoulders as he shoved his way through the ring of dancers, heading for Marjory and Alasdair, who hadn't yet noticed his approach.

She looked away before he reached them, not wanting to see Marjory's anguish when her brother tore her from the man she'd set her heart on.

Instead, Isobel turned to Grim, the man who—according to Grizel—held secrets she needed to hear.

For a beat, she thought she saw the crone and her enchanted white stag in the shadows of the pines, the two of them looking her way, watching.

But when she blinked, they were gone.

Grim remained, offering the best smile he could for a

man with such a hard, rough-hewn face. "Norn will no' be letting him push her around, ne'er you worry." He glanced her way, his lips twitching at the sight of Kendrew and Alasdair going toe to toe against each other, clearly arguing.

Marjory looked cool as spring rain, untroubled and sure of herself.

She didn't look anguished at all.

But Isobel's heart raced wildly. Kendrew in a temper was a sight to behold. Almost, but not quite, as glorious as when his blue eyes blazed with passion, his gaze locking with hers as he lowered his head to kiss her...

Isobel tore her gaze from him, not wanting his friend to read her emotions. "I am worried for my friend, Lady Marjory." It wasn't a lie. "She knows her mind and—"

"Kendrew will no' treat her wrongly." Grim clearly misunderstood her concern. "He aye does right by her and aye will. His temper will have cooled by the feasting this e'en. He'll be in fine fettle then."

Isobel doubted it.

But she did need to speak to Grim. Such an opportunity might not arise again so easily. And he'd already proven himself an ally, of sorts.

"Grim..." She went to the viands table, pouring him a generous cup of ale. "I would speak with you about a certain matter. Something that might"—she waited until he accepted the ale—"go against your loyalties to discuss with me."

His face turned a shade less convivial. "I am a true man, my lady. I do not betray bonds of blood or oath, not for anyone."

"I would not ask you to do the like." She wouldn't, knowing her own honor was just as proud.

But she wasn't above taking all advantages open to her, as long as trusts weren't broken.

"I wouldn't wish you to tell me anything I shouldn't know." She hooked her arm through his, leading him away from the other celebrants. Stepping hopefully, she steered him toward the only place she could think of that would be empty this day: the walled kitchen garden.

That he went with her gave her courage.

"Then what would you know, my lady?" He waited while she unlatched the garden's wooden gate.

"I would hear of Rannoch Moor." She held the gate open, letting him step onto the gravel path. "I know Kendrew visits the women there and—"

"Is that what you've heard?" He stopped, looking at her in surprise.

"Why, yes." Isobel didn't understand.

Everyone knew how often he journeyed there.

"You heard rightly." Grim angled his head, his eyes sharp now. "He does go often to Rannoch Moor. But his visits have nothing to do with the women there. He has another reason for making the journey."

"Oh?" Isobel's heart would've skipped with joy if not for the shadow that crossed Grim's face. "Is it something bad, then?"

"Nae, my lady, though it is sad." Grim glanced up at the clouds and then pulled a hand down over his chin before he looked back at her. "Kendrew goes to the moor to visit his mother."

Isobel blinked. "His mother?"

"Aye, herself and no other." Grim nodded. "The lady is buried there."

*   *   *

Unbeknownst to Isobel and Grim, or any of the friendship and dedication ceremony celebrants, another guest took much interest in the day's activities.

He was Daire.

He'd been along with Kendrew and his party for the whole journey from Nought to the erstwhile trial by combat battling ground. He'd had a time of it, keeping pace with them. Sometimes he'd fallen behind. But he'd still done the clan proud, dressed in full battle array and even donning a shining, plumed helm. He'd considered tossing a bearskin over his shoulders, but he rather appreciated the sheen of mail. Sadly, no one in the glittering entourage of Mackintosh warriors had spared him a glance. Not that he'd expected one, all things considered.

He'd been delighted to drift along in their wake, grateful that such a possibility existed for him.

Afterlife could be worse, he was sure.

Indeed, except for a certain nagging ache in his heart, he was much blessed.

Now, although he'd rather partake of the ale and victuals spread upon the viands table, he hovered patiently near where Kendrew had been staring so fixedly only a short while before. Here, close to the dense, black-looming edge of Haven's pine wood, he had a splendid view of the festivities. But he didn't risk the unpleasantness of having one of the dancers accidentally whirl through him.

Suchlike did happen now and then.

And perhaps it was vanity, or maybe just wistful longing for his old life, but he didn't like being reminded that he no longer "was."

He *was* still here, after all.

Leastways, he was after a fashion.

So Daire—the proudest of all Mackintoshes—swelled his chest a bit and made sure his mail shone brightly as he held his position a few inches above the damp, needle-covered entrance to the woodland path.

Truly not a boastful man—certainly not in his long-ago mortal existence—he did bend tradition by allowing himself the title of "proudest."

He figured the style was well-earned.

Unlike others of his name, the weight of centuries gave him ample time to ponder his clan's greatness. He understood the glory of Nought. The heart-stopping splendor of sheer cliffs and dark mists, the rock-strewn vale of dreagans, so sacred and dear to him. He also knew the strength, pride, and fearlessness of the men who, all down the ages, had called his beloved home their own.

Now, much to his sorrow and annoyance, he had to look on as Kendrew, the present chieftain, narrowed the clan's notable traits to pride.

That, and—Daire squared his shoulders, trying to hover a bit straighter—the most irksome abomination of all: stubborn foolhardiness.

The young chieftain needed to learn that little good comes of strutting about like a vaunting peacock.

Sooner or later, someone salts your tail.

Or the day arrives when you meet someone whose sword is longer and faster than your own. In a blink, you face an enemy whose ax blade is sharper and more deadly than the one in your hand.

Daire knew the feeling well.

In his day, he'd failed to win everlasting peace in the glen by kitting the perfect love matches he'd planned so carefully. He'd had a knack for the like. Rodan the traitor had seen to the end of those hopes and aspirations when he'd shown his true face, bringing hordes of callous mercenaries and slaughtering men and dreagans alike. Darkness descended as they ravaged Nought, ripping apart the cairns, searching for silver and gold they'd never find.

Nought's treasure was the strength of its high, noble peaks, the freshness of pure mountain air, the goodness of cold, rushing rivers, and the endless maze of jumbled rock that so often deterred invaders. Wealth could also be found in the richness of Nought's upland grazing, hidden places dressed in lush, sweet grass that made Mackintosh cattle the finest in all the Highlands.

But the greatest prize was the people who called Nought home.

Proud men and women who loved their land so fiercely that even the price of death wasn't too dear if it meant holding on to the beloved glen that held their history and blood, the promise of distant days yet to come. So long as a Mackintosh held Nought, the world was good.

Daire meant for things to stay that way.

When he walked—rather than *floating*—he'd done a fair job. Now, insubstantial as he was, he could only observe and, at times, use his ghostly skills to lend a few helpful nudges. Like the day he'd kept pushing the top stones off Slag's Mound so that Kendrew would be forced to deliver them to Castle Haven for the memorial cairn.

Still...

He couldn't fight flesh-and-blood men.

Those days were past.

Yet war bands roamed the glen. And—Daire shuddered—they were bold men well able to come close to Kendrew and his warriors in an affray. For sure, they'd wash the lower reaches of the glen, Cameron and Mac-Donald territory, with bright, fast-running blood. And they'd laugh the while, enjoying their horrible deeds and caring for no one.

Once, Daire, Slag, and the other dreagan masters and their beasts could've banished such dastards in the blink of an eye. Even the most fearsome fighter ran when a blast of dreagan fire melted his sword.

But those days were gone.

Daire's might held all the substance of a curl of mist. And even if Slag had fared better in the Otherworld and still retained his former strength, Daire had no idea where the beast was.

They couldn't confront the cravens prowling the glen. Men who lived for mayhem and slaughter and only wished to leave the Glen of Many Legends in smoking ruin.

Stopping the fiends fell to Kendrew.

Yet Kendrew believed himself as invincible, as untouchable, as Daire was now.

Daire would give anything to touch again. To once more rest his hand on the shoulder of the big, stony-scaled friend he missed more with each passing century.

Time didn't heal wounds.

It sharpened the ache.

Kendrew should enjoy the chance to revel and laugh with new friends. Good men who would make fine allies, strong fighters at his back. Fearless champions at his side, men unafraid to stand in a shield wall. Above all, he should admit he'd lost his heart to the raven-haired Cameron lass.

She would be good for him, Daire knew.

She had the soul of a Norsewoman. And no female could be finer than that.

Regrettably, Daire's means of persuading the lad to embrace rather than repel such bounty were limited.

He'd already done what he could.

Just now he drifted a bit away from the wood, his gaze seeking the big, hard-faced warrior called Grim and the Cameron beauty, Lady Isobel. They'd moved deeper into the walled kitchen garden, standing in deep converse in the shadows of the gardener's tool shed.

Watching them gave Daire hope.

The warrior Grim had a good heart. He could tell the maid truths that would help her turn Kendrew from his foolish, destructive path.

Thinking it prudent to give Grim a few nudges in that direction—only if need be, of course—Daire smoothed a hand down over his mail shirt and prepared to float up and over the circle of whirling dancers, then into the tiny, stone-walled garden.

But before he'd flittered more than a few paces, a loud crashing noise reached him from somewhere in the piney woods behind him.

Daire stopped at once, hovering in place.

Something large, heavy, and awkward was trundling through the trees, cracking branches and trampling underbrush, making an unholy din.

It was an unmistakable racket.

A furor only those in his realm would hear, and—his pulse quickened—the kind of noisy passage no entirely whole dreagan would make.

Drago the three-legged dreagan was near.

Excited, Daire ceased listening in on Grim and Isobel in favor of trying to catch Drago before the proud beast could lumber away.

It was a pursuit Daire often attempted to no avail.

Drago's pride went deeper than ambling about just to prove he could.

He was also a one-man dreagan.

He answered only to his own master, a man long dead, and one who must sleep peaceably, because unlike Daire, he no longer roamed the glen.

Drago walked alone, coming to no man.

Except—Daire freely admitted—Grim, who gave the creature food. It scarce mattered that Drago didn't actually eat the offerings. The glen's magic was such that the same treats appeared on Daire's and Drago's sides of the veil that separated the worlds.

So the three-legged dreagan loved Grim.

And, Daire hoped, perhaps some of this day's blessing would soften Drago's heart and he'd answer when Daire called to him. If so, a most troubling riddle might be solved. Daire might learn something that would bring him closer to finding his long-lost friend.

Drago was the last soul to see Slag alive.

So Daire hurried on, pumping his wispy legs though he knew fine that doing so wouldn't make him float any faster.

He owed it to his friend to try.

Chapter Thirteen

✤

Isobel looked at the huge Mackintosh warrior with his full-bearded, battle-hardened face and felt her heart splitting. "Is it true?" She glanced to the side, over the kitchen garden wall, but didn't see Kendrew in the throng. "Kendrew goes to Rannoch Moor to visit his mother's grave?"

"So he does." Grim's eyes held only truth.

Deep gray and compassionate, they were the same color as the rain clouds just beginning to blow in from the west. And in addition to honesty, they held a look that told Isobel he was someone who'd walk over jagged, razor-sharp knife blades for a man he called friend.

Isobel regarded him, his words echoing in her head.

"I thought he went to see..." She brushed at her sleeve, uncomfortable finishing the sentence. "I didn't realize he'd have other reasons."

To her surprise, a wash of color spread across the big man's face.

"Och, he kens the ladies there well enough. All men

hereabouts do." The tops of his ears were turning red. "But he pays them little mind. He spends his time on Rannoch at Lady Aileen's cairn. He cuts back the heather and bracken to keep the stones from being covered. And"—he hesitated—"he leaves sprigs of meadowsweet."

"Meadowsweet?" Isobel's brow creased. The common strewing herb wasn't known as something to be left at graves.

But Grim nodded. "Nought's seneschals have aye mixed meadowsweet with the floor rushes," he explained. "Lady Aileen liked the herb's freshening qualities. Sadly, the meadowsweet was the only thing she did like at Nought. Kendrew remembers that, so—"

"He leaves the herb for her now." Isobel had to remind herself to breathe.

Seeing her struggle—her chest felt so tight—Grim's eyes clouded with concern. His sympathy let her heart squeeze all the more.

"So it is, my lady." His words made it worse. "He has surely carried more meadowsweet to Rannoch Moor than would fill this glen."

Isobel swallowed against the thickness in her throat. "He must've loved her very much."

"He hardly knew her." Grim glanced at the neatly laid rows of lettuce near where they stood. When he looked back at her, he studied her face for a long moment, as if deciding if he should say more.

Above them, a cloud slipped over the sun, darkening the little garden around them. The smell of rich, loamy earth, onions, garlic, and herbs grew stronger, the pungency heavy in the air.

A sharp wind swept down from the hills, chill, damp,

and heralding rain. Isobel shivered, gooseflesh rising on her arms as Grim's meaning dawned.

"You're saying he was very young." She made the words a statement, knowing.

Grim's nod confirmed her guess.

"He was a wee lad when she died." He held her gaze as he spoke. "But he never forgot her fondness for meadowsweet. And, aye, he did love Lady Aileen. He still does, though I suspect part of the reason he visits her so often is guilt. He feels responsible for her death."

Isobel blinked. "What?"

Surely she'd misheard him.

"It is true, my lady." Grim glanced at the lettuce again, and then at a tidy cluster of rosemary. He was large and solid as an ox, and his shoulders were broad enough to blot her view of the revelry on the field behind them. Silver rings glinted in his beard, adding to his air of fierceness. But in that moment—as he studied the ground—he appeared weighted by a burden he couldn't shake.

A deep sorrow, Isobel sensed, that frustrated him because he couldn't besiege it.

"Kendrew believes his mother wouldn't have died if he hadn't been born." Grim looked up then, his tone proving she'd guessed rightly.

He wasn't a warrior who lost a battle gladly.

Yet this with Kendrew—whom he clearly loved—wasn't a skirmish fought with steel and strength. It went deeper, to a place Grim couldn't go.

"I'm sorry..." Isobel touched the ambers at her neck, confused. "I don't understand. He was only a child, a very young one at that. How can he blame himself for a parent's passing?

"Sad though it is"—she had to say it—"such sorrows aren't infrequent in these hills. Life is hard. Winters cold, our larders often lacking, and no one will deny clan feuding claims a great toll."

"To be sure, that is so, my lady." Grim agreed easily. "Kendrew wouldn't argue any of that. He knows the harshness of our lands better than most. He feels as he does because his mother died while trying to take him and Marjory away from Nought."

He frowned a little, pausing. "She didn't want her children raised there and left Kendrew's father. She was taking them to her family in Glasgow, but—"

"She died on the journey?"

"She did, aye. Flooding rains struck when they were only halfway across the bog. Lady Aileen and her escort were trapped there for days." Grim looked down, nudging the path's gravel with his boot. "Kendrew's mother caught a fever. The ladies of Rannoch saw their fire and went to help. They took Lady Aileen into their care, doing what they could. But—"

"She didn't make it." Isobel tightened her fingers on the ambers.

"She was lost, aye. Most regrettably, she passed the morning Kendrew's father arrived at the Rannoch ladies' encampment, searching for her." Grim glanced up from the gravel. "Lady Aileen died in his arms, with Kendrew and Marjory looking on."

"Dear God." Isobel dashed a hand across her cheek.

Now she knew why the Rannoch light-skirts were so welcome at Nought.

Shame at her resentment of the women swept her, twisting her insides. She pressed her hand to her breast and closed her eyes, breathing deep. Pain, sharp and lancing, stabbed the deepest part of her. Images of Kendrew and Marjory as wide-eyed, terrified children burned across her mind. She also imagined a large, stern-faced man, broken and on his knees, tears damping his cheeks as he clutched his wife to his chest, unable to revive her.

It was too much.

The images were ghastly, more heartbreaking than she could bear.

"It was long ago, my lady." Grim looked a little embarrassed, as if he regretted telling her. He shuffled his feet, fingering one of the silver rings braided into his large black beard. "Kendrew will no' have wanted me to—"

"I am glad to know this." Isobel tried to put him at ease.

She glanced at the darkening sky, not surprised that the afternoon light was fading. Rising wind lashed the trees, tossing branches as the air turned chillier and the low, angry clouds swept ever closer. Soon, the heavens would break, rain chasing the celebrants from the field into Castle Haven's great hall.

Secretly, Isobel wished for a downpour.

Truth was she'd always loved rain.

And just now...

If the storm raged powerfully enough, Kendrew would be forced to abandon his wish to return to Nought. He might do so if Marjory wasn't along. But she was. And Isobel knew he'd not subject his sister to riding through teeming rain and cold, howling wind.

But there were still things she didn't know. And they were nagging questions that needed answers. She wouldn't have any peace without prodding.

Blessedly, she doubted Grim would mind.

"Why"—she turned back to him—"did Kendrew's father need days to track his wife?" Isobel puzzled over this, her heart lurching at the whole tale. "Surely he knew Rannoch Moor as well as anyone in these parts? And if she'd set out for Glasgow, he could've easily followed her, knowing the route she'd have to take."

"Aye, and that would've been the way of it." Grim didn't hesitate. "Sadly, Kendrew's father didn't know she'd headed south. Lady Aileen knew he'd come after her and so she told him she wished to visit a cousin who'd married into Clan MacKenzie, up Kintail way."

"I see." Isobel looked at him, beginning to understand.

He continued. "She tricked him, aye. It wasn't until a passing minstrel begged a night's lodging at Nought and mentioned having seen her and her party crossing Rannoch that Kendrew's father realized what she'd done." He paused as the strutting pipers marched past the garden gate, waiting until they moved on. "He set off at once, at great speed, but by then days had passed, and—"

"It was too late." Isobel spoke softly.

"That it was, aye." Grim's tone matched his name.

"What a tragedy." Isobel blinked against the stinging heat pricking the backs of her eyes. "And so..." She took a deep breath, trying to find the right words. "Why did Lady Aileen dislike Nought so much? Did she also not care for her husband then?"

Grim shrugged. "Who can say? I was but a bairn in those days. Clan graybeards tell that she loved Kendrew's father dearly. But she despised his home. She feared the wildness, hated the cold, and saw Nought as a stony province beyond the rim of civilization."

Isobel frowned. "I've never heard of a Highlander who didn't love wild places."

"She wasn't a Highlander." He said that as if it explained everything. "She was Glaswegian, used to the bustle of Glasgow and all the comforts and luxuries found there. Her father was a wealthy merchant and arranged the marriage so she would have a title to go with her genteel ways. Lady Aileen was a great lady, she was.

"So say all who knew her." His voice was low, his tone respectful. "The pity is her ladylike delicacy brought her doom. She didn't have the heart or backbone to love Nought as true Mackintoshes do. What we see as stirring, she viewed as desolate and barren, even threatening. The cold, dark mists carried doom, and falling rock from a landslide could strike her children.

"So..." Grim spread his hands. "Her fear for Kendrew and Marjory drove her away, turning them into orphans when she meant to save them."

"Yet they didn't need rescuing."

"Nae, my lady." He looked at her intently, seeming pleased by her words. "Nought land loves us as much as we revere each dark curl of mist and every inch of the rocky, broken ground, the deep, black lochans, and the sheer precipices of our cliffs. To us, such wildness is beauty and as much a part of us as if our own breath and blood pulsed through every stone.

"Alas"—he glanced over the garden wall at the sweeping green of the battle site, the thick pines edging the field's length—"even some Highlanders cannae appreciate the starkness that is Nought. For Lady Aileen, such a savage place felt hostile, seeming like hell."

"Nought would be heaven to me." The admission slipped past Isobel's lips before she could catch herself.

She didn't want to sound disrespectful of Kendrew's late mother, a woman whose sad fate was surely the reason for Kendrew's aversion to ladies—or perhaps better said, of his refusal to let a lady touch his heart.

Drawing boundaries kept one safe.

Yet she knew Kendrew was a brave man. A warrior more fearless than most, except in this one matter. But she was equally bold. She was also prepared to be as daring as necessary to win his heart.

Thanks to Grim, she could arm herself accordingly.

"You, my lady, are a treasure any man would be honored to call his own." Grim stepped forward and took her hand, lowering his head to brush his lips across the air just above her knuckles.

"Though, I must warn you"—he straightened, releasing her hand—"that Kendrew will never forget the past. He loves Nought fiercely, but he's vowed that no gentlewoman will ever again come to harm for—"

"Lady Aileen took a fever because she was trapped in cold and rain for days." Isobel lifted her chin, adamant. "She didn't fall ill because black winds raced across Nought's ramparts or a mist-wraith brushed past her, tragic though her end was."

Grim eyed her for a long moment, then the corner of his mouth quirked in a smile. "So I have told him many times, my lady."

"Then perhaps he should hear it from someone else?" Isobel returned his smile.

"That would be very fine." Grim's smile spread to his eyes.

"Then"—Isobel rubbed her arms against the day's

growing chill—"perhaps you might do what you can to ensure he stays for the feasting?"

"It would be my pleasure." Grim inclined his head respectfully.

"I am pleased to hear that, Sir Grim." Isobel folded her hands at her waist, hoping he couldn't see that she was much more than pleased.

Hope and anticipation quickened her pulse. Excitement made her heart beat faster, and she was sure that if Grim looked closely, he'd see the blood drumming low at the base of her throat.

It was all she could do to stand calmly by as he bowed and then turned to stride down the gravel path and out the garden gate.

For the first time since the trial by combat, victory hovered within her reach. Grim had given her the means to understand Kendrew. And the wonder of such an advantage curled like sweet warmth around her heart. If she used the knowledge wisely, she could make him see reason. He'd look past the barriers he kept around himself and realize they were meant for each other.

Nothing could go wrong.

But when she smoothed her hands down over her silver-and-gold-threaded tunic, preparing to rejoin the revelers at the memorial cairn, her amber necklace began to warm against her neck. The stones hummed and vibrated, the pulsing heat inside them increasing with each step she took along the kitchen garden's path.

"Nae." Isobel spoke the word firmly, denying what she didn't want to know.

Instead, she let herself out the gate and went in search of Kendrew.

There could be no danger in loving him.

The ambers erred.

And even if they were right, so be it.

She had no intention of heeding their warning.

Hours later, Kendrew stood in the shadows of Castle Haven's entry arch, trying not to notice that his men—all proud, battle-hardened warriors—had succumbed to the lure of well-filled ale cups and fetching, bouncing-breasted serving lasses. To a man, his gruff, hard-faced champions whirled and stamped across the cleared dancing space in the Cameron great hall. Each bushy-bearded bugger wore a foolish grin and held an enemy wench in his arms as they jigged, twirled, and leaped to the scream of pipes and the lively tones of an admittedly talented MacDonald fiddler.

It was galling.

Kendrew's Berserker heart took umbrage, his disgust so thick he could taste it.

He wanted no part of such folly.

So he folded his arms and resisted the urge to lean his weary shoulders against the curving wall. He was tired. And one of his feet had gone to sleep because James Cameron's ancient pest of a dog—Hector?—had sprawled across his foot and promptly fallen into a deep slumber. The dog's thin snores and the lightness of the beast's aged, bony body made it impossible to disturb him.

Kendrew was a warrior of great renown.

Countless enemies had tasted the bite of Blood Drinker's razor-sharp beard. And he'd cut down as many with a sword and spear, never sparing his challengers a blink before sending them into the Otherworld.

His bare hands served as well, when need arose.

Such was life for a Highland warrior.

But he wasn't cruel to animals, not even those belonging to his foes. He even tolerated Hercules, his sister's flea-sized excuse for a canine. He wouldn't even harm the wee beastie if the little bastard bit him. It took courage and heart for a creature so tiny to snarl at a man his size. And those were qualities he admired. Hercules also amused him. Not that he'd ever admit it.

He did allow himself a fierce scowl.

The needle-jab prickles in his foot were starting to creep up his leg. Cramps were setting in and twice now, his knee had threatened to buckle. As annoying, the rousing, energetic skirls of the pipes and fiddle offended his ears, the noise beginning to make his head ache.

His men's hoots and gleeful shouts irritated most of all.

The weasels had clearly forgotten where they were.

Kendrew hadn't.

Even in the vastness of the Cameron hall, now filled with smoke haze and the tantalizing smell of good, roasting meat, one scent lingered in the air. And its fresh lightness teased and taunted him, making him crazy as it seemed to repeatedly drift beneath his nose.

It was the scent of spring violets.

He suspected he only imagined the fragrance, which made its persistence all the more vexing.

When a man scented a woman even in her absence, he was in deep trouble.

Thor was also having a time with him, he was sure.

Why else would he rip open the heavens, letting great, boiling masses of black-green thunderheads race in to spoil the day's ceremony with torrents of drenching rain and cold, gusting wind?

Gods were aye jesting with mortal men.

And what better joke than trapping Kendrew at Castle Haven when all he wanted was to leave?

He would have done, too. Rain and wind be damned.

The truth was he thrived in such storms. The more wild and raw the weather, the faster his blood raced. But he wouldn't expose his sister to the elements. Not even if she did deserve a chilling to her marrow, a stout dousing that would bring her to her senses and banish her moony-eyed yearnings for a certain brine-drinking, web-footed jackal. She'd clearly taken leave of her wits.

And he—Kendrew's entire body stiffened—would swear the scent of spring violets was intensifying.

He also heard the soft swish of silk.

"Odin's balls." He fisted his hands and drew a tight breath as the lady herself sailed out of the crowded hall to stand before him.

Hector popped open his eyes and struggled to his feet, his scraggly tail wagging.

Kendrew wasn't about to show such adoration.

"Lady Isobel." He inclined his head, emphasizing her title.

"Laird Mackintosh," she spoke just as coolly. "You are missed on the dais. My brother saved a place for you at high table."

"I am fine here." He was anything but fine.

It wasn't easy to speak when he was trying not to breathe. Each time he inhaled, the heady scent of spring violets flooded his senses. He also could do without the torchlight shining on her glossy black hair, the sight making his fingers itch to undo her braids.

Indeed, he burned to do more than loosen her hair.

And the knowledge—his capitulation—infuriated him beyond reason.

"I can't sit at your high table." He knew he sounded the fool, but couldn't stop the words. "Blood Drinker isn't pleased propped in thon corner." He jerked his head to where all the men's weapons rested near the hall door. "He'll tarnish if I leave him."

"He'll do no such thing." Isobel glanced at the huge war ax, raging so much higher than the long swords leaning against the wall. "Though"—she looked back at Kendrew, her dark eyes twinkling—"I am much impressed by the lengths you go to avoid me.

"Why, next you'll tell me that Blood Drinker has advised you against consorting with black-haired females." Her lips curved in an irresistible smile.

Kendrew frowned. "You tread on thin ground, Lady Isobel."

She glanced at the floor, all innocence as she lifted her gaze to meet his. "I see solid stone strewn with rushes. Can it be"—she raised an elegant black brow—"that your eyes are failing?"

"Don't twist my words." His annoyance made her mouth curl into an even more dazzling smile.

The effect was devastating, slamming through him with as much impact as if someone twice his size and strength had run a spear into his chest.

He ached to kiss her.

Instead, he set his jaw and just looked at her, hoping his fierce mien would discourage her.

Unfortunately, it didn't.

As he should've known, she proved her mettle, stepping closer to him. Her scent and her sparkling eyes fuddled his wits until he was sure he'd splutter nonsense if he tried to argue with her.

The woman was a proper pest.

Gods how he wanted her.

She eyed him up and down, bold and brazen. "Someone needs to talk sense into you." She reached to stroke Hector's ears, the motion making her breasts shift beneath the shimmering veils of silver-and-gold silk she called a gown.

Kendrew knew in that moment that she wanted him dead.

She'd set upon a nefarious scheme to reduce him to a blithering idiot.

And it was working.

"What I need is no concern of yours." He spoke more harshly than he'd intended, but he'd required all his strength to tear his gaze from her silk-covered bosom. Everything conspired against him. The carouse in the hall kept all eyes turned from the entry. And, closer by, a wall torch flickered near Isobel, the flame glow casting a spill of golden light across her, gilding her curves.

Outside, thunder boomed and lightning flashed in the narrow slit windows cut into the wall. Rain hammered on the roof and wind howled, making him believe that Thor and all the other gods in Asgard were raising their mead horns, looking down at him and laughing.

This was what they loved best.

Watching mortals squirm.

"You won't get to me, Lady Isobel." The denial was meant to annoy the gods as much as to thwart her.

"From your posturing, some might say I already have." She smiled again, sweetly this time.

"You make my head ache, that is all."

"I say that is a start." She sounded almost merry.

"It is nothing." Kendrew was adamant. "There is naught between us except a most regrettable mistake."

"Indeed?" She lifted an eyebrow.

The increased rise and fall of her breasts showed he'd struck a nerve. "Think what you will." Her gaze didn't leave his face. "Thoughts won't alter what happened on Midsummer Eve. Nor will they change things that occurred many years ago and that had nothing to do with you."

"What things?" Kendrew refused to flinch. But something about the way her eyes narrowed, almost defiant, gave him a sinking feeling.

She was too smug, much more daring than usual.

So he narrowed his own gaze, preparing to expose himself in a way he'd rather not.

"You spoke with my captain of the guard in the kitchen garden." He resented letting her know he'd noticed, that even when he'd confronted Norn and Alasdair, his attention had hardly left her. "If he—"

"Sir Grim is a gallant." Her chin went up, a trace of color staining her cheeks. "He is a man of noble bent, chivalrous and mannerly. He only—"

"Grim is no courtier, my lady." Kendrew couldn't squelch the urge to shock her, to send her running back to her high table, never to plague him again. "Did you see the rings in his beard?"

"Yes."

"Do you know what they are?"

She didn't hesitate. "They hold the ends of his beard braids."

"Aye, so they do." Kendrew leaned close to her. "They are also warrior rings." He straightened, unable to keep his lips from quirking. "They are similar to the blue kill-marks on my arms and chest. Grim makes them from the sword blades of men he defeats in battle. He has a whole chest of them, choosing different ones to braid into his beard each morning. He's a bloodthirsty man, Grim is.

"Indeed"—he hooked his thumbs in his sword belt, grinning now—"he can take out a man's throat with a dirk faster than any warrior I know."

"You are not frightening me." The lady didn't turn a hair.

Far from it, she kept her chin raised. "Such a strong warrior does honor to Nought, do you not agree?" She pinned him with a stare, smiling at the rolling thunder shaking the walls. "Your land is too proud, too magnificent, to breed men who are weak."

Kendrew frowned, not liking her words.

He heard only that she called Nought proud and magnificent. And the way his heart jumped on hearing her praise boded ill for him. Seeing how her eyes shone, lighting as if she saw the same wonder he did in Nought, believing his land to be a wild and beautiful place, now that...

He took a deep breath, not wanting to consider the implications.

If he couldn't thwart her with tales of his men's brute fierceness, more drastic measures were required. Fortunately, he was good at the like. Squaring his shoulders, he glanced across the hall to the dais, his gaze going to the end of the high table where Norn sat flanked by two of his most formidable warriors. Dour men who'd love nothing more than flattening Alasdair MacDonald's nose if the brine-drinking lout so much as looked at Kendrew's sister.

Seeing Norn's peeved expression, it was clear that he'd dealt well with her.

He'd also handle Lady Isobel.

He just hoped the only other means open to him wouldn't circle round and bite him in the arse. The maid was a worthy opponent, much too skilled for his liking. She surely had more than one war stratagem.

He suspected they were all arse-biters.

Even so, he had to take the risk.

"You speak true, lady." He stepped closer, crowding her. "Nought doesn't spawn weaklings."

He ignored her praise of his land.

"Nought men are strong, bold, and daring." He set a hand on her shoulder, gripping firmly.

To his annoyance, rather than shrinking back, she met his gaze, her eyes lighting as if his words filled her with eager anticipation.

"Grim showed restraint when he spoke with you. He is aye a charmer. I don't share his smooth manners with ladies." He lowered his head as he spoke, knowing she'd feel his breath on her neck. "You should've let me be, Lady Isobel, alone in the shadows where I was content. Instead"—he nipped her earlobe—"you've provoked me into showing you just what a Nought man is: wild and dangerous."

"I am not afraid of wild." She matched his boldness. "And I find Nought more thrilling than dangerous."

"You should fear everything about me." He gripped

her chin, lifting her face. "Even here, away from Nought and in your own hall."

"Say you?" Her dark eyes flashed at him, her quick smile so enticing.

Her spring violet scent rose between them, heady and intoxicating. Torchlight spooled across her, making her hair shine. Above her low-cut bodice, smooth, creamy flesh gleamed, beckoning enticingly. Her nipples were taut, thrusting beneath the silk, begging attention.

She stood taller, putting back her shoulders so that her breasts lifted. Now he could clearly see the dark outline of those delectably peaked nipples. They rose even more beneath his gaze, pressing into the sheer fabric, which was little more than a breath of silk, letting him see so much. He inhaled sharply, wanting to taste her there, and elsewhere.

"I am beyond speech." He looked at her, not bothering to hide his desire.

His heart hammered, pounding hard against his chest. His body responded to her, tightening painfully as heat poured into his loins.

"You know what you do to me and"—he swore a tremor of excitement rushed through her—"I no longer care if anyone sees what you won't let me deny."

Need almost consuming him, he released her chin and curled his hand around her neck, thrusting his fingers into the cool silk of her hair. He swept his other hand down her back, splaying his fingers over her bottom and pulling her to him as he brought his mouth down on hers, kissing her hard, fast, and hungrily.

There could be no doubt that she'd feel his arousal.

He'd hoped the rampant proof of his wildness would flame her almost-maidenly cheeks and send her scrambling back to the safety of the crowded hall. That she'd run to the dais and the civility of the waiting high table, never looking back and glad to be rid of him.

But he'd hoped wrong.

The soft gasp of pleasure that escaped her proved his folly. As did her sweet womanly warmth as she twined her arms around his neck and parted her lips beneath his. She leaned into him, even rocking her hips against the granitelike agony at his traitorous groin.

Worst of all, he couldn't release her.

He pulled her more roughly to him, plundering her lips and drinking of her, knowing he'd never get enough of her honeyed kisses. He'd kill to hold on to the delicious torment of her hot, silken tongue twirling with his. Even the blending of their breath unmanned him, the intimacy so startling and heady that he had no choice but to deepen the kiss. A kiss that—something inside him railed—was more a bold and forceful melding of souls. Something so scintillatingly right, so good, that he didn't care if her brother, Alasdair, or even long-nosed Grim leered at him over her shoulder.

All that mattered was kissing her.

Until somehow he'd lifted her skirts, the silky material sliding over his wrist as he stroked his hand up the sleek length of her leg. When he reached the soft, female heat at the juncture of her thighs, his fingers brushing the downy curls there, his wits returned and he yanked back his hand as if she'd scorched him.

He released her at once, breaking the kiss and stepping away from her. Biding the remainder of his good sense, he used the broad width of his back to shield her from the crowded hall. Her lips were kiss-swollen, her hair mussed, and her lovely breasts flushed pink with the sweetest tinge of feminine arousal he'd ever seen.

She was without doubt the most desirable woman he could imagine.

She was comely, spirited, and so responsive that it was all he could do not to take her here and now, against the wall of the entry arch.

He knew she wouldn't say no.

Her rapid breathing and—he wished he hadn't noticed—the stunned, starry-eyed look on her face, were as telling as if she'd pinned her heart on her sleeve.

She fancied herself in love with him.

And that meant he had no choice but to convince her that she wasn't.

"You'd best right yourself." He let his gaze sweep her, lingering on her breasts, the pulse beating rapidly at the base of her throat. "You'll no' want to head back to your high table until you do."

"And you?" She surprised him with a level stare, her eyes glittering in the torchlight. "Will you now join us at the dais?"

Kendrew felt his brow furrow. He'd expected her to beg him not to follow her there.

Unfortunately he was now obliged to go.

Only by acting the scoundrel could he prove to her that he was one.

So he ignored the twinges of guilt pricking him and once more narrowed the space between them. Only this time rather than touching her, he backed her against the wall, trapping her by planting his hands on either side of her head. Leaning in, he looked into her eyes, making sure that his expression was his darkest.

"I will wait for you there, aye." He would, though he wished there was another way to be rid of her. "Be warned, I'll no' play the courtier. You've pushed me too far, Isobel of Haven."

"I am not afraid of you." One corner of her mouth lifted in a smile, secretive and knowing. "Indeed, I find our encounters most enjoyable."

Daring much, she lifted a hand to touch his face, trailing one finger along the side of his jaw. "As do you"—she held his gaze, not blinking—"though I know you don't wish to acknowledge the pleasure."

Kendrew scowled at her. "It's no' pleasure—"

"You are not a good liar, Laird Mackintosh." She had the boldness to deepen her smile.

Then she ducked beneath his arm and strode away from him, her head high as she disappeared into the shadows at the back of the entry hall.

A trace of spring violet drifted in her wake.

Fleeing the scent, Kendrew squared his shoulders and made for her brother's high table. When she returned to claim her place there, he'd put an end to this folly once and for all time coming.

He just wished he didn't have the dreadful feeling that his own folly had just done more than circle round and bite him in the arse.

He wasn't just arse-bit.

He was doomed.

And it wasn't even the potency of her kiss or the undeniable attraction of her full, creamy-skinned bosom that brought him to such a pass.

It was the way her face had lit when she'd spoken of his land.

His heart had split to see the wonder in her eyes. And having seen it, he doubted he could resist her much longer. A woman he desired and who also appreciated Nought was too great a temptation.

Unless he turned around and left the hall now, never looking on her again.

But he kept on, elbowing a path straight to the dais and the empty seat awaiting him there.

And as he neared the dais steps, the night's rain pounded down on the roof and the wind rose, great bursts of thunder booming with especial glee.

Thor was well pleased.

What a pity Kendrew wasn't ready to surrender. Isobel might be bold in the shadows, but she'd back down if challenged in the blazing light of her family's high table with kith and kin looking on.

She was a lady, after all.

And Kendrew was about to show her the meaning of *scoundrel*.

The gods and their jesting be damned.

Chapter Fourteen

❖

Isobel regretted nipping into the secret, hall-skirting passage as soon as its cold, dank air rushed to greet her. Eerie on any visit, the dimly lit corridor was especially unpleasant with rain and wind lashing the castle walls. Outside, thunder rolled ominously, the booms echoing in the gloom. But the little-used passage curved back to the dais, offering her a chance to tidy and calm herself before she reclaimed her seat at the high table.

She hoped everyone there would be too occupied feasting or watching the dancers to notice her slip in through the hidden door near the hearth fire at the rear of the dais.

She hurried on, willing it so.

She just wished the corridor wasn't rumored to hold more than chill, stale air and shadows.

Skald, the huge, snarling black dog that graced her clan's banner, was said to roam the passage. Many were the tales of his glowing red eyes appearing in the corridor's empty, least-lit stretches.

And the tragic clan ghost, Lady Scandia, a young, raven-haired woman believed to resemble Isobel, was also known to drift through the darkness here. Fortunately, Scandia hadn't been seen in a while, and most Camerons now suspected she'd found peace at last.

Isobel hoped it was true.

But she still stepped lightly, trying hard not to glance over her shoulder. The corridor's murkiness didn't feel exactly empty. So she took care to keep her ears alert to any sound besides her own footsteps and the powerful thunderstorm raging overhead.

It was too easy to imagine shifting figures in the deeper shadows.

She could almost see them, a lovely wraithlike woman, or a large, wolfish dog with fire-ember eyes, or other things that—she quickened her pace—were perhaps much more terrible than Scandia and Skald.

Pushing them from her mind, she breathed deep of the chill, rain-damp air filtering into the passage from the air slits set high into the outside wall.

She still felt shaky from Kendrew's long, deep kisses and needed the air to calm herself.

She also smoothed her hair and straightened her gown as she hurried along, hoping as well that she remembered where the passage's other well-kept secrets could be found: tiny bits of rubble that could be removed from the wall to access peepholes into the hall.

She didn't trust Kendrew to take his rightful place at the high table.

And if he went elsewhere, she wanted to know before she returned to the dais, trapping herself beneath James's watchful eye.

Kendrew was her concern.

And he wasn't escaping her.

So when she rounded a certain bend in the corridor, she began counting her steps past the iron-bracketed wall torch spluttering there. She paused after twenty-one steps, lucky seven times the sacred three. Then she steeled herself against the feel of the chill, damp stone and ran her fingers along the wall until she found a loose bit of rubble. Easing the rock from its niche, she took a deep breath and pressed her eye to the spyhole.

Her heart raced when she did.

Kendrew hadn't lied.

He was striding through the great hall, boldly using the center aisle. Head high and shoulders squared, he ignored the whirling dancers and was making straight for the steps to the dais.

His eyes glinted in the blaze of the torches and he moved quickly, walking with purpose. Isobel could scarcely breathe watching him. Worse, his gaze wasn't on the empty place of honor to James's right that she'd insisted her brother reserve for Kendrew.

He'd fixed his stare on her other brother, Hugh, who sat across from Isobel's seat.

And the longer she observed his determined, unerring path, the more she grasped his intent. He would chase Hugh from his place on the trestle bench so that he, Kendrew, could sit close to her.

Which meant...

"You, devil." She inhaled sharply, her entire body flaming.

Her heart raced, her palms dampening because she knew he planned something outrageous.

He'd warned her that he wouldn't play the courtier. Already his lips were quirking in a roguish, self-satisfied smile. Triumph rolled off him, giving him the air of a victor about to claim his battle booty. For sure, he meant to cause a scene, perhaps even plucking Hugh from the bench and plunking him onto the vacant spot next to James.

He'd do it with relish, Isobel knew.

Then he'd dust his hands and grin, pleased to draw all eyes so he could proceed to embarrass her.

The image of him striding onto the gravel beneath her bedchamber window, waving her blue cloak like a banner, flashed across her mind.

That night, too, he'd shown his daring.

Only this night...

She'd hoped to display her own mettle.

And she would, by God.

But before she could replug the peephole and hasten on her way, Kendrew paused with one foot on the first dais step. As if he knew she stood behind the wall, staring at him, he turned his head and looked directly at her.

Isobel froze, her hand holding the rock just inches from the little opening in the wall.

Her heart thundered and her mouth went dry.

Kendrew couldn't possibly see her.

But his eyes glinted in the torchlight, his gaze so intense, so challenging, that she'd swear he could. Worse, it was a look of such startling intimacy that she felt not only stripped naked, but as if her body was on fire. Unable to look away, she touched her hand to her breast, the cold hardness of the rock like ice against her flesh.

Beneath her fingers, she could feel the rapid beat of her

heart. Her knees weakened, her mind flitting back to just moments before when he'd held her so tightly, kissing her deeply and sliding his hands all over her body, making her want him so badly.

She did now.

And he knew it, the bold-eyed bastard.

As if in proof, he flashed a grin. Then he turned and bounded up onto the dais, heading straight for Hugh as she'd known he'd do.

"Oh, God." Isobel jammed the rock into the peephole, using the heel of her palm to wedge it in place. Her pulse rushed crazily and heat stung her face.

Her knees felt weak, and once she'd sealed the spyhole, she braced her hand against the wall to balance herself. She was sure the pounding of her heart echoed in the corridor, perhaps even loudly enough to be heard through the wall, in the great hall. Outside the passage, the wind howled with more force than before, shrieking past the corridor's high-cut air slits. From farther away came the more ominous grumble of thunder. Only now the low rolling booms sounded more like the storied dreagan roar she'd heard at Nought on the night of the Midsummer revels than any true thunder.

The ambers at her neck hummed as well, pulsing warmth beginning to heat her skin.

"I am not afraid." She drew a deep breath and pushed away from the wall. Straightening, she brushed at her skirts and then smoothed her hair.

Kendrew was a danger to himself, not to her.

But he could ruin everything if he caused a scandal at the high table.

She couldn't allow that to happen.

She hoped the charmed ambers weren't warning that it would. Even the worsening of the night's storm and the odd stonelike rumble of thunder seemed to hint that some kind of trouble that had been lurking just out of range was now preparing to rush in and cause havoc.

Touching her necklace, she curled her fingers around the pulsating stones, willing them to cool and be still.

Blessedly, they obliged, quieting at once.

Isobel's spirits lifted.

This night was crucial, a turning point that needed to bring the triumph she yearned for so fervently. Kendrew's glance at her a moment ago had melted her. Even if he hadn't actually seen her, he'd certainly sensed her behind the wall. The air between them had crackled, proving that she wasn't alone in her feelings.

He did care for her.

What stood between them had been a long time in coming. And it went much deeper than stolen kisses and forbidden touches. They were perfectly matched in all ways. Their bonding was powerfully right and—she was sure—absolutely inescapable. And although there wasn't a moment when she didn't yearn to feel his arms tighten around her, she also knew that the longing inside her was more than lust.

It was love.

And she couldn't bear the damage that would ensue if Kendrew offended Hugh and a fight erupted on the dais.

Hugh spun tales. He wasn't a warrior.

But he'd defend Isobel to his last breath—and if he challenged Kendrew, the result might very well be Hugh's final gasp.

And then . . .

Isobel pressed the backs of her fingers to her lips and hurried along the corridor. Worrying about a fracas she meant to prevent would solve nothing. Returning to the high table as swiftly as her feet would carry her was what she needed to do. So she kept on, ignoring the other peepholes she passed and pretending not to notice how the shadows seemed to shift and follow her as she hastened toward the hidden door that opened beside the dais hearth.

When she reached it, she set her hand on the latch, pausing for only a heartbeat.

Then she prayed the hinges wouldn't squeak and opened the door. She stepped through onto the well-lit dais. Her eyes rounded at the sight that greeted her, her jaw slipping as she stared at Kendrew and Hugh.

Kendrew towered over Hugh's still-sitting form, his expression so earnest it was almost comical.

Her brother Hugh was twisted around on the trestle bench, looking up at Kendrew with shining eyes, his ruddy face flushed with pleasure.

Hugh was preening.

And Kendrew was goading him, using Hugh's vanity to maneuver him into a corner.

The scene was strange, and entirely different from what she'd expected to find. Isobel could only stare at the two of them—as did everyone else at the high table.

No one even noticed when she slid quietly into her own seat.

"Och, nay…" Kendrew waved a dismissive hand, looking uncharacteristically humble as he peered down at Hugh. "Honored though I am, I have too much respect for bards to take your rightful place at the top of the table."

He placed a hand over his heart, shaking his head. "You've earned thon place beside your clan leader." He glanced there now, ignoring James's narrowed eyes. "If you'll treat us to one of your lays later, I'll gladly sit here where you've kindly warmed the bench for me."

"You do make a point..." Hugh swelled his chest a bit, his gaze flicking down the table to his usual seat, now cleared and held free for Kendrew. "I am rather accustomed to my own place at the table. And"—he pushed to his feet, stepping over the bench—"I will be telling tales by the fire later, after the feasting and dancing. Folks enjoy hearing them before they go abovestairs to their beds."

"I'll look forward to the pleasure." Kendrew claimed Hugh's seat with speed.

He didn't even glance at Isobel, but the foot he pressed down over hers beneath the table proved that he knew she was there.

And that he considered tricking Hugh a victory.

It was, too.

"Well done." Isobel looked across the table at him. She kept her voice low, but not so soft that he'd loudly prompt her to speak more clearly.

The glint in his eyes assured her that he wouldn't hesitate to do something so outrageous.

"You tempt me to do many things, my lady." His words proved it.

Lifting Hugh's left-behind ale cup, he took a long sip, watching her over the rim.

"Why else would I be here?" He set down the cup, arching a brow at her. "You know there is only one reason."

His deep voice rolled over her, its richness making her

pulse quicken. For such a big, burly man, he did have a beautiful voice. But it was the implication of his words and the intensity of his gaze that melted her. She could see her own feelings mirrored in his eyes, a truth he couldn't hide behind his bluster.

"You do not speak, lady?" His tone went a shade huskier, as if he knew what he did to her and reveled in watching her squirm.

"Be glad I can temper my tongue." Isobel lifted her chin, letting her eyes flash.

"And since you ask why you're here...Perhaps you wished to pay respects to the battle fallen and support friendship and amity between the glen clans?" She tried to pull her foot from beneath his.

He smiled and clamped down harder on her toes. "What the glen needs is strong men and sharpened steel."

"There are other ways to promote peaceful living." Isobel held his gaze.

"No' for warriors." Kendrew raised his voice, looking round at the other men at the table. "Men speak with their swords. Mackintoshes"—his tone rang with pride—"let their axes talk for them."

Near James, Alasdair set down his eating knife. "I agree with Lady Isobel." His gaze lit briefly on Marjory, still trapped between two stony-faced Mackintosh guardsmen. When he looked again at Kendrew, his expression was direct, almost challenging. "Our host, James Cameron, and my lovely sister, his wife, Lady Catriona, prove that connubial bliss serves as well as any blade to foster goodwill between warring clans."

Marjory's cheeks turned pink and the wine cup she'd been about to lift to her lips nearly slipped from her fingers. "He speaks true, Kendrew. Such unions have borne fruit and ended feuds throughout the Highlands. Wedding an erstwhile enemy does have merit."

She didn't look at Alasdair.

But she didn't need to.

Her own troubles forgotten, Isobel held her breath, waiting for Kendrew's outburst.

It came as a smile. And it was a slow, damning smile that spread across his face as he turned to fix his sister with a chilly stare. "Marriages between allies are better." He looked around the table again, as if expecting agreement. When no one spoke, he picked up his ale cup and drained it, slapping it down with a loud clack.

"That's why"—his gaze once again pinned Marjory— "I've just decided to find you a husband amongst the many Norse nobles in the north. A fine Orkney earl or a Norwegian prince—"

"Here, here!" James leaped to his feet, rapping the table with the hilt of his meat knife. "Now isn't the time for such talk, Mackintosh."

Up and down the table, men agreed.

Kendrew scowled, but held his peace. "As you wish," he conceded, sending a glare at Alasdair all the same.

Alasdair fisted a hand on the table, returning the look with equal boldness. "No Highland woman used to the grace of our fair glen should be made to suffer endless winters of blackness in places where nothing grows but frost and ice."

"My sister loves the cold." Kendrew flashed a look at her. "Isn't that so, Norn?"

Marjory tightened her lips, calmly buttering a bannock rather than responding.

"Did you not have a special announcement to make this night?" Alasdair turned toward James, purposefully showing Kendrew his shoulder. "Something that should cheer all present, though there will surely be one or two"—he hesitated only a beat—"exceptions."

His words earned chuckles from the Camerons and MacDonalds on the dais.

With the exception of the two Mackintoshes flanking Marjory, and Grim, who was seated at a nearby long table, Kendrew's own men were dancing.

Kendrew muttered something under his breath that sounded like he'd "show Alasdair an exception."

Grim heard and shot him a dark look.

But Kendrew only snapped his brows together, glaring back at his thick-bearded friend.

Isobel leaned forward, trying to send Kendrew her own silent warning.

Ignoring her, he cleared his throat. "I ken what would please me, and without exception." He emphasized the last word, tossing a look of scorn at Alasdair's back before turning his attention on James. "Can it be the tide has finally washed away the foundation of Blackshore Castle? And MacDonald is leaving the glen to seek new lodgings far and away from Loch Moidart with its aye rising water?"

"Kendrew." Isobel abandoned caution and reached across the table to squeeze his arm.

"The like must be said." Undaunted, he smiled, seemingly pleased by the frowns aimed his way from up and down the table. "It's only a matter of time before that pile o' stanes falls into the loch."

"Blackshore is a fine holding." Isobel hoped Catriona hadn't heard him.

Looking toward her friend, Isobel saw that Catriona and her brother, Alasdair, had their heads together, speaking low as they peered up at James.

And—Isobel blinked—apparently they were no longer paying Kendrew any heed.

He wasn't looking at them either. His gaze was back on her, his blue eyes watching her intently.

Beneath the table, he kept his foot on hers.

Only now, his knee also rested against hers, the intimate pressure sending strings of pleasure rippling up and down her leg. Her skin tingled with excitement, and try as she might, she couldn't take her hand from his arm. She could feel the solid, rock-hard strength of him through his sleeve and—even though everyone could see her touching him—she couldn't bear to pull away.

As if he knew, he broke the contact for her, jerking free as he narrowed his eyes at her. "I told you once, my lady, you tread where you shouldn't."

"And you?" She met his gaze, leaning her knee more firmly into his. "What are you doing?"

"Making you see your folly." He gave her a bold look surely meant to unsettle her.

Instead, she felt herself melting—especially when he stopped merely pressing his knee against hers and used it to rub her thigh. And he was doing so most deliberately, in a knowing and provoking manner.

Isobel swallowed, her body quickening with excitement. Delicious warmth flooded her, tingling sensation that pooled low by her thighs, sweet and insistent.

She bit her lip, hoping he wouldn't guess.

He cocked a brow, proving he knew.

Then he lifted his ale cup, sipping slowly, his gaze

locked on hers as he continued to caress her leg with his knee.

"Friends, kinsmen!" Still standing, James rapped his dirk hilt on the table again, the interruption bringing Isobel to her senses.

She blinked, knowing she had to keep her wits if she meant to turn this night's opportunity to her advantage. Allowing Kendrew to distract her—to seduce her at her own high table and in the presence of others—when she most needed to pay attention would only thwart her chances of seizing the right moment when it came.

And seize it she would.

Such a chance as having Kendrew held captive across the high table from her might never come again.

This must be her night of triumph.

Chapter Fifteen

❧

M y friends—your ears!" James called out again, looking round Castle Haven's crowded great hall. Smoke from wall torches and the candles burning on every long table hazed the air. But high expectation could still be seen on the faces of the celebrants as they turned toward the dais. Even the guards lining the walls gave James their attention, though they were too well trained to leave their posts or loosen their grip on their spears.

Servants bustling about carrying ale jugs and platters of food paused to listen from the shadows beyond the hall's main aisle.

Isobel sat up straighter, aware of what was coming. She just hoped that someday she and Kendrew could make a similar announcement.

She bit her lip, not wanting to consider the consequences if they couldn't.

Her wishes and the sacred pact with her friends weren't just about her attraction to Kendrew, her appreciation of

Nought and its deep roots in the northern culture that drew her so strongly. The love for Kendrew that she knew burned deeply in her heart.

So much more was at stake.

Bitter memories needed erasing. Peace in the glen should last longer than an ever-fragile truce. So many wounds needed healing; scars could rip open again if ignored. A forever bond must be forged, guaranteeing amity and goodwill that would last lifetimes and beyond.

The importance of her task made her heart pound and dried her mouth. She didn't dare glance at Kendrew. A man used to fighting hard and walking away victorious, he wouldn't surrender easily.

This night, she needed to be the winner of battles.

So she sat proud, keeping her gaze on her brother.

In the center of the hall, the music stopped then and the energetic dancing slowed, the crowd surging forward to catch his pronouncement. James waited until all shuffling and shifting stopped and everyone quieted. When the hall fell silent, he lifted his voice.

"My lady wife and I have tidings!" He set a possessive hand on Catriona's shoulder, pride ringing in his words, shining on his face. "In honor of the new memorial cairn gracing this land, the child that Catriona carries beneath her heart shall bear the second name of Cairn. Whether a boy or a girl, the babe's middle name will become tradition, passed from one generation to the next so that none may forget the proud and noble sacrifices made to bring peace and goodwill to this, our beloved glen."

Cheering and whoops greeted his words. "Hail the babe, Cairn!" the cry rose from all lips. Well-wishes filled the smoke-hazed air, men slapping others' backs, some pounding fists on tables. "Long life and many blessings on Lady Catriona and her child!"

The din shook the rafters.

At the next table, two guards just returned, cold and drenched from patrol, argued about shadows one man claimed to have seen. The other guard denied anything had been there, telling his friend that if his eyes were so poor, he needn't be out on patrol.

Everywhere else men and women beamed. Cavorting castle dogs joined in with a chorus of barks and howls. James raised a hand and nodded to the musicians, giving them his permission to begin playing again.

And they did, the skirling pipes and screaming fiddle even livelier now, as was the dancing, which resumed with renewed vigor.

Only two souls in the hall weren't smiling.

Kendrew sat as if carved of granite, his face hard and stony.

And his sister, Marjory, in turn, could've been fashioned of marble.

Isobel's heart squeezed for her friend. Alasdair had used the ruckus to leave the high table. No doubt hoping to avoid a full-fledged fight with Kendrew, he'd joined his guardsmen at a lower table on the far side of the hall. He'd taken a seat in their midst, jesting with the men and seeming glad for their jovial company.

Although...

His besotted gaze kept straying to Marjory.

But then Marjory glanced at Isobel and her stricken expression changed. It was replaced by a tightening of her jaw and a determined light that suddenly shone in her sparkling blue eyes.

Marjory was up to something.

Proving it, she leaned past the huge Mackintosh warrior to her right and fixed Kendrew with a dazzling smile, its brilliance a sure warning.

"My brother." The lightness of her voice was equally telling. "You see now"—she tossed a look at James and Catriona, surrounded by well-wishers—"the blessings that come of such unions."

"I see you trying to needle me." Kendrew proved she wasn't fooling him.

"Then you see wrong." Marjory held her ground. "I haven't declared to a well-filled hall that I'll be seeking a Norse or Danish bride for you."

"Hah!" Kendrew slapped the table edge. "So that's the string you're harping on. And"—he leaned toward her—"you can keep on plucking it, because the last time I looked, it's aye fathers and brothers that find husbands for their daughters and sisters.

"It's ne'er the other way around." He paused as a surge of agreement rose from the men sitting near. "Even if it was, I'd be having none of it."

More chuckles and hoots from the men.

Marjory sat up straighter, readying for an assault.

Isobel looked right at her, opening her eyes wide in a silent appeal to get her friend to leave Kendrew be. The last thing Isobel needed was for him to become aggravated and storm from the dais.

But Marjory wasn't finished.

"If you wish to ruin my life, then perhaps you should be the Mackintosh to wed an erstwhile foe." She threw down her gauntlet, challenging him.

Isobel wanted the floor to open up and swallow her.

It was painfully clear that Marjory was attempting to steer her brother in Isobel's direction.

Unfortunately, he threw back his head and laughed, slapping the table again. And his levity was attracting attention. Men, women, and even the serving lasses stopped to turn and stare at him.

"I cannae marry, Norn." He wasn't laughing now.

But the earnestness of his tone was exaggerated, the glint in his eye showing his amusement. "You know that, my sister." He looked at her, shaking his head. "There isn't a maid in all the land I'd allow to wear my ring. Even if"—he spread his hands as if to prove the futility—"I had one to offer, which I don't."

"I say you do." Grim appeared at Kendrew's elbow, his fingers working one of the braids in his big black beard. "There!" He pulled a silver battle ring from the loosened twists of his braid. Thrusting his arm high, he waved the bauble in the air.

"Behold—a ring!" He looked pleased by the shouts of encouragement.

Even James appeared more intrigued than outraged, his gaze shifting between Grim, Kendrew, and Isobel.

Kendrew's levity vanished. "You're a bastard, Grim. A conniving, meddlesome lout who—"

"I but mean well for you." Grim didn't turn a hair.

Isobel sat frozen, a strange blend of horror and exhilaration rising inside her.

This was about her.

She knew it, as surely as she breathed.

"Finest silver it is, my friend." Grim turned the ring so that it caught the torchlight.

Kendrew jumped up, trying to snatch the ring from his friend. "You're a madman."

"Nae, that's you if you don't make use of my gift." Grim leaned around him and set the warrior ring on the table.

"Bluidy hell, I will." Kendrew lunged past him, grabbing at the ring.

His fingers brushed its edge, causing the ring to shoot across the table. It sped into Isobel's ale cup, stopping with a little *ping*.

Grim—and others—started laughing. Along the table and everywhere on the dais, men began thumping their elbows on the tabletop. Some stomped their feet, while more than a few used big, scar-backed hands to dash tears of laughter from their grinning faces.

The merriment spread throughout the hall, men and women crushing forward to see what had happened to ignite such a ruckus.

Only Kendrew frowned, staring at the little silver battle ring as if it'd turned into a red-eyed, writhing snake and meant to bite him.

"Bluidy hell," he said again, apparently seeing, as Isobel did, that all eyes were on them.

People knew there was something between them.

The knowledge stood on every face. It hung in the air, thick and tangible, as if the hall held its breath, waiting for the inevitable.

"She'd ne'er have me, you gawping fools." Kendrew addressed the hall at large, but his gaze was fixed on Isobel. A muscle twitched in his jaw and the color was visibly washing from his face.

He shook his head slowly, a warning. "She knows better."

"I know no such thing." Isobel picked up the ring, seizing the moment. "I believe a union between our two houses would be good for the glen."

Kendrew stared at her. "Good for—"

"For us as well, Laird Mackintosh." Isobel smiled as brilliantly as she could, with her heart hammering against her ribs.

Then she slipped the warrior ring onto the third finger of her left hand, her gaze never leaving Kendrew's stunned face. "I do accept your offer."

Kendrew's eyes flew wide, filling with disbelief. "Now, see here, Lady Isobel—"

Before he could finish his protest, a thunderous swell of applause rose in the hall, the tumult drowning any possible objections.

The deed was done.

And Isobel could see in Kendrew's eyes that his honor wouldn't allow him to naesay their match. To do so now would shame her.

He was hers at last.

Unfortunately, winning this battle didn't mean the fighting was at an end. The hardest part of her journey stretched ahead of her.

She had to make Kendrew love her.

Unless...

As she was half certain she'd seen in his eyes more than once, he already did.

Much later, long after Kendrew had resigned himself to his plight and trudged wearily to his guest chamber at Castle Haven and—a floor above him—his soon-to-be lady wife had slipped quietly into her own bed, her mood decidedly higher, another soul was wide awake, braving the wind and rain still sweeping the glen.

And although Daire didn't wish to admit failure, he couldn't deny that he'd lost Drago's trail.

The three-legged dreagan was nowhere to be seen.

Daire should also leave.

The cold, wet night didn't bother him. But the gusting wind proved a trial. It was hard to float along when the world turned into such a fury. And while the thick pines surrounding Castle Haven provided a buffer of sorts, he'd stopped counting how often a strong gale had lifted him high in the air, turning him this way and that, before dashing him into a tree.

Not that the impact hurt him.

But as a once-mighty dreagan master, finding himself tangled in dripping, tossing pine branches was an affront to his dignity. So he disentangled himself from the clinging boughs once again, brushing at his rain-streaked mail shirt with hands too wispy to do much to improve his present appearance.

Not that Drago would care how bedraggled Daire looked at the moment.

The dreagan would fare no better.

"You fool!" Daire stopped where he was, doing his best to hover in place. He also fought the urge to slap his brow with his palm.

Drago was the proudest of dreagans.

Dignity mattered to the three-legged beastie who only roamed so often and so far, simply so everyone would see him and know that he could.

Yet...

Drago sometimes lost his balance when hard rains made the ground wet and slippery.

And he didn't like to be seen stumbling.

Remembering, Daire felt hope for the first time since setting off to find the creature.

He'd been looking in the wrong place, expecting to spot Drago lumbering through the thick, mist-hung pines. But the dreagan would be elsewhere, taking shelter in an empty, disued cave or beneath a stony overhang until the ground no longer resembled a slick, running morass that would send Drago crashing to his knees.

So Daire let the wind carry him back the way he'd come: out of the wood, across the battling ground with its newly dedicated cairn, and up the side of the deep, narrow gorge cut into the hills behind Castle Haven.

He found Drago crouched in relatively dry comfort beneath a jutting rock ledge at the top of the Haven falls.

"Drago..." Daire spoke low, approaching the dreagan respectfully. There was no need for the beast to guess that Daire knew why he'd sought shelter.

Dreagans, like men, deserved to keep their pride.

Daire also went gently because Drago's deep, stony snores revealed that he slept.

But even Daire's careful, feather-light passage across the broken stones and boulders that edged the falls caused a flurry of loose pebbles to skitter down the steep, rocky wall of the gorge.

Drago's eyes snapped opened. Looking at first disoriented, recognition dawned swiftly on his long, gray-green face. He struggled against a yawn. Then he stretched, seeking to push to his feet before Daire, whom he clearly recalled as a master of dreagans.

"Stay as you are, my friend." Daire ducked under the

ledge, dropping to his knees beside the creature. "I am most tired this night. And I am weary of the downpour." He rested a gentling hand on Drago's shoulder. "I'll bide a while with you, if I may."

Drago gave a grateful sigh and sagged back into his crouch, a few bluish curls of stony-sweet smoke escaping from his nostrils.

Pleased by the beast's trust, Daire released a sigh of his own, glad indeed to be out of the racing wind and wild, wet weather.

"You've wandered far this day." Daire chose his words with care, making sure to lace his tone with admiration. "I'm aware you make such journeys often, even traversing the whole of our glen."

A low rumble rose from deep in the dreagan's chest, letting Daire know that Drago appreciated the recognition of his ramblings.

"I traipse about as well." Daire's own pride kept him from saying he drifted.

Once, he *had* traipsed.

And strode, marched, stormed, ran, and—when the mood took him—ambled, enjoying the day and the wonder that was the Glen of Many Legends.

To his mind, such experience was good enough to allow him to claim he traipsed even now.

He also just liked the sound of the word.

But he wasn't here to ponder poetic musings. He had a most serious purpose.

He needed to find his friend.

Slag was also excellent at sniffing enemies. Together, they could track the jackals roaming the glen. Daire knew they were hard, brutal men. The kind who lived to raid and burn, leaving a bloodred trail behind them, then raping and stealing women when they left.

Such folk weren't welcome in the Glen of Many Legends.

And if only Daire could find his old companion-in-guarding-the-glen, they might be able to help Kendrew banish the sorrow-bringers before they could leave their bloody mark on the glen and its people.

So Daire turned to meet Drago's steady red gaze and tried to keep the desperation from his voice. "You were fond of Slag." He spoke true words, his heart swelling to form his friend's name on his tongue.

He also didn't mention the brigands, not wanting to frighten this dreagan who was more proud than brave. "I have heard you were the last to see Slag before—"

Rodan and his men unleashed hell upon the dreagan vale?

Daire heard Drago's gravelly answer in his head, the words as clear as his own.

It is true. Another thread of smoke curled from Drago's nose. *I was the last to see Slag.*

"I seek my old friend, Drago." Daire hoped the dreagan would recall how much he loved Slag. "We were separated on the day. I know Slag doesn't sleep in his old lair as most dreagans do. I would feel his heartbeat beneath the stones if he did. The cairn is empty. Nor have I been able to track him in the glen." Daire put words to the sorrow that consumed him. "I fear"—he did—"that Rodan visited an especial horror on Slag, knowing he was my companion.

"If that is so, I would hear the truth, whatever it is." Daire looked deep into Drago's eyes, willing the dreagan to understand his need. "Most of all, I would know where Slag is—if you can tell me."

Slag escaped Rodan. Drago shifted, sending another scatter of pebbles down the hillside. *A shame he left when he did—he missed seeing Rodan's mercenaries turn on him when no gold was found beneath our nests.*

A look of reminisce glimmered in Drago's eyes. *It was a grand sight.* He turned his head, fixing Daire with his glittering eyes, clearly pleased to recall Rodan's downfall. *He went wild, Rodan did. Storming about, ordering his men to tear apart every cairn, throwing our stones hither and thither, digging deep holes into sacred earth.*

Then, when the last stone rolled and the final shovel- ful of earth was dug, the fiends' efforts left them empty- handed. Rodan's face ran even more red and he cursed them, accusing them of stealing the treasure when he wasn't looking. He swore not to pay them.

It was then—Drago closed his eyes for a moment, breathing deep—*that they threw aside their picks and shovels and drew their swords.*

In the face of such an angry horde, Rodan turned into a woman.

Daire's lips twitched, nodding. He'd always suspected his archrival of cowardice.

Shameful it was—Drago shuddered, his stony scales rippling at the memory—*seeing him shriek and run, fear- ing for his life. The mercenaries took it, too, cutting him down where his stone now stands.*

The monolith tilts because we—the dreagans that were slain that day, at his command—gathered our remaining strength and tried to push it down.

Drago looked at Daire, pride on his beautiful dreagan

face. *We couldn't knock the stone to the ground, but perhaps it is more fitting that it leans, showing how he ran.*

"Indeed." Daire agreed wholeheartedly.

But much as it pleased him to finally learn Rodan's true fate, he needed to find Slag.

"You said Slag escaped Rodan, that he'd left the dreagan vale. Do you know what happened to him?" Daire's heart lifted, hope welling in his chest because Drago surely must have some knowledge.

I do not. Drago glanced aside, avoiding Daire's eyes.

Daire bit back his disappointment. "But you were the last to see him."

I saw him run away, Drago answered reluctantly.

Cowardice was a failing second only to disloyalty amongst dreagans.

"He ran?" Daire couldn't believe it. "There must be a mistake. Slag would've fire-blasted Rodan and a whole army of hell-fiends. Never would he run—"

He didn't run from Rodan. Drago's eyes filled with pity. *There was a storm blowing that night, the worst to sweep the glen in all the ages. It was the storm that sent Slag galloping from the dreagan vale.*

Daire listened, stunned.

Shamed, too, because he hadn't been there to calm his friend when he'd needed him.

Slag's fear of thunder had been their secret.

Now ...

A hard, cold knot formed in Daire's chest, guilt pressing down on him. "Did you see where he went?"

Drago shook his great head, regret in his eyes.

But he did slide his long tail out from under him, uncurling its length to point north, back toward Nought.

"He is at Nought?" Daire was doubtful. He hadn't felt his friend's presence in centuries.

Slag could be there. Drago swished his tail to point in each of the three other directions. *He could be anywhere. In his fright, he ran in circles, his path ever widening until I saw him no more.*

"I see." Daire nodded, understanding at last.

His instinct hadn't failed him these long years he'd searched for his friend.

Slag was no longer in the Glen of Many Legends.

He'd run from his greatest fear and likely didn't stop until he was so far from home that the way back was forever lost to him.

And it was Daire's fault for leaving him alone that day.

It scarce mattered that Rodan—his superior—had sent him on a false errand to the outermost reaches of Nought land. Rodan had insisted Daire go on his own, claiming he wished Slag at his side that afternoon, intending to use him to train younger dreagans.

Daire had even been proud to see Slag chosen for such an honor.

He'd never seen his friend again.

But his search wasn't over. And he refused to give up hope.

The good thing about being a ghost was having all the time one needed.

Daire would take advantage.

Chapter Sixteen

✦

Kendrew's first thought on awakening in his annoyingly comfortable guest bed at Castle Haven was that his poor, aching head would split apart any moment. The Thor's hammer that he always wore about his neck had somehow taken on a life of its own, growing in size and menace to pound viciously on his temples.

Even the inside of his head rang with the hammering.

And someone must've crept into his room in the night and poured sand into his eyes.

Then the devious buggers had set fire to the backs of his eyelids. Sure of it, he pressed both hands to the sides of his face and groaned loudly.

Never had he suffered such agony.

Lady Isobel was responsible.

If his wretched, besotted self hadn't felt such a need to sit across from her at the high table, he'd never have obliged himself to spend the after-feasting hours sitting on a stool before the hall fire. He'd have been spared the misery of listening to Hugh-the-bard-who-was-anything-but spin his long-winded tales.

But honor-bound men do strange things.

So he'd dutifully perched on a wobbly, three-legged stool beside the hearth. And he'd schooled his features into an equally dutiful look of appreciation until Isobel's clapper-tongued brother finally reached the end of his monotonous repertoire.

The wind-brewer's tales had proved so boring that he'd been able to tolerate them only by repeatedly tossing down cups of Clan Cameron's surprisingly good ale.

He didn't quite remember, but he suspected some pernicious fiend had also plied him with a generous supply of uisge beatha, the Highland water of life, spirits so strong and fiery a thimble-sized draught could fell an ox.

From the pounding in his head, he must've downed barrels.

He was going to kill Isobel.

Grim would be treated to agonies worse than death.

But first he'd have done with the dimwitted arse hammering on his guest room door. The window shutters were still tightly shut, but it was plain to see that the sun hadn't even tinged the horizon.

It was well before cockcrow, making the door-banger the worst sort of moron.

The persistent knocking also intensified the drumming at his temples.

Such a disturbance—and to a guest's chamber—was beyond bearing.

It was fiendish—and, he suspected, deliberate.

Furious, Kendrew pushed up on his elbows and cracked his eyes just enough to peer into the gray, murk-filled room. He didn't recall where he'd thrown his clothes before he'd more or less fallen into bed. But he did see the glint of Blood Drinker's long-bearded ax head winking at him from the far corner.

Easing his legs off the high mattress—every muscle in his body railed against the motion—he pushed shakily to his feet, trying not to notice the room swaying around him as he clutched the bedpost.

He was half tempted to seize his ax and throw open the door, naked and threatening.

But he doubted he had the strength.

He did manage to lift the ewer on the bedside table and tip the jug's icy water over his aching head.

The effect was startling.

"Grrrr." He grabbed a linen towel someone had thoughtfully left folded beside the ewer's basin and scrubbed his face, slowly coming back to life.

Unfortunately, the door knocking didn't cease.

"Odin's swinging knackers!" Scowling, he thrust the linen before his groin—just in case the pest was Isobel—and stomped across the room.

He yanked open the door. "Can a man not sleep in this foul place?"

Emptiness answered him.

The shadow-filled passage was deserted.

But the knocking rang even louder here. Hollow and hellishly annoying, it echoed in the corridor, filling his ears and maddening him.

"A good morrow, sir," a small lad's voice came from the dimness to his left.

Whipping that way, Kendrew saw a thin-shouldered boy on the landing. Barely eight summers, perhaps younger, the lad clutched a wicker creel of tallow candles and was clearly a kitchen helper.

He couldn't possibly be responsible for the din.

"Thon knocking"—Kendrew eyed the lad, trying hard not to scowl—"is that something done here every morning, what? Mayhap your chief's way of getting his men up and stirring from their beds?"

"Oh, no, sir." The boy shook his head. " 'Tis the new memorial cairn, it is."

"The cairn?" Kendrew blinked, wondering if he was still dreaming.

But the lad nodded. "Aye, sir. It be the cairn, right enough."

Shifting the candle-creel against his hip, the boy swelled his chest. Apparently it wasn't often he had the chance to be a tidings-giver.

"The storm last night blew the top right off the cairn. Stones were spread everywhere this morn, they were." He came closer, lowering his voice. "There be some folk in the kitchens who say one of your dreagans did it."

"Pah." Kendrew made a dismissive gesture, realizing too late that he'd used the hand that held the toweling before him. Jamming the linen back in place, he gave the lad his best reassuring smile. "The only beasties hereabouts are your master, James Cameron, and his web-toed, brine-drinking friend, Alasdair Mac-Donald.

"That I promise you." He winked at the lad.

"I dunno..." The boy didn't look convinced.

"Well, I do." Kendrew spoke with authority. "There were Nought stones in the top layer of the cairn." Leaning down, he chose words he hoped would ease the lad's fears. "No dreagan would dare to touch them once they were put in place."

The boy looked much relieved. "You think so, sir?"

"I know so." Kendrew reached out with his towel-free hand and tousled the lad's hair. "Dinnae fash yourself about dreagans. 'Tis right fond o' wee laddies they are. And in a good way, ne'er you worry."

He winked again, remembering when he, too, was so young and trusted in dreagans. "They'd like you fine, they would."

The boy's eyes lit. "Then I should like to see one someday."

"And so you might." Kendrew kept his smile in place.

But it was hard with his head splitting and his eyes still on fire.

"Tell me, though"—he gripped the boy's arm when the child started to move away—"what *is* the knocking?"

"Oh! I thought I said." The boy's cheeks turned a bit pink. "My laird sent some men to rebuild the memorial. They've been at it for an hour or so, gathering the fallen stones and setting 'em back on the top of the cairn. That's making the knocking, sir."

"I see." Kendrew nodded, and then patted the boy's shoulder before the lad hurried off down the passage.

It wasn't until the boy rounded a corner at the end of the corridor that Kendrew went back inside his room, closing the door behind him.

When he did, he sank down on the edge of the bed and wished he had more cold water to dump over his head.

He needed his wits about him.

He knew what had happened to the fool memorial cairn.

And it wasn't wind or dreagans.

It was the gods.

More specifically, it was Thor, Odin, and every other Nordic deity feasting and drinking in Asgard. Unlike dreagans, gods could do anything.

Norse gods were stronger than most.

And they knew he'd brought sacred Nought stones to Haven. They knew that he'd lost his heart to Isobel Cameron. Most damning of all, they'd also seen that thanks to Grim's meddling, the lady now wore a fine silver battle ring on her betrothal finger.

And they were mightily displeased.

Damaging the cairn was a warning.

If such foolery continued, there was no accounting for the trouble that would visit the glen. Strange things had already been happening. He was still not wholly convinced he'd seen only mist-wraiths drifting about behind the cookfires at the Midsummer Eve revels.

And if something was afoot, he didn't need the gods angry at him.

He'd have to put an end to any furor before something worse happened.

So he dressed as quickly as he could—given his weakened, aching state—and went in search of James. He had a plan that he believed Isobel's brother would heartily endorse: He would take Isobel to Nought, showing her his land's most fearsome attributes.

Once she'd seen them, she'd realize her folly.

She'd beg him to return her to Haven.

Their betrothal would end before it began.

The only difficulty was that as Kendrew finally made his way down the tower stairs to seek out James, he found his feet stepping slower and slower. And when he reached the landing just before the great hall, he felt an inexplicable urge to lean against the wall, stare out the nearest arrow slit, and heave a great sigh.

He did want to take Isobel to Nought.

That wasn't his problem.

The trouble was that he knew she'd love every terrible inch of his land that he could show her. She'd ooh and ahh, and his heart would swell to see the wonder in her eyes. Isobel Cameron was a woman who loved wild places. Cold wind was an elixir to her. The scent of stone more dear to her than the costliest perfume.

And if he threw his bearskin around his shoulders and drank mead from a rune-carved horn, she wouldn't call him a fool for longing for the old ways. Her eyes would shine and she'd reach for his mead horn, begging a sip.

She'd raise her children to be no different.

All that Kendrew knew.

And Odin help him, the knowledge filled him with a greater joy than he'd ever felt.

Taking Isobel to Nought wouldn't end their betrothal.

It would bind them forever.

"Have you ever breathed air so fresh and clean?"

Isobel stood on the narrow stone ledge of the most formidable bluff in all of Nought and pressed both hands to her breast, inhaling deeply. Her face glowed and her eyes shone with rapture. Her words hung in the cold, brisk air she'd praised several times now, while the awe in her tone curdled Kendrew's gizzard.

He had not brought her to Dreagan Falls hoping to hear accolades.

His reasons were just the opposite, and the lady was dashing each one of them. He'd known she'd react this way, yet there'd been a slight chance he might be mistaken. She *was* a lady. And excepting his sister, he hadn't met one yet who could face Nought full on and not run for her life. He owed it to Isobel to take the risk.

If she quailed, he'd be rid of her.

Her life would be her own. She would forget him swiftly, turning her passion to a man better suited for a gentlewoman of a place as tame as Haven.

He would've done right by her.

It was a gamble he'd lost.

She was winning this battle, and he wasn't a man who enjoyed defeat.

So he stood a bit taller than usual, hoping to appear as harsh and daunting as the jagged peaks soaring above them. He also tried to think of something suitably off-putting to say to her. Words that would prove how dark, untamed, and desolate Nought truly was.

Inspiration came when she took another long breath, closing her eyes in appreciation.

"The air here is often so filled with mist that you can't see the spray from the falls, my lady." Kendrew kept a firm grip on her arm as he spoke. "You are fortunate to be here on a bright afternoon. One wrong step"—he pulled her closer, already regretting having chosen this site to show her—"and there is nothing but a sheer drop straight down to the Dreagans' Bath."

"Do they truly bathe there?" She leaned forward, peering over the ledge to the sparkling blue pool far below. "I would joy to see them if they do."

"Sakes!" Kendrew yanked her back from the edge.

"Have a care. This is not your Haven with its pinewood and gently rolling meadows of primrose."

"I thought to see if a dreagan swam." She glanced at him, her face alight with whimsy. "You didn't answer me."

"I thought I heard them splashing about down there once, aye." Kendrew set his mouth in a hard line, hoping to lend more seriousness to such folly. "I was but a boy at the time," he added, speaking honestly.

"Though..." He looked off into the distance, beyond the soaring peaks. "Some of our clan graybeards insist the beasts come here still, just as they did in the days before this earth was weaned. On such days, when the mist is too thick to see your hand before your face, our storytellers do claim that one can hear the creatures bathing here."

He slanted a glance at Isobel.

If he hoped to scare her, he failed.

Instead, she smiled. "The pool is a perfect place for them. I should like to bathe there myself."

"You'd freeze." He frowned at her, trying to close his ears to her wonder.

Regrettably, his heart betrayed him, beating harder on each word of her praise.

No gentle-bred lady should admire a place of such treacherous beauty.

Made of rock and mist and the roar of the falls, this was a calamitous spot—one that many believed cursed. Even stags avoided Dreagan Falls, and the barren pinnacles rising all around the falls were so bleak even eagles went elsewhere to make their eyries. And the narrow footpath that led through a crevice in the cliffs, the only entrance to the ledge where they now stood, was so tight in places that a man could only pass by squeezing in his gut and going sideways.

Isobel hadn't blinked when they'd pressed through the constricting space.

She'd cried out in delight as they'd stepped through onto the bluff.

"I have never seen anywhere more magnificent." She repeated the same words she'd said moments ago.

"Men have plunged to their death here, my lady." It was true. "Most living creatures shun this place."

"Then they do not know how to look at the world through their hearts, do they?" She made it sound so simple.

"And"—she tossed back her hair, turning to look at him—"I doubt the men who fell were Mackintoshes. That is so, is it not?"

Kendrew tightened his jaw, defeat inching ever closer.

Could she read him so easily?

He inhaled deeply, feeling more trapped than he had inside the bone-squeezing cliff passage. "Nae, they were not Mackintoshes. Nought men ne'er fall off mountains. We are bold and sure-footed, always. I would no' have brought you here otherwise."

"I know why you brought me here." She glanced down into the rock-walled ravine, even thrust out a hand, wriggling her fingers in the shimmering clouds of spray.

When she looked back at him, Kendrew knew she'd overheard his words to James that morning. The challenge sparking in hers was telling.

"You thought to frighten me with Nought's boulders and fissures, the rough and rocky heights." Her words proved it, shaming him.

He had hoped to scare her away.

But with good, sound reason.

Dangers lurked in wind and mist. Rocks could crush a man if he had the misfortune to stand in their hurtling, downward path. In winter, Nought held snow-shadows that no fire could warm. Autumn brought more than bright, golden leaves. Cold wind and rains swept the land then, hinting at the deeper chill to come, and the long, dark nights that never ended. And in spring, rather than flowers blooming, gales blew and the spates turned torrential.

Summer passed too swiftly to bear mention.

Knowing he was about to treat her in a way that would reinforce every slur folk hurled at him, Kendrew gave her a look he hoped was feral. A piercing glance sharp enough to chase the wonder off her face.

"See here, lass." He lifted her hand, turning her fingers so that Grim's warrior ring caught the sunlight. "You should be wearing a fine ruby or sapphire ring. A grand lady's jewel set in purest gold."

He released her hand, gripping her shoulders. "Your husband-to-be should be escorting you through glittering halls thronged with nobles and other ladies of gentle birth." He held her gaze, each word ripping his heart. "You belong in an elegant place where the greatest danger is having a musician's inept string-plucking offend your delicate ears. Nought is no place for..."

He couldn't finish, sure that the rock-face behind them heard and was scowling.

The truth was Nought needed Isobel.

He certainly did.

"Did you never think, Kendrew"—she spoke his name for the first time, breaking his gaze to look thoughtfully at the falls' leaping spray—"that greater jewels are to be found here than in any courtier's sparkling hall?"

Kendrew stopped breathing, her words wrapping round his heart, squeezing.

He didn't speak.

The last thing he wanted was to splutter like a fool. Or worse, let her guess that the sudden sheen in his eye was caused by something other than the wind.

"I see you haven't considered the matter." She didn't look at him, her gaze still on the clouds of shimmering spume from the waterfall.

"So-o-o..." Now she did turn back to him. And he knew that her perceptive dark eyes could see straight into his soul. "I ask you this: are there not rubies in autumn-red bracken? Or in the bright scarlet berries of the rowans growing out of cracks in this very bluff?

"And you speak of sapphires..." She tipped back her head, peering up at the sky. "What of the clear deep blue above us, not marred by a single cloud? And gold?" She turned back to him again, shaking her head slowly. "Can it be you have never gazed on a Highland sunset?"

Kendrew swallowed before the thickness in his throat could worsen. "Lady Isobel..."

"Isobel, please." She smiled, a dimple flashing in her cheek, melting him. "Do you not see? I love this place and I would rather be here, with you, than anywhere else in the whole of the world."

"You say that now." He couldn't believe her. He did reach to touch her face, briefly. "When winter comes and the nights are long and dark, wind howling—"

"We will have good reason to stay abed and breed sons." She looked at him, beaming.

Kendrew almost choked. "You are beginning to convince me, lady."

"I can do more than that." She tilted her head, her smile turning seductive. "I can prove it to you."

Before he could respond, she gripped her skirts, pulling up her gown so that the material bunched around her hips. Her long, shapely legs took his breath. Praise Odin she held her skirts in such a way that the sooty curls of her womanhood were hidden from view.

Even so . . .

He knew they were there.

He'd brushed his fingers across the tantalizing softness of those curls. The intimacy still scorched his memory. Just now, merely thinking about it set him like granite.

"Lady—Isobel, what are you doing?" It was so hard to keep his gaze on hers.

Everything in him demanded that he look down, drinking in the beauty of her legs until the pounding at his groin gave him no choice but to pull her into his arms and crush his mouth over hers, kissing her again and again as he claimed what he needed from her.

Her spring violet scent wafted around him, urging him on.

He bit back a curse, hoping she wouldn't see how close she was to winning.

"You're not looking, Kendrew." Her voice was teasing.

Her *words* were killing him.

"To be sure, I'm no' looking." He wasn't about to do so.

He still wasn't sure this betrothal—or a marriage between them—would work.

And if he looked where she wanted him to, he'd be lost.

Every shred of restraint would leave him.

"It's only my Thor's hammer." The rustle of cloth proved she'd hitched her skirts even higher. "I want you to see it. Once you do, you'll understand why I've always been drawn to Nought."

Kendrew frowned, puzzling. "You wear a hammer amulet?"

He'd only ever seen her amber necklace.

To his surprise, she laughed. It was a light, wondrous sound that did him such good. Warmth began to curl around his heart, chasing his resistence.

Almost he could believe her, trust that they could...

He pushed the possibility from his mind. Honor kept him from letting her see how easily he was capitulating. If she was weak, yearning for a match that would surely end in sorrow, he needed strength.

He inhaled sharply, bracing himself. "If you wear Thor's amulet on a chain about your waist"—he'd heard of such adornments—"I dinnae wish to see it."

He did, fiercely.

"Lower your skirts." He put a thread of steel in his voice. "Your amulet chain—"

"I do not wear the hammer." The dimple in her cheek flashed again. "It's a beauty mark, low on my belly and just above—"

"Dinnae say it." Kendrew pressed his fingers to her lips, stopping her before she said something that would surely make him even more uncomfortable.

He cleared his throat, his heart thumping hard. "There is a hammer mark on you?"

"Thor's very own." She sounded pleased. "It's small, but the same shape as the amulet. If you look, you'll see."

And this time he lowered his gaze.

She hadn't lied.

Tiny, but distinct, the perfect outline of Thor's hammer winked at him from the left side of her lower abdomen. Wonder filled him. Never had he seen anything more beautiful. The mark was proof that she, of all women, could love Nought as no one else, that she wouldn't just dwell here, but would thrive in this place of wild and primordial splendor that meant so much to him.

She was Thor's blessed.

And...

Kendrew lost the battle. If she were a man, an opponent on the field of combat, he'd be flat on his back now, his life spent.

As things stood, he dropped to his knees, looking at the mark more closely. "Lady, you take my breath." He glanced up at her, almost overwhelmed by emotion. "Why did you not tell me of this before?"

"When?" The hint of a smile that had been playing about her lips turned warm and delightfully wicked. No, triumphant. "You have done everything imaginable to keep me from having the chance."

Kendrew returned the smile, something inside him splitting wide. Warmth, sweet and golden, rushed through him. And from somewhere even deeper than his heart— perhaps his soul?—a great floodtide of happiness swept over him so swiftly that he felt almost dizzy.

"I was a fool." *And I would've loved you with or without Thor's mark on you.*

But now...

"Sweet Isobel. You are mine and I shall never let you go." Leaping to his feet, he pulled her roughly against him, running his hands over her shoulders and her back, kissing her hard and deep.

"I will show you Nought's glory, take you to places you never dreamed existed." He tore his mouth from hers, trailed kisses across her cheek and down the side of her neck. He reveled in the smooth warmth of her skin, the heady freshness of her spring violet scent. "I will share wonders with you that will make you believe Thor himself carved this land. You'll see more beauty than—"

"I already do." She laughed, the sound beauty in itself. Her joy making his heart swell so much that it hurt.

But then she took his face in her hands and kissed him even more passionately than he'd just kissed her. And as she did, he forgot everything except the glory of her and how deeply he'd fallen in love with her.

Who would have thought it?

Thor, perhaps, who'd see a great jest in sending him the temptation of a lady.

And what a temptation she was. He should have known from the start that he wouldn't be able to resist her. He could hear the gods' laughter in Asgard. And his mind reeled with the brilliance of their mischief.

Most of all, he appreciated their wisdom.

And his in bringing her to Dreagan Falls.

No one would disturb them here. He'd left a guard on the far side of the cliff passage. No one could see them from the sheer rock walls surrounding this sacred place. And the thunder of the falls would dampen any lustful cries Isobel made when he finished what they'd started at the dreagan stones.

"Sweet lass, you might already love my land"—he slid

an arm around her waist, pulling her closer—"but we are only beginning."

He made the promise against her hair.

And then he did something he had never thought he'd do. He closed his eyes, took a deep breath, and prepared to make love to a lady.

His lady.

And he was going to claim her right here in the heart of dreagan territory.

How wonderful that felt.

Chapter Seventeen

❧

Isobel knew she'd won when she felt a tremor rip through Kendrew's big, strong body as he held her so closely. She also sensed it in a shifting of the air around them. Even the light changed, seeming brighter. And the patches of rough heather and bare cliff almost glowed. Something had happened. Perhaps Dreagan Falls was more than just a special place, made extraordinary by the foaming white water plunging down its high, tight-walled ravine.

There was surely a touch of magic here.

How else could she feel so strongly that the rocks and even the cold, spray-drenched air embraced her? This sacred-to-Kendrew site letting her know that now, at last, she held his heart.

That it was so stood certain.

She'd seen it on his face when he'd reached for her. And it'd been there again when he'd shut his eyes and inhaled just now. She'd watched him carefully. And her hopes had soared because he'd looked as if he were drawing sustenance, like a man gathering strength before he slid into a deep, dark abyss of no return.

She was that abyss.

And she could feel the need, desire, and love thrumming inside him. Longing as fierce as hers darkened his eyes. Yearning and want quickened his breath, the look on his face saying so much more than words.

He might be battle-hardened and powerfully muscled, but he hadn't been able to hide those oh-so-exhilarating signs of his capitulation.

But—oh, how her heart lifted—theirs was a shared victory.

As if he agreed, he looked down at her, his gaze heating. Slowly, he measured the length of her, the appreciation in his eyes warming her. Although she'd dropped her skirts, he glanced again and again at the place where he now knew she bore Thor's brand. Seeing him look there made her breasts tighten with desire. And tingles stirred in the lowest part of her belly.

They were delicious tingles.

And she could tell by looking at him that he was equally roused.

She'd never dreamed her Thor's hammer beauty mark would affect him so fiercely.

She'd hoped.

Just as she'd known the mark proved that she belonged at Nought: beside him, and as his lady.

"So you are Thor's chosen. I am well-pleased. But I would know what other secrets you are keeping from me." He lifted a brow, his tone teasing.

He was so devastatingly good-looking. "Will you tell me? Or must I seek such treasures myself?"

"I..." She bit her lip, her pulse racing. "I have no other secrets."

"But you have treasures." His voice deepened, exciting her. "I have seen them once. And I have ne'er forgotten. In truth, you haunt my dreams."

"You wish to charm me." The words escaped her before she could catch them.

"It is you who beguile me, Isobel." He studied her face, his gaze steady as he looked deep into her eyes. "You have done so for long now. In truth"—he pressed a kiss to her hair—"just as you bear the mark of Thor, I carry your name carved on my heart."

"Oh!" Isobel felt her knees weaken.

He took her breath. Everything about him, and this place he clearly loved, made her skin prickle with anticipation. His words melted her. She loved him so much that it almost hurt to look at him. Just now, wind tore at his plaid and whipped his rich, auburn hair, making her want to plunge her fingers into the tossing mane. She'd grip tight and pull his head down to her for more of his devouring kisses.

But she couldn't move.

The way he was looking at her was too delicious. She couldn't bear to do anything that would break their sizzling eye contact.

"Can it be, my sweet"—he urged her back against the rock wall—"that you burn for me as hotly as I ache for you?"

"You know I do." Isobel lifted her chin. Never had she been so bold. But her heart hammered wildly and every part of her hummed with desire. She felt exhilarated, incandescent with happiness. She tilted her head back so

she could hold his gaze, certain she could look into his
clear blue eyes forever and always want him.

She'd waited so long for this triumph.

And now...

Victory made her almost light-headed.

She took a deep breath, her gaze locked with his. She
couldn't wait to see what he would do next. The slow
smile beginning to tug at one corner of his mouth indicated he had something most wicked in mind. The hungry
look in his eyes proved her right.

"As you have no more secrets, Isobel, I will share one
with you." He swept his hands up her back and over her
shoulders, reaching round to cup and mold her breasts.
"I would have you naked. Stripped bare here at Dreagan
Falls, your lush bounty mine alone to enjoy."

She melted, the thought sending rivers of molten heat
pouring straight into the tingly woman's place between
her thighs.

"So you dinnae mind?" His fingers were already
undoing her bodice laces. He opened her gown quickly, a
muscle jerking in his jaw as he looked down at her nakedness. Cold air washed across her, chilling her skin and
tightening her nipples. Clearly pleased, he took the material in both hands, easing it down to her waist.

"Gods, but you're lovely." He splayed his fingers across
the full rounds of her breasts, plumping and squeezing.
When she closed her eyes, shivering at the wondrous sensations, he began circling the taut crests with his thumb.
Wind whistled past them, but he kept her pressed to the
rock wall. He slid an arm around her, bracing her as the
gusts buffeted them, each chill blast bringing the heady
scent of clean, icy water and cold, wet stone.

"Being here would make any woman beautiful." Isobel tipped back her head and breathed deep, reveling in the wildness, her breasts now tingling with the same thrilling female need as the dark, secret place between her legs. And still, he rubbed her nipples, rolling the hardened peaks between his fingers, and then making her gasp when he splayed his big hands over her flesh, palming her.

She arched her back, pressing into him, needing his touch. She ached for a deeper, more tantalizing intimacy, the kind he'd shown her so briefly in the shadows of Castle Haven's entry hall when he'd slid his hand up her thigh, his fingers just barely grazing her neediest place.

"Kendrew..." She could hardly speak, her voice a breathless gasp she didn't recognize as her own. "I want... I need more. Touches like—"

She broke off, stunned she'd admitted such a thing. Hot color stung her face and she was sure she must be glowing like a balefire.

If so, he didn't seem to mind.

"Och, I'll touch you, lass." He grinned, the look in his eyes bolder, hotter than ever.

"I'll ne'er tire of touching you." He stepped back then, seizing her bunched gown. With a flick of his wrist, he whipped it down over her hips so that her skirts pooled around her ankles. Slanting his mouth over hers, he claimed her lips even as he thrust his hand deep between her thighs, cupping her possessively.

He kissed her hard and fast as he stroked her, using his knee to nudge her legs apart, giving him greater access. "You are sweet, my lady." He breathed the words against her cheek. Then he nipped her ear before he brought his mouth back down on hers, kissing her even more deeply now. "But you have not yet felt the bliss I wish to give you."

"Indeed?" She swayed as he teased her with his tongue, each tantalizing swirl of his tongue over and around hers giving her more pleasure than she could bear.

Her entire body trembled. Heated darts of incredible intensity tingled all over her deepest places, making her rock her hips against him.

"You err." She ground herself against him, not caring if she behaved wantonly. She needed to intensify the pressure. Any moment, she'd shatter from the wonder of what his hand was doing to her, the maddening thrill of his kiss. "There can be no greater pleasure than this."

"Say you?" He spoke against her cheek, letting her feel his grin as he formed the words.

Then he circled his thumb over what felt like the center of all pleasure. The world caught fire and she gasped, her eyes snapping wide, her knees almost buckling beneath her.

"Tell me again that I err." He circled that place again, rubbing deliberately.

Isobel was going to die.

The world no longer just burned. It disappeared, leaving only the rushing wind and the roar of the falls. The heady scent of cold, damp stone flooded her senses, intoxicating. And, most glorious of all, Kendrew's hand stroking her so wickedly, his thumb circling round and round...

"Just breathe, lass. I have you." His arm tightened around her, lifting her against him so that her feet left the stony ground. "Better yet..." His voice came as if from a distance. Deep, familiar, and oh-so-rousing, but blurred as if he spoke through a haze.

"Better yet," he repeated, "let me breathe with you."

Isobel did as he asked, parting her lips and then nearly dying of pleasure indeed when he brought his own mouth down hungrily on hers.

"Breathe with me, sweet." He slid his tongue between her lips, letting it glide and tangle with hers as they shared breath. The intimacy was almost too startling to bear. "Let me drink of you, and"—his thumb still rubbed her, circling purposefully—"bring you bliss such as you've never known. Just breathe and feel, drift away . . ."

"I'm falling, I am . . ." Isobel tensed in his arms as she split apart. Great waves of pleasure rolled through her, washing over her entire body.

Somewhere in the madness, she saw Kendrew watching her. His smile was dark, his gaze locked on hers. His eyes flashed with triumph and he said something she couldn't hear because of the thunder of the falls.

Or perhaps it was the roar of her own blood in her ears.

She didn't know.

But she did notice that he was carrying her. He'd lifted her into his arms and was striding along the narrow ledge, making for a spill of large, tumbled boulders at the overhang's far end. The rocks looked smooth and were lichened, some covered with a thick carpet of moss.

"Here, sweet"—he set her down beside them, gesturing to the largest boulder, covered with deep green moss—"a bed of emeralds, for you."

Isobel touched a hand to her breast, happiness suffusing her because she knew what he meant.

"There is no finer bed in the land." Her heart swelled when her words made him smile. "You could not have chosen better."

"Now you err, my lady." He shook his head, his gaze not leaving her as he threw off his plaid and then lifted his heavily muscled arms, pulling his mail shirt over his head as if it weighed nothing.

He flashed a glance at the boulder, the deep green of its mossy cushion.

"I would ne'er have noticed these emeralds had you not opened my eyes." He'd left his ax strapped to his saddle, but now he unbuckled his sword belt, letting the wide leather belt and his short, stabbing blade drop to the rock-strewn ground. Still watching her, he bent to tug off his boots and then he made short work of the rest of his clothes until he stood before her as naked as she was.

And oh, but he was magnificent.

Late-afternoon sun slanted across his broad, powerful chest and the shimmering spray from the falls sent rainbows of color across the swirling blue kill-marks on his arms and chest. He truly did look like a wild, pagan deity from the mead halls of his beloved Valhalla.

Isobel sat on the moss-grown rock, sure her legs wouldn't support her if she tried to stand.

Seeing him naked was almost too much.

It was a joy she'd never tire of.

So she let her gaze flicker over him, loving how his gleaming auburn hair whipped about his strong, wide-set shoulders. It also excited her to see the tantalizing wedge of dark gold hair that glinted on his chest and then arrowed down across his abdomen, joining a vertical scar there before thickening around his manhood.

His proud, rampant manhood that proved beyond doubt how much he wanted her.

"Oh, my." Isobel knew she was flushing.

Kendrew set his hands on his hips and grinned. "Mackintosh men are well blessed, what?"

"Yes!" Isobel blurted the truth, laughter chasing her blush.

His audacity was just one of the things she loved so much about him. She would never have lost her heart to a man of soft words and gentle manners.

But she couldn't resist teasing him. "They have overlarge opinions of themselves as well."

"And rightly so." He didn't turn a hair. But he did step closer and lean down to brush a quick kiss across her lips. Before he straightened, he nuzzled her neck, growling something she didn't catch against her hair.

It'd sounded like *I love you.*

Then he was lowering back onto the mossy boulder and urging her to wrap her legs about him as he climbed over her, settling himself between her thighs.

"Kendrew..." She twined her arms around his neck, clutching his hair and pulling him down to her for more kisses. "I have dreamed of this—"

"You have no more need of dreaming." He braced himself on his powerful arms, looking into her eyes as he nudged her most vulnerable place, finally taking her again as he'd done on Midsummer Eve.

"I am now yours, Isobel. You fought well and besieged me. Though I will ne'er call it a fair fight, know that." He grinned down at her, taking the sting from his words with a kiss to her nose. "You were a formidable foe. One of the worst I have ever stood against."

"The stakes were high." Isobel gloried in what he was telling her, each word bringing her such joy. "I had to fight well."

"And you did." He stilled inside her, holding her gaze. "The battle is yours. Now and for all time to come, nothing will ever come between us." He thrust deep then, the long, thick length of him filling her. "That I swear to you, here in this sacred place."

"I make the same oath." Isobel clung to him, running her hand down over his shoulders, needing to explore him. She wanted to brand the feel of him onto her skin so that she carried him with her always.

"We are one, now and forevermore." She lifted her hips, matching his rhythm as he moved into and out of her, the pleasure rising, spooling through her entire body. "I swear it on my Thor's hammer—"

"And I on mine." His gaze darkened when she locked her legs more tightly about his hips. He moved faster now, thrusting a hand between them to rub the special place that had already brought her such pleasure. "You are mine, Isobel. I will never let you go."

"You won't have to—o-o-oh!" Tingling waves of bliss rushed over her. Even more powerful this time, they blurred all but the feel of Kendrew's strong, hard body riding her so deeply. She clutched at him, her innermost place clenching around him with equal need.

"That's my lass…" His hips were pumping now, muscles straining in his arms and along his neck. "Isobel." He tipped back his head, staring up at the sky as he rode her, sweeping her into a dazzling place of spinning light and bright, wondrous seas of scintillating pleasure.

She was melting, splitting apart. And she wanted the glory, the rightness, to never end.

Then, through the haze, she heard a long, deep

rumbling. It was a terrible sound, almost a feral growl. But then Kendrew nuzzled her neck, nipping her ear and grazing her skin with his teeth. And just when he bit hardest, the sweetest, hottest flames swirled across her center, liquid fire spreading deep inside her.

Kendrew's seed, she knew. It could be nothing else, for he stilled above her, his manhood jerking in his release.

"No return now, my lady." He looked down at her, his gaze hot, burning.

Isobel lifted a hand to touch his face, not caring if he noticed that her fingers weren't steady. "I have looked this way for long. I have no wish to turn elsewhere. Most especially now.

"Can it be that Mackintosh men"—she couldn't keep from smiling—"have one fault among their many proud attributes? Can it be they keep wax in their ears?

"It must be so or you would know I am here to stay." She curled her hand around his neck, pulling him down for more kisses.

He gave them gladly.

Or so she thought, though she really didn't know how other men kissed. Nor did she have any wish to learn, wanting only this man and no one else.

"Oh, Kendrew—"

"Kendrew! Love of thunder, man!" a deep voice echoed through the cliff passage. "Hie yourself out here. Now!"

"That's Grim." Kendrew leaped to his feet, glancing round as he snatched up Isobel's clothes and tossed them to her. "Make haste, lass."

He was already pulling on his boots, yanking on his tunic, and then dragging his mail shirt back over his head.

"Something's happened." He bent to scoop up his sword belt. "And it willnae be good."

"Kendrew!" Grim called louder, his shout joined by the sound of running footsteps crunching over stone. "Niall's dead! Two others with him, butchered!"

"Niall?" Isobel stared at him, not recognizing the name.

"My second captain of the guard." Kendrew shoved a hand through his hair, his voice tight. "He took Grim's place on patrol so Grim could ride with me to Castle Haven for the dedication ceremony."

"Dear saints." Isobel's heart dipped. Her blood ran hot and cold.

She grabbed her amber necklace, not needing to touch the stones to know they'd sprung to life. The heat pulsing inside them burned her skin.

But it was the horror on Kendrew's face that terrified her. Looking as if the earth had just opened to swallow them, he seized her hand and pulled her swiftly along the ledge, back toward the gap in the cliff-side.

He didn't speak, but he kept his free hand on the hilt of his stabbing sword as they ran. She knew he'd grab Blood Drinker as soon as they reached the horses. The urge to kill stood all over him, his Berserker rage breaking loose.

He was also concerned for her.

And that meant . . .

Before she could finish the thought, Grim burst from the passage. His face was ashen, his eyes deeply shadowed, as if he'd seen something unspeakable.

"It was at Slag's Mound." He bent over, bracing his hands on his knees, panting as he stared up at them. "The cairn was split wide and"—he looked like he was going to be ill—"Niall and two other guardsmen were found savaged."

He paused, breathing hard. "Not much remains of them, but what does is scattered across the rubble."

"Our men?" Kendrew's voice was cold, his arm around Isobel's waist tight as a vise. "Are they riding out? Searching for who did this?"

"The bastards left no trail." Grim straightened. "But a patrol is looking, aye."

Isobel rubbed her arms against the cold. The sharp blue of the day was dimming now, the light fading.

Kendrew nodded, not even glancing at her. "Send a man on to Nought." He spoke directly to Grim, his words damning because Isobel knew what they'd be even before she heard them. "Have him muster my fiercest fighters to escort Lady Isobel back to Castle Haven."

Grim frowned, glancing from Kendrew to Isobel. The pity in his eyes hurt almost as much as Kendrew's words.

"I'm sorry, lass." Kendrew finally turned to her, setting his hands on her shoulders. "It would seem I did err. This is no place for you, after all. Not after this. I cannae allow you to stay here."

"No-o-o." Isobel shook her head, feeling the blood leave her face. "Now, especially, you need me here. I am not afraid. You know that. Please..."

But he wasn't listening.

And his face, as he turned from her, was shuttered.

Then he followed Grim into the cliff-passage, pulling her along behind him.

It was over.

She hadn't won at all.

And whatever tragedy had happened, she knew in her

heart she wouldn't be able to convince Kendrew that it had nothing to do with them.

Many heather miles away, in a small but well-appointed room set off Castle Haven's great hall, James sat in his favorite chair feeding bits of beef rib to his dog, Hector.

The hour wasn't all that late. And even though the door was closed, he could hear the murmur of voices in the hall. He also caught the sounds of eating and drinking. And, from somewhere, the soft plucking of a lute drifted into his little privy solar. The lute-picker would be his brother, Hugh. Not that it mattered.

What did was that this was his quiet hour, and he was enjoying the chance to sit alone and ponder names for his soon-to-be-born son.

Hector helped by twitching an ear if a name held possibilities.

Neither of them considered names for a daughter.

James knew his firstborn child would be a boy.

Pride welling, he stretched his legs to the fire and prepared to test a few more options on his dog. He was just reaching for a bit of beef rib—Hector appreciated a treat for each ear twitch—when the door to his privy solar swung open, the din and smoke from the hall rushing in to spoil his quiet evening.

Pushing to his feet, he swung round, ready to order Hugh from the room. His younger brother was the only soul at Haven who felt privileged enough to breach James's most sacred sanctuary.

But his scolding died on his tongue when he saw the stout and matronly figure of Beathag, the cook's wife, filling the open doorway.

Her already-fearsome face was set as if the worst rain-storm of the century was pouring straight into the hall. And she held a small, thin-shouldered boy by the hand. A kitchen lad who rose each day before cockcrow and crept silently through the castle, taking tallow candles to the bedchambers so that no one need rise in darkness.

The lad's name was Tam.

And he looked terrified, his eyes round and unblinking.

"Beathag." James strode past her and shut the door, closing her and the boy in the room with him. "What's the meaning of this?"

He wasn't of a mood to tolerate anyone frightening innocent castle bairns. Most especially not the tallow lad, as James held a special fondness for the boy.

So he crossed his arms and frowned at Beathag. "What have you done to the lad?"

Tam looked at the floor, avoiding James's eyes.

Beathag huffed, swelling her formidable breasts. "It's glad you'll be that I've brought him here—once you've heard his news."

"His news?" James looked between them, puzzling.

"So I said, just." Beathag gripped the boy's chin, lifting his face. "Tell the chief what you saw, Tam." The softening of her tone saved her a later reprimand from James. "Tell him just as you did me, in the kitchens."

"He'll be mad, he will." Tam wriggled free of her grasp. Looking down again, he shuffled his feet in the floor rushes. "I wasn't supposed to be up on the moors. And now I wish—"

"Speak, Tam." James dropped to one knee before the boy, set a hand on his shoulder. "What's this about?"

"There's bad men about, there is." Tam lowered his

voice, glancing over his shoulder as if he feared someone would leap at him from the shadows. "I saw them up on the moor when I was—when I went to see if I could find the Makers of Dreams. I know no one ought to be pestering them, but I wanted to see Rannoch, the white stag everyone talks about.

"But then"—he turned back to James, rushing the words—"I got lost and that's when I saw the men. They were MacNabs and they—"

"MacNabs?" James angled his head, frowning. "They hardly leave their own glen, lad. They have nothing to seek hereabouts and"—he paused as Hector shuffled between them to lean against Tam, as if the old dog knew the boy was frightened and needed a friend—"that whole clan knows better than to cause trouble here or anywhere.

"Their laird is an old, feeble man." That was true enough, James knew. "His sons are no threat, some ailing. They aren't fighters. Most of them wouldn't know a sword from a candlestick. They've raided us in years past, aye, taking a stray cattle beast or snatching fish from the MacDonalds' loch.

"But now..." James made sure his tone was reassuring. "They aye run from danger these days. They ne'er bring it, I promise you."

"They're still bad men." Tam curled a hand in Hector's fur, adamant. "I know what I saw."

"And what was that?" James tried to be patient.

"They were big men, sir."

"Most Highland men are. Someday you will be, too." James gave the boy's shoulder a gentle clap. "A few years and you'll be taller than me."

But Tam only shook his head, clearly frightened. "They weren't just big, sir. They were laughing and drinking as they crossed the moor. And—and"—he took a great, shuddering breath—"their plaids were bloodied. It was shiny, fresh blood that was all o'er them."

"Ah." James stood, understanding at last.

"Then they might well have been MacNabs, aye." He was suddenly sure of it. "Like as not, their larders are empty and they came here to poach. Our glen is richer in game than the rocky hills of their own Duncreag."

"They weren't here to hunt, sir." Tam shook his head. "They were doing bad things."

Something about the fear in the boy's eyes finally reached James as well.

His heart began a slow, wary thumping and the fine hairs on his nape lifted. "What makes you say that, Tam? Tell me true, for I need to know."

Tam swallowed, looking miserable.

Then he took a deep breath and spoke. "They were carrying heads, sir."

"*Heads?*" James stared at the boy, horror sluicing him.

"That's what I saw, sir." He nodded briskly. "One of the men had three men's heads. And he was carrying them by the beards."

James felt the floor tilt beneath his feet, one truth hitting him like a steel-shod fist in the gut: Men of the vilest order were in the glen.

And his sister wasn't in the safety of Castle Haven's walls.

But she was with Kendrew Mackintosh.

For the first time in his life, James thanked the saints

that Kendrew was such a fierce, ax-swinging bastard. He wouldn't let any harm come to Isobel.

But what in God's name had happened to the peace in the glen?

Something needed to be done, and swiftly.

Chapter Eighteen

✣

"I do not send you away lightly, my lady." Kendrew's tone was terse, his words sending little ripples of shock through Isobel.

"Then don't." She glanced at him as they rode across the rough terrain just beginning to narrow into the high-walled vale of the dreagans.

"You know I must." He edged his horse closer to hers, the regret in his eyes making her heart quake. She couldn't tell if his troubled gaze held remorse that he was ending their relationship or guilt that he'd allowed it to even begin. Either way, the look on his face boded ill.

Dark clouds might have swooped down from the heavens, shuttering his thoughts from her.

Gone was the man who'd surveyed the glories of his lofty, windswept world and then pulled her into his arms on the ledge at Dreagan Falls, kissing her so deeply and with such fervent possession. Even his wildness had fled, leaving no hint of the bold warrior who boasted of his Berserker blood and was known to brag that one good fighting man was better than a hundred fine-spoken courtiers.

What remained was a man turned to stone.

His face was hard, as grim-set as the towering granite peaks already closing in on them, blotting the day's sun.

"This can be an ill-favored place, lady." He glanced at the sky where, unlike the clear blue at Dreagan Falls, angry gray clouds were now blowing in from the west, bringing colder wind and the smell of rain. "I should've known it was folly to bring you here."

"Nought is showing you its worst side." His blue eyes glinted, challenging her to deny it.

She did, gladly. "The attack on your men had nothing to do with Nought. Such an ambush, or whatever it was, could've happened anywhere."

"Anywhere does not concern me." He guided his horse around the huge lichened boulders that formed the first crude dreagan cairn. "This is my land. And I'll have no peace until my hands are stained red with the blood of the jackals who slew my guardsmen."

"You should want vengeance." Isobel sought to reason with him. "Any Highlander would—"

"And do you know what I'd do if you'd been hurt?" His jaw tightened, his voice turning hard. "Vengeance would be redefined, my lady. Once I found those responsible, I'd flood the ground with so much blood that all the Highlands would be a morass."

Isobel shivered, sure he spoke true.

That meant he did care for her, and greatly.

She might yet be able to persuade him not to send her back to Haven.

"Stop trying to outwit me." He kneed his horse even closer, and then reached to grasp her wrist. "I know what you're thinking and it'll serve no good purpose. As soon as your escort arrives from Nought, you're away from this place." He tightened his grip on her, his gaze locking on hers, bold and fierce. "I'll tell your brother I'll steal all his cattle and harry his territory for the rest of my days if he e'er allows you to set foot on Nought land again."

The threat made, he released her, his face as cold as a stranger's. "We're almost at the cairn. I'd warn you to brace yourself.

"Better yet"—he narrowed his eyes at her—"dinnae look at all."

Isobel bristled. "I have seen dead men before."

Kendrew didn't reply, the muscle jerking in his cheek answer enough.

They'd arrived at what was left of the great cairn Isobel remembered from the revels. Only the horror before them was nothing like her memory of this place. What she saw now set her world to reeling.

"Dear God." Isobel clapped a hand to her mouth, her stomach roiling.

She'd always believed a woman learned how strong she was only when put to the test.

Slag's Mound now proved hers.

Drawing rein before the damaged cairn, she slipped down from the saddle, hoping that Kendrew couldn't see how badly she quaked inside. She also didn't avert her gaze from the grisly sight before her.

Now more than ever, Kendrew needed to see her mettle.

She hoped it wouldn't fail her.

Already she needed the iron-hard resolve of all her Viking forebears to keep from dropping to her knees before the torn and bloodied remains of Kendrew's three guardsmen. The slaughter was terrible, much worse than Grim's accounting. Even the carnage of last year's trial by combat couldn't compare to this sullied place.

"Sons of Valkyries." Kendrew had his ax in his hands, holding the huge-bladed weapon as if it weighed nothing. He started pacing, slapping the ax haft against his left palm as he moved about the destruction.

His mouth was a hard, tight line. And a deep red flush now stained his face, fury rolling off him, his outrage almost crackling the air.

Isobel understood.

These men hadn't just suffered cuts and slashes as if set upon by men wielding swords, spears, or axes. Battle wounds were common in the Highlands. They were much too common, to her way of thinking. There was nothing common about what had happened to these men. They'd suffered atrocities. They'd been squashed and ripped asunder.

"Turn your back, Isobel." Kendrew was striding back to her, stepping before her to block her view.

His eyes blazed, though she knew his fury wasn't directed at her. "I told you no' to look."

"How can I not?" She held his gaze, not flinching.

His tone put her back up. Even more cold and distant than on the ride here, the chill in his voice put an invisible barrier between them. It also scared her, unsettling her more than any sword-swinging marauder could.

He'd clearly dismissed her, already shutting her out of his life.

As if he knew she was about to rebel, he took a step toward her. He reached for her and then swore beneath his breath when she sidestepped him. "See here, Lady—"

"You must be speaking to a lady I do not see." She lifted her chin, glaring at him. "I never turn my back."

She wasn't about to now.

I don't run away either. She let her eyes flash those words, not wanting to push him too far.

His gaze narrowed dangerously. "In this, you will do as I say." He was on her in two strides, turning her swiftly to face the horses. "Stay here and dinnae give me reason to come back and argue with you."

"I am not yet your wife." Isobel turned right back around.

"You are as good as such." He scowled at her, his gaze flicking to the silver warrior ring on her finger. Then he wheeled about and strode over to his men. They stood in a small knot, speaking in low voices, near the edge of the wide-scattered rubble.

Only then, when he could no longer see her, did she take a long, steadying breath.

His glance at her ring gave her hope. He still thought of her as his betrothed.

But the horror here was great. And so severe that he wished her gone. In truth, she didn't know any man who would act otherwise, given the circumstances. Yet she knew with a woman's instinct that if she allowed him to send her away, he'd never let her return to him.

The honor he tried so hard to hide would keep him from letting her come to a place where he believed she might be threatened.

He'd rather tear them apart.

Hoping she slept—that she was trapped in a terrible dream—she closed her eyes tightly and then reopened them.

Regrettably, nothing had changed.

She still stood in the heart of the dreagan vale, before Slag's Mound. But unlike its look on the night of the Mid-summer Eve revels, the massive cairn now bore an ugly gouge at its middle. The dreagan nest's carefully laid stones spilled from the cairn's center, scattered like a skirt of rock across the broken, red-stained ground.

Split as if opened from within, Slag's Mound could be easily repaired. The tumbled stones washed, perhaps blessed, and reset in their original positions, making the ancient dreagan lair whole again.

The three men who'd died here...

No stonemason's skill, or even the world's strongest magic, could fix them.

Again, Isobel pressed a hand to her lips and tried not to gag. She truly did understand Kendrew's concern. Why he didn't want her to look upon the carnage.

The men's heads were missing.

Their limbs and innards...

A shudder ran through her, hot bile rising in her throat. Her heart raced, blood roaring in her ears. She felt light-headed, more hollowed the longer she stared at the terrible scene before her.

Niall, Kendrew's second captain of the guards, was easily recognizable by the rich cloak still draped across his shattered ribs. The exceptional quality of the heavy war shield, now cracked in two and lying near his leather-gloved hand, also hinted at his higher status. Even less remained of his two companions.

Blood was everywhere.

And worse things that she didn't wish to peer at too closely.

Yet...

She had to look, because something bothered her. And whatever it was went deeper than the horror of the scene. A long-ago memory nagged at her, clawing up from the oldest, darkest corner of her soul.

"Kendrew..." She started toward him, ignoring the shakiness of her knees. He stiffened, aware of her approach, but not looking at her. "Something isn't right here. I know it, but I can't say—"

"To be sure, something isn't right." He whipped around to face her, his expression fierce. "You should be at Haven now. No' here where hell has wakened to stalk my land and slaughter good men who—"

"There's a message here, in these deaths." Isobel's chin went up. "This was not a chance attack. I can't say how I know, but I do."

"Men lose their wits when the battle joy comes over them, my lady. Spears or axes in the hands of such men wreak great destruction." His tone allowed no compromise. "The blood lust is what you're seeing here."

"I say fury, too." Grim joined them, his gray eyes solemn. "Anger born of thwarted greed. Niall and the other two men must've been passing by when brigands broke into the stones." He lifted a hand, rubbed the back of his neck. "They'd surely heard the old tales about hoards of silver and gold buried beneath the cairns. There can be no other explanation. Not for the likes of this."

"Hell waking." Kendrew hooked his thumbs beneath his sword belt. "That's what they stirred when they ripped open Nought's sacred earth only to find peat and pebbles. Truth is"—he glanced at Grim, then the other guardsmen—"I've suspected for long that such cravens have been tracking through the glen. I've caught glimpses of them.

"Yet I could ne'er be sure." His mouth was a hard line again. "Each time I saw them, they were gone in a wink. I thought my eyes were playing tricks on me or that I was seeing bog mist.

"Even so"—he looked again at Isobel—"when I thought I spotted mailed spearmen up at the cataracts behind Castle Haven, I told your brother. The fool didn't believe me, claiming his lookouts would've seen them."

Isobel started to defend James, but just then her ambers turned icy cold.

They'd been on fire, humming, ever since Grim appeared on the ledge at Dreagan Falls.

Now...

She glanced to where the other guardsmen walked about the tumbled stones. They'd removed their plaids, using them to collect the mangled remains of their friends.

When she turned back to Kendrew, Grim had moved away to join the other men in their grisly task. Kendrew looked after him, his entire body tensing when she stepped closer and put a hand on his arm.

Isobel took a breath, knowing so much depended on her words. "Nought isn't hell waking. Hell has *been* here. There is a difference."

"Either way"—Kendrew set his hands on her shoulders—"it changes nothing. I'd know you back to Haven, into the care of your brother. I'll not have you here now."

"Men did this." Isobel spoke as firmly as she could, given how fast her heart was beating, and with the bitter heat of bile so thick in her throat. "Men are everywhere, good and bad. I feel safest with you."

She couldn't allow Kendrew to send her away.

If he did, she'd never reach him again.

So she kept her chin high, her gaze level on his. "Answer me this: Could a Berserker wreak such devastation? Legends tell of their raging. They are said to possess unnatural strength when fury besets them."

Kendrew stared at her, his expression darkening. "You think my own men did this?"

"Not your men, no." Isobel shook her head. Ideas—old memories—began to whirl across her mind, taking shape at last. "But perhaps men who wished to make it look as if Nought men did this. Or a dreagan—"

"The only dreagans hereabouts are moldering bones." Kendrew shot a glance at Grim and the other men. "The cairns are empty and have been so long as I can remember."

He took Isobel's arm, leading her away from the others, toward one of the nearby outcrops. "Stories of Slag fascinated me as a lad because he was said to be the most terrible of all the dreagans.

"Legend tells that he feared nothing and could turn a man to stone with a single glance." He paused, pulled a hand down over his chin. "I wanted to see him. One day when my father was away and I still young enough to believe in suchlike, I came here and climbed onto Slag's Mound. I shifted some of the stones and lowered a torch into the cairn, hoping to catch a glimpse of the sleeping beast."

"And you saw nothing?"

"Only old stones and dirt. A large empty space, filled with darkness and nothing else." He sounded disappointed. "I never told anyone, not wanting to spoil Slag's fame." He glanced again at his warriors. "Men stop believing in dreagans about the time they grow beards. But…"

He turned back to her, shaking his head. "They then develop a taste for gold. They crave gold, silver, women, and drinking. Many also live for a good, hard fight, raiding, and any other form of bloodletting."

"And you think such men did this." Isobel rubbed her arms, feeling chilled.

"I am sure of it." There was a flash of distaste in Kendrew's eyes.

"I still think there is more." Isobel looked up at the bare pinnacles rising above them. Nought could be the edge of the world with its soaring cliffs and rock-edged ravines. It was a place to be cherished and prized, not dishonored with spilt blood and snuffed lives.

She curled her hands into fists, wishing in that moment that she, too, could swing a huge war ax.

Whoever killed the three guardsmen had willfully stained a sacred place as well.

Men capable of such callousness deserved no mercy.

"I have an idea." She bit her lip, glancing back at Niall's broken rib cage, the proud blue cloak spreading beneath him. "I agree greed-driven cravens, looking for treasure, could've attacked the men. I'd take it further." She waved off his objection. "Men seeking to scare folk from Nought by making the attack look as if dreagans had wakened and done this. Or"—she tapped her cheek, thinking—"we have men hoping to put blame on Berserkers—"

"What are you saying?" Kendrew frowned, first reaching to stop her and then striding after her when she went to stand beside Niall's bloodied cloak.

"Look here." She waited until he joined her, then nudged the edge of the mantel with her foot. "I think if you lift away his cloak, you'll find the blood-eagle."

She didn't know how she knew, but she did.

"The blood-eagle?" Kendrew stared at her. His brows lowered fiercely. "No man today carves one. Only a true Berserker would do such a thing."

"Indeed." Isobel glanced again at Niall's ribs, needing all her strength not to shudder. "And doesn't everyone in the Highlands know you're always claiming proud descent from those half-mythic beings?"

"Humph." Kendrew's frown deepened. "You think someone wishes to besmirch my family name?"

Isobel flicked a speck of lint off her sleeve. "I'd say it is possible."

She shivered again, for the wind was quickening, the air turning colder.

Her ambers were icy now, each stone feeling frozen to her skin.

And the chillier they grew, the more clear her memory of an old clan tale: a Viking yarn of how the Norsemen sometimes dressed their slain, cutting the dead man's ribs from his spine and then lifting out his lungs to spread them like wings across the back.

The blood-eagle.

It was a surefire means of striking terror into the hearts of enemies.

Or, in this instance, an excellent way to make their nefarious deeds look as if men from Clan Mackintosh—

warriors who prided themselves on their Berserker ancestry—were responsible.

"I dinnae believe it." Kendrew's frown turned blacker. But he leaned down and whipped away the cloak, dropping it as quickly when Isobel's guess proved true.

Niall's remains did wear the blood-eagle.

Kendrew straightened at once, blanching. "How did you know that?"

"I didn't—I guessed." Isobel tossed back her hair, grateful that Kendrew's broad back spared her the view. "An old clan bard told a terrifying tale of the blood-eagle whenever his stories mentioned my ancestor, Ottar the Fire-worshipper, and another forebear, Lady Scandia, whose mother was a Norsewoman. They lived in Viking days."

"It makes no sense." Kendrew rubbed his neck. "Why go to the trouble to carve the blood-eagle on Niall's back and then also gouge a hole in Slag's Mound?"

Isobel shrugged. "Perhaps they hoped to scare off as many good folk as possible? Those who believe in the like will accept that a dreagan escaped and is wreaking havoc in the glen. And"—she reached to straighten Kendrew's plaid—"those who fear the great name Mackintosh, men of Berserker origin, will run from here. They'll be fleeing your fury."

"A threat they underscored with the blood-eagle." Kendrew nodded, grimly. Then he began to pace. "Those were good men, lady." He wheeled to face her. "They patrolled only. They were not looking to fight anyone. Their sole task was to keep peace and"—he shoved a hand through his hair—"to watch for stray cattle beasts and guide them back to the herd at the summer grazing.

"Who could do this to such men?" Kendrew rubbed his eyes.

"I don't know." Isobel didn't.

But she did go over to him, gripping his arm when he made no move to stop pacing. "Tonight at Nought we can think about it and then—"

"There will be no 'tonight at Nought.'" He looked at her, incredulous. "Not with you, there won't be. I'll think on this myself."

"Then we must think now." Isobel stepped back and tightened her cloak against the rising wind. Even more dark clouds were gathering in the west. If she delayed him long enough, a storm would break, giving her time.

He glanced at the sky and then back at her. "I'll not be tricked, Isobel." His words proved he'd guessed her plan. "Thon is a grave matter." He jerked his head toward the damaged cairn and the torn bodies. "This is no place for a—"

"I am not just any lady." Isobel knew what he was about to say. "I stitched terrible wounds after the battle last autumn. And"—this was important—"I never looked away during the fight. It didn't please me, none of it did. But I saw everything. I am not one to wilt when dark winds blow through this glen. Nor do I run and hide when blood flows." She let all the pride of a Highland woman ring in her voice.

"Humph." Kendrew rubbed his chin and glanced aside, not meeting her gaze.

But a muscle twitched in his jaw, encouraging her.

She was reaching him.

Putting a hand to her brow, she looked around, deliberately avoiding the carnage. "This place is surrounded by rocks, sky, and mountains. A natural fortress as strong as Nought's own walls, wouldn't you say?"

He didn't answer her.

He did wrap his hands around his sword belt, knuckles white.

"Sometimes"—Isobel picked up a small, round stone, rolling it in her palm—"even the mightiest defenses are breached. As far back in time as one looks, dark chapters can be found, staining history and blighting the land we love so dearly. Yet no matter how calamitous the tragedy, our glen lives on to bless us on the morrow."

"Do you aspire to be a poet, lady?" Kendrew tightened his lips, still not looking at her.

"I speak words you need to hear." Encouraged because he didn't storm off, she stepped closer to him, slipping her hand through his arm.

"After every storm, the clouds are swept away, giving us a sky of clear, deep blue." She spoke easily, believing. "The waters of our shores and lochs sparkle anew, glittering like jewels. And the cliffs rising around us gleam like polished silver in the afternoon light."

She squeezed Kendrew's arm, leaning into him. "The jewels we spoke of at Dreagan Falls are here, too. Even now, in such a dark moment. To pretend they aren't is unfair to every soul who ever loved this land. And"—now she did glance over at the carnage—"to your guardsmen who fell trying to defend their home."

"You will still be returning to your home." Kendrew finally looked at her.

"I am home." Isobel stood firm.

"Aye, and you soon will be. You'll be safe in your linen-dressed bed at Castle Haven, lying back against your finely embroidered cushions and nibbling cream pasties off a silver tray." He shook free of her grasp, frowning. "That is your future, Isobel.

"You don't belong here." He made his tone final.

Isobel squared her shoulders. "I won't let you bring me meadowsweet, Kendrew."

His brows shot upward. "Who told you of meadowsweet? Wait, I know who it was." His gaze shot to Grim, who appeared to be examining tracks leading away from the cairn. "That long-nosed, meddlesome—"

"He is your good and loyal friend." Isobel defended Grim. "Not the kind who can be bought with a flash of coin or a jug of wine. It is good that he told me what he did." She didn't mention Lady Aileen, hoping there would be time later to address that sorrow.

This moment was theirs.

Yet Kendrew looked furious. "I will cut the tongue from that interfering bastard."

"And I promise you that I will always love Nought, and you." Isobel refused to be intimidated. "Nothing will ever chase me away." She set her hands on his shoulders, lifting up on her toes to kiss him. "Not the cold and all the rock. Not hardship, strife, nor any vicissitudes that might befall us."

She paused, swallowing against the thickness in her throat. "Not even you, my lord."

"Isobel—" He reached for her, pulling her close. "You don't know what you're saying. Three well-armed, battle-hardened warriors have been torn apart. That proves this can be a benighted place, not safe for you. It doesn't matter how much you love—"

"I am not afraid—"

The sound of approaching riders cut her off. They were coming fast, the thunder of their horses' hooves loud on the stony ground. Even as Kendrew and Isobel broke apart and turned, a hard-riding party of warriors pounded up to them. Cameron guards, they called a quick greeting as they swung down from their saddles, hurrying over to Kendrew.

Their faces were grim-set, their gazes swiftly taking in the carnage. They exchanged telling glances as they neared.

Isobel recognized one of her brother's best guardsmen. Named Sorley, he was an older man, incredibly loyal. He came forward with long strides, carrying a bulky, red-stained leather pouch.

"Ill tidings, Mackintosh!" Sorley set the pouch on a large, flat-topped rock. "Like as not to do with this! Three brigands were seen on the high moor above Castle Haven and"—he glanced at the sack—"they carried a grisly package."

Isobel's stomach dropped. She knew what the bloodied sack held.

"I know what's in that pouch." Kendrew gripped Sorley's arm, his gaze flashing to the sack, then back to the guardsman. "Were the bastards killed? Did you get their names? Why they did this?"

The other Cameron guards exchanged glances. One of the two looked again at the slaughter field. Only Sorley met Kendrew's eye.

"Nae, we didn't catch them." Sorley appeared uncomfortable. "We tried, scouring the hills for hours. I'm not sure we even saw them. It was the strangest thing." He ran a hand through his hair, glanced at Isobel. "Tam, our tallow lad at Haven, saw them and told our chief. But by the time we ran out to look for them, they were gone."

"Yet you have three heads in thon bag." Kendrew released Sorley's arm and looked to his own men who'd pressed near. "Where did you get them?"

"That's what's so odd." Sorley shifted, but didn't look away from Kendrew's fierce gaze. "We saw a mailed warrior up by the castle falls, the cataracts in the gorge behind Haven. We all saw him—a big, hard-faced man carrying a spear. But his mail shone like the sun and he wore a great plumed helm such as men haven't used in ages.

"He stepped to the edge of an overhang up on the gorge and beckoned to us." Sorley shook his head, as if disbelieving his own words. "We saw then that he couldn't have been one of the blood-drenched brigands Tam described. The man's armor didn't bear a speck of blood."

"And the heads?" Kendrew prodded.

"We found them in a pool up beside the falls, just about where the mailed warrior beckoned to us." Sorley rubbed the back of his neck. "Thing is, the man was nowhere to be seen when we reached the overhang. He'd vanished as if he hadn't been there at all."

"Humph." Kendrew folded his arms. "Men dinnae disappear into the thin air."

"Some do." Isobel spoke softly, recalling the big, hard-faced warrior she'd seen at the Rodan Stone, the night of the revels.

He, too, had vanished like the mist.

And he matched Sorley's description.

"So the cravens who did this escaped?" Kendrew started pacing, his fury palpable. "No one even saw them close enough to guess who they were?"

Again Sorley glanced at the other Cameron guards. "Wee Tam thought they were MacNabs."

Kendrew snorted. "They're a pack o' poets and women."

"We have other cause to suspect them." A frown appeared between Sorley's brows. "Some of us went up onto the high moors after we found the heads. It was there, on the outermost fringes of our land, that we again saw the mailed warrior. A storm was blowing in and mist swirled around him, but we were sure it was him."

"He raised his spear at us." One of the other Cameron guards stepped forward, his frown even deeper than Sorley's. "Then"—he crossed himself—"when we started toward him, he swung the spear around, pointing it to the east, in the direction of Duncreag."

"And did you catch up with him this time?" Kendrew's gaze was piercing.

"We couldn't, lord." The guard looked to Sorley.

"He disappeared again." Sorley shrugged, spreading his hands. "He could have run off into the mist, it was thick enough, the rain just beginning to hammer down on us. Who can say? We saw him, that's certain.

"And"—Sorley's voice held no doubt—"we believe he was telling us MacNabs killed those men."

"I cannae believe it." Kendrew threw a glance at Grim.

His friend came to stand beside him. "MacNabs have aye been unfriendly."

"They're hermits, not murderers." Kendrew pulled a hand down over his chin. "Nor can I see Archie MacNab harboring such men beneath his roof."

"James thought the same, sir." Sorley was respectful. "He's sending a party to Duncreag to—"

"I will take men there." Kendrew's tone was harsh, final. "Good men who can climb up to Duncreag without using their fool goat track and"—his chest swelled a bit—"men who won't be seen until they're inside the bailey, swords and axes drawn if need be.

"You"—he spoke directly to Sorley—"ride back to Haven and tell Cameron to scour his own lands and send word to Alasdair MacDonald if he hasn't yet done so. My men and I will see Lady Isobel to Nought." He flashed a look at her, his face unreadable. "She can stay there until all danger has passed. Nought is closer or I'd send her away with you. Now begone and make haste."

Turning to Isobel, he gripped her arm, pulling her toward their horses before Sorley and his men had mounted their own and ridden off.

"Now you'll see why Mackintoshes are night-walkers, my lady." He swept her up into his arms—not to kiss her as she'd hoped he'd do, but to swing her onto her saddle and thrust the reins into her hands. "I dinnae believe for a heartbeat that old Archie MacNab had anything to do with this. But I do think something's amiss at Duncreag.

"Charging up to their castle gate as your brother would've done will serve naught if my suspicions are well founded." He mounted his own horse, signaling his men to ride. "You'll be safe at Nought. When I return—"

"You'll see me back to Haven." Isobel saw it on his face.

"So I will, aye." His tone brooked no argument.

"And I say you won't," Isobel disagreed anyway.

Not that her defiance mattered.

Kendrew was already spurring ahead of her, his men dutifully circling their mounts around hers, shielding her from any trouble they might encounter as they rode after Kendrew, making for Nought.

The stronghold she'd so hoped would be her new home.

It would be, too, if she was ever able to talk sense into Kendrew.

What a shame she no longer believed such a day would come.

Chapter Nineteen

❖

Hours later, in a dark and remote glen that ran parallel to the Glen of Many Legends, and that Kendrew secretly believed was truly benighted, he learned the reason he'd been plagued by neck-prickles for long. The answer to the riddle peered up at him from a quaking, mud-filled pit beneath the rocky crag that held Duncreag Castle, ancient seat of Clan MacNab.

Except...

This cold, mist-drenched night it appeared as if the MacNabs had a new home.

Their naked, butchered bodies filled the reeking muck pit that had once been a moat. Hundreds of years before, until some long-ago MacNab chieftain decided their lofty stronghold's unassailable position made the trouble of maintaining a moat unnecessary.

"Sons of Thor." Grim stood at the pit's edge, looking down at the mangled remains. The stench was sharp, bearable only because the light rain washed the air. "There are women and children down there, I'm sure of it. And old men, feeble and bent..."

Kendrew agreed, choosing not to look again.

The first time he had, he'd imagined Isobel down there, knowing that any fiends capable of such atrocities would take especial pleasure in getting their hands on such a prize as a gently born lady.

So he kept his back to the horror and looked over his men, making sure they, like him, were prepared to become night-walkers.

"Talon"—he narrowed his eyes at a burly, square-faced warrior—"take off your Thor's hammer and rub more peat and soot onto that ugly face of yours."

"I forgot I had it on." Talon nodded, complying at once, removing his amulet and slipping it into a pouch tied to his peat-blackened sword belt. As quickly, he dipped his fingers into a second pouch, dabbing soot onto his nose and forehead.

"Are all blades smeared?" Kendrew walked down the line of his men, examining their sword and ax blades, making sure that, like his own weapons, they'd been well-coated with peat juice so that nary a glint of silver would reveal their presence as they slipped round behind Duncreag's massive bluff and quietly scaled its heights.

It'd been long since he'd truly night-walked.

And he felt more than naked without his Thor's hammer and arm rings. He'd need days to clean the caked muck from the links of his mail shirt. And he'd have to polish Blood Drinker's huge, long-bearded head for hours if he wished to assuage the mighty war ax's pride.

Even the wolf pelts that he and his men had thrown

around their shoulders—his bearskin was too heavy and cumbersome for such a climb as stood before them—had been well blackened and now reeked of goop and bog water. But the pelts would help shield them from view, and nothing else mattered. A wise warrior bent on ambush led a careful approach and then attacked in a rush, taking his foe by surprise.

"Then come"—he started forward past the broken rocks at the base of Duncreag's cliff—"it is time we avenge Niall and his men."

"And rid these hills of such a scourge." Grim crept along beside him, bent low to take advantage of the sheltering rocks and scrub.

They hadn't gone far before two men stepped from a bramble thicket, barring their way with spears.

"Looks like our pit is about to overflow," the nearest man jeered, tossing a glance at his companion. "Wolf-men have come to visit the MacNabs."

"You're headed the wrong way, my friends." The second man grinned, jabbing his spear-point at Kendrew and Grim, who led their party.

"He speaks true," the first man sneered, thrusting with his spear as well. "You'll find the MacNabs behind you, in the corpse pit."

"Then say them our greetings." Kendrew returned the men's grins.

It was the last thing they'd ever see, because in that moment, Talon and another Mackintosh appeared behind them, clamping firm hands over their jeering mouths. In a flash, two Mackintosh war axes rose and fell, ending the men's interference, silencing their taunts.

"Wolf-men." One of Kendrew's warriors spat on the

ground. "I'll have that bastard's skull for an ale cup when we're done here."

"Drag them in the brush for now, lest anyone see them from above." Kendrew glanced up at Duncreag's ramparts. "The rain will keep them from peppering us with fire arrows, but I'd no' have them see something's amiss and start throwing down logs or boiling water to knock us off the rocks."

Craning his neck, he scanned the high walls, trying to see through the drizzle.

All seemed quiet, but thick mist and cloud obscured the tower, making it difficult to see how many guards patrolled the battlements. The soft glow of a fire hazed the night sky where he supposed the kitchens lay, indicating the stronghold was occupied by more than the two men they'd killed.

Somewhere distant thunder rolled and the wind picked up, the rain beginning to fall harder. Within moments, the stronghold's massive outline blurred even more as great curtains of rain and mist swept in on the freshening wind. Icy water pounded them, washing away the peat-and-soot smears they'd so carefully rubbed onto their faces and arms.

"Damnation." Kendrew scowled, wondering why he hadn't thought to bring swathes of black linen. Cloth they could've used to wrap around their sword and ax blades, and even themselves.

He knew why he'd forgotten.

Worry over Isobel dimmed his wits.

Furious, he tossed a glance at his men. "We climb now. If any man makes a noise, my dog, Gronk, will have the bastard's bollocks for his supper."

"And if you're that bastard?" Grim cocked a peat-blackened brow.

"Then he'll have my bollocks, you arse." Kendrew glared at his friend. "Now hold your flapping tongue and scale this slope with me."

Turning back to the bluff, Kendrew took the lead, putting his foot on a jutting rock. Quiet as the night, he hoisted himself up onto the steep rock face, and immediately stretched to reach the next toehold. The best climber of his men, he was halfway up the crag before the others had even left the wet, soggy ground.

But they followed quickly, each man scaling the steep, rain-slicked rock as effortlessly as if they were walking across Nought's feasting hall.

Mackintoshes excelled at the like.

The only thing they did better was swing their war axes, bringing death to their foes.

So the day—or night, for the hour was late—seemed theirs when they at last reached the top of the crag and, with great stealth, slipped over the rampart wall and onto Duncreag's battlements.

"Ho, you there!" A guard came running, his sword already drawn.

"I am Mackintosh." Kendrew waited for the man to reach him and then swept his ax in a killing arc, slicing deep into the guardsman's throat.

He looked down at the dead man, wiping his ax blade on his thigh. "Blood Drinker thanks you—he was thirsty!"

Looking round, he searched for other watchmen, but Duncreag was quiet. There was no sound except the hiss of rain on stone and the whistling night wind. But cooking smells drifted from the keep's entrance, and it was in that direction that he now led his men.

Surprise was aye good.

Surprising men with full bellies and addled by wine was even better.

But it was his turn to be stunned when the hall door flew open and two big-bearded men with wild hair and cold eyes appeared in the aperture, outlined by the smoking torchlight behind them.

The men weren't alone.

They held Isobel and Marjory, dirks pressed hard against the ladies' throats.

Kendrew stared, disbelieving. Somewhere terrible thunder boomed, though in some still sane part of himself, he knew it was only the roar of his own blood in his ears. Chills swept him, hot and cold, his fury boiling and breaking free in a horrible roar so loud even the two men holding his women took a backward step.

Torchlight from a wall sconce fell across Isobel then and he saw a trickle of blood on her neck.

It was then that his world turned red.

The Berserker rage took him.

Bellowing, he charged across the cobbles, swinging Blood Drinker as he ran. To his surprise—or perhaps not—the men holding Isobel and Norn dropped their dirks and fled, racing across the bailey toward the outbuildings clustered against the curtain wall.

A dozen Mackintosh blades stopped them, swords and axes wielded with deadly accuracy until both men lay sprawled on their backs, their blood staining the cobbles as they twitched and jerked in their death throes.

Kendrew scarcely noticed, grabbing both Isobel and

his sister and dragging them away from the open hall door.

"What's the meaning of this?" He pulled them into the lee of a wall near the gatehouse, his voice shaking with rage as he glared at them.

"You're cut." He wiped blood off Isobel's neck with his thumb.

"It's only a scratch." Isobel caught his hand, kissed his fingers. "I'm fine."

Behind them, his warriors fought with the men pouring out of the great hall. Big, wild-eyed men with huge beards and, unlike the two guards who'd run from Kendrew's fury, weren't afraid to face Mackintosh axes.

The ring of steel was loud, the sound of sword and ax blades slicing through mail and flesh, a sickening accompaniment to the clatter of falling weapons. Groans and cut-off cries filled the air as men thrashed on the cobbles, writhing in their final struggle for breath.

"Tell me I'm no' seeing you here." Kendrew scowled at the two women, flashed a quick glance over his shoulder, relieved to see Grim and Talon holding his back. "I can only be having a fearing dream, for no female would be so foolhardy to walk into an ambush."

"You're hurting us." Isobel jerked against his fierce grip, pressing a hand to her breast when he released her. "We weren't afraid, neither of us. We knew you'd—"

"I dinnae matter!" Kendrew roared. "I'd hear why you're not at Nought. Dinnae tell me you followed us?" He struggled against shaking the answer from her, fought harder not to grab her face and kiss her senseless, despite the danger all around them.

Isobel was brazen enough to have trailed him.

Norn was little better.

But he could've wept to know them safe.

"Answer me!" He gripped Isobel's shoulders, fury heating his entire body like a raging flame. "How did you get here? Have your wits left your head?"

"They came thanks to your stable hand, Angar." A deep voice rose from the gloom beyond Grim and Talon. "The price of your ladies' journey here was the promise of any wealth he wished from Duncreag's treasure pit."

"Angar?" Kendrew didn't know any such man. He did whirl to face a huge, thick-bearded man who seemed more amused than concerned that Grim and Talon held spear points at his mail-coated belly.

"I ne'er heard of Angar." Kendrew tossed Blood Drinker from one hand to the other as he approached the other man, clearly a leader. "I would know who you are. I like to ken a man's name before I feed his blood to my ax."

Thick-beard smiled. But it was a cold smile that only emphasized the hard glint in his eyes. "I am Ralla the Victorious, Laird Mackintosh." His voice was smooth, confident. He was clearly unaware that he had only a few moments to live. "You've no need to know my name, because your gods in Asgard already do.

"I've sent many men to Odin's feasting hall." He glanced to where Kendrew's men still fought his own, shrugging when he saw that no Mackintosh had yet fallen. "Perhaps you will be the first of your race to reach Valhalla this night."

"Who is Angar?" Kendrew moved with lightning speed, setting Blood Drinker's blade beneath Ralla's chin.

"He came looking for a new lord some weeks past,

saying he needed work." Norn stood next to Isobel, the two women holding hands. "He was so quiet, I forgot to mention him. Indeed, I'd forgotten him entirely until he appeared in the ladies' solar, branding an ox knife and threatening to cut us if we didn't go with him."

"Where is he now?" Kendrew pressed the ax blade deeper into the soft skin under Ralla's chin. "I'll show him why an ax is better than an ox blade."

Ralla laughed. "No need. He's already dead. After he brought your women here, I told him he could choose his treasure from the Duncreag hoard pit.

"He was surprised to learn that the treasure I'd meant was the MacNabs' moldering bones." Ralla's voice turned cold. "I've no use for a man who'd betray his master."

"And I've no use for you." Kendrew whipped back his arm, bringing Blood Drinker down in a vicious swipe that cleaved Ralla's head in two.

"Dear God," Isobel and Norn gasped as one, turning away as the big-bearded man lurched awkwardly on his feet and then toppled onto the cobbles.

Kendrew felt no such distaste, only the blind fury still roiling inside him. Striding over to his foe—the fiend who'd taken the two women most dear to him in the world—he placed his foot on the corpse, breathing hard.

"Grim! Talon!" He called to his men. "Guard my ladies. We're almost done here." Then, not bothering to clean Blood Drinker's blade, he sprinted across the bailey, eager to plunge into the fighting still going on near the door to Duncreag's hall.

The cobbles already ran red and the air no longer smelled of just the cold, wet night and cook smoke, but now reeked of blood, hot and metallic. The Berserker rage was on Kendrew's warriors and they hacked and chopped like wild men at their opponents, men whose numbers were lessening with each furious drop of an ax blade.

Losing heart as well as blood, the brigands grew clumsy, their feet slipping on the slick cobbles, a few men losing their grip on their swords—then paying with their lives when their weapons slipped from their fingers.

"Fight me, you bastard!" A large man, Kendrew's equal in size, leaped from the shadows, challenging. "I'm Ralla's brother," he snarled, swinging a well-reddened sword. "Let me send you to join him in hell!"

"A pox I will!" Kendrew lunged, cutting down swiftly with Blood Drinker, but the man was quick, whirling aside and taking only a glancing blow to his shoulder.

Kendrew hefted his ax again, grinning now. He appreciated a worthy opponent. "Your name, bastard," he growled, sweeping his ax wide.

Again he missed, Blood Drinker slicing only air. "I'll cut you to ribbons, bit by bit, until you tell me."

"I am Atil." The man spun a feint, whipping round and nicking Kendrew's cheek.

"Your people?" Kendrew ignored the hot blood trickling down his face.

"I have none." Atil sounded proud.

"Then you'll gain plenty in Valhalla." Kendrew lunged again, meaning to send him there.

"I'm not going anywhere." Atil danced around Kendrew, whipping his sword in flashy figure eight circles.

"You're the dead man, and after you, your warriors. Then my lord will give me—" He howled when Kendrew swung Blood Drinker, slicing his sword arm clean through.

"Give you what?" Kendrew waited until the man fell to his knees, clutching his arm stump with his left hand. "Who is your lord?"

But Atil clamped his jaw, glaring defiantly at Kendrew. "A man far greater than you."

"But no' great enough to save you, eh?" Kendrew stepped back, holding Blood Drinker loosely now.

To his surprise, Atil surged to his feet then, his sword gripped in his left hand as he lunged, swinging the blade in a wicked arc aimed at Kendrew's neck.

It was a foolish move.

Kendrew might've let him live otherwise—he valued brave men.

As things were...

"Greet Odin!" Kendrew let Blood Drinker sing, whipping the ax with such speed and force that its long, curving blade sliced through Atil's ribs, nearly lodging in his spine.

But Kendrew yanked the blade free with even greater speed than he'd given the killing blow, and dropping to one knee as Atil fell, he grabbed the man's left hand, clutching his dying fingers around Blood Drinker's haft. "Live well, brave Atil, in the mead halls of Valhalla."

Ignoring his men, who must've finished off the remaining brigands, for they now stood circling him, looking on as he knelt beside Atil, Kendrew waited until the last breath rattled from Atil's throat.

Then he peeled the dead man's fingers from Blood Drinker and jumped to his feet, looking round for the only person who truly mattered to him...

Isobel.

But she was gone again.

Norn stood shivering against the curtain wall, clutching one of his men's wolf pelts around her shoulders. Pushing past his men, Kendrew strode over to her. "Where is Isobel?" He roared the words, rage beginning to pump through him again. "Dinnae tell me—"

"She's there"—Norn lifted her chin, fixing him with the same cool stare she used on him at Nought when she meant to vex him—"with old Archie MacNab and a slave girl, taken by Ralla and his war band."

Kendrew blinked. "MacNab's here?"

Turning, Kendrew saw them now. Isobel, flanked by Grim and Talon, the old MacNab chief, looking more frail and gray than Kendrew remembered him. And a slender wisp of a flame-haired girl, dressed in tatters, and—like Norn and Isobel—clutching a peat-blackened wolf pelt around her shoulders. They made a motley sight.

And Kendrew had never seen anything more beautiful.

Nor had he ever lost anything so dear as the raven-haired woman standing so still on the entry steps of Duncreag's great hall.

Except that wasn't quite true.

Once, he had lost someone who meant the world and more to him. And now, after this night, he was more determined than ever that he'd never lose anything so precious again. He certainly wasn't going to lose his bride.

He might lose his face when he told her so.

But that scarce mattered.

What did was getting her out of the cold wind and rain. Somehow—he hadn't even noticed—the heavens had split wide and rain now poured down in rivers, already washing clean men and the bloodstained cobbles.

Wind howled, lashing at Duncreag's walls, while above them, lightning streaked across the heavens, the thunder deafening.

They couldn't leave in such a storm.

But he could get Isobel inside Duncreag, keep her warm, tend the nick to her neck, and—if she'd still have him—hold her in his arms the whole night through.

"MacNab!" Kendrew started forward, sprinting across the courtyard, knowing the cantankerous old chief would accept only gruff respect. "I'd beg lodgings this night for my men and"—he reached the hall's entry, ducking under its sheltering arch—"for my soon-to-be bride and myself, if you've room to spare for us?"

"That I do, boy!" Archie stood straighter, lifting his grizzled chin. "You and your lady shall have my best quarters. If"—he blinked, for a moment, looking shamed—"thon hell-bred brigands you've rid me of haven't left the room in too great a ruin."

"I'll see to the chamber." The red-haired girl stepped forward, her voice revealing her to be Irish. "It's the least I can do." She glanced at Isobel and Norn, smiling warmly. "I know who you are from your lady and your sister. They spoke so highly of you. They gave us such hope, promising that you'd come and rescue us all."

"Is that so?" Kendrew lifted a brow.

"Of course it is." Isobel went to him, slipping her arm through his, heedless of the rain and the blood soiling him. "Could anyone who knows you ever doubt you? I even told Breena"—she glanced at the Irish girl—"that you'd arrange for Alasdair MacDonald to take her on one of his ships back to Ireland. But she—"

"Aye, to be sure." Kendrew turned to the girl.

"MacDonald isn't fond of me, but I doubt I'd have a problem persuading him to see you home."

"Thank you." The girl bobbed a curtsy, but her gaze was troubled when she glanced at old Archie.

"You don't understand, my heart." Isobel squeezed Kendrew's arm. "Breena no longer has any family in Ireland. Ralla and his men sacked her village, burning everything and killing all but the few villagers they sold into slavery."

Kendrew frowned, fiercely. "Then she shall come to us at Nought." He looked back at the girl, nodding as if it were settled. "You'll be welcome there, lass. Ne'er you fash yourself."

"Kendrew..." Isobel nudged him, nodding her own head in the old chief's direction.

Archie MacNab seemed to have shrunk. His bony shoulders sagged and his rheumy eyes glistened a bit too brightly. He started shuffling his feet, his bristly chin lowering as he avoided gazes.

"He's become like a grandfather to the girl, see you?" Isobel drew Kendrew away from the others, speaking low. And finally, she saw the comprehension dawn on Kendrew's face. At last, he recognized that with Archie having lost his sons and everyone else at Duncreag, and Breena seeing her village left a ruin, the old man and the young girl had no one else to call their own.

"I've a better idea, MacNab." Kendrew let his voice boom, speaking as loudly as Isobel had just whispered. "With so much room here these days and"—he smiled at Breena—"a fine and able lassie to run your household, I'm wondering if you'd do me a favor, what?"

"To be sure!" The old man stood tall again. "What are you in need of, laddie?"

"Och, no' much." Kendrew slid his arm around Isobel, drawing her near. "I could use some extra grazing land on your high moors in summer. And"—he glanced at his men, his gaze lighting on the ones he knew to be married with sons—"I'd appreciate it if you could take on some fine, eager Mackintosh lads as squires?

"I'd send along a garrison to help with their training. And"—he sounded pleased, as if the decision was his reason for coming here—"you'd be helping me, because Nought is about out of space for brawling young boys."

Archie MacNab swallowed, the brightness in his eyes brimming over. "I'd be honored, Mackintosh. And you couldn't have a better fostering home for the lads than Duncreag. Truth is"—his chest puffed a bit—"I was once quite a fine fighting man myself."

"Then it's done." Kendrew nodded solemnly.

It was all he could do to keep his lips from twitching.

Archie MacNab could hardly handle a meat knife, as everyone for miles around knew.

But he wasn't about to remind the old goat.

He did need to settle matters with Isobel.

And while he was most pleased to help MacNab, even enjoying the way the old chief now strutted about his hall, making plans, Kendrew's reputation stood to be tarnished if he played the gallant too long.

He rather liked being known as a howling madman.

So he put back his shoulders, set a grin on his face, and grabbed Isobel, sweeping her up in his arms. "I need some words with my lady." Again, he let his voice boom, wanting all present to hear him. "We'll see you at the high table anon"—he flashed a look at Archie—"or, perhaps no' at all this night, depending on my lady."

"Kendrew!" Isobel felt her face flame.

"That's me, aye." Proud of it, he marched straight down the center aisle of Archie MacNab's great hall, making for the tower stairs.

"Where are you taking me?" Isobel squirmed in his arms, laughter and joy bubbling up inside her because—as she'd always known—she loved Kendrew's wildness and wouldn't want him any other way.

"Everyone is staring after us." Propriety made her offer a protest.

"Let them." Kendrew laughed and only clutched her tighter against his chest as they reached the torchlit arch of the stair tower.

He took the stairs two at a time, climbing the winding stone steps swiftly. "We're up to the battlements, lass, a place where we'll be high enough to see the peaks of Nought when I ask you what I must."

"But it's storming." Isobel didn't care about the booming thunder, but she did worry a bit about lightning.

"We'll no' step out of the stair tower." Kendrew set her down when they reached the top landing and threw open the door. "We can see Nought from here."

He pointed. "Look there, to the north."

Isobel did, at once seeing Nought's proud peaks through the rain and mist, the highest crests shining silver-white with each burst of lightning. Icy wind streaked across the ramparts, howling and blowing sheets of stinging, pelting rain, already beginning to drench them.

It was a storm the likes of which probably hadn't been seen in these hills for centuries.

Isobel shivered, sure she'd never seen anything so magnificent.

Except, perhaps, Nought's master.

"What did you want to ask me?" She turned to him now, circling her arms around him, leaning into his warmth. "You already know how Norn and I—dear saints, look!"

But Kendrew was lowering his head, about to kiss her. "No' just yet, lady. One kiss, and then—"

"No, *look*!" Isobel broke free and ran to the far corner of the wall-walk, clutching a rain-soaked merlon. "There, high above those pines"—she pointed to a stony ledge near the top of a neighboring hill—"I swear there's a mailed spearman standing there. A man, and—nae, it can't be…"

She leaned out across the merlon to see better, one hand pressed, disbelieving, to her face. "It's a dreagan, come look! And he's huge, standing right beside the spearman. I vow I do see them. They're near what appears to be the narrow entrance of a cave."

"You see rain and mist." Kendrew joined her, wrapping an arm around her waist. "There's nothing there but—sons o' Valkyries!"

Kendrew's jaw dropped, his eyes rounding as he, too, stared at the sight before them.

A tall, hard-faced warrior stood proud, his mail coat and great plumed helm brighter than the sun. He held a long spear in one hand and rested the other on the flank of a huge, stony-scaled beast with large kindly eyes that glowed red. Glittering blue puffs of smoke rose from the beast's nostrils, and when he glanced down at the warrior beside him, Isobel was sure she'd never seen such adoration.

The warrior smiled, too, the warmth in his eyes transforming his hard features into a handsome, roguish face.

Then he raised his spear high above his head, pointing its tip to the north.

"Live well, my friends. May peace and gladness be yours, all your days." The words came on the wind, a whisper, and then they were gone.

The warrior and the dreagan were also no more, vanished into the mist of fable where, perhaps, they'd always been.

But this night, for a sliver of a second, they'd come to show themselves.

And to bless the union that Isobel always knew was so perfect.

"Oh, God..." Isobel dashed at her eyes, hot tears blinding her. She turned to Kendrew, reaching up to frame his face, certain that the wetness on his cheeks was just as hot as hers. "Did you see them?"

"See what, lady?" He lifted a brow, surely feigning ignorance.

"The shining spearman and his dreagan." Isobel twisted round, glancing back at the now-empty ledge. "They were there, you had to have seen them."

"I saw only rain and mist." Kendrew remained stubborn.

But the sheen in his eyes and the catch in his throat gave him away.

Someday, perhaps when they, too, were as old as Archie MacNab, she'd wheedle the truth out of him. For now, she'd let it be.

Clearing her throat, she rested her hands on his shoulders and looked up at him, the love in his eyes almost splitting her heart.

That, at least, he wasn't hiding from her.

"What did you want to ask me up here?" She couldn't believe her voice was steady.

So much depended on this night, what would happen on the morrow.

"Only this, my lady"—he tilted her chin up and kissed her softly—"from this vantage point you can see Nought to the north and Haven to the east. I would know..."

He kissed her again, more deeply this time.

"Tell me true," he said, when he released her, "which direction you'd have me take you when we leave here in the morning. Home to Haven or—"

"You can't be serious." Isobel threw her arms around his neck, clinging to him. "There is only one way I wish to go, as you should know well."

"I'd hear the words all the same." He looked down at her, his eyes suddenly just a bit vulnerable.

"Oh, Kendrew. I love you so." She leaned into him, kissing him this time.

When she pulled back at last, her eyes were burning again. And this time, she didn't bother to dash away her tears. They were happy tears, after all. Ones she'd waited so very long to shed.

So she lifted up on her toes and nipped Kendrew's ear, telling him what he needed to hear.

"I want to go home to Nought." Gladness swept her as soon as the words left her lips. "There, with you, and nowhere else for all our days."

To her surprise, Kendrew threw back his head and whooped.

Then he grabbed her up into his arms and whirled her around and around. When they stopped, he pulled her to him again and kissed her long and hard.

"Home to Nought we shall go then." He grinned and shook the rain from his hair.

Then he winked and said four little words she'd once begged him to say for her.

"So mote it be."

Epilogue

❧

THE GLEN OF MANY LEGENDS
AT THE DREAGAN STONES
AUTUMN 1397

*O*nly my brother would wear mail and carry his ax at his wedding revels."

Marjory glanced to where Kendrew spoke with James and Alasdair near the well-laden feasting tables. Catriona sat on a nearby stool, her cloak drawn against the wind, her hands folded atop her swollen belly.

"You'd think he still expects marauders to leap from behind an outcrop." Marjory narrowed her eyes at her brother. "He boasts often enough of ridding the glen of Ralla and his war band, yet…"

"He isn't worried about brigands." Isobel didn't say what she suspected. She did follow her friend's gaze, her pulse quickening to see her new husband so gloriously arrayed in full warring armor. He'd even thrown his bear-skin over his shoulders, wearing the cloak proudly.

It was a badge of his Berserker lineage.

Just like the golden Thor's hammer at his throat and the many silver-and-gold rings lining his arms. His mail shirt and Blood Drinker's curving, long-bearded blade shone bright in the afternoon's cold sunlight.

He dazzled her.

As he'd done ever since he'd marched so boldly onto the field at the trial by combat, his great Norse ax in his hand, grinning roguishly as if he welcomed the fierce fighting about to commence.

Isobel's heart swelled looking at him.

Truth was, he'd always dazzle her.

She told him so often, unable to resist his flashing smile and boyish pleasure each time she praised him. He didn't need to impress her. So she suspected he'd had other reasons for coming to their wedding feast armed like a returning conqueror awaiting accolades.

"He's hoping Alasdair or James will give him cause to fight." Marjory put Isobel's suspicion to words.

"He wouldn't dare." Isobel knew he would. "Not this day."

"He'd relish nothing more." Marjory sounded sure. "He'd especially enjoy bloodying his hands on Alasdair. Did you hear how he growled his greeting when the Mac-Donalds arrived?

"I'm surprised swords weren't drawn then." Marjory's gaze flickered to Alasdair, worry creasing her brow. "Alasdair would surely have left if he didn't wish to offend you."

"He stayed because of you, my dear." Isobel smiled when her friend's cheeks bloomed pink. "He might be keeping his distance, but his eyes haven't left you since he arrived."

"If that is so, Kendrew will make trouble." Marjory glanced at her little dog, Hercules, tucked comfortably into her arm. He returned the look, sagely. "You see"— she stroked his tufted head—"even Hercules knows Kendrew will do as he pleases.

"He won't challenge Alasdair or James." She kept petting Hercules. "He'll provoke them into picking a fight. He's that clever, my brother."

Isobel couldn't deny it.

There was reason for concern. The enmity between the three chieftains hadn't wholly vanished, though each warrior tolerated the others. James and Alasdair had even grown friendly, to a degree.

And they'd all agreed to stay in convivial spirits throughout the day's celebrations. No heated words were to fall, or even to be implied. No bloodletting of any kind.

Isobel, Marjory, and Catriona had insisted, using what influence they could.

So far it was working.

Nothing marred the fine, crisp day. A brisk wind blew in from the west and not a single cloud broke the brilliant blue of the afternoon sky. Nought's soaring granite peaks sparkled in the sunlight, while autumn-red bracken shone like jewels on the moors. Yellow and gold leaves skittered along the rocky ground, adding whimsy. And the air was fresh and clean, smelling of woodsmoke and, as always at Nought, the heady tang of cold, damp stone.

The Glen of Many Legends was smiling.

It was just a shame that Marjory was not.

"You are too hard on him." Isobel softened words that might sound traitorous by gently tucking a strand of Marjory's hair behind her ear. "Kendrew only desired to show his rivals a bit of bluster. This is his day, after all. You weren't in the hall early this morn when he spoke to his younger warriors.

"He paced back and forth in front of them, warning them how to behave at the wedding feast." Isobel smiled, remembering. Kendrew hadn't known she stood in the shadows, watching. "He cautioned them not to get too ale-headed, not to quarrel, and to be gallant to visiting womenfolk, dancing with and complimenting them all."

"He would forget every word if Alasdair claimed me for one dance." Marjory drew a breath, her gaze once again on Alasdair.

"So he would, yes." Catriona joined them, slowly lowering herself onto a large, flat-topped boulder at the base of a cairn. "He's taunting my brother, Alasdair, with his plans to see you wed to a Norse nobleman.

"He claims"—Catriona glanced between Isobel and Marjory, and then at the three warriors—"he's already heard from several keen to wed you."

"Pah!" Isobel dismissed the possibility.

It was true, sadly.

But now wasn't the day to spoil Marjory's enjoyment of Alasdair's company, however sparse any contact between them proved.

"I've heard nothing about a Viking husband for Norn." Isobel set a hand on Catriona's shoulder, squeezing lightly to warn her not to disagree.

"I will not wed such a man if he finds one." Norn set down Hercules, brushing her skirts in place when she straightened. "I've waited long to fulfill my part of our pact." Her voice was strong, unwavering. "You both know—Alasdair and I have feelings for each other. I'll not allow Kendrew to ruin my chance at happiness."

"We won't either." Isobel knew she spoke as well for Catriona.

When Catriona nodded, her gaze dipping to Isobel's ambers, Isobel understood her friend's message.

Agreeing, she reached to remove the precious necklace, fastening them as swiftly around Marjory's neck. "You must wear these ambers now, dear friend. And"— she gripped Marjory's upper arms and kissed her on both cheeks—"you must see them returned to Blackshore Castle, their true home."

"But..." Marjory curled her fingers around the stones, her lovely blue eyes glistening. "If Kendrew sees me wearing them, he'll grow suspicious."

"He'll do no such thing." Isobel had ways of distracting him. "If he says anything, we shall tell him—"

"Tell me what?" Kendrew spoke from the end of the cairn. He leaned back against the stones, his arms folded, his gaze locked on Isobel.

"Why..." She completely forgot what she'd been about to say.

Kendrew did that to her.

Especially looking as he did this day, the sun and firelight making his mail glitter. The heat in his eyes stirred a thrilling response deep inside her. And—her heart fluttered—especially to see him so magnificent here in the vale of the dreagans where their story had begun.

She turned to her friends, hoping they'd help her wriggle out of an awkward situation, but Marjory and Catriona were gone. They were moving swiftly across the stony ground, making for the feasting tables. Catriona had her hand tucked securely into Marjory's arm. Little Hercules trotted in their wake, his head and tail held high, his gait jaunty, as if he was part of a conspiracy.

Which, of course, he was, as her friends had plainly deserted her.

So she did what anyone would do in such a position and stood straighter, putting back her shoulders. She also lifted her chin, letting her eyes snap.

Only then did she trust herself to face Kendrew.

"How long have you been standing there?" She tried for indignation.

"Long enough for my ears to ring." He gave her one of his crooked smiles.

It was the same roguish smile that melted her at the Midsummer Eve revels.

"I..." Isobel felt her knees weaken, images and memories whirling across her mind.

"Is aught amiss?" The smolder in his eyes showed he knew what ailed her. The way his gaze roamed over her revealed that he was also recalling all that had happened here, in the shadow of these stones.

"Can it be"—he pushed away from the side of the cairn and strolled toward her, setting both hands on her shoulders as he looked down at her—"that you are no longer wearing your ambers?"

Isobel lifted a hand to her bare neck, guilt sluicing her. "I gave them to your sister. She has a greater need for them than I do now."

That was true.

"She needs them?" Kendrew arched a brow.

Isobel nodded vigorously. "I've told you the ambers are enchanted. They warn of danger and—"

"I've dealt with any threats hereabouts." Kendrew leaned down and kissed her, long, slowly, and thoroughly. "No woman in this glen need close her eyes in fear at night. No trespasser would dare set foot here again. Word has spread—they'll know the welcome they'd reap."

He swept his arms around her, lowering his head to nuzzle her neck.

Isobel leaned into him, delicious tingles rippling across her nerves when he nipped her ear.

"I gave Marjory the ambers because I felt sorry for her." She did, but not in the way she was leading Kendrew to believe. "I thought they'd take her mind off watching her two best friends wed while she is still a maid."

Kendrew straightened, looking fierce for a moment. "She'll marry soon enough."

Isobel hoped so fervently—to the man Marjory loved, Alasdair MacDonald.

If the fates were kind, the MacDonald ambers would protect her, signaling if a Norse betrothal should indeed loom on the horizon.

Such a help wasn't much, but it was better than nothing.

The three women could then prepare their defenses, readying for the next battle.

Until then...

Isobel slid her arms around Kendrew's neck and lifted up on her toes to kiss him deeply. When she pulled back, she glanced at the huge cairn behind them. "This place feels blessed now, at peace."

"So it is, my lady." Kendrew scooped her up in his arms and started walking down the side of Slag's Mound, following the same path into the shadows as he'd taken the night of the revels. "Nought has a fine new mistress who loves every lichened stone and each blast of cold, racing wind."

"Perhaps Slag and his master are at rest now?" Isobel reached to trail her fingers along the cairn's stones. "I'm sure it was them we saw that night from Duncreag's battlements. They were on a ledge in the storm. Do you remember?"

Kendrew glanced at her. "I remember you pointing at rain and mist."

"You're just being stubborn." Isobel knew that was true.

"And you dinnae ken the first law of a good legend." His voice held a teasing note. "If you spoil the riddle, the tale is a legend no more."

"That's not an answer," Isobel protested.

"It wasn't meant to be." He pressed a kiss to her brow.

Before she could argue, he carried her around a red-berried rowan tree and then set her down. They'd entered a dense thicket, shielded by a jutting outcrop. Two plaids, Mackintosh and Cameron, covered the ground. And a wicker creel of feasting goods rested near a clutch of heather. A wine jug peeked out of the grass beside the plaids, while several tasseled cushions indicated why Kendrew had brought her here.

"This day we make our own legends." He was already throwing off his bearskin cloak, his flashing smile encouraging her to reach for her bodice laces.

He slanted a glance at the plaids, tossed his cloak onto the heather. "A meet celebration, what?"

"Oh, yes." Isobel stepped out of her gown, the cold wind chilling her skin. Her heart began to pound, her pulse racing.

"I started loving you here, Isobel." He pulled her hard against him, tangling his fingers in her hair as he looked down at her. "You stole my heart the night of the revels. Now I'll never let you go. You are mine forever. Woe be the man who even dares to glance at you."

His words thrilled her.

"And you didn't want a lady." She couldn't help but tease him.

"I didn't, it is true." He gripped her face with both hands and kissed her soundly.

When he released her, Isobel saw so much love in his eyes that her heart almost burst with happiness. "I'm so glad I persuaded you—"

"You tempted me, lass." He kissed her again. "I couldn't resist you."

Isobel refrained from telling him that it was *she* who hadn't been able to resist him.

Men didn't need to know everything.

So she melted into him and gloried in his kisses as he lowered her to the bed of plaids. Then, as their guests drank mead and made merry, and clean, cold wind swept the dreagan vale, Kendrew kept his word...

New legends were born that day, in a wondrous place that already held so many.

And somewhere in a distant world beyond man's hearing, the dreagans rumbled approval.

"The Devil" of the Highlands
knows no weakness—until
a flame-haired beauty
tempts him to abandon
his loyalties.

Please turn this page
for a preview of

Sins of a Highland Devil

The first book in the Highland
Warriors trilogy

The Legacy of the Glen

❖

Deep in the Scottish Highlands, three clans share the Glen of Many Legends. None of them do so gladly. Each clan believes they have sole claim to the fair and fertile vale. Their possessiveness is understandable, because the glen truly is a place like no other. Bards throughout the land will confirm that the Glen of Many Legends is just that: an enchanted place older than time and steeped with more tales and myth than most men can recall.

Kissed by sea and wind, the vale is long and narrow, its shores wild and serrated. Deeply wooded hills edge the glen's heart, while softly blowing mists cloak the lofty peaks that crowd together at its end. Oddly-shaped stones dot the lush grass, but the strangeness of the ancient rocks is countered by the heather and whin that bloom so profusely from every patch of black, peaty earth.

No one would deny the glen's beauty.

Yet to some, the Glen of Many Legends is a place of ill fame to be avoided at all costs, especially by the dark of the moon. Strange things have been known to happen there, and wise men tread cautiously when they must pass that way.

But the MacDonalds, Camerons, and Mackintoshes who dwell there appreciate the glen's virtues above frightening tales that may or may not have credence. Good Highlanders all, the clans know that any storyteller of skill is adept at embroidering his yarns.

Highlanders are also a proud and stubborn people. And they're known for their fierce attachment to the land. These traits blaze hotly in the veins of the three clans of the Glen of Many Legends. Over time, their endless struggles to vanquish each other have drenched the glen with blood and sorrow.

Peace in the glen is fragile and rare.

Most times it doesn't exist at all. Yet somehow the clans tolerate each other, however grudgingly.

Now the precarious balance of order is about to be thrown into dispute by the death of a single woman.

A MacDonald by birth, and hereditary heiress to the MacDonalds of the Glen of Many Legends, she was a twice-widowed woman who chose to live out her days in the serenity and solitude of a nunnery.

Sadly, she neglected to set down her last wishes in a will. This oversight would not be so dire if not for the disturbing truths that her first husband had been a Cameron and her second, a Mackintosh.

On her passing, each clan lays claim to the dead woman.

Or, it can be more aptly said, they insist on being her rightful heirs.

Soon land-greed and coveting will once again turn

the glen's sweet grass into a sea of running red and many good men will lose their lives. But even when the last clansman sinks to his knees, his sword sullied and the end near, the real battle is only just beginning.

When it is done, the Glen of Many Legends will be forever changed.

As will the hearts of those who dwell there.

Chapter One

❧

BLACKSHORE CASTLE

THE GLEN OF MANY LEGENDS

AUTUMN 1396

A battle to the death?"

Alasdair MacDonald's deep voice rose to the smoke-blackened rafters of his great hall. Across that crowded space, his sister, Lady Catriona, stood frozen on the threshold. Alasdair's harsh tone held her there, but she did lift a hand to the amber necklace at her throat. A clan heirloom believed to protect and aid MacDonalds, the precious stones warmed beneath her fingers. She fancied they also hummed, though it was difficult to tell with her brother's roar shaking the walls. Other kinsmen were also shouting, but it was Alasdair's fury that echoed in her ears.

His ranting hit her like a physical blow.

Her brother was a man whose clear blue eyes always held a spark of humor. And his laughter, so rich and catching, could brighten the darkest winter night, warming the hearts and spirits of everyone around him.

Just now he paced in the middle of his hall, his handsome face twisted in rage. His shoulder-length auburn hair—always his pride—was untidy, looking wildly mussed, as if he'd repeatedly thrust angry fingers through the finely burnished mane.

"Sakes! This is no gesture of goodwill." His voice hardened, thrumming with barely restrained aggression. "Whole clans cut down. Good men murdered and for naught, as I and my folk see it!"

Everywhere, MacDonalds grumbled and scowled.

Some shook fists in the air, others rattled swords. At least two spat on the rush-strewn floor, and a few had such fire in their eyes it was almost a wonder that the air didn't catch flame.

Only one man stood unaffected.

A stranger, Catriona saw him now because one of her cousins moved and torchlight caught and shone on the man's heavily-bejeweled sword belt.

She stared at the newcomer, not caring if her jaw slipped. She did step deeper into the hall's arched entry, though her knees shook badly. She also forgot to shut the heavy oaken door she'd just opened wide. Cold, damp wind blew past her, whipping her hair and gutting candles on a nearby table. A few wall torches hissed and spat, spewing ashes at her, but she hardly noticed.

What was a bit of soot on her skirts when the quiet peace of Blackshore had turned to chaos?

When Alasdair spoke of war?

As chief to their clan, he wasn't a man to use such words lightly. And even if he were, the flush on his face and the fierce set of his jaw revealed that something dire had happened. The stranger—a Lowland noble by his finery—didn't bode well either.

Men of his ilk never came to Blackshore.

The man's haughty stance showed that he wasn't pleased to be here now. And unlike her brother, he'd turned and was looking right at her. His gaze flicked over her, and then he lifted one brow, almost imperceptibly.

His opinion of her was palpable.

The insolence in that slightly arched brow, a galling affront.

Annoyance stopped the knocking of her knees, and she could feel her blood heating, the hot color sweeping up her neck to scald her cheeks.

The man looked amused.

Catriona was sure she'd seen his lips twitch.

Bristling, she pulled off her mud-splattered cloak and tossed it on a trestle bench. She took some satisfaction in seeing the visitor's eyes widen and then narrow critically when he saw that the lower half of her gown was as wet and soiled as her mantle. She had, after all, just run across the narrow stone causeway that connected her clan's isle-girt castle with the loch shore.

She'd raced to beat the tide. But even hurrying as she had, the swift-moving current was faster. She'd been forced to hitch up her skirts and splash through the swirling water, reaching the castle gates just before the causeway slipped beneath the rising sea loch.

It was a mad dash that always exhilarated her. As she did every day, she'd burst into the hall, laughing and with her hair in a wild tangle from the wind. Now she might look a fright, but her elation was gone.

"What's happened?" She hurried forward to clutch Alasdair's arm, dread churning in her belly. "What's this about clans being cut down? A battle—"

"Not a true battle." Alasdair shot a glance at the Lowlander. "A trial by combat—"

"I see no difference." She raised her chin, not wanting the stranger to see her worry. It was clear he'd brought this madness. That showed in the curl of his lip, a half-sneer that revealed his disdain for Highlanders.

Alasdair noticed, too. She hadn't missed the muscle jerking in his jaw.

She tightened her grip on him. "If men are to die, what matters the name you cast on their blood?"

Behind her, someone closed the hall door. And somewhere in the smoke-hazed shadows, one of her kinsmen snarled a particularly vile curse. Catriona released her brother's arm and reached again for her amber necklace. She twirled its length around her fingers, clutching the polished gems as if they might answer her. Her own special talisman, the ambers often comforted her.

Now they didn't.

Worse, everyone was staring at her. The Lowlander eyed her as if she were the devil's own spawn. He surely saw her fiery-red hair as the brand of a witch. Almost wishing she was—just so she could fire-blast him—she straightened her back and let her eyes blaze. MacDonald pride beat through her, giving her strength and courage.

She turned to Alasdair. "You needn't tell me this has to do with the Camerons or the Mackintoshes. I can smell their taint in the air."

A Scottish warrior chieftain
faces the battle of his life
when he falls for a Viking's
promised bride.

Please turn this page
for a preview of

*Seduction of a Highland
Warrior*

The final book in the Highland
Warriors trilogy

The Honor of Clan Donald

❖

In the beginning of days, before Highland warriors walked heather-clad hills and gazed in awe across moors chased by cloud-shadows, old gods ruled the dark and misty realm that would one day be known as Scotland. Glens were silent then, empty but for the whistle of the wind and the curl of waves on sparkling sea-lochs.

Yet if a man looked and listened with his heart rather than his eyes and ears, he might catch a glimpse of wonders beyond telling.

For Manannan Mac Lir, mighty god of sea and wind, loved these rugged Scottish shores. Those who haven't forgotten legend will swear that stormy days saw Manannan plying Highland waters in his magical galley, *Wave Sweeper*. And that on nights when the full moon shone bright, he favored riding the edge of the sea on his enchanted horse, Embarr of the Flowing Mane. All tales claimed that wherever he was, Manannan never lost sight of Scotland's cliff-fretted coast. One stretch of shoreline was said to hold his especial attention: a place of such splendor even his jaded heart swelled to behold its wild and haunting beauty.

That place was the Glen of Many Legends.

Storytellers agree that when the day came that Manannan observed a proud and noble MacDonald warrior stride into this fair land of heather, rock, and silvery seas, he was most pleased.

Those were distant times, but even then the men of Clan Donald were gaining a reputation as men of fierce loyalty and unbending honor.

They were the best of all Highlanders.

Even the gods stood in awe of them.

So Manannan's pleasure grew when this MacDonald warrior, an early chieftain known as Drangar the Strong, chose this blessed spot to build a fine isle-girt fortress. Here, Drangar the Strong would guard the coast with his trustworthy and fearless garrison. And—the talespinners again agreed—the great god of sea and wind surely believed Clan Donald would blossom and thrive, gifting the Glen of Many Legends with generations of braw Highland warriors and beautiful, spirited women.

The world was good.

Until the ill-fated day when Drangar the Strong took a moonlit walk along the night-silvered shore of his sea-loch and happened across a lovely Selkie maid who no red-blooded man could've resisted.

Her dark hair gleamed like moonlight on water and her eyes shone like the stars. Her lips were seductively curved and ripe for kissing. And her shapely form beckoned, all smooth, creamy skin and tempting shadows.

MacDonalds, it must now be said, are as well lusted as their hearts are loyal and true.

Drangar fell hard, succumbing to the seal woman's charms there and then.

But such passion flared hotly only for a beat, at least for the woman-of-the-sea, who soon suffered unbearable longing to return to her watery home.

Nor is any Highlander unaware of the tragedies that so often befall these enchanting creatures and the mortal men who lose their hearts to them. Such tales abound along Scotland's coasts and throughout the Western Isles, with every clan bard able to sing of the heartbreak and danger, the ills that can break good men.

Or, perhaps worst of all, the tears of children born to such unions.

Drangar could not allow such sorrow to visit his people.

Nor did he wish to see his seductress in sorrow, for he did indeed love her.

So he did as all good MacDonalds would do and followed his honor.

Rather than carry her into his castle and make her his bride, he took her shining sealskin from the rock where she'd discarded it, and returning the skin to her, he'd stood by as she vanished into the sea.

Then—the bards pause here for effect—before the waves settled, Manannan himself rose from the spume-crested depths and made Drangar a great gift of thanks for his farsightedness and his honor.

The gift was an iron-bound treasure chest heavy with priceless amber.

These were enchanted gemstones that, according to legend, would bring Clan Donald fortune and blessings, aiding them always in times of trouble.

But life in the Highlands was never easy.

And even magical stones can't always allay feuds, strife, and the perfidy of men.

Years passed and then centuries. Times were good and then also bad. Bards embroidered Manannan's fame and nearly forgot the role of the seal woman in explaining Clan Donald's chest of ambers. Soon other tales were added, until no man knew what was real or storied.

Then the day came when even Drangar the Strong slipped into the murk of legend.

Worse fates followed, and the MacDonalds' once-mighty fortress was torn from their grasp.

But the clan never lost its honor.

Centuries later they even regained their home.

Now a new Clan Donald chieftain rules there. Alasdair MacDonald is his name, and he's a man of such valor and integrity that Drangar's heart would've burst with pride if he could have known him.

To Alasdair, honor is everything.

Yet he lives in troublesome times. And although his beloved glen is quiet, the truce that keeps it so is fragile. Two other clans now share the Glen of Many Legends, and while one can be called an ally, the other remains hostile. Many would credit Alasdair's patience and authority that, so far, disaster hasn't struck.

Those less generous would say the strength of his sword arm is responsible.

Whatever one believes, he is a man well respected.

Unfortunately, ill winds are blowing ever closer to the fair glen, once so loved by Manannan and Drangar.

Alasdair's passion for the glen is equally great.

But soon his love for a woman will challenge him to abandon everything he holds dear.

When he does, he will lose more than his honor.

His actions will unleash a calamity worse than the Glen of Many Legends has ever seen.

And every man, woman, and child there will be marked for doom.

THE DISH

Where authors give you the inside scoop!

♥ ♥ ♥ ♥ ♥ ♥ ♥ ♥ ♥ ♥ ♥ ♥ ♥ ♥ ♥ ♥

From the desk of Caridad Piñeiro

Dear Readers,

I want to thank all of you who have been writing to tell me how much you've been loving the Carrera family, as well as enjoying the towns along the Jersey Shore where the series is set.

With THE LOST, I'm introducing a much darker paranormal series I'm calling *Sin Hunters*. The stories are still set along the Jersey Shore and you'll have the beloved Carreras, but now you'll also get to meet an exciting new race of people: The Light and Shadow Hunters.

Why the change? There was something about Bobbie Carrera, the heroine in THE LOST, that needed something different and something very special. Someone very special. Bobbie is an Iraq war veteran and she's home from battle, but wounded both physically and emotionally. She's busy trying to put her world back together and the last thing she needs is more conflict in her life.

But I'm a bad girl, you know. I love to challenge my characters into facing their most extreme hurts because doing so only makes their happiness that much sweeter. I think readers love that as well because there is nothing more uplifting than seeing how love can truly conquer all.

Bobbie's challenge comes in the form of sexy millionaire Adam Bruno. Adam is different from any man she has ever met and Bobbie feels an immediate connection to him. There's just one problem: Adam has no idea who he really is and why he possesses the ability to gather energy.

That ability allows him to do myriad things; from shape-shifting to traveling at super speed, to wielding energy and light like weapons. But these powers are challenging for Adam: as his abilities grow stronger, they also become deadly and increasingly difficult to control.

Enter Bobbie Carrera. Bobbie brings peace to Adam's soul. Adam feels lost in the human world, but in Bobbie's arms he finds love, acceptance, and the possibility for a future he had never imagined.

But before he can reach that future, he must deal with the present, and that means battling the evil Shadow Hunters and facing the shocking truth about his real identity.

I hope you will enjoy the Sin Hunters series. Look for THE CLAIMED in May 2012, which will feature someone you meet in THE LOST. Not going to spill who it is just yet, but keep in mind I just love stories of redemption. . . .

Thank you all for your continued support. Also, many thanks to our military men and women, and their families for safeguarding our liberty and our country. THE LOST is dedicated to you for all the sacrifices you make on our behalf. God bless you and keep you safe.

♥ ♥ ♥ ♥ ♥ ♥ ♥ ♥ ♥ ♥ ♥ ♥ ♥ ♥ ♥ ♥

From the desk of Jennifer Haymore

Dear Reader,

When Serena Donovan, the heroine of CONFESSIONS OF AN IMPROPER BRIDE (on sale now), entered my office to ask me to write her story, I realized right away that

I was in trouble. Obviously, there was something pretty heavy resting on this woman's shoulders.

After I'd offered her a chair and a stiff drink (which she eyed warily—as if she's never seen a martini before!), I asked her why she had come.

"I have a problem," she said.

I tried not to chuckle. It was obvious from the permanent look of panic in her eyes that she had a very big problem indeed. "Okay," I said, "what's the problem?"

"Well—" She swallowed hard. "I'm going to get married."

I raised a brow. "Usually that's reason for celebration."

"Not for me." Her voice was dour.

I took a deep breath. "Look, Miss Donovan. I'm a romance writer. I write about love, blissful marriages, and happy endings. Maybe you've come to the wrong place." I rose from my chair and gestured toward the door. "Thanks for stopping by. Feel free to take the martini."

Her eyes flared wide with alarm. "No! Please . . . let me explain."

I hesitated, staring down at her. She seemed so . . . desperate. I guess I have a bleeding heart after all. Sighing, I resumed my seat. "Go ahead."

"I do respect and admire my future husband. Greatly. He's a wonderful man."

"Uh-huh."

"But, you see, he—" She winced, swallowed, and took a deep breath. "Well, he thinks I'm someone else."

I frowned. "You mean, you told him you were someone you're not?"

"Well, it's not that simple. You see, he fell in love with my sister."

"O . . . kay."

Her eyes went glassy. "But, you see, my sister died. Only he doesn't know that. He thinks I'm my sister!"

"He can't tell that you're not her?"

"I don't know . . ." Her voice was brimming with despair.

"You see, we're identical twins, so on the outside we're alike, but we are such different people . . ."

Oh, man. This chick was in big trouble. "And you want to fashion a happy ending out of this, how?" I asked.

"But I haven't told you the whole problem," she said.

I thought she'd given me a pretty darned enormous problem already. Still, I waved my hand for her to elaborate.

"Jonathan," she said simply.

"Jonathan?"

"The Earl of Stratford. He's a friend of my fiancé and the best man," she explained. She looked away. "And also, he's the only man I've ever—"

"That's okay," I said quickly, raising my hand. "I get it."

She released a relieved breath as I studied her. I really, really wanted to help her. She needed help, that was for sure. But how to forge a happy ending out of such a mess?

"Look," I said, flipping up my laptop and opening a new document, "you need to tell me everything, okay? From the beginning."

And that was how it began. By the time Miss Donovan finished telling me her story, I was so hooked, I had to go into my writing cave and write the entire, wild tale. The hardest part was getting to that happy ending, but it was so happy and so romantic that it was worth every drop of blood and sweat that it took to get there.

I truly hope you enjoy reading Serena Donovan's story! Please come visit me at my website, www.jenniferhaymore. com, where you can share your thoughts about my books, sign up for some fun freebies, and read more about the characters from CONFESSIONS OF AN IMPROPER BRIDE.

Sincerely,

Jennifer Haymore

♥ ♥ ♥ ♥ ♥ ♥ ♥ ♥ ♥ ♥ ♥ ♥ ♥ ♥ ♥ ♥

From the desk of Sue-Ellen Welfonder

Dear Reader,

Does a landscape of savage grandeur make your heart beat faster? Do jagged peaks, cold-glittering boulders, and cauldrons of boiling mist speak to your soul? Are you exhilarated by the rush of chill wind, the power of ancient places made of stone and legend?

I love such places.

TEMPTATION OF A HIGHLAND SCOUNDREL, second book in my Highland Warriors trilogy, has a truly grand setting. Nought is my favorite corner of the Glen of Many Legends, home to the series' three warring clans. These proud Highlanders prove "where you live is who you are."

Kendrew Mackintosh and Isobel Cameron love wild places as much as I do. Kendrew boasts that he's hewn of Nought's soaring granite peaks and that he was weaned on cold wind and blowing mist. He's proud of his Norse heritage. Isobel shares his appreciation for Viking culture, rough terrain, and long, dark nights. She stirs his passion, igniting desires that brand them both.

But Isobel is a lady.

And Kendrew has sworn not to touch a woman of gentle birth. Isobel is also the sister of a bitter foe.

They're a perfect match despite the barriers separating them: centuries of clan feuds, hostility, and rivalries. Bad blood isn't easily forgotten in the Highlands and grudges last forever. Kendrew refuses to acknowledge his attraction to Isobel. She won't ignore the passion between them. As only a woman in love can, she employs all her seductive wiles to win his heart.

The temptation of Kendrew Mackintosh begins deep in his rugged Nought territory. In the shadows of mysterious cairns known as dreagan stones and on the night of his clan's raucous Midsummer Eve revels, Isobel pitches a battle Kendrew can only lose. Yet surrender will bring greater rewards than he's ever claimed.

Kendrew does open his heart to Isobel, but they soon find themselves caught in a dangerous maelstrom that threatens their love and could cost their lives. The entire glen is at peril and a brutal foe will stop at nothing to crush the brave men of the Glen of Many Legends.

Turning Kendrew loose on his enemy—a worthy villain—gave me many enjoyable writing hours. He's a fierce fighter and a sight to behold when riled. But beneath his ferocity is a great-hearted man who lives by honor.

Writing Isobel was an equal joy. Like me, she feels most alive in wild, windswept places. I know Nought approved of her.

Places do have feelings.

Highlanders know that. In wild places, the pulse beat of the land is strong. I can't imagine a better setting for Kendrew and Isobel.

I hope you've enjoyed watching Isobel prove to Kendrew that the hardest warrior can't win against a woman wielding the most powerful weapon of all: a heart that loves.

With all good wishes,

Sue-Ellen Welfonder

www.welfonder.com

♥ ♥ ♥ ♥ ♥ ♥ ♥ ♥ ♥ ♥ ♥ ♥ ♥ ♥ ♥ ♥ ♥ ♥

From the desk of Sophie Gunn

Dear Reader,

Some small-town romances feature knitting clubs, some cookie clubs, and some quilting clubs. But my new series has something else entirely.

Welcome to Galton, New York, home of the Enemy Club.

The Enemy Club is made up of four women who had been the worst of enemies back in high school. They were the class brainiac, the bad girl, the princess, and the outcast. Now, all grown up, they've managed to become the best of friends. But they're friends with a difference. They've promised to tell one another the truth, the whole truth, and nothing but the truth so help them Gracie (the baker of the pies at the Last Chance Diner). Because they see things from their very (very!) different points of view, this causes all sorts of conflicts and a nuanced story, where no one has a lock on the what's right or wrong.

In *Sweet Kiss of Summer*, Nina Stokes is the woman with the problem, and she's going to need everyone's help to solve it. Her brother lost his life in the war. On his deathbed, he asked a nurse to write Nina a letter, instructing her to give his house back in Galton to his war buddy, Mick Rivers.

Or did he?

How can Nina know if the letter is real or a con? And even if it's real, where has Mick been for the past two years, during which Nina tried everything to contact him to no avail? How long should she be expected to keep up the house in this limbo, waiting for a man who obviously takes her brother's last wish lightly?

So when a beautiful man claiming to be Mick roars up Nina's driveway one summer afternoon in a flashy red car, demanding the house that he feels is rightfully his, every member of the Enemy Club thinks that she knows best what Nina should do. Naturally, none of them agree. The themes of friendship, duty, and honor run deep in Galton, and in *Sweet Kiss of Summer*, they are all tested. To whom do we owe our first duty: our family, our friends, our country—or ourselves?

What I loved most about writing *Sweet Kiss of Summer* was that there was no easy solution for anyone. As I wrote, I had no idea what Nina would do about her dilemma. Mick struggled with an even thornier problem, as his secrets were bigger than anyone in the Enemy Club could imagine. I could understand everyone's point of view. There is just so much to consider when you're not only out for yourself, but for your country, your community, your family, and ultimately, something even bigger.

I hope you'll enjoy reading about these characters as much as I've enjoyed writing about them. Come visit me at SophieGunn.com to learn more about the small town of Galton and the Enemy Club, to see pictures of my kitties, and to keep in touch. I'd love to hear from you!

Sophie Gunn

www.sophiegunn.com

Find out more about Forever Romance!

Visit us at
www.hachettebookgroup.com/publishing_forever.aspx

Find us on Facebook
http://www.facebook.com/ForeverRomance

Follow us on Twitter
http://twitter.com/ForeverRomance

NEW AND UPCOMING TITLES

Each month we feature our new titles
and reader favorites.

CONTESTS AND GIVEAWAYS

We give away galleys, autographed copies,
and all kinds of exclusive items.

AUTHOR INFO

You'll find bios, articles, and links to personal websites
for all your favorite authors—and so much more.

GET SOCIAL

Connect with your favorite authors, editors, and
other Forever fans, and share what's important to you.

THE BUZZ

Sign up for our monthly romance newsletter,
and be the first to read all about it.

VISIT US ONLINE

@ WWW.HACHETTEBOOKGROUP.COM

AT THE HACHETTE BOOK GROUP WEBSITE YOU'LL FIND:

CHAPTER EXCERPTS FROM SELECTED NEW RELEASES
•
ORIGINAL AUTHOR AND EDITOR ARTICLES
•
AUDIO EXCERPTS
•
BESTSELLER NEWS
•
ELECTRONIC NEWSLETTERS
•
AUTHOR TOUR INFORMATION
•
CONTESTS, QUIZZES, AND POLLS
•
FUN, QUIRKY RECOMMENDATION CENTER
•
PLUS MUCH MORE!

BOOKMARK HACHETTE BOOK GROUP
@ WWW.HACHETTEBOOKGROUP.COM